Dear Readers,

Many years ago, when I was a kid, my father said to me, "Bill, it doesn't really matter what you do in life. What's important is to be the best William Johnstone you can be."

I've never forgotten those words. And now, many years and almost 200 books later, I like to think that I am still trying to be the best William Johnstone I can be. Whether it's Ben Raines in the Ashes series, or Frank Morgan, the last gunfighter, or Smoke Jensen, our intrepid mountain man, or John Barrone and his hard-working crew keeping America safe from terrorist lowlifes in the Code Name series, I want to make each new book better than the last and deliver powerful storytelling.

Equally important, I try to create the kinds of believable characters that we can all identify with, real people who face tough challenges. When one of my creations blasts an enemy into the middle of next week, you can be damn sure he had a good reason.

As a storyteller, my job is to entertain you, my readers, and to make sure that you get plenty of enjoyment from my books for your hard-earned money. This is not a job I take lightly. And I greatly appreciate your feedback— you are my gold, and your opinions *do* count. So please keep the letters and e-mails coming.

Respectfully yours,

WILLIAM W. JOHNSTONE

THE FIRST MOUNTAIN MAN
FORTY GUNS WEST

THE FIRST MOUNTAIN MAN
PREACHER'S PEACE

PINNACLE BOOKS
Kensington Publishing Corp.
http://www.kensingtonbooks.com

PINNACLE BOOKS are published by

Kensington Publishing Corp.
850 Third Avenue
New York, NY 10022

This novel is a work of fiction. Names, characters, places, and inci-
dents are either the product of the author's imagination, or are used
fictitiously. Any resemblance to actual persons, living or dead, or
events is entirely coincidental.

All Kensington Titles, Imprints, and Distributed Lines are available at
special quantity discounts for bulk purchases for sales promotions, pre-
miums, fund-raising, and educational or institutional use. Special book
excerpts or customized printings can also be created to fit specific needs.
For details, write or phone the office of the Kensington special sales
manager: Kensington Publishing Corp., 850 Third Avenue, New York,
NY 10022, attn: Special Sales Department, Phone: 1-800-221-2647.

Pinnacle and the P logo Reg. U.S. Pat. & TM Off.

First Pinnacle Books Printing: November 2006

10 9 8 7 6 5 4 3 2 1

Printed in the United States of America

THE FIRST MOUNTAIN MAN:
FORTY GUNS WEST

BOOK ONE

Don't tread on me!

1

The townspeople of the long-settled eastern village never really grew easy with Preacher around. The mountain man walked like a big panther, silent and sure. A few of the town and the area's bully-boys felt compelled to call him out for a tussle. They very quickly learned that Preacher fought under no rules except his own. One bully-boy lost an eye, another was abed all winter with broken ribs, and the third—and final man to challenge Preacher—was buried one cold February morning.

"I reckon," Preacher said to his pa and ma one day, "I best be thinkin' of headin' back to the High Lonesome."

"It's been so good to see you, son," his mother said, placing her hand over his. "But I fear for you here."

"You don't need to be fearful for me, Ma," Preacher said. "That bully-boy pulled a blade on me. I had no choice in the matter."

"Your mother's right, son," Preacher's father said, stuffing his old pipe full of tobacco. He knelt by the fire and picked out a lighted twig and puffed. Back in his chair, he said, "You've left us money a-plenty to last for the rest of our years. I don't want to see grief come to you. And it will come if you stay around here."

Preacher knew his parents were right. He just didn't

want to admit it. But he knew he'd out-stayed his welcome in town. He just didn't fit in. Preacher was all muscle and bone and gristle. He was tanned dark by the sun and the wind, he carried the scars of a dozen deadly battles, and he operated under no moral or legal code save that of his own. And nobody was going to make him conform to any standard except that which he considered fair. But in his own peculiar way, Preacher was a highly moral man for the time, this year of our Lord, eighteen hundred and forty. He had the utmost respect for womanhood. He loved the land and the critters on it. He could not abide injustice. He didn't like lawyers and thought the country in general was going to Hell in a handbasket.

Preacher nodded his head. "You're both right. My good brothers won't even come around whilst I'm here."

His mother smiled. "They're afraid of you, son. They belong to order and families and the clock. You belong to the wilderness. Their lives are routine. Your life is like the wind. They don't, can't, understand that."

Preacher cut his eyes to the west. "For a fact," he muttered, "I have missed the mountains."

His father's old eyes twinkled. "I see where you've packed your gear. You must have been thinking about leaving."

Preacher laughed and gently placed one strong hand on his father's stooped shoulders, bent from years of brutally hard work, clearing the land and wrestling a living from the soil. "I reckon I'll pull out come the mornin'. Ma, if you'll make me a little poke of food, I'd be obliged." He stood up.

"Where are you going, son?" his mother asked.

"Oh, I think I'll take me a little stroll through the town. Give the good folks one last look 'fore they're shut of me." He looked at this parents. "You know when I leave this go-round, I prob'ly won't be back."

They nodded their heads.

Preacher stepped out of the house into the cold early March air of Ohio. A thin covering of new snow the past night had laid a carpet of white over the land. Preacher checked on his horse, Thunder, and then decided to stretch his legs and walk the short distance into the village. A town, actually. Darn near five hundred people lived all crowded up like ants.

Preacher still drew stares from the citizens but he paid them no heed, just walked on to the combination coach stop, hotel, and tavern and opened the door. The buzz of conversation stopped when he padded silently up to the bar, the soles of his high-topped moccasins making no more than a whisper on the floor. He leaned on the bar and ordered a whiskey with a beer chaser.

Several ladies who had stopped there for the night and were waiting on the afternoon coach began whispering behind their fancy fans. Preacher paid them no mind. From the looks of them they were city women, all gussied up to beat the band. Preacher took a sip of whiskey and a sip of beer. He hid a smile as the few locals who were lined up at the bar backed away, clear down to the end, getting as far away from Preacher as they could. It had been in this very tavern, just two weeks past, that Preacher had killed that feller who shucked out his knife during what Preacher had thought was just a friendly fist-fight. Preacher had left him on the floor, cut from navel to neck.

The door opened and a frail boy of about nine or ten entered. They boy's clothing was ragged and the soles of his shoes were tied on with string. He carried a small bucket with a lid on it. The top of the boy's head just did reach the lip of the bar. He placed the bucket on the bar and said, "A bucket of beer for Mister Parks, please, sir."

The barkeep took the bucket to rinse it out and the boy looked at the free lunch on the table, hunger in his eyes. His pinched face was pale and his eyes held a strange brightness.

"You hungry, boy?" Preacher asked.

The boy's eyes were scared as they fixed on the mountain man. "Yes, sir. Some."

"Then fix you a sandwich or two."

"That food's for customers!" the barkeep hollered.

"The lad just bought a bucket of beer, didn't he?" Preacher asked. "So that entitles him to food. Fix you something to eat, boy."

"I'll slap you, boy!" the barkeep barked. "You stay away from that food, you . . . woods' colt."

Preacher gave the barkeep a disgusted look as he walked to the table and fixed two huge meat and cheese sandwiches and gave them to the boy. "You sit over there by the stove and eat and get warm, boy." He turned to the barkeep. "You want to slap me?"

The man paled. "Ah, no, sir!"

"Fine. Now you pour that lad a big glass of milk and then go on about your business and leave the boy alone."

The boy fell into a hard fit of coughing that reddened his face. Bad lungs, Preacher thought. A wonder he lived through the winter.

Hard footsteps slammed on the boards outside the coach stop and the door was flung open. The hard and big bulk of Elam Parks filled the doorway, his face mottled with rage. He held a quirt in one hand. He pointed the quirt at the boy. "What the hell do you think you're doing, Eddie?" he shouted. "I didn't give you permission to eat."

"No. But I did," Preacher said.

In the time Preacher had been in town, he'd seen enough of Elam Parks to last him two lifetimes. Parks was an important man about the community. He owned several farms, a couple of businesses, and about fifty percent of the local bank. His brother was in tight with the governor, or senator, or some damn blow-heart politician. Parks thought himself the bull of the woods around these parts. He was a bully and a slave-driver to those who had the misfortune to work for him. He gave

Preacher the same type of look he might give a roach. Then he turned to the boy.

"Get up and get back to work, you worthless whelp!"

"When he finishes his meal," Preacher said.

Parks turned to face Preacher. He was a big'un, all right. Preacher guessed him at about six feet, one inch, with the weight to go with it. A big man with hard packed muscle. "This is none of your affair, Mountain Man," Parks said, contempt dripping from each word. "So stay out of it. The boy is bound to me and does what I tell him to do."

"Bound, huh? I thought that practice stopped a long time ago. I never did hold with it. It's just a fancy word for slavery. I don't hold with that either. You eat your meal, Eddie. This big mouth can wait."

Elam started stuttering and sputtering, his face beet red. People just didn't talk to him in such a manner. He pointed the quirt at the Preacher and shouted, "I'll have you run out of town, you, you . . . *trash!*"

Preacher smiled and finished his whiskey. He sat the cup on the bar and said, "You figure on doin' that all by yourself, or you gonna call some boys to help you?"

Preacher cut his eyes to the little boy. Eddie was gobbling down his sandwiches as fast as he could. It was evident to Preacher that the sick little boy had not had sufficient food in a long time.

Elam dropped his quirt on the table. "Mountain Man, you have had your way in this town for long enough. You been strutting about like a peacock. You need to learn a hard lesson, and I am just the man to teach you."

"Is that a fact?" Preacher hesitated for a moment, not wanting to bring any further grief to his parents. "Well, mayhaps you're right. I brung mountain ways to this town and expected folks hereabouts to accept 'em. I do apologize for that. But I don't apologize for standing up for the lad yonder. He's a mighty sick little boy. And he's got marks on his face that I just noticed under all that grime. Have you been beatin' on him, Parks?"

"The boy lacks discipline and motivation. Besides, he's bound to me and what I do is no concern of yours. But now that you have backed down from this issue, we'll call it even and forget it."

"Whoa!" Preacher said. "I ain't never backed down from no man. So don't you be puttin' the cart ahead of the horse." He looked at Eddie. "You want some pie or cake, boy?"

"Now, that's all!" Elam blurted. "I have had quite enough of this foolishness." He moved swift for a man his size. Elam slammed a heavy hand down on Eddie's shoulder and jerked him to his raggedy shoes. He flung the boy toward the door. Eddie struck the wall and cried out in pain.

Preacher took two steps forward and started his punch from down around his knees. The big hard right fist caught Elam on the side of the jaw and stretched the man out on the floor, blood leaking from his mouth.

"Oh, my God!" a local blurted. "Somebody run get Doctor Ellis."

Preacher knelt down beside Eddie. There was a bump on the boy's head and a slight cut oozing a tiny bit of blood. "Gimmie a wet cloth," Preacher said. When nobody moved, he added, "Now, damnit!"

One local ran out the door for the doctor while another handed Preacher a dampened cloth. Preacher gently bathed the frightened boy's face then picked him up and sat him in a chair. "You just take it easy 'til the doc gets here, boy."

"Mountain Man," a fancy dressed dude said, "you'd best haul your ashes out of here. Elam Parks is a big man in this state. You're prison bound when he wakes up."

Preacher ignored the warning. Obviously, Elam Parks had the whole damn town buffaloed. He looked up as his older brother rushed into the tavern.

The older man looked at the prostrate Parks and blurted, "My God, Art! Have you taken leave of your senses? That's Elam Parks."

"No kiddin'? I'd a swore it was a brayin' jackass and nothin' more." He pointed to Eddie. "What's the story on this here boy, Brother?"

"He's a woods' colt. Elam bound him out of the orphanage to work for him. Nobody gives a hoot about that brat."

"Wrong, Brother. I give a hoot." The doctor ran in and started for the still unconscious Parks. Preacher grabbed his arm and halted him. "You check the boy first, Doc. Then you tell me about him."

Dr. Ellis hesitated, took a short look into Preacher's cold eyes, then shrugged his shoulders. He checked Eddie, put some antiseptic on the small cut and took Preacher's arm, leading him away from the boy.

"The boy is dying, Mister. Lung fever. It's a miracle he lived through the winter. The next winter will kill him for sure."

"All right. Now you can go check on stupid over yonder." He walked over to Eddie, past the out-of-town women who were vigorously fanning themselves, their faces flushed from all the excitement. "You got any belongin's, boy?"

"A few, sir."

"Go fetch them. You're shut of this town and its sorry people. You're comin' with me."

The boy's sad eyes brightened. "Really?"

"Really. Go on. Get back here as quick as you can." Preacher walked over to the bar and finished his beer. He watched through amused eyes as several men tried to get Parks up on his feet. "You best get you a hoist," he called. "It'll take it to get that moose up."

Parks finally managed to sit up on the floor, but his jaw was swollen and his eyes were glazed. Dr. Ellis bathed his face and the man's eyes began to focus. Pure hate was shining through, all of it directed at Preacher.

"Was I you, Parks," Preacher said, "I'd be real careful what come out of my mouth right about now. As upsot as you are, you just might let your butt overload it."

Preacher's brother rushed over to help Elam get to an upright position. He brushed at Elam's coat, all the while apologizing for Preacher's actions.

"That's right, Brother," Preacher drawled. "Suck up to him."

Elam shoved the men away from him. "Mountain Man, if you're in town an hour from now, have a gun in your hand."

"I'll prob'ly be in town. And if I am, I'll have a gun to hand, Parks. But you best remember this, Parks: I ain't no poor sick little boy. You level a pistol at me and the undertaker will be givin' you your last tidyin' up."

Parks snorted his reply and stalked out of the tavern just as Eddie was returning. He drew back his hand to strike the boy and Preacher said, "I'll break your arm, Parks."

Elam lowered his hand and stomped off. Preacher looked at the rags Eddie had stuffed into a sack and tossed them into a corner. "We'll get you some new duds, Eddie. But first we get you a bath and a haircut. Then we'll dust this town."

"Where are we going, Mister Preacher?"

"Where the air is pure and clean. Where them lungs of yours can heal. West, boy. To the mountains."

2

The barber was nervous as he cut Eddie's hair, but he managed to get the boy looking presentable without snipping off anything other than hair. Then it was into a hot tub with a bar of strong soap. While Eddie was washing off the grime, Preacher went to the general store and bought him new clothes, from underwear out.

Preacher checked his awesome four-barrel pistol and holstered it. He carried only the one pistol while in town; but even that made the local constable nervous. The county sheriff was half a day's ride away.

Preacher was under no illusions. He knew that Parks was no coward. If he said he'd come looking for Preacher, he'd come. Preacher returned to the barber shop and found a brand new boy waiting for him. Good lookin' kid, too. Preacher looked at the wall clock. He had about twenty minutes left 'fore Parks would start on the prowl. He walked the boy down to the livery and bought him a pony. The horse was small, but strong limbed and Preacher guessed it had plenty of staying power. He bought a saddle and saddle bags.

"You know where Elm Street is, Eddie?"

"Yes, sir, Mister Preacher."

"I'm Preacher, boy. Not mister. You go over to Elm.

Second house on the right. Wait there for me. My ma and pa is there. You tell Ma I said to get that poke of food ready. I'll be along shortly."

"Mister Elam's a bad one. He's kilt men before, Preacher," Eddie warned.

"Not as many as I have. Go on."

Preacher made sure the boy was on his way, proudly riding his new pony, and then he stepped out into the street. The town lay silent under the cold sun. Preacher walked right up the center of the main street.

"You there!" the constable called to Preacher from under the awning of his office. "I order you in the name of the law to cease and desist."

"Go suck an egg," Preacher told him.

"I'm the law around here!" the man bellowed.

"Congratulations. Now go back into your office and drink coffee. Stay off the street."

"You can't talk to me like that!"

Preacher ignored him and kept on walking. A block ahead of him, Elam Parks stepped off the boardwalk and into the street, a pistol in each hand. The two men began closing the distance.

"This don't have to be, Elam!" Preacher called. "You abused the boy and got socked in the jaw for it. Now it's done and past. It ain't nothin' worth dyin' over."

But for Elam, time for talking was gone. He had been humiliated in his own town and had to redeem himself in the eyes of the citizens. He lifted a pistol and fired. The ball missed Preacher by several feet.

"You better make the next one count, Elam," Preacher called, his own pistol still holstered.

Elam fired his second pistol. Again he missed.

"Now it's over, Elam," Preacher called. "You took your shots and you missed. I ain't gonna fire. Go on home. You'll not see me nor the boy never again."

Elam was frantically reloading. "You son of a whore!" he yelled at Preacher.

Preacher's eyes hardened and he stopped in the street. "Insult me all you like. But don't never slur my mother's name. You hear me, Elam."

"You sorry, filthy trash!" Parks shouted. "Son of a whore!" He lifted a pistol and Preacher drew, cocked, and drilled him clean, the ball driving the third button of his shirt clear to his backbone. Parks stumbled and fell to the street, on his back.

The stores along the street and the houses behind them and on the side streets emptied of people, all gathering around the dead Elam Parks. Preacher reloaded the empty chamber and turned his back on the crowd. He walked to the house on Elm street. His parents had heard the shots and were waiting in the front yard, behind the picket fence.

Preacher's older brother came running up, all out of breath. He stood for a moment, panting, and then blurted, "My God, Mamma, Daddy. Art's done shot and killed Mister Elam Parks."

"He had it coming," the father said. "It's long overdue. I'm just sorry it had to be you who done it, Art."

"Had it coming!" the older brother said, horrified. "Daddy, how can you say things like that? Why, Mister Elam was a fine man. He . . ."

"Was a crook and a no-count," the father said. "Maybe with him dead and gone, now you can get that brown spot off your nose, boy."

Preacher laughed at the expression on his brother's face. The older brother turned toward him, his face red and his hands balled into fists.

"I'd think about it, brother of mine," Preacher said. "I'd give it real serious thought."

The brother stared at Preacher for a moment. "You're no brother of mine, Art. You've turned into a godless savage, just like the heathen Indians."

Preacher wanted real bad to hit him, but didn't want to do so in front of his mother. However, he figured his pa would probably enjoy seeing it. But he contained the urge to deck his brother and instead turned his back to him. The brother snorted and walked off. Preacher kissed his mother and held her close, both of them knowing this would be their last goodbye. He shook hands with his pa.

"You take care, son."

"I'll do 'er, Pa."

"God bless, son," his mother said. "I put a sack of food on your saddle."

"Y'all take care." Preacher walked to the small barn, Eddie keeping up with him. Two minutes later, they were riding out, heading west. Preacher did not look back. He would not have been able to see his ma and pa through the mist in his eyes.

"I thought we were going to head west, Preacher," Eddie remarked.

"We are, boy. But we'll head south for a time. Tell me about yourself."

"There ain't much to tell, Preacher. My ma and pa died with the fever when I was little. I don't even remember them. I was passed from pillar to post for a time, then the orphanage took me in. I was sick a lot, and no one wanted a boy who couldn't work. Mister Parks got me last year. I reckon I'd a died working for him."

"Prob'ly. But you gonna get well with me." Preacher paused. "At least some better. I think what you need most of all is good vittles, clean air, and rest."

Eddie tired easily and Preacher was in no hurry. He stopped often and made evening camp much earlier than he normally would. He avoided towns as often as possible. But he was under no illusions about what lay behind him. If Parks was the big-shot people thought him to be, there would surely be warrants out for him by now. But he wasn't worried too much about that, either. Worryin' caused a man to get lines in his face and gray in his hair.

Preacher skirted the town of Cincinnati and crossed the Ohio River by ferry and rode into Kentucky.

"That was some river, Preacher!" Eddie said, all excited.

"Wait 'til you see the Mississippi, boy. The Ohio runs into the Mississippi down in Southern Illinois."

"Will we see that?"

"We might. I was goin' to Saint Louie, but I think I'll skip that town this run. I'll take us down through Arkansas and then cut west from there."

"You're thinking that Mister Parks's friends might be after us, aren't you?"

The boy was very quick and very sharp. The lad didn't miss much at all. "Yeah," Preacher said. "That thought has crossed my mind a time or two."

"How old were you when you went west, Preacher?"

"Not much older than you, Eddie. My, but that was a time, back then. Back in the mountains. Why, you could go for months without seein' another white man. Now ever' time a body looks up, they's a damn cabin bein' built."

That was not exactly the truth, not even close to it. But people were moving west. It would be a few more years before the flood gates of humanity were thrown open and the real surge westward began. Many, if not most of the mountain men resented the pioneers' drive westward. They were, for the most part, solitary men—in some cases legitimately wanted by the law for various crimes—and they felt the vast West was theirs alone. But that was not to be. The mountain men were credited, however, with the carving out of much of the Far West. By 1840, the mountain man's way of life was very nearly a closed book, as beaver hats faded from vogue and the mountain men faded from view.

Many of the mountain men would drift back onto a civilized way of life, opening stores or turning to farming or ranching on a small scale. But many others either could not or would not change. They elected to stay in the mountains and eke out a living. Others, like Preacher, became scouts and wagon masters. And, like Preacher, living legends.

As the days on the tráil drifted into weeks, and the weather warmed, moving silently into spring, Eddie began losing his cough and his face and forearms first blistered, then tanned under the sun and the wind. The boy began putting on weight and his face lost the sickly pallor and his eyes lost their feverish tint. Then, as Preacher and Eddie were making camp one afternoon in Arkansas, Preacher realized that the boy had not coughed up phlegm even one time that day.

All he needed was a chance, Preacher thought. Someone to take an interest in him and show him the right paths to take.

The mountain man and the kid drifted down to Little Rock. Preacher had been this way back in the twenties. He'd run up on them two kids, Jamie and Kate MacCallister. They'd been headin' for the Big Thicket country of East Texas, running from Kate's pa and a bunch of bounty hunters. Jamie and Kate, Preacher had heard, had gone on to have a passel of kids and Jamie later made quite a name for himself during the Texas fight for independence.*

Preacher had heard that shortly after the fall of the Alamo, Jamie and Kate had pulled out for the Rockies in Colorado. Mayhaps he and Eddie would drift up that way and visit them.

Preacher provisioned up in Little Rock and didn't dally in doing it. Leaving Eddie with the horses, sitting in the shade and sucking on a piece of peppermint candy, Preacher stepped into a tavern for a drink and news. If there were warrants on his head, or bounty hunters after

*THE EYES OF EAGLES—Zebra Books

him and the boy, the tavern would be the place to hear it.

Preacher ordered whiskey and leaned against the plank bar, listening. It did not take long for him to learn the bad news.

"I'll not take up the trail of that mountain man," he heard a man say. "Not for five hundred dollars, not for five thousand dollars."

"I'd foller Ol' Nick hisself straight into the gates of hell for five thousand dollars," another said.

"Yeah, me too," another agreed. "Man, that's a life-time's wages."

The first man said, "How you gonna spend it ifn you're dead? Man, this is Preacher we're talkin' about. He's nearabouts as famous as Carson and Bowie and Crockett and Boone."

"He's just one man traveling with a snot-nosed brat," the man who would traverse the gates of hell said.

Preacher was glad he had left the boy hidden in that little glen outside of town. He was suddenly conscious of eyes on him. He sipped his whiskey and then turned his head, meeting the direct gaze of the man who professed to have no fear of hell.

"Howdy, stranger," the man said. "Ain't seed you 'round here afore."

"Just passin' through," Preacher replied. "Come up from South Texas headin' north. Who you boys be talkin' 'bout that's so fearsome?"

"Some old mountain man called Preacher. He kilt an important gentleman back up in Ohio and taken a boy west with him. Big money on his head. Dead or alive."

Preacher nodded his head slowly. "I know a little some-thing 'bout Preacher, boys. I trapped the High Lonesome for some years 'fore the fur price dropped. Preacher ain't old. I'd figure him for maybe thirty-five or so. And he's a ring-tailed tooter who was born with the bark on. I ain't never met him, but I know lots who has, and they'll all tell you the same thing . . . that you better let Preacher alone."

"See, I told you!" the first man said to his friends.

"He ain't but one man," the fellow with the desire to meet the devil persisted. "I'm supplyin' up and pullin' out in the mornin'. I am to get me a sack full of gold coins."

"Me, too," his two friends said in unison.

"Well, I wish you boys good luck," Preacher said, draining his cup. "Me, I'm headin' up toward Canada. Mighty pretty country up yonder."

Seated way in the back of the tavern, in the deep shadows, an old man wearing stained and worn buckskins sat, nursing a jug of Who Hit John. The old man smiled secretly and knowingly. He'd recognized Preacher the instant the mountain man had entered the saloon. Wolverine Pete had come to the high mountains back in the late 1790's, blazing a solitary trail and earning a reputation as being a man to ride the river with. He picked up his jug, corked it, and quietly slipped out the back of the tavern. He walked to the livery and saddled up, riding to the edge of town and reining up on a rise.

It was a good move on his part. About ten minutes later, Preacher came riding along, leading a packhorse. Pete rode down the trail and intercepted Preacher.

"Wagh!" Preacher said. "Wolverine in the flesh. I heard you got kilt up on the Cheyenne last year."

"I took me an arry in my back for a fact. I'm a-headin' for Saint Louie—in a roundabout way—to get 'er cut out. It's botherin' me fierce. They's big money on your butt, Preacher. That shore must have been some important uppity-up feller you kilt."

Preacher told him what happened.

Pete grunted. "Sounds to me like you give him ever' chance in the world to back off. But that don't mean you gonna get any slack cut you. I figure 'fore it's all said and done, they'll be forty or fifty men lookin' to collect that gold."

"They're welcome to try," Preacher replied.

"I wished I didn't hurt so bad, I'd go with you. Sounds like fun to me."

"I'll try to avoid 'em. I don't want the boy to get hurt."

"Sounds like you took a shine to this lad."

"He just needed a chance, and I aim to see that he gets it."

"You want me to lay up on a ridge and kill them fellers you was talkin' to in the bar?"

Preacher shook his head. "I'm obliged, but no. They didn't look like much to me. When they see how hard the trail is, I'm thinkin' they'll give it up."

"They might. You take care of yourself, ol' hoss."

"I'll do it, Pete."

Back at the shady glen, Preacher said, "We got manhunters on our trail, boy. We got to shake them if we can. But we got to cross them damn plains 'fore we get to the mountains. Let's ride, son. We got hell nippin' at our heels."

3

"Were you the first mountain man, Preacher?" Eddie asked.

"Oh, no, boy. There was lots of men in the High Lonesome long 'fore I come along. I got there right in the middle of it all, though. We had some high ol' times, we did."

Eddie loved to get Preacher going on some of his exploits. The boy wasn't that sure that Preacher was telling him the truth all the time, but the tales were lively and entertaining and they helped pass the hours between supper and bedtime.

Preacher was teaching Eddie the ways of the wilderness as they crossed the Arkansas line and headed into the Territories. "Wild country from here on in, Eddie. And it gets wilder the farther west we go."

"Will we see heathen Indians, Preacher?"

"I'd just as soon we didn't, but we prob'ly will. I best start your learnin' about Injuns, Eddie."

"They attack and scalp people," the boy said.

"Well, some do and some don't. Personally, I don't think Injuns started that scalpin' business. I think they learned that from the white man some years back. Your Sioux and Cree Injuns, to name a few, place a lot of value on scalps, but other tribes place much more value on countin' coup on an enemy or the stealin' of his horse. And Injuns ain't bad folks, Eddie." He paused. "Well, maybe with the exception of the Pawnee. I ain't *never* been able to get along with them damn Pawnee. The Injun just ain't like us, that's all. Their values is different. You don't never want to show fear around an Injun. Remember that always. Courage is something an Injun respects more than anything else."

"Preacher?"

"Yeah, boy."

"You know there are men following us?"

"Oh, yeah. I been knowing that since yesterday afternoon. I wanted to see when you'd pick up on it. That's the way it is, Eddie. People look at lots of things, but very few actually *see* anything. I think it's them loud mouths I met back yonder in Little Rock. I don't want to have to hurt none of them, but I'll be damned ifn I'll let them hurt us."

Preacher had armed the boy and stopping often along the way, had taught him how to shoot both rifle and pistol. Preacher still carried his muskets, but back in Ohio, he'd picked up a couple of 1836 breech loading carbines, and one kiss 1833 Hall North breech loader rifle. The breech loaders gave him a lot more firepower because they took a lot less time to load.

"What are you going to do about those men back there, Preacher?"

"I don't know, boy. Yet. But I got to discourage them and that's a fact."

"Is there a reward posted for you?"

"Yep. I don't know how much, but I 'spect it's a princely sum for the news of it to have traveled this far." Preacher pointed to a meandering creek, lined on both sides by cottonwoods. "We'll face them down over yonder."

Preacher took his time making camp, and making certain that Eddie was safe from any wandering bullets, then squatted down by the tiny fire he'd thrown together and boiled some coffee. He figured the men behind him would show up in about half an hour. He checked his guns and waited.

He didn't miss the time mark by more than a few minutes. Three mounted men reined up when they spotted Preacher, sittin' big as brass by the fire, drinking coffee right out in the open, making no attempt to hide himself.

At that distance, Preacher couldn't be certain, but the men looked like those who'd been braggin' back in Little Rock. They rode toward the camp, muskets at the ready.

"Hallo the camp!" one hollered.

"Come on in," Preacher returned the shout. "If you're friendly, that is. If you're not, you best make your peace with God, 'cause if you start trouble with me, you'll damn well be planted here."

The trio hesitated, then rode on. "You!" the man who wanted to shake hands with the devil blurted, as the men reined up close to the camp.

"In the flesh," Preacher said, standing up, his hands close to the butts of his terrible pistols. "What are you three doin' doggin' my back trail?"

"We're a-lookin' for a wanted desperado called Preacher."

"You found him, hombre. Now what are you goin' to do about it?"

The men exchanged glances. Preacher had the advantage, and the men, although unskilled in man-hunting, were fully aware of that fact.

The man who held a kinship with the devil cleared his throat and said, "In the name of the law, I command you to surrender."

Preacher laughed at him. "The Injuns call me Ghost Walker, White Wolf, and Killing Ghost. Now, before you push me to show you why I'm called that, you boys best turn them ponies around and head back to Arkansas."

"Cain't do that," the second man said. "We done made our brags back to home that we'uns was gonna bring you in—dead or alive."

"You boys is makin' a bad mistake," Preacher warned them. "That shootin' back in O-hi-o was a fair one. I give that Parks feller more'un a fair shake. Now back off and let me be."

The man who warned to sit down with the devil got his wish. "I can feel that gold in my hands now," he said. Then jerked up his rifle and leveled it at Preacher.

Preacher snaked the big, heavy four-barreled monster from his leather holster and blew him out of the saddle. The double shot took him in the chest and face, making a mess out of the man's head.

The man's companions fought their spooked horses for a moment. One of them lost his musket in the process. When they got their horses calmed down, they sat staring at Preacher. The mountain man now stood with both hands filled with those terrible-looking pistols.

"You kilt Charlie Barnes!" one man said after finally finding his words.

"Shore looks that way," Preacher said. "Either that or he's mighty calm."

"Whut do we do now?" the remaining man asked.

"You boys dismount, careful like, and I'll tell you."

The two men carefully dismounted and stood before Preacher.

"Lay all your guns on the ground," Preacher ordered.

Guns on the ground, Preacher said, "Now bury your buddy."

"We ain't got any shovel!"

"Then use your hands and a stick! Move!"

While the men were struggling to gouge out a hole, Preacher stripped their horses of saddle and bridle. He kept their pack horse and supplies.

Charlie Barnes now planted in the earth, Preacher said, "Now strip down to the buff, boys."

"Do what?"

"Strip, boy! Are you deef?"

The men took one look at the eight barrels pointing

at them and quickly peeled down to bare skin. "This is plumb humiliatin'!" one said.

"Now get on your horses and ride," Preacher ordered.

"Bareback? Like this?" the other one shrieked.

"Like that. Or I'll shoot you both and leave you for the buzzards. What's it gonna be?"

"But they's highwaymen back yonder. We ain't got no means of protectin' ourselves."

"One look at you two, nekked as a jaybird, and any outlaws will laugh themselves silly at the sight. You got ten seconds to get clear 'fore I start shootin'. If I ever see either of you followin' me again, I'll lay up and ambush you. And that's a promise."

Ten seconds later, the two would-be man-hunters were gone, moaning and complaining about their discomfort.

Preacher chuckled and stoked up the fire. "Come on out, Eddie. Let's fix us something to eat and see what we got new in supplies."

"Those men are gonna sure be rubbed raw and sore time they get back to town," the boy said.

"I 'spect so. Break out the fryin' pan, boy. I'm hungry."

While Eddie cut slices of bacon, Preacher inspected the newly acquired supplies. The men had provisioned well. The added supplies would take Preacher and the kid a long ways. Preacher stripped the saddle and bridle from the dead man's horse. It was a fine animal; too fine to be turned loose. Preacher could trade the horse for something later on up the trail. The men had brought along enough powder and shot to stand off an army. One had brought along a fowling piece, a fine double barreled shotgun that just might come in handy along the way. There was nothing like a shotgun all loaded up with nuts and bolts and the like to take all the fight out of a trouble-maker. Preacher had seen men cut literally in two with a shotgun.

"Those men might try to come back," Eddie said, laying strips of bacon in the pan.

"Yep. I 'spect they will, boy. Tonight I 'spect Charlie Barnes will have company come the dawnin'."

"We could move on."

"We could. But we ain't. Learn this, boy: You start takin' water from one man, pretty soon you gonna take it from another. Then runnin' away becomes a habit. Eddie, out here, a man's word is his bond and a man's character, or lack of it, stays with him forever. I tried to warn them three back in town. They didn't pay no heed to my words. Barnes paid the price. Them others will too, I reckon. We'll see."

The boy smiled shyly. "If I was set loose in the wilderness bare-butt nekked, I figure I'd try to get my clothes back too. Wouldn't you?"

Preacher returned the smile. "I 'spect."

Preacher lay in his blankets and listened to the two Arkansas men as they made their return to the camp by the creek. He had to suppress a chuckle as the barefoot men stepped on rocks and thorns and oohhed and ouched and groaned along, trying their best to be quiet, but losing the game something awful. He figured it was right around midnight.

Preacher slipped from his blankets and picked up the club he'd chosen hours before. He really did not want to kill these two, just discourage them mightily. He glanced over at Eddie. The boy was sleeping soundly, a habit that he would soon break if he wanted to survive out here.

Preacher slipped like a ghost out of camp and away from the dying eye of the fire. By now he had the men spotted. It wasn't all that hard to do. Their lily white skin was shinin' in the faint light like a turd on top of a white-icin' birthday cake. Preacher slipped around and camped up behind them, his moccasins making no sound as he moved from tree to tree. Preacher had to put a hand over his mouth to keep from laughing at the sight. The men had wrapped

some sort of leafy vine around their waists. Looked to
Preacher like it was poison ivy. The men must have tore the
stuff down in the dark, not realizing what they were wrap-
ping around their privates and over their buttocks.

They'd damn sure know come tomorrow, what with all
the itchin' and scratchin' they'd be doin'.

Preacher whacked the one in the rear on the back of
his noggin, and when the man in front turned around,
Preacher laid the shillelagh across his forehead. Both
men dropped like rocks.

Being careful to avoid the poison leaves, and it was
poison ivy, Preacher tied them up, back to back, ankle
and wrists, and left them on the ground. He returned to
his blankets and went to sleep, a smile on his face.

The men probably realized it would only lead to more
knots on their heads if they hollered during the night,
so they remained silent until Preacher was up just before
first light, coaxing some coals to fire and making coffee.

"Mister Preacher?" one called. "We is in some awful
discomfort over here."

"I don't doubt it," Preacher called, setting the coffee pot
on the rocks. "You got poison ivy wrapped all around you."

There was a long moment of silence. "Well, hell,
Jonas!" the second man said. "No wonder I been itchin'
all night."

"Mister Preacher?" Jonas called.

"What is it?"

"Ifn you'd give us back our clothes and saddles, we'd
git so far gone from here by noon we wouldn't even be a
memory in your mind."

"You ain't gettin' your supplies back."

"You can have 'em, Mister Preacher. With our blessin's."

Preacher had already piled their clothes up and had
them ready. He cut the men loose. "You boys head on
down to the crick and pat mud all around your privates.
It'll help take the itch out of that poison ivy."

"I know better than to wrap myself in poison ivy,"

Eddie said contemptuously, watching the men gingerly make their way to the creek. He looked at Preacher. "You could have killed them."

"Yeah. I could have. But they're followers, not leaders. That Charlie Barnes, he talked them into this. There's a time to kill and a time to talk, boy. I think it says something like that in the Good Book. I need to get me a Bible. It's right comfortin' to read them words. Had me a Bible. Lost it last year. I think I left it with Hammer."

"Hammer?"

"My old horse. Some scum kilt him. I tracked them and kilt them. Hammer was a good horse. I miss him. We rode a lot of trails together."

Jonas looked at his companion, both of them sitting in the creek, letting the water momentarily ease the itching and burning. He whispered, "That mountain man tracked down a bunch of men who kilt his horse and kilt them."

"I heard. I knowed we was makin' a mistake when we let that Charlie Barnes talk us into this. Jonas, you ain't never gonna say nothin' about this, is you?"

"No, not a word."

"You promise?"

"Cross my heart and hope to die."

"Let's spit on it."

The men spat and their secret was sealed.

Both Eddie and Preacher noticed the men were a mighty sorry lookin' pair as they climbed up the creek bank and joined them around the fire. They walked funny, too.

Preacher had cooked bacon and pan bread and he told the pair to sit and eat.

"We'll eat and be proud to do it," Jonas said. "But if you don't mind, we'll stand."

"I understand. You boys stop ever' now and then on your way back home and bathe the infected areas with mud if you can't find no goldenseal root to powder up and put on it. Apple cider vinegar is real good too."

"Much obliged, Mister Preacher."

"Think nothin' of it. But in the future, you boys best choose your company with a tad more care."

"You can bet on that," the younger of the two said. "Our days of man-huntin' just begun and ended with this trip."

"Wise decision, son," Preacher said drily.

4

Preacher and the kid were gone within the hour. As they rode, Preacher pondered what Jonas had told him just before the two would-be man-hunters—now officially retired—rode out for home, both of them sitting in their saddles very carefully.

"The way I heard it, Mister Preacher, they's forty or fifty men huntin' you. Maybe more than that. Prob'ly more than that. For they's big money on your head. Several thousand dollars as of a couple of weeks ago. That must have been a real important man you kilt back east."

"Them men behind us know I'll be headin' to the mountains, Eddie," Preacher told the boy after only a few minutes on the trail. "If any of 'em has any smarts, and I 'spect some of them do, they've headed straight west and will be tryin' to get ahead of us, for an ambush."

The boy looked at Preacher. "So if they think we're going straight to the mountains, we don't go."

Preacher smiled. "You catch on real quick, lad. That's right. We don't go . . . leastways not right off."

"Where are we going, then?"

"North. Straight north. We got staple supplies to last us a long time. I'll kill us a deer or two and show you how to make jerky. We'll keep the skins and make you some proper clothing, or I'll have some fitted buckskins tossed in when I trade that spare horse. We're gonna be skirtin' the edge of Pawnee country, and me and them damn Pawnees never has got on worth a damn. Once they know I'm in their territory, and they'll know, bet on that, we'll have us a fight on our hands. But I get along with the Sioux and the Crow and most others."

The mountain man and the boy turned their horses and rode toward the plains. When Eddie caught his first glimpse of the plains he was speechless. It seemed to stretch forever. Mile after mile of waving grass and an endless horizon that seemed impossible to ever reach.

Preacher smiled at the boy's expression. "Takes your breath away, don't it, lad?"

"Yes, sir."

"I've knowed people to go mad out here. Wind blows all the time. It's the vastness of it all. And the buffalo, boy, I can't describe 'em. I've seen thousands and thousands of them on the move. Maybe they was millions of them. The Good Lord alone knows. The earth beneath your feet trembles when they pass. The buffalo is life itself to the Plains Injuns. The buffalo and the horse. The Injun is a fine horseman. They worship the horse. Call him Spirit Dog, Holy Dog, Medicine Dog. The Injuns make their tipis from buffalo skins, they wrap up to keep warm in buffalo robes, they eat the buffalo, they use the soft skin of a buffalo calf to wrap newborn babies in, and the hide of a bull or cow will be used as a buryin' cloth. They use parts of the hide to make drums, moccasins, shirts, leggin's, and dresses for squaws. They use buffalo hair to make rope. The horns of a buffalo is used for drinkin' cups. The bones is used to make all sorts of Injun tools. The paunch of a buffalo is used as a cook pot. Without the buffalo, the Injun would prob'ly cease to be."

"You like the Indians, don't you, Preacher?"

"Most of 'em, yeah. I've lived with 'em and I've fought 'em. I've had me a squaw now and then. I been captured and tortured by 'em, and I've laughed and joked and ate with 'em." He reined up and swept a strong hand across the panorama that lay before himself and the boy. "Look at it, Eddie. The plains. Far as I know, they ain't another sight like it in the whole wide world. And there never will be again. For when the white man comes, and he's comin', they'll junk it all up and try to change it. They'll plow lines in the earth and change the flow of rivers and kill off all the buffalo herds. They'll kill off the wolves 'cause the settlers is ignorant of the ways of the wilderness. Each animal is dependent in some ways on other animals. The wolves kill off the old and the weak in a herd. Without them, the herds wouldn't be healthy. But the white man don't understand that. They *could* understand it, but they won't. I tell you, boy, there ain't nothin' prettier in the world than layin' in your blankets at night and listenin' to wolves sing and talk to one another."

"Won't they attack you?"

"Naw. Them's old wive's tales from scary people. There ain't never been no healthy, full growed wolf ever attacked no human person that I ever heard tell of. Hell, I've had 'em for pets. A body just has to understand the ways of the wolf and respect 'em, that's all. But they's do's and don't when it comes to wolves. Don't never corner one. You do that, you got big trouble on your hands. Don't never get between the he-wolf and his mate. They don't like that. A wolf pack is a real complicated type of society, Eddie. They have leaders and co-leaders. They real protective of their young. The male and the female take turns carin' for their pups." He smiled at the boy and lifted his reins. "Now you see why some Injuns call me White Wolf. I'm a brother to the wolf. I had one big ol' buffalo wolf stay with me for weeks one time. He must have weighed a hundred and fifty pounds. I'd toss him scraps of food and at night he'd sleep so close to me I could feel his breath. But I never touched him and he never touched me. But we was brothers. I knew it, and he knew it."

"What happened to him?"

"I don't know. One day he just veered off and was gone. He sat on a rise and watched me ride off. He threw back his head and talked to me until I couldn't hear him no more."

"That's sad."

"Yeah, it was. I ain't never forgot it, neither."

"I think I would have liked to have been a mountain man," Eddie said wistfully.

"You'd have made a good'un, boy. I saw right off you got what it takes."

Eddie smiled the rest of the day.

Just a few miles from where someday the town of Wichita would stand, men had gathered. And what a strange collection of men it was. Some were eloquently dressed in the most up-to-date sporting clothes on the market. Others wore homespun, and some were dressed in buckskins. A few carried the most modern hunting rifles, made especially for them, while others carried long flintlock rifles and shotguns. Some carried short-barreled muskets. But despite their difference in dress and speech and weaponry and levels of education—or lack of it—they shared one thing in common: they were bounty hunters. Most were here for the money, but a few were here solely for the enjoyment of the blood sport of man-hunting—the most skilled and elusive game on earth. The ultimate sport. At last count, taken that morning, there were sixty-five gun-totin' men gathered, twelve servants, four cooks, one hundred and five horses, and twenty pack mules. Oh, yes, and seven reporters.

There were two Englishmen, two Frenchmen, two Prussians, one Austrian, and one nobleman from Spain. The men had been communicating by letter, mapping

out this expedition for two years. They had originally
planned to travel Out West and shoot Indians. But after
they had all gathered at a grand hotel in New York City,
and heard of this Preacher person, why, this seemed like
it would be so much more fun. One could always find a
savage to kill. All the servants and cooks were in the
employ of the "hoity-toity," fancy-dressed foreigners.
They all beat it across the country just as fast as they
could.

They called themselves professional adventurers, and
to most men they were brave; they had traveled the
world in their quest for the ultimate game animal. They
had faced hardships and they were certainly not lacking
in courage. Although it would be safe to say that they
were all a tad shy on the common sense side. They were
arrogant, aloof, and looked down on anyone who wasn't
nobility. They all had some fancy title stuck in front of
their names like sir, count, duke, baron, or prince.

On the other side of the coin, so to speak, were the
bulk of those about to take out after Preacher and the
boy. Most of them were the hard ones. Professionals in
in the art of man-hunting and tracking. There were
about ten men who were along for the adventure of it
all, or what they thought starting out would be adventure. They would all soon learn that trying to track down
and kill Preacher was no grand adventure. Sixty-five men
were riding deeper on to the Plains that next morning.
By the time they reached the Rockies, only about forty
would be left. Forty guns against Preacher and the kid.
One of the trackers leading the bounty-hunters was a
renegade Pawnee called Dark Hand, so named because
of the strange, large birthmark that covered nearly his
entire right hand. Dark Hand despised Preacher. Hated
him with a wild fury that was almost blinding in its intensity. Preacher had killed Dark Hand's older brother and
Dark Hand had fought Preacher twice over the long
years that followed, and twice Preacher had bested him,

the last time leaving him for dead. But Dark Hand lived . . . and hated.

At that moment, Preacher and Eddie were no more than seventy-five miles away, west and slightly north of the location of the bounty hunters, camped along the Walnut.

A tiny band of wandering Cherokee, fleeing from the Big Ticket country of Texas after the death of their chief, Diwali, approached the camp of Preacher and Eddie and made the sign of peace.

"Come on in," Preacher called, knowing the Cherokee probably spoke English better than he did. Preacher had just killed a deer and told Eddie to start slicing it up.

"Ghost Walker!" one of the older Cherokees said, as he dismounted. "I saw you some years ago, when I was with a scouting party north of Bent's Fort."

Preacher shook hands all around and invited the Cherokee to sit, rest, and eat.

While the venison was cooking, the leader of the band said, "There are many men gathering only a few days' ride from here, Ghost Walker."

Eddie and Preacher exchanged glances, Preacher knowing that the furtive exchange would be caught by the vigilant Cherokees.

"You know any of them?" Preacher asked.

"Bones Gibson."

Preacher grunted. Bones Gibson was a first class manhunter. He was first class in everything, including his ruthlessness. Some say, and Preacher didn't doubt it, that Bones had killed more than a thousand Indians and more than a hundred white men during his long career as an Indian fighter and man-hunter. It was also said, and Preacher didn't doubt this either, that Bones had never lost a man once he got on his trail. But Bones had never been west of the Mississippi and had no experience with the Plains Indians.

Preacher looked at Eddie. "I won't lie to you, son. We're in for it."

The boy nodded his head, a solemn expression on his face. Even he had heard of Bones Gibson.

"The men have with them a Pawnee tracker called Dark Hand."

Preacher cussed under his breath. Again, he looked at Eddie. "Dark Hand hates my guts, Eddie. I killed his brother and whupped him twice. The last time I thought I killed him. I should have made certain. Goddamnit! Bones is gonna have half a dozen hard-cases that have been with him for years. Andy Price, George Winters, Horace Haywood, Mack Cornay, Cal Johnson, and Van Eaton, I'm sure. Van Eaton is a bad one. Just as bad as Bones, and maybe a little worser."

"We are moving north to Canada," the spokesman for the Cherokee said. "Perhaps there we can find peace." He looked around and received nods of approval from the other men. "Why don't you and the boy ride with us? Your pursuers are looking for two sets of tracks, not many."

Preacher shook his head. "No. 'Cause when they find us, and they will, they'd kill you all for helpin' us. And don't think they wouldn't. But I do 'preciate the offer."

The Cherokee ate and socialized and then moved on, leaving Preacher and the boy alone by the small fire. "We got to move fast, Eddie. We got to reach the mountains. Once we's in the High Lonesome, them ol' boys will play hell takin' us. I know places there that even the Injuns don't know about." Preacher was thoughtful for a moment. "We can move a lot faster than that mob behind us. But we'll be riding right through Kiowa and then Southern Cheyenne country, after that it'll be mostly Utes. I get along all right with the Cheyenne. Kiowa and Utes can be right testy. You never can tell about them. Let's hit the blankets, boy. We ready steady tomorrow."

Bones Gibson sat on his horse off to one side of the gathering and watched with a sort of grim amusement on his hawk-like face as the many men tried to get packed and mounted up. The sun was just beginning to peek over the horizon. Horses were pitching and bucking as their riders were getting the kinks out of them, mules were braying and snorting, and men were cussing and hollering. All in all it was a scene of chaos and confusion.

Bones's right-hand man, Van Eaton, a heavily muscled, sour-faced man who was little more than a brute, said, "I don't see why you let them igits come along."

"Preacher will kill probably twenty or twenty-five of them long before we finally corner him. We can use their supplies and mounts as ours give out."

"I don't like them reporters along."

"We couldn't refuse them. Freedom of the press, and all that. But if they can't keep up, that's going to be their hard luck."

Van Eaton curved his thick lips into something vaguely resembling a smile. "Yeah. I see what you mean. Accidents do happen along the trail."

"Exactly."

"Bones?"

"Yeah?"

"Preacher ain't no pilgrim. And we all best keep this in mind: When we get up into them mountains, all of Preacher's friends is gonna be lined up solid agin us."

"That's true. But from what I've been told, there are few real mountain men left at this date. Certainly not enough of them to cause us any real worry. And I got that from a very reliable source."

But Van Eaton was far from convinced. He shook his

head. "When we hit them mountains, we best double the guard and sleep with one eye open."

Bones glanced at his long-time friend and ally. "I don't remember you ever being this worried before."

"Ain't none of us ever been this far west, Bones. We been all over the Smokies and the Blue Ridge and the Adirondacks and the Greens and so forth, but never out here. I ain't never seen no country like this. It's . . . there . . . well, there ain't nothin' out here, Bones. It's . . . *empty*."

"Except for thousands of Indians," Bones reminded him. "But you and I have fought Indians hundreds of times."

"We also knew the country, Bones. And we ain't never fought no Plains Injuns. We're gonna lose men on this job. Lots of men. If it wasn't for all that money them silly foreigners offered to pay us, I'd say to hell with it."

"Van, those guns they's carrying is worth thousands of dollars, and they got thousands more in cash money with them. I seen some of it. The rings they's wearin' is worth a fortune. No, Van, them fancy pants, nose-up-in-the-air gentlemen ain't never gonna come out of the mountains alive. But we are. Rich enough to retire."

Van Eaton smiled. "You got it all worked out, don't you?"

"I always do, Van. I always do."

5

Knowing that their chances for survival were nil if they were caught out in the open plains by sixty-five or so men, Preacher and Eddie packed up, saddled up, and rode out before dawn that morning, heading straight west. Seventy-five or so miles away, the gang of man-hunters finally pulled out, about two hours after.

Indians from several tribes saw Preacher and the boy as they crossed the great expanse of rolling hills and waving grass, but they made no hostile moves toward them. They all knew Preacher and most felt he was as one with them. If the boy rode with Preacher, then he too was one with them.

The Indians also saw the huge group of heavily armed and mounted men coming up behind Preacher. They watched the trackers study the ground and knew the men were after White Wolf and his pup.

But this was not their fight. And it would not be their fight unless the large group of men attacked them. For the Indian to mount an attack against such a large and well-armed army of men would be foolhardy. Nothing could possibly be gained by it.

"Preacher will not run long," one Indian remarked.

"No," another said. "There will be blood on the moon when Ghost Walker has his belly full of running."

"I think he runs because of the boy," yet another said. "When he finds a place where the boy will be safe, he will turn and make his move."

"It would be interesting to watch," the first one said.

The others smiled. "But dangerous, and would not serve us in any way."

That was true, the Indians agreed, then wheeled their horses and rode back to their village.

Preacher finally found what he was looking for. The country had turned higher and drier, the grass shorter, and the landscape dotted with buttes, cliffs, and mesas. Preacher stowed Eddie and told him to stay put. He tied sacking over the hooves of Thunder and Eddie's pony, and walked the horses back to where he'd found a blind canyon. There, he removed the sacking and rode the horses deep into the canyon. Then he replaced the sacking and walked them back out, staying close to the wall and carefully removing all signs of his departure.

He picketed the horses and then ran back to fetch Eddie and the other horses. He found a small creek and led them back along it. By the time Bones and his men reached the creek, the water would have cleared and the hoof marks would be long gone.

"Now, Eddie," Preacher told him, "we got about a day and a half, maybe two days, 'fore those men reach us. I know that Bones and Van Eaton don't know this country. What I don't know is whether Dark Hand does. I'm bettin' that he don't know this is a blind canyon. I got to shorten the odds some. And this is how you and me is gonna do it . . ."

"Preacher rides into the canyons to try to lose us," Dark Hand said to Bones. "But it is a clumsy attempt. I find his tracks going in. Nothing coming out."

"Is there a way around it?" Van Eaton asked.

"There is a way around everything," the Pawnee said, making no attempt to hide his contempt for the white man. "But we would lose much time. But time is what we have. I do not like this canyon country. I say we go around."

"Be lots of twists and turns in there," said Mack Cornay, a thug from Maryland. "Preacher could do 'most anything. Head in any direction, or circle around and come in behind us."

Horace and Haywood and George Winters had dismounted and were studying the tracks that were plain before them. There was no doubt about it. Preacher and the kid and their pack horses had entered the pass and had not come out.

"I say we got no choice but to foller," George said. "If we don't, we run the risk of losin' them."

Bones looked up at the sun. Not yet noon. They had plenty of time. He made up his mind. "Let's go. We might trap him in there and end this show here and now."

High atop the mesa above the entrance to the blind canyon, Eddie and Preacher looked at each other and grinned.

"They took the bait," Preacher said. "I can't believe it, but they done it. All right, Eddie. You know what to do at my signal."

The boy nodded and then Preacher was gone.

The reporters from New York and Boston and Philadelphia did not like this canyon. It was hot and still and not one breath of breeze entered to fan them. John Miller, on assignment from a New York City paper, glanced at the Philadelphia journalist and saw that Raymond Simms was not happy about it either. William Bennett, writing for a magazine out of Boston was behind them, and one look at his face told Miller that he too was very unhappy about this present situation.

When their editors had handed them this assignment, all the men had been thrilled beyond words. They would be going into wild, savage, untamed, and unexplored country. They could all write books about their adventures, make a lot of money, and perhaps aid in bringing an outlaw to justice. But back in Missouri they had been told by a dozen well-placed gentlemen that Preacher was no outlaw. He had worked for the government and was a highly respected scout and trail-blazer. And they had finally realized that Bones Gibson and his men were nothing more than common murderers, thugs, and hooligans, under the dubious disguise of bounty-hunters.

But it was too late to turn back. The reporters were depending on the bounty-hunters to guide them back to civilization. In other words, the eastern reporters were all lost as a dim-witted goose.

Dark Hand had fallen back to the middle of the column. He did not like these twisting canyon trails and he felt in his belly that Preacher had set up some sort of trap.

"I say," Sir Elmore Jerrold-Taylor said, twisting in his saddle and looking around him, "isn't this grand fun?"

Baron Wilhelm Zaunbelcher agreed, adding, "But I am so disappointed that we have not been able to kill any savages. Let's hope our luck will change."

Duke Sullivan said, "But what magnificent country we've seen. The vastness of it boggles the mind."

His mind hadn't been boggled just yet. But it was about to be.

All of a sudden, the trail ended against a sheer rock wall. For a moment, Bones was stumped. That confusion abruptly ended when the man next to him, Bill Front, toppled from his saddle, shot through the head. Cal Johnson screamed as Front's brains splattered all over the front of his shirt.

Dark Hand had leaped from his horse before the echo of the shot began reverberating around the canyon and jumped for the protection of a rock overhang.

Boots Baldwin was the next to go down, the front of

his shirt suddenly stained with fresh blood. He fell dying against another man and took him to the ground with him.

Preacher and Eddie had worked for most of a day and a half rigging another surprise for Bones and his party. At Preacher's yell, Eddie slapped Thunder on the rump and the animal jumped, stretching the rope taut. "Haww!" Eddie yelled, and the animal strained and a wooden platform gave way, spilling hundreds of pounds of rocks of various sizes down into the narrowest part of the canyon trail. The rocks took other rocks with them as they tumbled down the incline, some of them huge boulders, and within a matter of seconds, the trail was blocked by a pile of boulders twenty feet high and fifty feet deep.

Preacher had both hands filled with those terrible pistols of his and was wreaking havoc on those trapped inside the narrow walls of the dark trail.

Preacher had gathered up bushes to dry and he lit them and began throwing them onto the canyon floor. Then he started throwing small bags of black powder into the flames. The results were even better than he had hoped for. The concussion of the explosions brought down more rocks, hopelessly blocking the trail in a half dozen more locations. Horses were bucking and jumping and screaming in fright, throwing riders all over the place. Dead, dying, and wounded men were lying on the sand, many of them calling out for help that no one was able to give.

A warrior's smile on his lips, Preacher ran around the lip of the blind canyon to where Eddie was, and together, they got the hell out of there.

None of the reporters had been hit by any of the rounds Preacher had fired, but they had experienced the sensation of having the crap scared out of them.

Bones squatted down after he realized that no more shots were coming their way and assessed the situation. It was terrible. It was going to take them a good day and a half, maybe longer, to dig their way out of the huge piles of rocks blocking the trail in half a dozen places. And they'd lose another four or five days tending to the wounded. Normally, Bones would have left the wounded to fend for themselves. But with the reporters along, he couldn't do that. They would write him up as a monster or worse.

"Damn you, Preacher," he softly offered the oath. "Damn your eyes."

Dark Hand squatted down beside him in the churned and bloody sand. "I tried to warn you about Preacher. Do not underestimate the man. Not ever."

Bones ignored that. "How many men down?"

"Eight dead. Nine others wounded. Two of them will not live through the night."

"One man and a snot-nosed kid and they take out nineteen men and we never even got a glimpse of them."

Sir Elmore Jerrold-Taylor turned to one of Bones's regular gang and said, "Your Mister Preacher appears to have no fair play in him, whatsoever."

Andy Price looked at the Englishman for a long moment, then shook his head, which had a big knot in it from a falling rock, muttered something under his breath, and walked off to help move the tons of rock.

"Brutish lout!" Sir Elmore said.

"This here's Big Sandy Crick, boy," Preacher said, reining up and stepping down. "We'll make camp here."

They had been riding steady from before dawn to nearly dark for several days. Preacher figured they were at least a week ahead of the man-hunters and could finally afford to relax and rest the horses.

"How far to the big mountains, Preacher?" Eddie

asked, as he gathered up dry wood for a smokeless fire without having to be told. Preacher was as proud of the boy as if he were of his own blood.

"Five days easy ridin'."

"Preacher?" Eddie's tone was soft.

"Yeah, boy?"

"I know you been thinking I'm all better and such, but I know the truth. I ain't gonna make it, Preacher. There are too many scars on my lungs. And the sickness affected my heart, too. It's weak. Right now, with me all tanned and such, it's like the quiet before the storm. But I can't get no better."

"Boy . . ."

"No, Preacher." Eddie shook his head and smiled. "I know. Believe me, I do. But I'm not afraid of dying. Really, I'm not. I've been baptized. And I believe in heaven. So let's you and me just have a real good time for as long as it lasts, all right?"

Preacher looked long into the boy's eyes and saw the truth there. He sighed and said, "All right, Eddie. We'll have a high ol' time until who flung the chunk. I got cold mountain lakes for you to see and catch big trout out of. I got waterfalls and wild rushin' streams for you to witness. And meadows bustin' with flowers of all colors. We'll have us a summer of fun, you and me. But mayhaps you be wrong about yourself, boy."

But Eddie only smiled sadly.

Bones and company buried their dead and tended to their wounded and the reporters noted it all in their journals. They carefully coded their words in case Bones or some of his men who could read might get their hands on the journals, for they were not being kind to Bones or any of the other men with him. The reporters now realized, after listening to some of the men talk, that Preacher was no desperado, and the shooting back in Ohio had been a fair one. The thousands of dollars now on Preacher's head was not an officially sanctioned reward, but money put up by friends and family of Elam Parks. And the reporters now were having doubts that any of them would live to tell of this terrible travesty of justice. For, to a man, they believed Bones and his men intended to kill them, and the so-called noblemen who were on this blood sport.

The reporters began to make friends with one of the men who had come along for the adventure of it, a man from St. Louis who was having a lot of second thoughts about this trip. His name was Jim Slattery.

On the evening before they were to resume the hunt, Jim came to the reporters' fire and squatted down, pouring himself a cup of coffee. In a soft voice, he said, "I figure in about a week, we gonna be about sixty-seven miles north and some east of Bent's Fort. I'm fixin' to leave this den of thieves and murderers and head there. Y'all want to come with me?"

"I've heard of that place," the Boston reporter said. "We could perhaps hire an escort back east from there."

"I'm sure you could," Jim agreed. "They's supply wagons rollin' in and out all the time, so I was told. Boys, I got me a real bad feelin' about the company we're in. I think them foreigners are in for a rude surprise. If Bones and his bunch has their way, I don't believe none of them hoity-toity barons and dukes and counts and the like is gonna come out of this alive. But they're a nasty lot themselves, so I don't hold out a lot of sympathy for them."

"Nor do we," another reporter said.

"All right then. That's settled. When I'm ready to make the jump, I'll give you boys the high sign. Stay loose."

"Mr. Slattery, what do you think is going to happen to this Preacher person?"

Jim grinned. "Preacher is a war hoss, boys. That little deal back in the canyon should have warned off any reasonable-thinkin' man. Damn shore did me. What do I think is gonna happen? Well, I think these ol' boys is gonna chase Preacher and the sick little boy until they catch up with them. And when they do, they're gonna be the sorriest bunch of people east or west of the Mississippi River. That's what I think."

"We are all in agreement with that. Tell us, Mister Slattery, why we have not seen any savages."

"They've seen us. You can bet on that. We're too big a bunch for them to attack. Now, I ain't gonna lie to you, when we leave the main body, we're gonna be in considerable risk. We're gonna have to ride light, fast, and cautious. But if we have any kind of luck at all, we'll make it. We're all armed, and from what I've been told, it'll take a big bunch of savages to attack us. Dyin' young ain't real attractive to an Injun." He stood up. "Stay ready, boys. Night."

Across the way, Van Eaton had been watching the Missouri man and the reporters through very suspicious eyes. "I think them reporters is plannin' on pullin' out when they get a good chance," he said to Bones.

"Good," the leader of the group said. "I hope they do. They'll be fair game for any band of hostiles who spot them. None of those reporters can shoot worth a damn. The reason we haven't been attacked is because of our size. Wherever those nitwits are thinking of heading, odds are they'll never make it. With them gone, it'll be a whole lot easier for us to kill Preacher and the kid."

"Bent's Fort," Van Eaton said. "That's the only place they could be heading."

Bones was thoughtful for a moment. "Let them go. Even if they do make it through and tell their story to the Army, and the Army decides to do something about it, this hunt will be long over before patrols can find us. I say good riddance."

"That kid had something to do with that ambush back

yonder," Van Eaton said, his eyes shining hard and cruel. "I want that little puke alive. I'll skin him and listen to him holler."

"You can sure have him. Might be fun listenin' to him squall. Say, cut me off a hunk of that venison, Van. Talk like that makes me hungry."

6

While Eddie and the horses rested, Preacher prowled around and found what was left of three wagons. He looked at the shaft and head of an arrow still embedded in the charred wood of a wagon bed. Kiowa. They had probably been on a raiding party and come up on these poor folks, he mused. But he could find neither graves nor bones. He rambled through the burned wreckage looking for anything that might be salvageable. He found a saw and laid it to one side. He had a use for that. He found a good sized piece of lead and a bullet mold, which he took. He also found a small Bible. He opened the cover and tried to make out the writing, but the weather had blotted the words. He saved the Bible; most of it was still readable and Preacher did find comfort in the words of the Good Book. Besides, he felt that Eddie might like to have it. The boy had said he liked to read the Bible.

That got Preacher to feelin' maudlin, and with an effort, he shook off the depression. When the boy's time came, it would just have to be. Eddie seemed resigned to it.

Back at the camp, he hauled out the shotgun and went to work cutting off most of the barrel. He cut it down and hefted it. Now it was one of the most dangerous weapons man ever devised. A sawed-off shotgun at close range could stop just about anything that moved.

Eddie carried two smaller caliber pistols hooked onto his saddle, with two or more in the saddlebags. Whether he would use them against a human being was something that Preacher did not know, but he had a hunch that Eddie would not hesitate to cock and fire if it came right down to the nut-cuttin'.

Preacher stowed the now short-barreled shotgun and gave Eddie the battered Bible he'd found. "Figured you might like to have this, boy. I found it in what was left of some wagons over yonder."

"I wonder who they were?"

"No way of knowin', boy. There ain't a sign of a grave nowheres." He shrugged his shoulders. "But that really don't mean nothin'. Even if they was buried, it was prob'ly in a shallow grave and the critters dug 'em up and et 'em then scattered the bones." He watched the boy shudder at that prospect and said in a softer tone, "That'll not happen to you, Eddie. I give you my word on that."

"That makes me feel better," the boy replied, a somber expression on his thin, tanned face. "Preacher? Are there any towns out here?"

Preacher chuckled, "No, boy. Nothin' like a town. Some south of us is Bent's Fort and it's sorta like a town. Further on west they's a big adobe buildin' with log walls around it where some mountain men live with Mexican and Injun wives. I understand they taken to farmin' now. Don't know how long that will last.* But towns?" He shook his head. "There ain't no towns 'til you hit the West Coast. And that's a far piece."

*Not long. Fremont visited there in 1842 and reported all was well. The next year when mountain men came through, the place was deserted. The town of Pueblo was started around 1860.

"I'd like to see the ocean," Eddie said, a wistful note to his words.

"Mayhaps you will, boy."

Eddie smiled. "No," he said softly. "I won't. But you have. Will you tell me about it?"

Preacher leaned back against a fallen log and stuffed and lit his pipe. He pondered that question. "The Pacific Ocean. First time I seen it I couldn't believe my eyes. The water was blue. And when it come crashin' up aginst the rocks along the shore it made a thunderous noise and spray and foam went to flyin' ever'where. Liked to have scared my horse to death, and my heart beat some faster too. I rode down there and took me a swaller of that water. Spit it out fast. Salty water. Ain't fit for man nor beast. I can't see how a fish could live in it, but they do. And they's monsters in the ocean that eat folks. Now, I ain't never seen none of them monsters, I won't lie about that, but I was told about 'em by some sea-farin' men. They tell me they's somethin' called an octo-pussy that's got about twelve arms that's twenty-five feet long each and the arms has got suckers on it; that's what holds you whilst the thing eats you." Preacher and Eddie both shuddered at that thought.

"It was a whale in the sea that ate Jonah," Eddie offered.

"Say! You're right, it was. Tell you what, why don't you read some aloud from the Bible whilst I rustle up some vittles?"

"Any passage you favor, Preacher?"

"Naw. I'll leave that up to you."

The boy turned to Psalms and read aloud the 23rd. Preacher soon realized that the boy had that one memorized, but said nothing about it. Must be plumb awful to be so young and knowin' that any day could be your last, Preacher thought. That there is a mighty brave little boy. He's got more courage in his big toe than a lot of men have in their entire body.

Eddie had stopped reading and Preacher saw that the boy had read himself to sleep. He covered Eddie with a blanket and set about making supper as quietly as he could. He thought to himself, "Another day of rest and then we head for the mountains. I got a lot to show the boy, and prob'ly not a lot of time to get it done."

Shortly after crossing into what would someday be Colorado, the reporters, led by Jim Slattery, slipped away from Bones and his men and simply vanished into history. Somewhere between the White Woman and Bent's Fort, the small party of men met their fate. But no one knows what that fate was. Not one trace of them, their horses, or their equipment has ever been found. Their newspapers and magazines hired scouts to try to find out what happened, but to no avail. It was doubtful they became lost, for historians have noted that Jim Slattery was an experienced woodsman and a fine warrior. Over the years that followed their disappearance, several hundred Indians from numerous tribes were asked about the party of men. If any of the Indians had any knowledge about the eight men, they went to their graves carrying the secret.

The West holds many such mysteries, and it yields its secrets reluctantly. Only one man is reported to have known what happened to the reporters and to Jim Slattery, and he did not solve the mystery until almost a quarter of a century after their disappearance. He died an old, old man, near the turn of the century. It is said that the old mountain man told only one person, the legendary gunfighter that he helped raise: Smoke Jensen.

But that is quite another story.

"Well?" Bones demanded impatiently.

Dark Hand and two other trackers stood up and

shook their heads. "Lost it," the Pawnee admitted. "These are not their hoof prints."

Bones threw his hat on the ground in frustration. Three weeks had passed since the ambush in the blind canyon and Preacher and the kid seemed to have vanished into the air.

Only the noblemen seemed unperturbed by the delay in finding their prey. It didn't make any difference to them if the hunt took five weeks, five months, or five years. They all had more money than they could spend in ten lifetimes. Besides, this was good fun. The air was clean and fresh and quite invigorating, the scenery magnificent, the food tasty. The company was lousy and the conversations lacking in grammatical correctness and substance, but one couldn't have everything.

"I say, old boy," Sir Elmore Jerrold-Taylor called to Van Eaton. "Do calm yourself and try some of this wonderful pâté, won't you?"

Van Eaton told the Englishman where to put his pâté, and stalked off. He walked to Bones and said, "Let's give this up and head on back, Bones. We ain't never gonna find them two in all this wilderness."

That idea was becoming more and more appealing to Bones. They were camped on the eastern side of the Rockies and Bones had to admit he had never even dreamed of country such as this. Mountains two miles high, in country that looked so rough it seemed incredible that any human being could possibly live there.

Bones was beginning to understand why that breed of men called mountain men were held in such awe and respect. He just thought he'd seen mountains and rough country in the Smokies.

"All right," Bones said. "Let's talk to the fancy-pants crowd and see what they say."

"Why, heaven's no!" Jon Louviere said. "The hunt must continue. We're paying you to guide us, so guide on."

Bones put it to his men.

"Arapaho and Cheyenne behind us, Ute in front of us and all around us," Dark Hand pointed out. "Is not good."

"I figure we been real lucky to get this far without havin' trouble with the savages," Jimmie Cook said. "I think we're pushin' our luck to go any deeper. But if them lords and the like want to go on payin' us . . . I'm for it."

"Exactly where the hell are we?" Sam Provost asked.

"Just east of Ute Pass," Dark Hand said. "None of you have seen rough country yet. The Rockies are just beginning here. Preacher does not know it, but I left my tribe and spent two years in these mountains. I do not know them as well as he does, but I am not lost."

"You really think we can find them?" Bones asked.

The Pawnee was honest in his reply. "We will be lucky if we do. Or unlucky," he added.

Bones nodded his agreement with both remarks. He did not know whether to go north, south, or west. But he did feel strongly that Preacher had not doubled back to the east. Bones had forty-eight men left, six of them still suffering from wounds that had left them just able to sit in a saddle and not much more.

"In your opinion, Dark Hand," Bones asked, "where do you feel in your heart Preacher went?"

"Deep in the mountains," the Pawnee answered quickly. "West and slightly north of here."

"You've been there?"

"One time only. It is wild country. And do not allow yourselves to be trapped in there when the winter comes. You will surely die."

"Do mountain men live up there in the winter?" Willy Steinwinder asked from the group of noblemen.

"Some of them. But they are used to hardships. It does not bother them."

"Bah!" the Austrian scoffed. "This is nothing compared to my Alps. Let us push on."

"Yes. Quite right," Burton Sullivan said. "And if we see

painted hostiles, we shall engage them. I feel the need for some blood-letting."

The Pawnee looked at the Englishman. "You are a fool!" he said bluntly. "The Ute, the Arapaho, and the Cheyenne have all been watching us since we approached the shadows of the mountains. You think that pack horse broke loose the other night? Bah! A warrior slipped into camp and took it. That is sport with my people. You all sleep like the dead. If you continue to sleep in such a manner you will all *be* dead." He walked off.

"The guard is doubled from here on," Bones said. "Dark Hand knows what he's talking about. We push on at first light."

As the crow flies, Preacher and Eddie were only about seventy miles from where Bones and his man-hunters were camped. But traveling through that country is not counted in miles, rather in days and even weeks. They were camped along a tiny rushing stream in a camp so cleverly disguised that Bones and party could ride to within twenty-five feet of it and not know it was there. The Utes knew it was there, but they did not bother Preacher and the boy. They knew some sort of deadly hunt was taking place, and they were curious about that. They were both amazed and appalled that such a large band of white men would want so desperately to kill so frail-looking a boy. The Utes shook their heads and again thought how silly white men were.

Preacher had been their enemy and he had been their friend, as he would be again. For that was the way of things. But for now, the Ute and Cheyenne chiefs passed the word: Leave Ghost Walker and the boy alone. And leave the stupid white men alone. Steal their horses if you like, but let them play out this game to its end.

"The Indians know we're here, don't they, Preacher?"

Eddie asked. He wasn't feeling well and Preacher had made him a soft bed of boughs and was letting him rest.

"Oh, yeah. I see sign of them near'bouts ever' day. They're curious and puzzled 'bout what's goin' on. Injuns is naturally curious folks. And the ways of the white man is real strange to them. It's puzzlin' to 'em why all them men is chasin' us. They can't figure out what harm we is to them." Preacher looked over at Eddie and saw the boy was asleep. He walked over to him and put a hand on Eddie's forehead. Hot. Real hot.

Preacher had found some catnip plants and he crushed some and made a tea. While he was letting it steep, Eddie moaned and opened his eyes. Preacher was at his side. "Ain't feelin' so good, right?"

"I'm hot, Preacher."

"I can fix that." He poured some of the vile smelling liquid in a cup. "It don't smell very good, but it's good for you. Sip it, Eddie. Trust me."

Eddie wrinkled his nose at the smell. "Smells like old dirty socks."

Preacher laughed. "Yeah, it do, don't it. Wait 'til you taste it. It tastes even worser. But it'll knock that fever right out. My mamma used to have us drink this ever' day, and we never was sick. I want you to drink three cups a day, Eddie. Ever' day. You start sippin'."

Preacher found some wild onions and Indian potatoes and started up a venison stew. The broth would be real good for Eddie. "A body don't have to starve in the wilderness, Eddie," Preacher talked as he worked. "But to survive in the wilderness, you got to work with nature, not aginst it. You drink your tea and sleep. Sleep is good for a body. When you wake up, this here stew will be ready to eat and it'll be larrepin' good. If you wake up and I ain't here, don't worry. I'll be prowlin' around."

Preacher sat the kettle to one side so it would simmer slow, and rifle in hand, he worked his way up the mountain until he found him a vantage spot. He took his spy-glass from his pouch and extended it, then slowly looked the country over. He saw a few plumes of smoke, but they had been there for several days, and he knew that it was a small camp of Utes about fifteen miles off. He saw no other signs of life.

He wondered for a moment if Bones had given up the hunt. But he shook that off. Bones wasn't known for givin' up. He had to take a prisoner from the group and find out what the hell was going on. The only problem was, he couldn't leave the boy alone.

Well, there was one thing he could do: He could take the boy down into the Ute camp and see if they'd take care of him. He'd rather go into a Cheyenne camp, for he'd always gotten along well with the Cheyenne—except for a few minor skirmishes over the years—and the Cheyenne revered children. But he didn't know of any Cheyenne village close by. So it was the Utes or nothing.

Preacher worried about that all the way down the mountain. But when he reached his camp, he stopped worrying about getting into and out of a Ute village alive.

About a dozen Ute warriors were waiting for him, and one of them had a hand on Eddie.

7

The man with a hand on Eddie lifted his other hand, palm out, in a gesture of peace. Preacher lifted his hand as recognition flooded him. The Ute was a tribal chief called Wind Chaser.

"Ghost Walker," Wind Chaser acknowledged. He patted Eddie's shoulder "Boy sick."

Preacher deliberately laid his rifle aside and walked away from it, a move that did not go unnoticed by the other Utes. "Yes, he is, Wind Chaser. But I'm gettin' him well."

"No get well running all over the mountains," Wind Chaser said.

"I was gonna bring him to your village and see if you'd take care of him whilst I checked my back trail."

That pleased the Ute. He solemnly bowed his head. "My woman take good care of him. How is he called?"

"Eddie."

"Ed-de," Wind Chaser repeated. "Means what?"

This was always difficult to explain to an Indian. Indian names meant something, or stood for an event or happening. "He's named after his father."

"Ummm. Confusing. But I have never understood the white man's ways Why men chase you and boy?"

This, too, was chancy and Preacher chose his words carefully. "The boy was a slave. His master was cruel. You can see what condition he left the boy in. I took the boy and the man came after me with a gun. I kilt him. The man's friends put a bounty on my head."

"Ummm," Wind Chaser said. "Yes. This is true. My warriors have been close to their camp and heard them talk. But there is more."

"More?"

"Yes. But my warriors did not understand it, and I do not understand it. There are men of great importance among those who hunt you and Ed-de. Men who have slaves who see to their needs. Cook for them, wash their clothes, and saddle their horses. It is all very strange."

Damn sure was. Preacher sat down by the fire and poured a cup of strong coffee. He took a sip and passed the cup around. It was returned empty and he poured more until the pot was empty. He stirred the stew. He shook his head. "I don't understand it, Wind Chaser. It's confusing to me, too. But it's noble of you to offer to care for the boy whilst I scout the camp of my enemies."

Wind Chaser shook his head. "It is nothing. I remember a winter when Ghost Walker provided meat for my old father and my family while we were away at war. A debt is something that must be repaid."

Preacher had forgotten all about that. That had been a good fifteen years back. Preacher went and fetched the horse that Charlie Barnes had ridden. He handed the reins to Wind Chaser and spoke to the chief in his own tongue, using sign language when the Ute words did not come to him. "The boy is very sick and knows he is going to die." Wind Chaser's eyes widened at that. "Eddie wishes to have a set of buckskins like mine before he passes from this world to the next. Please accept this horse from me to you in exchange for the buckskins."

Wind Chaser rose and carefully inspected the horse, his eyes shining at the sight of the animal. "One small set of coverings is not enough for such a fine animal. I will have my woman make you a fine set of buckskins. Is that fair?"

"That's fair."

"Eddie is a brave boy," Wind Chaser said, kneeling down and stroking the boy's hair. He faces death like a Ute, without whimpering and whining. He will be warm and safe in my own lodge. When you return from your scouting, you will be welcomed in my village like my brother. We go!"

"See you, boy," Preacher said to Eddie with a wink. "I'll be back in a couple of weeks. You mind your manners, now, you hear?"

Eddie smiled and nodded his head. This was a grand adventure for the boy, and he showed no signs of fear.

Wind Chaser slashed down with a hand and a big brave picked up Eddie and gently carried him to Eddie's paint pony, already saddled. That told Preacher that the Utes had watched every move he and Eddie had made since coming into the mountains.

"I will not lead those men to your village, Wind Chaser," Preacher said.

Wind Chaser shook his head. "You come when and how you like, Ghost Walker. If those men hunting Ed-de come to my village, they will be fed a good meal and then we shall see how well they die. Do not worry yourself about Ed-de. He will be cared for."

The Utes left like wisps of smoke, flitting silently through the timber.

Preacher sat for a time, eating the stew and drinking coffee. The Utes would take care of Eddie and defend his life to the last man. If an Indian gave his word on something, chisel it in stone. Preacher rose and began construction of a crude corral for the pack horses and a cache for his supplies. The animals had access to water and forage and if food ran out, or a puma or bear threatened them, they could easily break out of the brush enclosure. Preacher erased all signs of the camp, packed a few things, saddled up Thunder, and was gone that afternoon.

Dark Hand looked nervously around the camp. He had just returned from his afternoon's prowling and did not like what he had seen, or rather, what he had *not* seen.

"What's wrong with you?" Van Eaton snarled at the Pawnee. "You're makin' me nervous."

"We are alone," Dark Hand said.

"What do you mean, alone?"

"No Ute. No Cheyenne. No Arapaho. We are alone."

"Why . . . you ninny! That's good."

"That's bad," Dark Hand contradicted. "That means the chiefs have met and agreed to stay out of the fight. That means that Preacher is on the hunt. For us. He is probably out there now, looking at us. Waiting. Watching."

"Now, just how did you come to that?"

"It is the only thing that makes any sense."

"Well, it don't make no sense to me," Van Eaton said sourly.

"Yes. That makes sense to me, too," Dark Hand said haughtily.

Van Eaton watched the Pawnee walk off. He figured he'd been insulted but he didn't quite know how. He looked all around him. Birds were singing and feeding, squirrels were hopping around, all having grown used to the presence of the large body of men. Van Eaton snorted. "Preacher out there," he muttered. "Hell, he ain't within fifteen minutes of his camp."

Preacher was about two hundred yards away, lying on his belly in some brush. Part of him was clearly visible to the naked eye, if anyone would just make a very careful visual inspection of their surroundings. But he knew none of the men would. What Preacher was doing was one of the oldest of Indian tricks—hide where your enemy would least suspect.

Preacher was puzzled by what he saw and the few words that he could hear. He couldn't figure out who those fancy-dressed men were, and what they were doing with the likes of Bones Gibson. Nothing about this made any sense to Preacher. Those duded up men had servants and cooks waitin' on them hand and foot. So why were a bunch of rich folks like them tied in with Bones, and why were they hunting him?

Preacher saw Dark Hand looking carefully all around him. He immediately averted his eyes so he would not be staring directly at the Pawnee. Dark Hand spoke with Van Eaton for a moment, and then walked away.

Preacher watched the Pawnee until he disappeared and then backed away from the scant cover and into the thicker brush and timber. He didn't think Dark Hand had spotted him, but he wasn't going to take any chances. He made a slow half circle of the camp until he found a good spot to lay under cover until dark and he could make his move, or until one of them in the camp came out alone to answer a call of nature.

A half a dozen came out to the area together and Preacher could do nothing except listen to them swear, grunt, and make other disgusting sounds. Then his ears perked up when he heard one say, "Them royal folks has upped the ante on Ol' Preacher and the kid."

"Yeah, I heared," another said. "But what they want is foolish to me. They want us to take Preacher alive, and then turn him a-loose unarmed and on foot so's they can hunt him down for sport."

Preacher blinked at that. *Sport?* What the hell kind of people were these fancy-pants men? Royal folks? What in the world did that mean?

"But Van Eaton wants the kid," a third voice was added. "What did the kid do to get on Van Eaton's bad side?"

"I don't know," yet another voice said. "But Van Eaton

ain't got but one side, and it's all bad. He's even worser than Bones, and that's sayin' a lot. He says he's gonna skin him alive slow-like just to listen to him holler."

Preacher felt a coldness wash over him with those words. A dark and deadly hand touched his heart. Any man that would torture a kid, of any color, was too low to let live. And if Preacher had his way, Van Eaton would not be counted among the living for very much longer.

Skin Eddie? What matter of men were these people? How low-life could man be? Preacher figured he was right close to just about the lowest of the low.

Preacher fought back with some effort an urge to rise up and blast these men into eternity. But doing that would only wound the tip of the snake's tail. He wanted Bones, Van Eaton, and those fancy-dressed men. And he wanted just one man from this bunch to question. And if he didn't want to talk to Preacher, Preacher knew a way to loosen his tongue—he'd just turn him over to the Utes.

Preacher lay under cover until dusk. Then he got his chance to grab one of Bones's men. A man he'd heard call John Pray wandered over to the area, alone, and started to drop his trousers. Preacher coshed him with a leather pouch filled with dirt and the man hit the ground unconscious. Preacher tossed the man over one shoulder and quickly took off.

When John Pray awoke he fully expected to get whacked on the head, like had happened three times already that night during the ride from camp. His head hurt something fierce. But no blow came. He tried to move his hands, but they were tied behind his back and his back was hard up against a tree. He looked across a hat-sized fire into the hard and cold eyes of a man dressed all in buckskins.

"You be Preacher?" John croaked out the question.

"I be Preacher."

"Are you gonna torture me?"

"If I have to. And believe me, John Pray, I will."

John believed him. Oh, how he believed him. "What do you want to know?"

"Everything. Front to bottom and side to side. You tell me ever'thing you know about this gang that's chasin' me and the boy, and I'll cut you loose. And that's a promise. You can either hook up again with Bones, or clear out. It's up to you. Start talkin', John Pray."

John Pray was a brigand and a scalawag, but he was no fool. He opened up and talked for a full ten minutes, nonstop. So complete was his confession, Preacher didn't have to ask him a thing.

When John Pray fell silent, Preacher hauled out his Bowie and cut him free. Preacher gestured toward the coffee pot. "Help yourself."

"Mighty nice of you," John said sarcastically. "Considerin' that you're sendin' me to my death."

"I ain't sendin' you nowheres, John Pray."

John sipped and smiled. "You know damn well I can't go back to Bones. They'd know I talked and kill me for sure. I ain't got no hoss and no guns. The savages will kill me 'fore I get ten miles from here."

Preacher picked up John Pray's brace of pistols, shot and powder, and knife. He tossed them to him. "I took the liberty of unloadin' them pistols. You got ample shot and powder. 'Bout ten miles from here, anglin' south, they's a crick. Follow it down to Ute Pass. Stay southeast 'til you come to another crick. That's Rock Crick. Follow that and you'll come to a settlement. Mex and Injun women and mountain men that's done takin' up plowin' and plantin'. You got money in your purse 'cause I seen it. They'll sell you a horse. Bent's Fort is due east of there. Keep ridin' and don't never come back to these mountains. If I ever see you again, I'll kill you, John Pray. Now, git gone!"

John Pray was gone in a heartbeat, not even looking back. Preacher immediately doused his fire and took up Thunder's reins and was gone in the other direction, putting miles between the man-hunter and himself before he settled down for the remainder of the night in a cold camp.

At dawn, Preacher gathered dry wood and built a tiny fire under the overhang of branches and boiled water for coffee. He was so angry he had to struggle to keep his emotions in check. A bunch of goddamn foreigners were planning to use him like some wild animal to hunt down . . . for sport. Preacher had a dirty opinion of people who hunted animals for sport and trophy and not for food. And Indians took an even sourer view of folks like that. Indians hunted animals for survival. They never killed what they couldn't use.

Preacher calmed down some and drank his coffee and chewed his jerky. He mulled over his situation. Counting the cooks and servants, he was outnumbered about fifty-some-odd to one. He knew that common sense told him to get Eddie and head deep into the mountains. Bones and them goddamn foreigners would never find them. Preacher knew that. But Preacher didn't much cotton to runnin' away. That cut against the grain. It wasn't that he hadn't run from trouble before, because he had. There was a time to fight and a time for a feller to haul his ashes. Said that plain in the Bible—sort of. But damned if Preacher was gonna run from the likes of Bones Gibson and a bunch of fancy-pants counts and barons and dukes and princes and so forth.

Now, about the boy. Eddie was safe in the Ute village. Bones would never attack an Indian village, even if he could get close enough without bein' seen, which he couldn't. Bones was arrogant, but he wasn't stupid.

Preacher drank the last of his coffee and made up his mind as the fire began dying down to coals. All around him lay the magnificence and majesty of the Rockies. Birds were singing and squirrels were playing and chattering.

He had done nothing to any of those men huntin' him. They wanted to do harm to him and Eddie. They wanted to use Preacher like some poor chased animal. But that would never happen. They wanted a war. Well, all right. That could happen. Preacher could damn sure give them a war. But this war would be on Preacher's terms—Preacher would lay down the rules of warfare. And they would be harsh. This would be a war like none they had ever seen. Count on that.

Preacher doused his fire and covered all signs of the camp. He saddled up Thunder and packed his few supplies and stepped into the saddle.

He rode for about fifteen miles before topping a rise and there, staying in the timber, he surveyed his surroundings. This was his country. The High Lonesome. The Big Empty.

And it was about to run red with blood.

8

Bones had shifted his camp.

It only took Preacher about one minute to determine which direction they'd gone. He did not immediately follow the tracks. Instead, Preacher threw together a small fire, made some coffee, and then sat for a time, ruminating.

Bones and Van Eaton had assumed rightly that John Pray would blab, telling Preacher everything that he knew. Dark Hand would point out that he'd been right all along in saying that Preacher was close-by, watching. So the smart move would be to shift locations. But this time it would be a much more secure camp, one that could be easily guarded and defended while the man-hunters made new plans.

The men had made no attempt to hide their tracks, so to Preacher's mind, that meant they wanted him to follow. "They think they gonna ambush you, Ol' Hoss," he muttered. "They got some boys layin' in wait for you to come amblin' along so's they can put a ball in your noggin. So you just sit right here and figure out where the main bunch is headin' and then circle around and do some dirty work of your own."

John Pray had told him that the Pawnee, Dark Hand,

had spent a couple or three years in this area. That was news to Preacher, but he didn't doubt the man's words. It made sense to him. Without someone who knew this country, Bones and his men would have been wanderin' about like a lost calf a-bellerin' for its mamma. So where would Dark Hand lead the men now that they knew Preacher was on the prowl?

That was a question that Preacher could not answer. Putting himself in Dark Hand's moccasins, he could come up with several dozen places where he'd go. But what he could do was pretty much determine the direction. Preacher carefully extinguished his fire and swung into the saddle.

"Let's go see what misery we can cause, Thunder. Then we'll go check on Eddie."

"We lost the mountain man!" Van Eaton said, an evil smile curving his lips.

"We will never lose Preacher," Dark Hand said sourly. "And he will not fall into your stupid and clumsy attempt to ambush him."

The men had taken a break and were watering their horses and resting after several hours of riding over rough country. Tatman, a Rogue out of Indiana, looked at the Pawnee, disgust in his eyes.

"'Pears to me, Injun, that you're 'bout half skirred of this Preacher."

Dark Hand smiled, sort of. "I fear no man. But I have much respect for many. Preacher has been in this country ever since he was a boy. He is respected, if not liked, by all. Songs are sung about him around the night fires, and stories are told and retold about his courage and cunning and fierceness in battle. Do not take your enemies lightly. To do so is to die. If you would but open your eyes and your brain, you would know that the Utes in this area have made a pact with Preacher. If you would have but looked at the signs back at our old camp, you would have seen one horse only. That means the boy is safe somewhere. Preacher would not have left him alone in the wilderness. This is grizzly and puma country. And this is also Wind Chaser country."

By now, the camp was silent, the men standing or sitting, all listening to the Pawnee speak.

"Wind Chaser is a war chief of the Utes. Very brave and very cunning in battle. I think the boy is in Wind Chaser's village. I know that we have been watched, and I think the watchers are warriors from Wind Chaser's village. For the time being, they are going to leave us alone. This fight is between us and Preacher. Any attempt to take the boy would mean instant death for us all." His eyes touched the eyes of every man in the camp. "Or a very long and slow and painful death by torture. Chances are slim that any of you will see one of Wind Chaser's warriors, but if by accident you do, do not shoot. Make no hostile moves toward any Indian you might glimpse. We must concentrate our efforts on finding and destroying Preacher. No one else."

Tatman snorted. "I still say you're skirred of Preacher."

Dark Hand cut his eyes. "You are a fool. I do not think you will die well."

"Injun," Tatman said. "You don't call me no fool!"

"He just did," Bones said. "And I would suggest we all pay heed to his words. Now mount up. Let's get out of here."

Bates and Hunter, the two men Bones had assigned to spring the ambush on Preacher, were growing restless. And more than a bit edgy. It was getting late in the afternoon. They both felt that Preacher should have been along hours before. And they both felt that Preacher had figured out Bones's plan and that the ambushers were now the hunted.

It was a feeling that neither of them liked.

Suddenly to their right and in the dark timber, came the unmistakable sounds of a mountain lion on the prowl. The cough and huff and angry snarl. Hunter and Bates both turned to face the chilling noise.

But they could see nothing. No movement of brush or low branches. The mountain wind died down to no more than a whisper and the men waited, their hearts thudding heavily in their chests. They were both uneducated men, neither able to read or write, and both very superstitious.

Preacher, crouched no more than fifteen feet away, suddenly split the high mountain air with the scream of a panther. Bates fired his rifle and hit nothing and Hunter peed his dirty underwear. Preacher screamed again and the horses of the men broke loose from their picket pins and went racing off, eyes wild with fear.

"Shoot your damn gun, Bates!" Hunter yelled, frantically reloading.

"At what?" Bates hollered.

Two young Ute braves, in their late teens, hiding and watching on the other side of the animal trail, had to shove their fingers in their mouths to keep from laughing at the antics of the two frightened white men. They knew it was Preacher on the other side of the trail, and not a panther. This was going to be a good story to tell around the night fires. They would entertain the whole village with its telling. They might even make up a dance, showing how frightened the silly white men were. Yes, they would definitely do that.

Hunter got his rifle charged and brought it to his shoulder just as Preacher picked up a rock and flung it. The fist-sized rock caught Hunter in the center of his forehead and knocked him down and goofy. His rifle went off and the ball missed Bates by about an inch, slamming into a tree. Bates yelled as blown-off bark bloodied one side of his face.

"You've shot me, you goose!" Bates hollered, dropping

his rifle and putting both hands to his bloody face. Bates suddenly stepped on a loose rock, lost his footing, and began flailing his arms in a futile attempt to maintain his balance. He lost and went rolling down the side of the rise, yelling and hollering for help. He banged his head on about a half dozen rocks on his way down and came to rest against a tree, totally addled.

The two young Utes were rolling on the ground, clutching their sides in silent hysterics at the sight unfolding before their eyes. This story and dance would be remembered and retold and danced for years to come. This was the funniest thing they had seen since Lame Wolf's fat and grumpy and ill-tempered wife, Slow Woman, sat down on a porcupine's tail while picking berries one day. Even Lame Wolf thought that was funny. Until she hit him in the head with a club and knocked him silly. Slow Woman never did have much of a sense of humor.

Preacher knew the young Utes were on the other side of the trail. They were good in the woods, but not as good as Preacher. And by now he could see them rolling on the ground in silent laughter. That was good. They would tell Wind Chaser and he would have them dance it out and the entire village would be amused.

Preacher stepped out of hiding and jerked the shot, powder, and pistols from the near-unconscious Hunter. He picked up both rifles and vanished into the timber. He caught up with their horses and led them off. Bates and Hunter were going to have some tall explaining to do when they caught up with Bones and party. If they caught up with Bones.

The two young Utes left in a run, back to their village. They could not wait to tell this story.

Wind Chaser was clutching his sides, his face contorted with laughter long before the young braves had finished telling their story. When they had finished, he wiped his eyes and said, "Our hunters have brought in much meat this day. We will feast and dance this evening. Ed-de will be entertained and be happy with this news." He pointed at the two young Utes. "You two go now and bathe and prepare your dance for this evening. You have both done well." He rose and entered his tipi to tell Eddie of the feasting and dancing and story-telling that evening. Good food, rest, and the attentions of the women had done the boy good. His fever was gone and he was able to walk about for short periods of time. Wind Chaser had talked it over with his wife and they had both agreed to ask Preacher if they could have the boy, for as long as Man Above allowed him time to live. If Preacher did not agree, well, that was the way it had to be. But Wind Chaser felt he could prevail upon the mountain man. He had known Preacher for a time, and known of Preacher for a longer time. And Preacher possessed uncommon good sense for a white man. Not as much sense as an Indian, of course, but one could not expect too much of a white man.

Preacher had found him a snug little hidey-hole for the evening. He had trapped a big, fat rabbit and it was on a spit. He was smiling about his day's work as he drank the strong black coffee and savored the good smells of food cooking.

Hunter and Bates had staggered into the camp of Bones and company just about dark. Both of them were footsore and weary, and both had knots on their heads.

Bones took one look at the pair and said, "I don't even want to hear about it." He turned and walked away.

Van Eaton took his plate of food and joined Bones, sitting down on the ground. "We got to talk, Bones."

"So talk."

"If Dark Hand is right, and I 'spect he is, and the Utes has taken a likin' to the kid, we can scratch him off the list. We won't be able to get within five miles of that Ute camp."

"Agreed."

"Preacher is playin' with us. He could have kilt both them men but didn't."

Bones nodded his head in sour agreement.

"I just don't like it, Bones. It's a black mood that's layin' on me. I get the feelin' that Preacher is tryin' to tell us that if we'll leave now, we can leave alive. But if we stay, he's gonna turn this game bloody."

"After seeing Hunter and Bates, I tend to agree with you. But them crazy foreigners has upped the ante, Van." He stated the amount and Van Eaton almost choked on his food. He swallowed hard and stared at Bones. Bones nodded his head. "You heard me right. We don't even have to think about robbing them. They're offering us enough money to retire on, Van. Think about it. With that much money we could both buy them farms and horse breeding stables and the like we've always talked about. We could live like gentry."

Van Eaton thought about that for a moment, his eyes shining with greed and cruelty and cunning. "Yeah. And oncest we got shut of the foreigners, we could kill ever'body 'ceptin' our own men and we'd have twicest the money."

"That's right. And them crazy lords and dukes and such has agreed to divvy up money right now if we'll stay. And they's this to think about: We might not even have to kill the men to get the money. You know damn well if we stay, Preacher is gonna kill fifteen or twenty, at least, 'fore we get him. Maybe more than that. Probably more than that. We could just take the money off their bodies and nobody would be the wiser."

"Is them lords and such carryin' that much money on them, Bones?"

"No. Of course not. But they are carrying bank drafts that's legitimate. All they got to do is fill them out and they're good. I know that for a fact. They're kill-crazy, Van. All of them. I ain't never heard tell of some of the things they claim to have killed. Rinossoruses and wild crazy-sounded animals all over the world."

Van Eaton blinked at that. "What kind of ossorusses? What the hell kind of animal is that?"

Bones shook his head. "I don't know. I never heard nothing like it. They may be tellin' great big whackers for all I know. What do you say, Van? Do we take the deal?"

Van Eaton slowly nodded his head. "Yeah, Bones. We take the deal."

"I got a plan," Bones said. "And it's a good one. The way I got it figured, it shouldn't take no more than a week to push Preacher into a pocket and let them fancy-pants foreigners kill him."

"And then we can get gone from this damn wilderness." Van Eaton looked around him at the night. The mountains were shrouded in darkness and it was cold for this time of the year. "I really hate this damn place, Bones. You can't get warm at night. Can you imagine what it's like out here in the *winter?*"

"No. And I don't want to find out, neither. I just can't imagine anybody in their right mind who would want to live in this godforsaken place."

At the Ute village, Eddie was having the time of his life watching the two young Indians act out what they had witnessed earlier that day. The boy was laughing and clapping his hands, his belly full of meat from the feast. Wind Chaser gently put his arm around the boy's shoulders and patted him.

Deep in the wilderness, Preacher snuggled deeper into his blankets and slept to the sound of wolves talking back and forth to each other. It was a comforting sound to the mountain man, for many people, both Indian and white, believed him to be a brother to the wolf. Some even went so far as to say Preacher was part wolf himself.

They were not that far from the truth.

9

Preacher rose from his blankets and squatted for a moment in the grayness of pre-dawn. In the brush and timber surrounding the little pocket of clearing where Preacher had made his camp, he could see gray and black shapes moving silently about, slowly circling him but making no attempt to enter the clearing.

"My brothers," Preacher said softly, his eyes on the big ever-moving wolves "You've come to warn me."

Low snarls greeted his softly-spoken words.

"So today it really starts," Preacher whispered. "They're really gonna come after me."

As one, their mission accomplished the wolves vanished, running deeper into the timber.

Kit Carson once said that Preacher was the"gawd-damnest feller" he'd ever seen. He had a way with animals like no man he'd ever known. Ol' Bill Williams said Preacher was spooky. He felt that Preacher could actually talk to animals, most especially with wolves. Jim Beckwouth once told a writer that of all the mountain men he'd ever known, the man called Preacher was the most fascinating. John Fremont confided in his friends that the mountan man Preacher was almost mystical in his dealings with animals. He swore that he actually witnessed a pack of wolves playing with Preacher one day, in a small meadow deep in the Rockies. He said that when they all tired of playing, they fell down on the grass and flowers and rested in a bunch, Preacher right in the middle of the huge wolves. Jim Bridger said that Preacher could be as rough as a cob, mean as a grizzly bear, and as gentle and compassionate as a mother with a baby.

Smoke Jensen, the West's most talked about, written about and feared gunfighter, whom Preacher took under his wing as a boy to raise after Smoke's pa died, wrote later in the biography, that the man called Preacher was a highly complex man, who lived under only one set of rules, his own. He said that Preacher was an inordinately fair man, but once his mind was made up, and his moccasins set on the path of his choosing, would brook no interference, from any man.

If those who made up the party who were now hunting Preacher for sport had known anything at all about the inner workings of the man, they would have immediately packed up and left the mountains as quickly as possible.

But they did not really know the matter or manner of the man they sought. And by the time they finally found out, it would be too late for most of them. It wasn't just that Preacher was a mountain man. For there were mountain men, albeit not many of them, who were as skittish as an old maid in a men's bath house. It was the individual himself that should have been studied closely. Bones had never had any experience with Preacher, or with men like him. His reputation as a successful man-hunter had come about by chasing down escaped convicts, weakened by physical abuse, poor food, and brutally hard work. He had chased down embezzlers who by the very nature of their work were not physically imposing people. Bones had chased down and captured—or shot dead—men who had killed their wives and wives who had killed their husbands. He had killed or captured ignorant farm boys who broke jail after some minor infraction. True, Bones had tackled some mean and vicious men and emerged victorious. But he had never taken on anyone who came even close to being in Preacher's league.

As for the royalty who were members of this party of man-hunters, to them this escapade in the wilderness was still nothing more than good sport and fun. Quite entertaining, really, don't you know? It was irritating to them that Bones had forbidden them to kill a savage or two, but perhaps when this Preacher matter was concluded, then they could hunt some Indians. They'd never taken a scalp, and that would be quite a novel thing to take back to show their friends. They were all looking forward to scalping some savages.

It just never entered their minds that they might be the ones to get killed and scalped.

Preacher struck first, three days after he'd waylaid Hunter and Bates. He still had it in his mind that he could maybe harass them into leaving the mountains. There was no way he could have known that the blood-hungry royalty had upped the ante on his head. He had checked on Eddie and found the boy was happier than he had ever seen him.

Wind Chaser was uncommonly blunt with Preacher. "My woman and I wish to keep Ed-de as our own, Preacher."

Preacher nodded his head. "And what does Eddie think about that?"

"He is a child. He does not know what is best for him. As adults, we do."

Preacher had to hide his smile. The Indian and the white man were so much alike, in so many ways, and yet, so far apart that their two cultures could probably never co-exist side by side.

"Well, when the time comes, I'll talk to Eddie. If it's all

right with him, it's all right with me, Wind Chaser." He smiled and to soften his words added, "And I'm purty sure it'll be just fine with Eddie."

Wind Chaser smiled. "The boy will want to stay with us. You will see."

"I 'spect you're right. I've cached supplies all over these mountains, Wind Chaser. So I'm gonna leave my horses with you and go this on foot."

Wind Chaser had noticed the huge pack and had suspected as much. He nodded his head. "This is no longer a game, White Wolf. Why don't you take some of the warriors and end this foolishness once and for all?"

Preacher shook his head. "This is personal, Wind Chaser. I talked to the wolves the other mornin'. They told me."

Wind Chaser felt the hair on the back of his neck hackle and he resisted the temptation to step back, away from Preacher. He had heard about Preacher and his relationship with the great gray wolves that roamed the countryside. It was just that sort of thing that made many people, Indian and white alike, believe the story that Preacher had been found as a baby and raised by wolves, suckled on their milk. Preacher had, of course, heard the story, and, naturally, being Preacher, he had never done anything to dispel the myth. Indeed, whenever he got the chance, he added a few words to strengthen the myth. The more Indians were spooked by him, the safer he was.

"Your brothers, the wolves, they were close to you?" Wind Chaser asked.

"'Bout as clost as me and you is right now."

"Ummm!" Wind Chaser said softly.

Smiling, knowing Wind Chaser would repeat the story and the legends about him would grow all over the Indian nation, Preacher walked out of the Ute village and made his way toward the timber. His pack would have bowed the back of a normal man. Preacher walked like he was carrying a pack full of feathers.

"Not a sign of him," the teams of men reported back to Bones after an all day search in an ever-widening circle around the base camp of the man-hunters.

"We seen savages," Mack Cornay said. "Plenty of them. But all they done was look at us. They didn't make no move, no gesture, nothin'."

"No tracks of that big rump-spotted horse he rides?" Van Eaton asked.

"No. Nothin'."

"He is on foot," Dark Hand spoke from where he sat on the ground. "He has hidden supplies all around and is now living with some wolf pack."

"Aw, hell!" George Winters said. "No human man lives with wolves. They'd tear him to pieces. All that talk is nothin' but poppycock and balderdash."

Dark Hand shrugged his shoulders in total indifference to what these foolish white men believed. Dark Hand and Preacher were about the same age, and Dark Hand had heard many things about the mountain man called Preacher over the years. Much of what was said about him was indeed nonsense. But some of the talk was true. Dark Hand knew that Preacher was not unique in his ability to get along with wolves. He knew of Indians who possessed the same talent. He also knew that Preacher did not sit with the spirits for guidance. Preacher was just a very highly skilled woodsman—as good as any Indian—and he had honed those skills to a knife blade sharpness.

Dark Hand also knew that Preacher had not killed the man called John Pray. He had scouted for miles the day after Pray had vanished and found where Preacher had taken him, tied him, questioned him, and then turned him loose.

And most importantly, he knew he would be much better off if he would leave the company of these foolish white men and strike out on his own. But the white men fascinated him. They were so ignorant about so many things. Dark Hand never tired of listening to the babble. They prattled on and on about the most unimportant subjects.

Tatman said sarcastically, "All right, Injun. You seem to think you more'un the rest of us. So what is Preacher gonna do now?"

"Start killing you," the Pawnee said matter-of-factly.

"Oh, yeah?" a big, ugly unwashed lout called Vic said, standing up. "I reckon you think this here Preacher is just gonna walk right in this camp and start blastin' away, huh?"

Dark Hand smiled knowingly. None of the white men had taken note that when he sat, he sat with his back to a boulder, or log, or tree. No one seemed to notice that Dark Hand utilized every available bit of cover even when in camp. How these men had lived this long was amazing to Dark Hand.

"No," the Pawnee said. "He will not come into camp firing his guns."

"Well, then," Vic said, his voice dripping with ugly sarcasm, "I reckon you think he'll call down lightnin' or something to strike us all dead? You seem to think this feller is some sort of god."

Dark Hand sighed. An instant later, Vic cried out and looked down at the arrow that was embedded deeply in his belly. Vic screamed as the pain hit him hard. His legs seemed to lose strength and he stumbled and sat down heavily on the ground. "Oh, mother!" he hollered, "Oh, my dear sweet mother!"

Dark Hand had bellied down on the ground before the first yell had passed Vic's lips, presenting no target at all for Preacher, and he was certain it was Preacher lurking in the dark brush and timber around the camp. The men started shooting wildly, hitting nothing and accomplishing only the wasting of lead and powder. Dark Hand suspected that Preacher had turned and slipped away as soon as he saw the arrow strike its mark. That was what he would have done, and Preacher could be as much Indian as he was white when he had to be.

When no more arrows came silently and deadly out of the brush, the men slowly began crawling to their knees and reloading. The cooks and servants of the gentry remained where they were, belly down on the ground, eyes wide with fear.

"Halp me!" Vic bellered. "Oh, sweet baby Jesus, halp me."

There was nothing anyone could do for the man. The arrow had torn through his stomach and when they laid Vic out on the ground and cut away the back of his jacket and shirt, they could see that the point was very nearly all the way through his back.

"Go ahead and shoot him," Jimmie Cook said. "I don't want to have to listen to all that hollerin' for days and nights."

Sir Elmore Jerrold-Taylor waved to one of his men. "Franklin here has received some medical training. See what you can do for this unfortunate wretch, Franklin."

Franklin knelt down and inspected the puncture wound. "I will have to push the arrow out the back, remove the barbed point, and then pull the arrow out from the front. But I fear the lining of the stomach has been penetrated front and back so all that would accomplish is a great deal of agony for the man. He will die no matter what I do."

"Oh, very well," Elmore said. "Wilson," he called to one of the cooks. "Be a good fellow and fix some tea, will you? I feel the need for something warm and soothing. Something to calm the nerves, don't you know?"

Preacher's big rifle boomed and Elmore's plumed hat

went sailing about twenty feet away. His Lordship yelped and unceremoniously hit the ground, belly down in the mud.

The Frenchmen, Louviere and Tassin, jumped behind a fallen log and landed right on top of the Prussian, Rudi Kuhlmann, knocking the wind out of him. Preacher's rifle boomed again and the Austrian, Willy Steinwinder, got a faceful of bark splinters as the heavy ball smacked into the tree he was trying to hide behind. One of Bones's men, Cal Johnson, sprinted for cover just as Preacher fired one of his pistols. Cal turned a flip in the air as the ball slammed into his right leg and sent him sprawling and hollering. Preacher fired again and the ball whined off the big iron cook pot and went ricocheting wildly and wickedly around the camp. One of the servants ran into a tree and knocked himself silly. Van Eaton jumped for cover and landed squarely in a big pile of horse crap. He was so afraid to move that he lay in the dung and suffered the indignity, cussing Preacher loud and quite emotionally. Bones had jumped behind a boulder as the rest of the camp sought cover wherever they could find it. Dark Hand lay safe behind a fallen tree and took silent satisfaction in watching the panic of the white men.

Just before Preacher took off for safer territory, figuring he had done enough damage for one day, he turned and unloaded his pistols into the panicked camp. The sound was enormous and the double-shotted barrels spewed lead in all directions.

Baron Wilhelm Zaunbelcher was just getting to his fancy, hand-made boots when Preacher cut loose and Horace Haywood jumped into the slight ground depression and landed right on top of the Baron. The Baron did not appreciate that at all and began roaring in German. Horace figured rightly that Wilhelm was giving him a sound cussing and rared back and slugged the Baron right on the royal snoot. Horace and Wilhelm, ignoring the whining lead balls, began rolling around on the ground, cussing and punching and kicking and biting and gouging, the blood and the mud and the snot flying in all directions.

Bones rose to his knees and looked at the fist-swinging, bleeding, cussing men, rolling around in the dirt. He shook his head in disbelief.

Horace tried to knee Wilhelm in the groin and then gouge him in the eye with a thumb.

"Oh, I say now!" Burton Sullivan called. "That's a foul. Unfair. Unfair. Fisticuffs is one thing, but ungentlemanly behavior simply won't be tolerated here. I must protest this. Why . . ."

Jack Cornell busted the duke in the chops and Burton went down, his mouth bloody. He jumped to his boots and assumed what was then considered a proper stance for bare-knuckle fighting—the left arm stretched out, left fist knuckles to the ground; the right fist held close to the face. "I'll thrash you proper!" Burton said.

"That'll be the damn day!" Jack replied and bored in. Much to his surprise, Burton Sullivan knocked him flat on his butt.

Dark Hand lay behind cover and smiled at the antics of the white men. With danger all around them, the fools were making war against each other. To Dark Hand's way of thinking, it had to be some sort of a miracle from Man Above that the white race had survived this long.

"Break them up!" Bones yelled to his men. "Right now. We can't afford this. Preacher might be back at any moment. Do it, damnit!"

The cussing and fighting men were hauled apart and led off, to be widely separated from each other until they cooled down. Cal Johnson's leg was bathed and bandaged by Franklin; but Cal was going to be out of action for a time.

Vic was moaning and carrying on something awful. Van Eaton walked over to the man. He stood looking down at him for a moment, then cocked and lifted his pistol.

Vic yelled, "No, Van! Don't do it, man. Please, no. For God's sake!"

Van Eaton coldly shot him in the head, abruptly silencing the moans. "Gettin' on my nerves," Van Eaton said, recharging his pistol.

The camp was silent for a moment. "Oh, well. What the hell? He wouldn't have lasted the night noway," Mack Cornay said. "I'll get a shovel."

"No!" Bones called. "We don't have the time. Just roll him over the side of that ravine yonder and let the buzzards have him. We're breaking camp."

"Where to this time?" Van Eaton asked.

"The scouts found a much better place. It'll be harder for Preacher to slip up on us." He looked around him. "I sure don't want a repeat of this day."

10

By the time the man-hunters ended the confusion in their camp and stopped fighting among themselves, Preacher was long gone. When Bones asked Dark Hand if he was going to attempt to pick up Preacher's trail, the Pawnee looked at the man as if he had taken leave of his senses.

"That's what Ghost Walker would like some of us to do," he told Bones. "I tell you, those who pursue Preacher now will not return."

"By God, I'll pursue him!" Tatman said, picking up his rifle and moving toward his horse. "That Injun's yeller. I knowed it all along."

Dark Hand shrugged that off and turned his back to the ignorant loudmouth.

"Take Brown with you," Van Eaton told him.

"I shall accompany the men," the Frenchman, Jon Louviere said.

"Suit yourself," Bones told him.

"I'll go with them," Burton Sullivan said. "I just don't believe this man is the will 'o' the wisp you people claim him to be."

"Good show, Burton!" Sir Elmore shouted.

"Hip, hip, hooray!" Robert Tassin yelled.

Dark Hand grimaced at the very premature congratulatory shouts and poured himself a cup of coffee. The Pawnee watched the four men ride out and thought: Some of you will not return.

"Hell, he's a-foot!" Tatman said, reining up about a thousand yards out of camp, leaning out of the saddle and studying the ground. "We got him now, boys. He's ourn for shore."

"Splendid!" Louviere said.

"Do push on," Burton urged.

About a mile from camp, a rattlesnake, as thick as a man's forearm and made as a hornet, came sailing out of the brush and struck Brown's shoulder and landed stretched out from saddle horn to Brown's thigh. Brown, terrified out of his wits, let out a wild whoop and left the saddle just as the snake bit him on the leg. The snake left the saddle with the frightened and yelling man, biting him several more times before Brown hit the rocky ground. Preacher screamed like a panther and the horses went into a panic and began pitching and bucking, doing their best to throw off their riders.

Burton Sullivan's butt left the saddle and he went rolling and squalling down the steep grade to the left of the trail. Jon Louviere dropped his rifle and grabbed onto the saddle horn as his horse became more panicked and started bucking more fiercely. His rifle discharged when it struck the ground and the ball struck Tatman in the shoulder, knocking him out of the saddle. He hit the ground, screaming and cussing the Frenchman. Brown was dying beside the trail, the rattler having bitten him a dozen or more times, the last few times on the neck and face. The bounty-hunter was already beginning to swell grotesquely.

Tatman landed about two feet from the horrible scene and clawed at his pistol. The snake shifted its attention from the dying man to Tatman and opened its mouth to strike. Tatman finally pulled the gun from behind his belt and shot the rattlesnake, blowing its head off.

Preacher picked up a rock and flung it, the heavy stone impacting against the side of Louviere's jaw and slamming him from the saddle. The Frenchman, out cold, landed on top of Tatman, knocking the wind from Tatman, and bringing a scream of pain from the frightened and wounded man.

Burton Sullivan, several hundred feet below, had no idea what was taking place above him. He was frantically attempting to claw his way up the rocky incline. He had lost his fancy rifle and one of his pistols and was thoroughly disgusted. He had busted his head on a rock and it was bleeding. His safari clothing was ripped and torn and he had lost one boot. All things taken into consideration, this day was not going well at all.

And it was about to get worse.

By the trail, Preacher had taken all the guns and powder and shot from the dead and wounded men. He was waiting for Burton Sullivan when the man finally, panting and grunting, hauled himself over the side.

"You lookin' for me, Fancy-Britches?" Preacher asked.

Burton gazed upward and into the coldest eyes the Englishman had ever seen.

"I say now, my good fellow," Burton gasped. "Can't we discuss this like civilized men?"

"Nope," Preacher said, and busted the man on the side of his jaw with one big fist.

The nobleman's feet, minus one boot, left the incline and down he went, rolling butt over elbows. He went back down the grade a lot quicker than he came up. He rolled over rocks, smashed into small sturdy trees, and uprooted bushes in a frantic attempt to halt his descent. He finally came to rest all tangled up in a pile of thorny bushes. He was so addled he thought he was a child back in England.

"Oh mummy," he muttered. "I'm afraid I've poo-pooed in my nightie."

"I'll kill you for this," Tatman told Preacher, pushing the words past the pain in his shoulder.

"I doubt it," Preacher told him, settling one moccasin against Tatman's big butt. Preacher shoved and Tatman began his journey down to join Burton Sullivan at the bottom of the incline.

After two trips, Burton had pretty much cleared the way, so Tatman didn't really encounter much in the way of obstacles on his way down. He must have been covering about fifty feet a second when he slammed into Burton Sullivan, who was just getting to his shaky boots, his back to the incline. Burton, his butt filled with thorns from the bramble bush, and his mind foggy, was staring dreamily down at a lovely little creek about twenty feet below when Tatman slammed into him. Both of them sailed over the edge and landed in the creek.

Preacher looked down at the pair and laughed at them, wallowin' around in the creek. Preacher knew that creek was snow-fed year round and that the water was icy cold. Them two down yonder was liable to come down with pneumonia.

Preacher hoped they did.

Van Eaton recovered the money the noblemen had paid to Brown, stuck it in his pocket, and then shoved the body over the side for the buzzards to eat. Van Eaton didn't give a damn about Brown, or anybody else for that matter, but this meant that Preacher was slowly whittling away at their strength. And the man was still playing with them. He just didn't seem to be taking this hunt seriously. It seemed to Van Eaton that to Preacher, this man-hunt was . . . well *fun!*

At that thought, the hired killer looked nervously around him. Van Eaton didn't like these Rocky Mountains.

He didn't like them at all. He quickly walked over to his horse, swung into the saddle and took off.

I should have killed him, Preacher thought, on his belly about two hundred yards from where he'd waylaid the four men. That Van Eaton is one cold hombre. He sure wouldn't give a second thought to killin' me.

But Preacher still clung to the rapidly fading hope that the men would give up this foolishness and let him be. Deep within him, however, he knew they would not. That sooner or later, he was going to have to start killing them on sight. The problem was, he didn't want to kill these men. Well . . . maybe Bones and Van Eaton. The world wouldn't miss them at all. These noblemen, now, that was something else. Preacher figured them to be nothin' more than just spoiled rich boys who'd suddenly got all growed up without the maturity that came with bein' an adult man. And he hadn't meant to hit that man with the rattlesnake. Problem was, when you start flingin' rattlesnakes about, you got to be careful, 'cause they can whip that head around and give you a fearsome bite. That knowledge sort of threw Preacher's aim off some. It wasn't that he was feelin' bad about Brown, 'cause he wasn't. After all, the man had been out lookin' to kill him.

Preacher looked carefully around him, then rose up and began trailing Van Eaton. Which wasn't a big deal. Any ten-year-old Injun boy could have done that with one eye closed. Van Eaton did not know this country and that would have been evident to anyone with any knowledge of the land. From all the smoke from cook fires he'd seen plumin' up into the air, Preacher had a pretty good idea where Bones had chosen to camp. He'd try one more time to warn these men off, to stop this foolishness. If they didn't heed his warnings, then Preacher reckoned, he'd just have to get nasty about this thing.

* * *

Jon Louviere's jaw was swollen up something frightful. He could just barely speak. Which came as a great relief to most of Bones's gang. Burton Sullivan sat gingerly on a pillow in front of a roaring fire, a blanket wrapped around him. The long and numerous thorns had been plucked from Sullivan's butt, his skin had lost its blue color from the icy waters, and he had stopped shaking. Both Louviere and Sullivan had been thoroughly humiliated by what had taken place. But their eyes shone wildly and silently spoke volumes of revenge.

Tatman was not badly injured, the ball punching a hole in the fleshy part of his left shoulder and passing through without doing any major damage, except to his pride. All during the cleaning out of the wound, he had cussed and spoke of dire consequences should he and Preacher ever meet again. Bones sat with his back to a large rock and listened to it all with a disgusted look on his face. It wasn't that any of the men lacked courage, for he knew that those who'd stuck with him thus far had more than their share of that. He was just sick of Preacher making fools of them all. Playing with them like this was some sort of kid's game.

Problem was, Bones didn't have a clue as to how to bring the hunt to a conclusion. He was going to use the boy, somehow get him away from Preacher and use the brat as leverage. But with the boy in the protective hands of the Utes, that was out. No one in their right mind would attack an entire Ute village; not with as few men as Bones had, anyway.

And to make matters even worse, Dark Hand had told the gang, with no small amount of satisfaction in his voice and smugness on his face, that the Indians were watching it all, spying on them. Ute and Cheyenne for sure, and probably Arapaho, too, and were making up dances and telling stories about how foolishly this large band of white men were behaving. Now Preacher was out-foxing them all and making them look stupid. That really rankled both Bones and Van Eaton. A bunch of filthy ignorant savages making light of them all.

Bones watched as Van Eaton rode back in and stripped the saddle off his horse and rubbed the animal down. No matter how evil the men were, they knew to take good care of their horses. Horses were life in this country.

"Any sign of Preacher?" Bones asked, after Van Eaton had poured coffee and walked over to squat beside him.

"No. But I shore felt his eyes on me. I 'spect he followed me here."

"Well, if that's the case, we best get ready for more fun and games from him. Make sure the guard is doubled and changed ever' two hours so's they'll stay fresh."

"Will do."

"Did you get the money from Brown?"

"Shore did. I stashed it in my gear."

"What'd he look like?"

"Turrible sight. All swole up like nothin' I ever seen afore." He shuddered. "I seen that big rattler, too. Damned if I'd pick that big ugly thing up alive and fling it at anybody. Personal, I think Preacher's 'bout half crazy. I was tole a lot of these mountain men is off the bean somewhat."

"I can believe it. This country would drive a body loony. What are you grinnin' about?"

"Thinkin' 'bout his majesty over yonder rollin' butt over boots down that hill and landin' in them briars. I'd a give a pretty penny to seen that."

He and Bones started snickering at the thought and had to cover their mouths so the others would not hear. Van Eaton sobered after a moment and said, "I'll tell you the truth, Bones. I ain't lookin' forward to the night."

"Neither am I," Bones whispered. "But just maybe Preacher feels he done enough for one day."

"I hope so. I ain't had a good nights' sleep in I cain't 'member when."

He wasn't going to get much sleep that night, either, for Preacher had found the camp and was planning his mischief with a grin on his face.

11

"Eight guards," Preacher muttered under his breath. "I got them scared, for a fact."

He had slowly circled the camp, then made himself comfortable and waited for the guards to change. Every two hours, he noted. These folks are learnin'. Man stays on guard more'un two hours, he tends to get careless.

Preacher waited until the shift changed at midnight, and then waited for another thirty minutes or so before he made his move. With all the supplies he'd taken from Bones's men, Preacher had gunpowder to burn . . . in a manner of speaking. Preacher slipped around to where the horses were picketed and went to work for a few minutes. Then, having to really struggle to keep from giggling, he took aim and chucked a bag of powder into what was left of a dying campfire. Coals aplenty to do the job. Preacher had already found a good spot to watch the show, and he almost made it. He had tossed a second bag of powder into another fire but he thought he'd missed the dying coals. Obviously he hadn't. The big bag of powder blew and the quiet camp turned into a scene of mass confusion.

The horses pulled their pins and jerked free of the picket line and stampeded right through the camp. Ever seen what fifty or so wild-eyed horses and twenty odd big runnin' mules can do to a camp? Preacher jumped behind a rock when the action started and the outcome went way beyond his wildest expectations. The explosions blew hot coals all over the place and set a dozen or so blankets on fire and that only added to the chaos. The horses ran right over the fancy tents of the gentry and Preacher had never seen such a sight as that. In the light from the fires, the gentlemen were exposed in their nightshirts. Several of them had what looked to Preacher like little bitty fish nets tied around their heads. Damnest sight he'd ever seen, for sure.

Sir Elmore Jerrold-Taylor got in the way of a big Missouri and that mule knocked him about twenty feet from point of impact. Sir Elmore landed right smack dab on his butt on that rocky ground and commenced to squallin'.

Bones got himself run down by a spooked horse and before the dust and smoke got so bad that Preacher couldn't see, Bones was on all fours, scurryin' away like a big ugly bug. Van Eaton had climbed a tree, so Preacher just hauled out one of his pistols and let 'er bang.

But the smoke and dust threw his aim off and the ball took a chunk of meat out of Van Eaton's butt. Van Eaton started screamin' and turned loose of the branch he was holding onto and fell about fifteen feet, landin' hard on the ground.

Preacher took aim at a running man and squeezed off another shot; the fall flew true and the man stumbled and fell, pitching face-first onto the ground.

Preacher changed locations, flitting soundlessly through the timber, staying low, working his way around the scene of wild confusion. The only one in the camp he was really worried about was Dark Hand, but his worry was needless. Dark Hand had left his blankets before the echo of the first explosion had faded and jumped into the narrow space between two boulders.

And there he sat. Dark Hand would choose his own time and place to confront Ghost Walker. And this night definitely was not the time nor the place. All the advantage was Preacher's.

Mack Cornay jumped onto the back of a galloping horse and grabbed a double handful of mane, trying to halt the frightened animal. But the animal was not to be stopped. The horse raced into the timber and Mack was knocked from the horse when his face impacted with a low limb. Mack hit the ground, his nose busted and his front teeth missing.

A man-hunter known only as Spanish made the mistake of taking to the timber after Preacher. Not a wise thing to do. Preacher noticed the movement behind him and to his left and waited, crouched in the brush. When Spanish drew up even with Preacher, he caught the butt of Preacher's rifle in his gut and doubled over, all his breath gone. Spanish lay on the cold ground, gasping for breath and unable to move. Just to be on the safe side, Preacher quickly tied the man's hands behind his back with a length of rawhide. Preacher tossed the man's weapons into the night and took off.

Preacher continued his circling of the camp, which by now was beginning to settle down somewhat. But the dust and smoke were still thick.

"He shot me in the butt!" Van Eaton hollered. "Feels like it's on fire!"

"My buttocks are on fire!" Willy Steinwinder yelled, frantically slapping at his rear end. A running horse had knocked him into some burning blankets and ignited his nightgown. Prince Rudi Kuhlmann tossed a bucket of water on him.

Preacher underwent a mental wrestling match for a moment, and better judgment won. He left the camp and headed for his hidey hole and safety. He needed a few hours sleep. He figured the bounty-hunters would spend the rest of the night trying to round up their horses and mules, picking up their scattered supplies, and seeing to the needs of the wounded. They'd be after him with vengeance come daylight, but by then, Preacher would have once more shifted locations.

At daylight, the man-hunters began assessing the damage done to their camp, and it was extensive. The tents of the royalty had been burned beyond repair. A lot of their supplies were either missing or destroyed. Two men were wounded and a half a dozen more were injured.

"Indians watched this," Dark Hand announced, returning from a scouting of the timber around the camp. "I don't know what tribe, but several were in the woods. They left heading north. That might mean nothing, or it might mean they were Arapaho."

"Preacher?" Bones asked.

"I lost his trail. He was heading east when I could no longer track him. He took to the rocks."

Dark Hand went to the fire for coffee, leaving Bones again doing some fancy cussing.

Van Eaton and Willy Steinwinder were laying on their bellies, Van Eaton due to the bullet from Preacher's pistol, Willy because of burned buttocks. Van Eaton's rear end was bandaged and Willy's spread all over with lard. Neither man was terribly pleased with their present situation but Willy did express his discomfort much more eloquently than Van Eaton.

Preacher was up at dawn and took a quick wash in a little creek . . . a very quick wash, for the water was ice cold. He boiled coffee, ate some berries for breakfast, and then packed up and moved out.

About a mile from his old camp, Preacher ran into some Arapaho. They grinned at him and the leader said, "You gave us much enjoyment last night, White Wolf. The behavior of the white men was funny. We will have a fine time retelling the story. We thank you. Go in peace."

The Arapaho rode off without another word.

"I ought to start chargin' admission," Preacher muttered, then shouldered his pack and moved on.

"How far back to Bent's Fort?" Bones asked wearily, his eyes sweeping the devastated camp.

"As the crow flies, 'bout two hundred or so miles, I figure," Andy Price said.

"Soon as we get the mules rounded up, take ten men and head there. We got to have supplies. His Lordship, Sir Jerrold-Taylor done made up a list and he'll give you the money. You ought to be safe with that many men. You 'member that valley we rode through southeast of here? We'll be there. We'll do nothin' 'til you boys get back. Last night's affair done scattered and ruint near'bouts ever'thing we got. Head on out."

"You want me to see about pickin' up some more men?"

"Yeah. If you can. But don't tell nobody who it is we're chasin'. Preacher is bound to have friends there." Bones gave the man some gold coins. "Just tell them we're after a murderer and they's big money in it. This here gold ought to get their attention."

The men were gone by midday. It was to be a long, hard trip, and no one in the camp expected their return in under a month. Three weeks at best.

"Pack it up," Bones ordered. "This time, by God, we'll secure our camp and do it right."

Preacher watched the men through his spy glass. He knew immediately they'd sent a party back for supplies. And he saw right off he'd have little chance of slipping into this new camp. The men were working steadily, clearing away brush, cutting down and hauling in logs, and laying out fields of fire. This was going to be a regular little fort.

"Somebody down yonder's had some military experience," Preacher said, collapsing his spy glass and standing up. "They're buildin' a stockade. This is a good time for me to check on Eddie."

Eddie was all decked out in a brand new set of fancy buckskins. He grinned when Preacher walked into the village. But the boy was not well, and there was sadness in Wind Chaser's eyes.

"He dies slowly before our eyes," the Ute said. "And there is nothing that anyone can do."

"Except make him happy," Preacher spoke in low tones.

"That we are doing. My woman, and the whole village. Come, Ghost Walker. Sit, eat. Let us talk about ridding ourselves of these silly white men who hunt you . . ." He smiled. "Or try to hunt you."

Over a thick, rich stew, Preacher said, "It's time for you and your people to be moving to the hunt, Wind Chaser. Past time, actually."

Wind Chaser smiled. "You are wrong if you think we stay because of Ed-de. We stay because the buffalo are late in coming this year. We are leaving soon, though. Ed-de wants to go with us."

Preacher nodded his head. "It'll be an adventure for him. Prob'ly his last one."

Wind Chaser's face tightened at that, but he said nothing. Privately, he agreed with Preacher's assessment. Neither man had any idea that it would be the last adventure for most of Wind Chaser's band.

The sounds of a horse ridden hard reached the men and they stood up. The young brave jumped off at Wind Chaser's lodge. "Crooked Arm says the buffalo are moving."

Wind Chaser gripped Preacher's shoulder. "You

should come with us, Ghost Walker. The hunt will be fun and we shall all feast until our bellies swell."

"I got business to tend to, Wind Chaser. I'll speak to the boy and then be gone. I know you got packin' up to do."

Preacher kept his goodbye brief. He didn't want to get all emotional, besides, Eddie was all flustered with excitement and rarin' to get gone huntin' buffalo. The boy was trembling with anticipation. Preacher suddenly had a bad feeling about this trip. But seeing that the boy was all set up to go, Preacher kept his feelings to himself.

"You mind your manners, now, boy," Preacher said, placing a hand on Eddie's frail shoulder.

"Yes, sir, Preacher. I will."

"I know you will, Eddie. You're a good boy. Might be a while 'til you and me hook up again. But we will. That's a promise. So you take 'er easy, you hear? You mind what Wind Chaser says, too. You hear?"

Eddie laughed. "I hear. I'll see you, Preacher."

Wind Chaser's band was not a large one to begin with, and many of the men had gone on ahead to scout for the buffalo. What was left was mainly women and kids and a few warriors. Preacher stood and watched them break camp and head out. He waved his farewells and then saddled up and rode out, in the opposite direction.

He made camp early that afternoon, high up and protected by huge boulders. That night, he woke up with a stir and listened. Seemed to him like he could hear the faint sounds of gunshots. But they faded away or were lost in the sighing winds and Preacher snuggled warm into his blankets and drifted back off to sleep.

Over bacon and pan bread and coffee, something in the far distance caught Preacher's eyes. He dug out his spy glass and extended it. He could just make out the circling of buzzards. A lot of buzzards, and they were already making their slow glide down to the ground to feast on the dead . . . whatever it might be, human or animal, and Preacher had a hunch it was human.

Preacher suddenly lost his appetite as a feeling of terrible dread settled over him, hanging on his shoulders like a stinking shroud. He knew that many buzzards didn't congregate over a lone dead animal. It would have to be a whole herd dead, and that just wasn't likely.

With an effort, Preacher forced himself to eat what he had cooked, 'cause in the wilderness, it was good practice to eat when you can, drink when you can, and rest when you can, 'cause you never knew when the chance might come again.

He drank his pot of coffee and then rinsed the pot and scrubbed out his frying pan and cached it with the bulk of his supplies. He made sure his stock had plenty of grass and water, and then slowly saddled Thunder.

"I know what's down there, Thunder. I know in my heart and it makes me sick to think about it. I don't wanna go down yonder, but I gotta. I gotta," he repeated, and then swung into the saddle and started for the valley far below and to the north.

He could smell the scene long before he reached it. The buzzards had torn open the bodies, exposing the innards to the air.

The first thing he came up on was Eddie's little paint pony, lyin' dead. The sorry man-hunting trash had cut its throat and let it bleed to death. Preacher looked at the pony for a moment.

"You was a good horse to a good boy when he needed some good in his life, pony. I won't let the buzzards have you."

He rode on, reading the signs as he went. They were easy. Wind Chaser and his band had made camp along the banks of a stream. That night, when they were settled in, Bones and his bunch had hit them, and hit them hard. He knew it was Bones's bunch 'cause the lone white man he found dead he'd seen several times before.

"I'll not bury you, you sorry son!" Preacher said, considerable heat in his voice.

He found Wind Chaser beside his woman. The chief had died protecting his woman and their children. It didn't take an experienced eye to see that the women had been raped, and used badly. Preacher felt a chill run over him when he saw that Bones and his men had even raped the little girls.

"Sorry white-trash," he muttered.

But he couldn't find Eddie. He didn't want to fire a shot and bring Bones and his people back, so he rode amongst the dead, using a Ute lance to knock the buzzards away. He really didn't have anything against the carrion-eatin' critters; they were just doing what God had put them on the earth to do, but damned if they were gonna do it in front of him. Least not with people he had known and liked.

Preacher rode around the circle of death twice, looking for the boy. He had steeled himself for the worst. But it was worse than even he had thought.

He found Eddie and almost lost his breakfast.

12

The boy had been dragged to death.

The boy's new buckskins were bloody and torn. Preacher just could not bear to look at him any longer. He dismounted and gently laid a blanket over what was left of Eddie. Preacher squatted down for a moment and tried to piece together what had happened.

He figured that Wind Chaser and his small band had been spotted by scouts from Bones's camp. John Pray had told him that the foreigners had expressed a desire to kill some Indians. Bones and his party had waited until the Ute camp had settled down and then had slipped up on them under cover of darkness. This was Ute country and Wind Chaser had felt no great need for a lot of security. How Bones and his men had managed to pull this off was a mystery to Preacher, and probably always would be. The important thing was that they had done it. And Eddie was dead.

With a sigh, Preacher stood up and began the task of burying the dead. And he had to do this right, for more than one reason. If Wind Chaser's scouts returned and found this massacre, the entire Ute nation would go on the warpath, and no white man would be safe for months or even years to come. Preacher couldn't allow that to happen.

Preacher built him a travois and began toting the bodies to a dry off-shoot of the creek. He placed Wind Chaser and his family together and carefully caved in part of the bank over them. He did that with all the Utes, choosing his spots with care. Then he took bushes and small saplings and transplanted them in the soil that covered the Indians. It took him most of the morning to get it done, stopping often to look around him for trouble and every fifteen minutes or so taking up his club to knock buzzards away from the remaining bodies.

He searched the area, gathering up everything that had belonged to the tribe and scattered it throughout the timber: clothing, utensils, tipi poles; everything he could find. Then he carefully cut squares of sod out of the earth, worked throughout the afternoon greatly enlarging the hold, dragged and sometimes having to muscle the pony into the hole, and then burying Eddie beside his little paint pony. Preacher carefully replaced the squares of sod and toted water from the creek to dampen the disturbed earth, making certain the grass would stay fertile and grow, ensuring Eddie a proper grave.

As the sun was setting, Preacher stood over the grave of the boy and took off his hat. It was rare for Preacher to be at a loss for words, but for a long time late that afternoon, words failed him.

"This here was a good boy, Lord," he finally said, the waning rays of the sun casting shadows about him. "He never done a harm to nobody. I reckon he was about ten years old and in all them ten years, he never knew much comfort. Shore didn't know no love and affection 'til he come to the Utes. They give him a home, and it was a good one."

Suddenly, Preacher realized he was crying, tears streaming from his eyes and rolling down his tanned cheeks. He remembered the last time he shed a tear it was over Hammer's body. He sure had liked this little boy.

He waited for a few moments, wiped his face, and said, "Eddie liked this little paint pony, Lord. So I'd consider it a debt owed if You'd let this here horse into heaven with him. I think You'll find they'll serve You well.

"Now them Utes I buried this day, well, they didn't have no fancy church buildin' like them so-called civilized Christians back East. But what they did have was a belief in Man Above, and that's You, and their church was the whole wide country around them. I think that's a fittin' thing, since it was You who created it all. Includin' the Utes.

"I reckon Eddie and his pony is standin' beside You now. Or maybe beside Jesus, or one of them appissles, or somebody up yonder. Leastwises I shore hope so. I'd hate to think I done all this for nothin'."

Preacher held up the Bible he'd given to Eddie after finding it amongst the ruins of the burned out wagons back on the Big Sandy. "This here is the Good Book, which I'm shore You can plainly see. I ruminated some about plantin' this with Eddie and his little pony. Then I decided I'd keep it and read it from time to time. I ain't no Christian man, but I do find the words to be right comfortin'. I'm a-fixin' to read it now, 'cause what I'm gonna read is one of Eddie's favorite verses. I ain't no real good reader, so You excuse my stumblin' around on any big words I might run acrost."

Preacher read the 23rd Psalm, then closed the Bible and tucked it away in his parfleche. "I reckon that about does it, Lord. I don't know what else there is to say. I'm gonna miss this boy. I liked him. That's all. Good evenin'."

Preacher turned to go, hesitated, then once more stood over the grave. "Well, there is somethin' else. Them no-count, trashy heathens over yonder behind them log walls in that valley done a terrible thing last night. They's rich men over yonder that's had a fancy education and all the trimmin's that most of us don't get. They knew better. As a matter of fact, all them men over yonder knew better. Now, Lord, there ain't no law out here in the wilderness. But they is justice, and I aim to see it done." He patted the buckskin parfleche containing the Bible. "I know that somewheres in the Good Book it says that vengeance is mine, sayeth the Lord. Well, I'm a-fixin' to relieve You of that burden for a time. Now, if You don't cotton to me doin' that, You best fling down a mighty lightnin' bolt to strike me dead. 'Cause that's the only thing that's gonna stop me." Preacher closed his eyes tightly and braced himself for a bolt from Heaven. When none came, he expelled air and said, "Thank You kindly. Now if You'll excuse my language, Lord, I'm a-fixin' to go kill me some sorry sons of bitches."

13

Bones had figured Preacher would come after him, and he had prepared for the visit. The fort in the middle of the pretty little valley had been reinforced with rocks and logs and dug up earth. Every bush had been pulled up, every tree cut down for hundreds of yards all around the stockade. Grass for several hundred yards all around the little fort had been repeatedly trampled down by horses and mules.

"You think you're smart, don't you?" Preacher muttered. "Well, you are, Bones. But you ain't near'bouts as mean as me. So that means I got it all over you."

After burying Eddie and the others, Preacher rode up into the high country to think things over and to clear his head. He knew better than to wage war when angry. Man has to be cold when he fights. Anger causes mistakes, and when outnumbered the way he was, Preacher knew he couldn't afford to make any mistakes.

Preacher sat his horse up on a ridge, in the timber, and ruminated for a time. Then he smiled and headed out. Maybe he couldn't get in that stockade, but he figured he sure knew a way to get them inside out. Might take him a couple of days to get it done, but he'd do it.

Willy Steinwinder limped down to the creek to get some water for coffee. He stood for a moment, looking rather confused. He closed his eyes, shook his head, and opened his eyes again. Same thing. He walked back to the stockade and up to Bones.

"There is no water in the creek."

"What?" Bones asked, looking up.

"The creek is dry."

"I don't believe it. That's impossible!"

"Go look for yourself."

"Well, I sure will!"

Everybody walked out to look. The creek had dried up to no more than a tiny trickle in the center. Dark Hand sat on the bank and chuckled.

"You find this funny, Injun?" Jack Cornell asked.

"Yes. Most amusing. Preacher has dammed up the creek. Now what are you going to do?"

Jack Cornell wasn't going to do anything. Not ever again. Preacher didn't think he could make the shot, but he did. He had Jon Louviere's fancy hunting rifle and it was about the best rifle Preacher had ever had his hands on. It was handmade for Jon, that was evident. The workmanship was flawless. So Preacher loaded 'er up, sighted in, and let 'er bang.

He held high because of the distance and dead centered Jack Cornell in the chest. Cornell was stone dead before he hit the ground, his spinal cord severed. The others scattered for the protection of the stockade or hit the ground.

But no more shots came. Preacher worked his way out of the valley by following a ravine when he could and bellying the rest of the way. He figured he had at least three weeks before the others came back from Bent's Fort, and since he was sure they'd bring back some more ornery ol' boys with them, Preacher had decided to whittle down those that stayed behind.

He figured he had a right good start this morning. He was aimin' to whittle down one or two more come this evenin'.

Bones sat behind the earth and long walls and cussed Preacher. Van Eaton sat on a pillow and joined in. Willy Steinwinder had a few choice words to say about the mountain man, but he soon recognized the futility of that and fell silent. The men knew they had to move; without water they could not last long.

"We could go upstream and tear down that dam," Jimmie Cook suggested.

"You want to volunteer to do that?" Bones stopped cussing long enough to ask.

"I reckon not," Jimmie replied.

"That's what I figured." Bones stood up. "Come daylight we're splittin' up into five man teams and takin' out after Preacher. I ain't havin' no more of this."

"Oh, good show!" Sir Elmore said, clapping his hands. "Good show."

Bones almost shot the man right then and there. But he had found out that the gentry might be a tad foolish, but they weren't stupid. The bearer bonds, or bank notes, or whatever in the hell they were, weren't worth a damn unless the signature matched up with the one on record back in St. Louis. And since Bones could just barely write his own name, there wasn't a chance in hell he could copy any of the gentry's handwriting, and he knew it. Torture was out, for the royalty would guess they would be killed anyway and just scrawl their name, making the certificates worthless. So they had to be kept alive and escorted all the way back to St. Louis. And that really irritated Bones.

"We managed to bring enough water up to water the stock and have some for ourselves," George Winters said.

"Will we come back here for the evenin' tomorrow?" Bones was asked.

He shook his head. "No. We'll meet up over yonder in the timber west of here. This place is worthless to us now." He walked to a gun slit and looked out. The sun was going down.

"You reckon Preacher will be back and try to Injun up on us tonight?" Spanish asked.

"He will return this night," Dark Hand said. He had not gone with the men on their raid against Wind Chaser and his band. Wind Chaser had befriended him one time, and he could not bring himself to do harm to one who had been his friend in a time of need. He wished desperately to convey that fact to Preacher.

And Dark Hand had already, several times, prayed to the Man Above that the group he was with did not run into any Utes. He had watched from a distance as Preacher very cleverly hid the evidence after the night raid. But he knew, as Preacher surely did, that it would not fool a determined search.

Dark Hand stood peering through a gun slit in the logs. He could sense Preacher's presence, ever more strongly as the last rays of the sun began to fade.

"You think he's out there, don't you, Dark Hand?" Robert Tassin asked.

"Yes."

"Well, he's a fool then!" a man called Cobb snapped. "What does he think he's gonna do? Attack this stockade? That would be stupid."

Dark Hand smiled as he turned to face the man. "It is dark now, Cobb. Do you wish to be the first to leave these walls to relieve yourself?" Cobb said nothing. "No?" Dark Hand said. "I thought not."

Preacher was working closer as the night fell softly all around him. He stopped his stealthy advance at the far side of the creek bank. He took his bow, strung it, and selected an arrow from the quiver. He waited, watching the stockade. Those inside had lit candles or lamps and they had a fire going. Stupid, Preacher thought. The gun slits were lit up like a chandelier: rectangular pockets of light in the darkness. Every so often the shape of a head would appear briefly, then pull back.

Preacher calculated the distance. Easy shot. He waited with the patience of a stalking panther.

Davidson walked to a slit and peered out. Everyone inside the walls heard the wet smack and turned. Davidson stood on his boots for a few seconds, the shaft of the arrow protruding from his forehead. Then he toppled over and fell on his back. When he hit the ground the pistol in his hand discharged and the ball just missed Bones's head by a few inches. Bones stretched out on the cool earth.

"Douse them candles and lamps!" Bones yelled, cold sweat covered his body. "Put out them fires."

"Drag Davidson's body out of here and heave it over the walls," Van Eaton ordered. He had watched Davidson put the money given him by the gentry into his pack. He'd get it before they pulled out in the morning. Easy money.

There would be nine teams and then some pullin' out, Van Eaton thought. That meant the odds of Preacher trailin' any particular team was one in nine. Not the best odds in the world but better than nothin'.

Van Eaton knew what Bones was planning. With nine teams working the area, there was a good chance they could box Preacher in and end this man-hunt. But they would all have to be very careful. Preacher was like a ghost in the woods.

Percy lit the stub of a cigar and another arrow came whizzing through a gunslit, this time on the other side of the stockade. The arrow thudded into a log, just missing Spanish, and the man yelped and flattened out on the ground.

"Good God!" Bones yelled. "Don't fire up no more matches."

"Isn't this exciting?" Sir Elmore whispered to his friend, Prince Juan Zapata.

Zapata's eyes were shining with anticipation of the up-coming hunt. "I cannot wait until the morning," the Spaniard replied. "The mountain man is indeed a worth-while adversary."

"We'll have to do this again sometime," Rudi Kuhlmann said. "It is fraught with danger but very exhilarating."

"Oh, quite," Burton Sullivan agreed.

"Igits!" Van Eaton thought, listening to the royalty whisper amongst themselves. "I ain't never in all my borned days seen such a goofy bunch all gathered up in one spot."

Preacher had worked closer, passing through the horses in a crude corral. He calmed them with touches and whispers and made his way to the log walls of the stockade. Bones had placed no guards outside the stock-ade. Not very smart of him, Preacher thought. Then he stopped cold.

No way! No way that Bones would not put guards out-side the log and rock and earthen walls. He wouldn't leave the horses unguarded. He wasn't that stupid. "Damn!" Preacher thought. "I been boxed. Unless I was awful lucky."

Preacher did not move, remaining as still as a rock. Only his eyes shifted, searching the darkness. And when his eyes touched a shape he almost jumped out of his moccasins. The man was no more than ten feet away. Preacher could make out the shape of the man's head, and the long barrel of his rifle. Fortunately for Preacher, the guard had his back to him. The night had turned cloudy, and there would be no moon. Already a few large drops of cold rain had fallen. If the dark building clouds held true, in a very few minutes this night was gonna produce a rain that would be a real toad-strangler.

Preacher pulled out his razor-sharp, long-bladed knife and held it close to one leg, so no stray glimmer of light would reflect off the blade.

"You see anything, Cleave?" the whisper came from a gun slit about a foot from where Preacher stood.

"Nothin'," the guard replied. "But the wind is fresh-enin' and it's gonna pour down any minute. That's when Preacher will make his move. Bet on it."

"I just spoke to MacNary on the other side. He ain't seen or heard nothin' neither. I'm bettin' Preacher has done his deed and got gone back to his camp 'fore the rain comes."

"I just want to kill that Preacher and get back to civilization," Cleave said. "I don't like these mountains."

"Knock off the talk!" Bones called. "You'll give away your position."

Cleave muttered something about Bones under his breath and leaned up against the logs, still with his back to Preacher.

Preacher cut his throat and lowered the body to the ground. He began working his way around to the other side of the stockade, moving very slowly. John Pray had told him about MacNary, and MacNary was a bad one. A thug and a brigand through and through, a man who would do anything to anybody, man, woman, or child, if the price was right. Preacher had come into the cleared area to stampede the horses, but Bones had used a length of chain to fasten the crude corral gate, and Preacher had to nix that plan.

Thunder began to rumble in the distance and that covered any slight sound that Preacher might make. The clouds began dumping a very light rain and Preacher decided he'd pushed his luck enough for one night. When the shape of MacNary came into view, Preacher shot him and then jammed the muzzles of those terrible pistols into a gun slit and began firing as fast as he could.

Inside the log walls, the wound and fury was enormous. The lead balls were slamming into the logs, whining off of cook pots, and terrorizing those who had thought themselves to be safe and secure. A thug called Dutch screamed as a ball took him in the side. An Arkansas man known only as Wilbur began choking on his own blood as a ball took him in the throat and put him down. The flashes from Preacher's multi-barreled pistols blinded those inside the logs and before their eyes could once more adjust to the darkness, Preacher was gone, running through the night.

The men rushed outside of the stockade. But the darkness of the night and the now heavy-driving rain obscured the fast fading form of Preacher.

About two hundred yards from camp, knowing he could not be seen, Preacher stopped and turned around. "I am Preacher!" he shouted. "The Indians call me Ghost Walker. White Wolf. Man Who Kills Silently. None of you will ever leave the mountains. You will all die. I have given you all the chances you will ever get. Make your peace with God. Some of you will die tomorrow."

"I was under the impression the man was a near cretin. Illiterate," Sir Elmore said. "That was a very eloquent little speech."

"Now how does he propose to carry out that rather ominous threat?" Rudi Kuhlmann asked, stuffing snuff up his nose. He sneezed explosively several times in a row and the bounty hunters standing close to him, their nerves stretched as tight as a guitar string, almost shot him.

Dark Hand was the only one who had not rushed outside. The Pawnee squatted near the gate to the stockade. "Preacher means what he says," Dark Hand said. "It is my suggestion that we all leave these mountains at first light and do not look back."

"Yeller," Tatman said, his arm in a sling, easing the pressure on his wounded shoulder. "I knowed you was yeller all the time."

Dark Hand did not reply. He had moved back from the door and was packing up a few belongings. He had made up his mind. He was going to look up Preacher and make his peace with the man. If Preacher would accept it, the two would never again make war against the other.

The Pawnee was very swift in packing. He was through before the others even thought about reentering the stockade. Dark Hand was not missed the next morning.

14

Preacher saw Dark Hand coming from a long way off. He got out his spy glass and scanned the country behind the Pawnee. No one else in sight. Then he noticed that Dark Hand was riding with his rifle in a boot and his pistols nowhere in sight. His bow was in his quiver, and not strung. He was riding with his big knife sheathed and hung by a cord around his neck.

"Wants to palaver," Preacher muttered. "That's odd."

Preacher stepped out from his camp into a clearing on the slope and waved his arms. He watched Dark Hand straighten on the horse's back, and then angle toward him. About fifteen minutes later, Dark Hand was reined up in front of him.

"Light and set, Pawnee," Preacher said. "I got coffee and bacon and bread if you feel like partakin' of my grub."

"You would feed me?"

"Sure."

"I accept. But watch closely my backtrail. There are a few in that bunch of blood-hungry fools who have the ability to track well."

"You left 'em?"

"Forever and ever." He dismounted and led his horse into Preacher's camp, picketing the animal with

Preacher's stock. He squatted down by the fire and took the plate of food and the cup of coffee Preacher handed him. "It is one thing to make war against men. But not women and babies. I took no part in that."

"I didn't see your moccasin tracks nowheres about there. I knew that Wind Chaser had befriended you a time or two. Eat. We'll talk when you're done."

When the Pawnee had finished, Preacher poured them both more coffee and they smoked. Dark Hand said, "It is one thing to hate when there is a reason for it. But my hatred for you had become unreasonable. My brother attacked you. You did not attack him. I attacked him. I attacked you, twice. You did not attack me. My hatred was stupid." He abruptly stuck out his hand and Preacher smiled and shook it. Dark Hand said, "From this day forward, we do not make war against the other. Is that agreeable with you?"

"Sure is."

"Good. Now I will tell you something. I was scouting the other day . . . two days ago . . . and came up on two Cheyenne. They were young men, and I have seen enough blood. I made peace and they did the same. We ate and smoked and talked. They had spoken with some Kiowa a few days before who had spoken with some Delaware who had just left the trading post on the river. A very large group of white men was there. They had just come in from the East. Far to the east. The Delaware told the Kiowa and the Kiowa told the Cheyenne and the Cheyenne told me that the men were buying huge amounts of supplies and they were all well armed. They also were a loud talking bunch and smelled bad. They did not bathe and the odor from their bodies was awful, the Cheyenne told me what the Delaware had told the Kiowa who told the Cheyenne. I believe these men will join Andy Price who should be at the fort by this time buying supplies for Bones and his people and the arrogant men with them.

"Preacher, my heart is very sad about the little sick boy who was killed. I saw where you buried him with his horse. That was a good thing you did. He will need his pony to cross to the other side of life. But his grave will not fool the Utes when they return to find out what happened to Wind Chaser. And they will return, Preacher. After the hunt. Listen, I have what I think is a fine idea. Why don't you ride to the strong Ute camp and tell them what happened? They will see to the fates of those who did that terrible thing."

"No," Preacher said with a shake of his head. "I can't have Utes killin' ever' white man who comes along. We're not all bad, Dark Hand."

Dark Hand grunted at that and Preacher understood and had to smile. The white man had not given the Indians many reasons to trust them. But the Indians hadn't exactly welcomed the white man with open arms, either. Preacher understood that there was right and wrong on both sides. There always is when two strong cultures clash. What was considered barbarism and savagery to the white man was an accepted way of life to the Indian.

"Well, if Bones has more men comin' out to join him, I reckon I best get on with whittlin' down the odds."

"I would say that you have made a fine start toward that," Dark Hand said, a distinct dryness in his tone.

The eyes of the Indian and the white man met, and both of them chuckled. Most whites felt the Indian did not have a sense of humor. They were wrong. The Indian had a fine sense of humor. They just didn't show it very often around whites.

Dark Hand finished his coffee and stood up. "I go now, White Wolf. You will not see me again while this silly war is going on. Months from now, should we meet again, remember that you will always be welcome in my camp."

"And you in mine, Dark Hand," Preacher said, extending his hand.

Dark Hand shook the hand and walked to his horse. He was gone seconds later.

Preacher stood for a moment. "First Pawnee I ever really made friends with," he muttered. "Damned if he didn't turn out to be a right nice feller."

"Tracks lead off yonder," Van Eaton pointed, reporting back to Bones. "I betcha that Injun went straight to Preacher."

"No matter," Bones said. "I'm glad to be shut of him. I never did really trust him."

The teams of men were packed up and ready to mount. The royalty had been separated at Bones's orders. He wanted to keep as many alive as possible. He wanted his money, and the gentry were no good to him dead.

"Let's go," Bones said, swinging up into the saddle. "We'll meet an hour before sunset."

One team was to head straight for the new camp and get it ready. The other teams were to concentrate on tracking and finding Preacher. They didn't know that Preacher was, at that very moment, making the search very easy for them.

"Got him!" Spanish called out. "He ain't near'bouts as smart as he thinks he is. Look here."

The team members, including Robert Tassin, gathered around. The tracks were plain as could be. They didn't know that Preacher had been laying down sign all morning, trying to get them to see the tracks. For this sign, Preacher had jumped up and down in one place, broke off a branch, and built a small fire. He figured if this didn't work he'd have to find him a white rag and stand out in the open and wave it at the men.

"We've got him!" the French aristocrat said excitedly.

"Let's press on, men." He spurred his horse and entered the timber.

"No, you don't," Spanish muttered. "Preacher is mine." He jumped ahead of Tassin and unknowingly and certainly unwillingly, saved the Frenchman's life.

Preacher's rifle boomed and Spanish went down, leaving the saddle like a sack of potatoes as the big heavy caliber ball blew a hole in his chest and shattered his heart.

"Merde!" Tassin said, jumping from the saddle and taking cover behind a tree. He looked all around him, but could see nothing. He looked over at Spanish. The man lay motionless on the ground, his shirt front bloody.

Tassin lifted his rifle, looking at where he'd seen a faint puff of smoke. If the Frenchman had been the man-hunter he thought he was, he should have guessed that as soon as Preacher fired, the mountain man would shift locations. The only thing that saved Tassin's life was the turning of his head as one of the team, a large, big-bellied, rather obnoxious fellow called Percy, stepped on a branch and it popped. Preacher's rifle crashed and the ball blew bits of bark into the side of Tassin's face, stinging and bringing blood. Had he not turned at the sound of the branch breaking, the ball would have blown a huge hole in his head.

Badly frightened, Tassin bellied down on the ground, presenting as small a target as possible. This was just not turning out well at all.

"You boys made a bad mistake," Preacher called from the brush. "You best say your prayers."

"Hell with you, Preacher," a thug called Hubert yelled. "We got you now."

"Then come get me," Preacher challenged. A second later he changed position, moving several yards to his left. Rifles boomed, the balls whizzing harmlessly to the position where Preacher had been.

"Oohhh!" Preacher moaned, trying to keep from laughing. "You got me, boys. Oohh, it hurts somethin' turrible.

Damn your eyes, you've kilt me. Tell my poor ol' ma good-bye for me, boys." He managed to suppress a giggle.

Hubert gave out a loud shout of triumph and lurched to his feet.

"Get down, you fool!" Percy hollered.

Hubert suddenly realized he had made a perfectly horrible error in judgment. He froze in wild-eyed and openmouthed fear and panic. Preacher dusted him, shooting him from side to side, the ball making a huge bloody hole as it exited. Hubert fell dead to the ground.

"Get out of here!" Percy yelled. "Work your way back. He's got us cold in this brush."

Paul Guy made a jump for his horse and Preacher's rifle boomed again. Paul's leg buckled under him and collapsed to the ground, crying out in pain.

Preacher slipped quietly away. He'd dealt this bunch enough misery. He figured rightly that all the shooting would bring the others at a gallop. Preacher was a brave man, but no fool. He'd fight this group of man-hunters on his own terms, not on theirs. He slipped over the crest of the rise and jumped into the saddle. He had him a brand new little hidey-hole all picked out.

Bones took one look at the sign that Spanish had found and snorted in disgust. He looked at what was left of this team of men. "He suckered you all."

"Whatever in the world do you mean by that remark?" Jon Tassin shouted, holding a bloody handkerchief to his face. "I demand an answer!"

"Tricked you, that's what I mean. Preacher deliberately left this sign, hopin' you'd be dumb enough to follow it. And Spanish was dumb enough." He savagely kicked the dead Spanish in the side. "Stupid, igit!"

"Let's proceed with the hunt!" Willy Steinwinder shouted. "After him, men!"

"Just hold on, hold on!" Van Eaton said. "That's what

Preacher wants you to do. He's layin' up in the brush or behind some rocks just over that hill yonder. Now just settle down."

"Van Eaton's right," Bones said. "We got to sit down in a safe place and plan this out, carefully."

"I'm for that," Percy said. "I've helped hunt down a lot of men. But I ain't never seen no human bein' like this here Preacher person."

"Yeah," Paul Guy said through clenched teeth, as he wrapped a dirty rag around the wound in his leg. Preacher is more like a wild animal that somehow got as smart as us."

A huge ignorant lout called Doyle said, "Preacher said last night that some of us would die this day." He looked nervously around him. "He was shore right."

Bones sensed the moment was getting spooky to some of the men. Down on the flats, he could see the rest of his party riding toward the ridges. He already had too many of the royalty gathered here. "Evans, you take Doyle and head off those other men. Preacher would love to catch us all bunched up near the timber."

Doyle and Evans didn't need a second invitation to leave this scene of blood and death.

Bones took off his hat and scratched his licy head. "We got to start actin' like an army and thinkin' like generals."

"I am a general!" Rudi Kuhlmann said.

"I thought you was a prince?" a man called Falcon said.

"I am. I'm a general too."

"Me, too," Wilhelm Zaunbelcher said. "And so is he." He pointed to Juan Zapata. "Well, why don't you start generalin', then?" a man called Flores asked.

Sir Elmore Jerrold-Taylor smiled. "We thought you would never ask. Catching this Preacher person is easy. We'll show you how."

"Oh, yeah!" Bones said beligerently.

"Oh, yes," Tassin said. "Just watch and learn."

15

"That's odd," Preacher muttered, watching the man-hunters through his spy-glass. They were all packed up and riding away. He watched the riders until they were no more than tiny dark dots in the distance. He collapsed his glass and tucked it away, then squatted down and gave this some thought.

"Them ol' boys want me to think they're pullin' out, when I know damn well they ain't doin' no such thing. Now, why would they want me to think that? Ummm." After a moment, he smiled and said, "So's I'd follow them and ride right into an ambush, that's why. Well, I ain't a-gonna do that."

Preacher thought a while longer and then began to break camp. He figured they would take the same route back that they took comin' in, so he'd just make a wide circle and see if he could get a few miles ahead of them. He'd be right there to greet them.

"This ain't a-gonna work," Flores grumbled. "We ain't seen hide nor hair of Preacher."

Bones and party, now led by the royalty, were on their third day of travel, and the thought was creeping into the minds of many of the man-hunters that

Preacher had not taken the bait and was not going to fall into the trap.

By late afternoon of the third day, the man-hunters had traveled about sixty miles from their last contact with Preacher. They had not seen one living human being. They did not know that most of the Indians were far to the north, hunting buffalo.

"Yeah," Bobby Allen said. "I'm a-gettin' hongry. I hope Mack finds us a good spot to camp pretty damn quick."

"Right purty," Mack Cornay said, looking at the coolness provided by the shady trees that lined both banks of the little creek. "This'll do just fine."

The man-hunters were in a long and narrow flat, running north to south between the snow-covered peaks of the Rockies. Cornay waited until the main body was in sight, and then began waving his hat. Rudi Kuhlmann, riding point, spotted the signal and angled the column off toward Mack and the creek.

Rudi could not understand why one minute he could see Mack, and the next instant he could not. He did not know the terrain ahead of him; did not know it was very deceptive, with ravines and gullies and wallows on the east side of the creek. And Mack Cornay was in no condition to be aware of anything. Preacher had thrown a fist-sized rock at the man, the stone slamming into the back of Mack's head and knocking him from the saddle. Mack lay on the ground, unconscious. Preacher had taken the man's weapons, his powder horn, and his shot, and vanished into the bog across the creek.

A knowledgeable man can traverse a bog, but he'd better know where to put each step, for there was mud there that could take a man down to his waist, or beyond. The bog ran for about fifteen hundred yards one way and was about half a mile across. Indians avoided the place, knowing it could be a death trap for both man and horse. Venomous snakes lay above the shallow water on clumps of grass, sunning themselves.

Rudi rode up to the creek and sat his saddle for a moment, looking down at Mack, thinking the man certainly chose a strange time and place to take a nap. Preacher's rifle barked and Rudi was slammed from the saddle, the ball tearing through his shoulder and almost blinding him with white-hot pain. He hit the ground on his belly, knocking the wind from him.

Bones and Van Eaton and a few of the others immediately left the saddle and bellied down in the knee-high grass. A few of the less-experienced, including all the royalty, raced their horses toward the wounded Rudi.

Preacher fired again from the bog and a man called Scott did a back-flip out of the saddle, dead before he impacted with the earth.

Wilhelm Zaunbelcher, shouting oaths in a guttural tongue, threw caution to the wind and galloped his horse through the creek. But the horse had more sense than the Baron. He refused to enter the bog, stopping quite abruptly. Zaunbelcher went flying out of the saddle and landed in the mud at the edge of the bog. He sank about six inches. Zaunbelcher thought he was in quicksand—he wasn't, but there was quicksand in the bog—and immediately panicked. He began screaming in fright, kicking his feet and waving his arms and flinging mud in all directions.

Sir Elmore Jerrold-Taylor drew a short saber from a saddle scabbard and shouted, "Charge, men!"

"Charge?" Bones said.

"I think that's what he said," Van Eaton replied.

This was the day of horse-sense. Elmore's horse refused to step into the bog, putting on the brakes and sliding to a halt. Like Baron Zaunbelcher, Sir Jerrold-Taylor left the saddle and went flying through the air, slowly turning as he flew. A Red-breasted Nuthatch flew past the Englishman and gave the huge creature a very strange look.

"Yna, Yna, Yna," the Nuthatch chirped, and flew on to

tell his mate there was something very weird going on in the bog.

"My word!" Sir Elmore said. He landed right next to the Baron and when he impacted with the mud, the point of his saber jabbed Zaunbelcher in the ass and the Prussian came roaring up out of the bog, looking and sounding very much like some terrible monster from a swamp.

Benny Atkins realized he had made a bad mistake by following the nutty foreigners up to the creek and had jumped from the saddle, heading for the trees. Preacher's rifle sang its deadly song and Benny took a ball in his hip, turning him around in a haze of pain before he collapsed to the ground. He tumbled into the creek.

Preacher let himself sink into the mud until only the top of his head and his nose remained above the surface. He was behind a clump of grass and could not be seen. His one rather fervent wish was that there was not a big rattler sunning on the clump. The sun would be cycling soon, shadowing the valley in darkness. Preacher would mud swim out of the bog under cover of night. He rather hoped that some of the men would step into the bog, but he knew that was not very likely.

Sir Elmore reached up and jerked Zaunbelcher back into the mud and safe from rifle shot and they lay quite still for several long moments before they began cautiously working their way back to solid ground.

"Oh, drat! I lost my saber," Sir Elmore said.

"Excellent," Zaunbelcher said. "I hope you never find the damn thing."

The rest of the man-hunters waited until shadows began casting long pockets of darkness before they moved. And even then, they did so very cautiously. None of them had been able to spot Preacher and they did not know whether he was still out there in the bog.

"Creep out of that swamp or whatever it is careful-like," Bones called to Elmore and Wilhelm. "Stay low leadin' your horses back here. We got to get gone." To

Van Eaton he said, "Have the boys start draggin' the wounded out."

"Right."

"What about Scott?" a man called.

"Leave him," Bones said, cutting his eyes to Van Eaton.

"You boys get gone," Van Eaton said. "I'll see to Scott."

Preacher heard the calling back and forth and let the men leave, noting which direction they took. Just in case they were trying to set up a trap—something he doubted— Preacher remained in the bog for an hour after they'd left. Then, at full dark he carefully worked his way out of the bog and back to his camp, about three miles away. He washed himself at a tiny run-off and brushed the now dried mud off his buckskins. Something was nagging at his mind but he could not bring it to full light. He shook his head and gave it up. It would come to him.

He cooked his supper and boiled his coffee over a tiny fire. As he ate and drank, he tried to figure out what was nagging at him. He knew it was something he'd seen, and seen that day, but whatever it had been remained elusive to him. He laid out his blankets and with rifle and pistols fully charged and close to hand, Preacher sighed and went to sleep.

He awakened with a grunt of anger about an hour later. Scalps. That's what he'd seen. There had been scalps tied to the manes of the horses of them silly foreigners.

And one of them had been Eddie's.

16

"So much for the generals leadin' us anywhere," Van Eaton groused that evening. "I told you it was a bad idea."

Van Eaton shrugged that off. He already knew it was a bad idea. He glanced around at his shot-up men. They were a pitiful-looking bunch and a lot of the enthusiasm for the hunt had been knocked out of them by Preacher. Bones had never before encountered such a man as Preacher. What Bones didn't know about any number of things would fill volumes, but just about any experienced mountain man would have behaved pretty much the same as Preacher as far as fighting ability went. Most mountain men would have been content to just run Bones and his so-called man-hunters out of the mountains, and then they would have gone on about their business. But there were a few who would have done just exactly what Preacher was doing.

"We got to find us a hidey hole and stay low 'til Andy gets back," Bones said. "The men just ain't in any shape to go much farther and they damn shore ain't in any shape to mix it up with Preacher."

"You mighty right about that," Van Eaton said.

Up until almost that very moment, if Bones and his

bunch had really wanted to give up the hunt, Preacher just might have let them go. But not after seeing Eddie's scalp tied onto the mane of that horse. That snapped it with Preacher.

Preacher lay for a long time in his blankets after the nagging thought had awakened him in all its horror. Bones and them knew that was a white boy they dragged and scalped . . . or scalped and then dragged, the dread thought came to him.

The dirty scum! He didn't give a damn if those that went for supplies came back with a hundred extra men. Anybody who joined up with Bones Gibson, Van Eaton, and them silly and savage foreigners was dead meat.

The longer he thought about that previous afternoon, the more scalps he could identify. Wind Chaser had a streak of gray right down the center of his hair. Preacher had seen that one tied to the mane of Van Eaton's horse. Wind Chaser's woman's hair had a sort of auburn tint to it, since she was the daughter of a mountain man. Bones had been displaying that one. And their kids had taken after their mother, with lighter hair than the others in the tribe. Preacher had seen their scalps, too.

Preacher looked up at the starry heavens. This high up, the stars seemed so close he could almost reach out and touch them. But Preacher was in no mood to appreciate the beauty of the night. He had something else on his mind.

Killing.

Preacher picked up their trail about mid-morning. And for a moment, it confused him. The trail led south and east. Dismounting, he studied the tracks. There was still the very faint outline of older tracks, and he recognized those as being the men who had left for supplies and returning from Bent's Fort. Horses and mules. Then he realized what Bones was doing. His bunch was pretty

well shot up and hurtin'. So he was tryin' to link up with
his other party, hopin' they was bringin' reinforcements.
Preacher figured that when they joined up, they'd hole
up for a time, and then come after him with a vengeance.

"Suits me," Preacher muttered. "Just fine. The more
the merrier, Bones. Bones. Somebody shore named you
right. 'Cause your bones is gonna bleach white as snow
in these mountains, you kid-killer. I swear it."

Preacher didn't follow Bones and the others. He
turned around and headed back north. He wanted time
to kill a couple of deer, make some pemmican, smoke
and jerk some meat, and just lounge around and eat
some venison steaks. He'd found him some wild peas
and prairie turnips and wild taters. Mix all that up with
some pieces of venison and toss in some rose hips and
sage and a body had him a lip-smackin' good stew.
Preacher got all hungry around the mouth just thinkin'
'bout it.

The weary and bloodied bunch linked up with Andy
Price and the gang of men he was bringing back from
Bent's Fort. Bones eyeballed the bunch and figured
about half of them would turn back once they took a
good look at the Rockies. Fifteen or twenty more would
pull out after the first sneak attack by Preacher. Those
that stayed would be lean and mean and hard and
tough.

"They's another bunch comin' up behind me," Andy
told him. "I tole 'em to head on back. This ain't no
game. But they're still comin' on. They're city toughs.
Some of them come all the way from New York and
Philly and Boston and them places. I don't understand
how they've made it this far. They don't appear to know
north from south. And you never in your borned days
seen so many different kinds of guns. One of 'em's got
two pistols. Each has a cylinder that holds six rounds and

revolves. He called them revolvers. Strange lookin' things."

"They're what?" Van Eaton asked.

"Revolvers," Andy repeated.*

"Damned if I know," Andy said. "But I don't think they'll ever catch on."

"How do they work?" George Winters asked.

"Did you hear anything about the hunt back at the fort?" Bones asked.

"Oh, yeah. That's about all that folks talk about. And that's strange, too."

"How so?" Van Eaton asked.

"Well, they was a goodly number of mountain men there, but none of them seemed to be a bit concerned about Preacher. Near'bouts all of them said the joke was gonna be on us. One big mountain man told a bully boy from New York—let's see, how did he put it? Oh, yeah. "'Ye'll nar leave them mountains ifn ye go yonder with a blood lust for Preacher. Ye been warned by us who knows White Wolf. Heed our words.'"

"How about Jim Slattery and them writers who left us?"

"They never showed up, Bones. Nobody there has seen hide nor hair of them."

"Injuns got them," Van Eaton opined.

Bones was thoughtful for a moment. "That mob comin' up behind us just might be what we need. Preacher will be so busy tryin' to figure out what to do, mayhaps some of us can slip off durin' the confusion and kill him."

*A Nichols and Childs belt model revolver. About .34 caliber. Only a very few were made. Manufactured about 1838 or '39. The cylinder revolved using a mechanical device called a pawl that was attached to the hammer.

Sir Elmore had walked up. He said, "Say now. That is an excellent thought. By jove, I believe you've quite probably stumbled upon the solution to our problem." He patted Bones on the shoulder. "A very admirable bit of ruminative prowess, my good man." He smiled and walked off to share the good news with his fellow adventurers.

Andy shook his head. "I was hopin' them fellers would learn to talk right whilst I was gone."

"No such luck," Van Eaton said. "They's even worser than before."

Preacher spent his time relocating his caches of supplies, jerking a goodly amount of meat, resting and eating and getting ready for war. He was completely unaware of the second band of men hunting him. While Bones was waiting for the wounds of his men to heal, and Preacher was preparing himself mentally to dispose of the entire worthless, no-count, disagreeable lot of them, summer came to the mountains in full bloom. The valleys were pockets of color in all hues.

Utes had returned from a very successful hunt and were puzzled by the disappearance of Wind Chaser and his small band. Warriors from Wind Chaser's village were frantically and desperately searching for their families. But so far they failed to search the little valley where Eddie and Wind Chaser and his band had met their deaths. But they would. The wilderness was vast, and it was impossible to look everywhere. The warriors from Wind Chaser's village mistakenly headed north and west in their search, and the little valley, now covered with summer's blossoms, remained untouched, for the time being.

Had they run into Dark Hand, he could have and would have told them what had happened, but Dark Hand had traveled north and east, to rejoin his own people, who were camped over in the unorganized territory that lay just south of the Missouri River.

Sir Elmore had found his saber but wisely kept it sheathed and out of sight because Baron Zaunbelcher had threatened to break it if Elmore ever drew it again.

Most of Bones's men were healed up enough to ride, and those that weren't properly healed could either suffer the discomfort and ride, or stay and be left behind. All chose to ride.

The second band of man-hunters was just about the most disreputable looking bunch of ne'er-do-wells that Bones had ever seen. And when the likes of Bones Gibson thought somebody was trash, they couldn't get much lower if they crawled under a snake's belly.

Bones had ridden back to eyeball the second bunch, to see if there might be any men in there that he could use. He found a few possibilities, but for the moment, would stay with what he had. He was back up to strength, just over forty men.

This bunch, he thought sourly, would not last a week in the mountains, not if just one of them made a hostile move against Preacher. Preacher would turn on them like a wild animal and run them all back to the Mississippi. If they made it that far. Bones wisely decided to distance himself from this mangy looking pack of so-called man-hunters.

"You there!" the gruff shout stopped Bones as he was just riding off.

Bones turned to stare at the burly lout who was striding toward him. "What do you want?"

"Where's this here murderer called Preacher?"

Bones laughed at him. "You want him, you find him."

"I'm Lige Watson." The man acted as though that was supposed to mean something.

"So?"

"I'm the toughest man in all of Pennsylvania."

Bones laughed at him. "Then you best head on back to Pennsylvania, Watson. 'Cause out here, you're nothin'."

"We'll see about that."

"Not for very long, you won't." Bones left it at that and rode away.

"Holy jumpin' elephants!" Preacher said, peering through his spy-glass. He took a second look just to make certain his eyes weren't deceiving him. They weren't.

It looked to him like about forty or so in the first bunch, and that would be Bones's men, for he could pick out Bones in the lead. Another forty or so in the second bunch, layin' back about a mile behind Bones.

"I shore ain't gettin' to be a right popular feller," Preacher muttered, putting away his glass. "Damned if that ain't a regular army down yonder. Forty in one bunch and forty in the other. They gonna be fallin' all over one another 'fore this is through." He smiled a wicked curving of his lips. "I'm gonna have me some fun come the night."

What was fun to Preacher could be downright unsettling to others . . . and sometimes lethal.

The floor of the long narrow valley was dotted with campfires, with a dark space about a mile in length between the two camps of man-hunters. Lige Watson, the self-appointed leader of the second bunch, walked through the camp, inspecting 'his men,' as he liked to call them.

To Lige, they looked like a very formidable army. In reality, they were about as sloppy a rag-tag bunch of losers as had ever gathered anywhere. The group was made up of those types of people who are constantly out for an easy dollar, who expect the world to give them a handout, who always blame others for their problems, who could never keep a job because the boss 'picked on them.' Among the second group were strong-arm boys, thieves, hustlers, pimps, forgers, murderers, rapists, and every other kind of no-good anybody would care to name.

Really, the social and moral difference between Bones's group and Lige's bunch was minuscule. There wasn't a man in either group worth the gunpowder it would take to blow his brains out.

"Lookin' rale good," Lige said to his friend, Fred Lasalle, after completing his walk-through of the camp. "I'd put these boys up aginst just about any group twicest our size."

"Did you git to talk to any of them royal highnesses?" Fred asked.

"Well, sort of. I spoke to one and he tole me that in all his years he had never stood so clost to such an odorous cretinous moronic specimen of foul humanity."

Fred blinked. "Well, you done good, then, din you?"

"I don't rightly know. I reckon so."

"What do all them words mean, Lige?" Derby Peel asked.

"Means we all right, I guess."

"Thought so."

With the exception of the rendezvous of the mountain men, which had now ceased to be, never had such a large gathering of white men occurred in the Rockies. The stench of unwashed bodies could be smelled for hundreds of yards. No self-respecting Indian would get within an arrow's range of such a group. The smell alone probably contributed to saving their lives from Indians looking for a scalp.

"Whew!" Preacher muttered, as he drew closer to the encampment. His nose wrinkled at the stench of unwashed bodies. A buzzard would have a tough time competing with this bunch, he thought.

Preacher lay on his belly in the tall grass less than fifty

yards from Lige's camp and looked over the scene that
unfolded before him. It was only slightly less than incredible. The fools had fires blazin' that were big enough to
roast a whole buffalo. The big ugly bully-lookin' man
someone had called Lige was probably the leader of this
skunk-pack, Preacher reckoned. He looked like a man
who had a real high opinion of himself the way he strut-
ted around. Preacher took an immediate dislike to him.
He'd seen men like Lige before, men who'd come to the
mountains and tried to fit in with other trappers. They
had not lasted long. Mountain men were hard to impress.

"Well, boys," Lige said to his friends who'd come west
with him. "Tomorrow we start huntin' down this
Preacher person. I don't figure on it takin' no more than
a week. Prob'ly less than that."

Preacher smiled and moved closer until he reached a
pocket of darkness. Then he stood up and slipped into
the camp. Many of the men were dressed in buckskins so
no one paid any attention to Preacher as he walked
through the camp and straight up to Lige.

"Howdy," Preacher said. "I got a message from Bones
if you be Lige."

"I'm Lige. What's on your mind?"

"Well, Mister Lige, don't get mad at me, I'm just deliv-
erin' the message. Bones said for your men to bring your
cups and come on over. They's whiskey a-plenty and
food for all. Says both our bunches had best get to know
one another. But he said for me to tell you to keep your
butt out of his camp. Says if you show up he'll stomp
your gizzard out."

"He said *what?*" Lige hollered.

"Oh, he said a lot, Bones did. But I dasn't repeat most
of it. It was right insultin' and personal."

"You tell me, mister!" Lige growled the words, as a
large crowd gathered around.

"Well, now, don't get mad at me," Preacher said.

"I'm not gonna get mad at you. You just tell me what Bones said."

"Well, he said you smelled worser than a skunk and prob'ly had about as much sense as a jackass. And he called your mamma some real turrible names, he did. I just won't repeat them slurs aginst a good woman. I just won't do it. God might strike me dead."

Lige was so mad he was hopping up and down.

"If you don't mind," Preacher said. "I'd like to leave that bunch of name-callers over yonder and join up with you, Mister Lige. I think Bones is settin' up an ambush for your boys. That's what it looks like to me. Besides that, I just cain't abide a man who'll call another man he don't even know a low-down, no-good, buzzard-puke-breath, dirty son of a bitch like Bones said you was."

Lige's eyes bugged out and his face turned red. His ears wriggled and his adam's apple bobbed up and down. "You stay here," he said to Preacher, finally finding his voice. "I think you a good man. Let's ride, boys. We got a nest of snakes to clean out."

Within seconds, the camp was deserted. Preacher grinned and began wandering through the camp, picking up what supplies he felt he might need. "Gonna be real interestin' over at Bones's camp in about five minutes. Real interestin'." Chuckling, Preacher faded into the night.

17

"Riders comin', Bones," a guard called. "Looks like that new bunch."

"Now, what you reckon that pack of ninnies wants?" Van Eaton asked.

"They certainly are coming in quite a rush," Baron Zaunbelcher remarked.

Lige and his group rode right through the camp, knocking over pots and scattering bedrolls and sending men scrambling to get out of the way.

"What the hell do you think you're doin', you half-wit?" Bones yelled to Lige.

Lige and his men jumped off their horses. "I got your message, you big mouth no-count!" Lige yelled, marching up to Bones. "And this is my reply." Lige rared back and flattened Bones with a right to the mouth.

Lige's men jumped at Bones's men and the fight was on.

Preacher could hear the shouts and yelling and cussing more than a mile away. Carrying several huge sacks filled with powder horns, food, weapons, candles, matches, and what-have-you, Preacher walked away toward the high-up country. He would have taken several blankets, but they all had fleas hopping around on them.

Bones jumped up and popped Lige right on his big snoot. The blood and the snot flew and Lige's boots flew out from under him and he landed on his butt.

Bob Jones had tied up with Mack Cornay and the two men were flailing away at one another. Derby Peel had squared off against Van Eaton and the men were exchanging blows, each blow bringing a grunt of pain and the splattering of blood. Fred Lasalle looked around for somebody to hit and his eyes touched on Sir Elmore Jerrold-Taylor, standing beside a fancy wall tent. Fred walked over to the clean shaven and neatly dressed Englishman and without a word being said, slugged him right on the nose. Elmore hollered and grabbed at his busted beak. He drew his hands away and looked at the blood. "I've been wounded!" he yelled.

Jon Louviere jumped on Fred's back and rode him to the earth while Stan Law busted Baron Wilhelm Zaunbelcher in the mouth. With a roar, the Prussian drew back one big fist and sent Stan rolling through the dirt, then turned and kicked Fred Lasalle hard in the belly with a polished boot. That put Fred out for the duration.

Will Herdman jumped on Andy Price and went to pokin' and gougin' and kickin' and bitin' until Andy threw him off and began stomping on him. That went on until Cantry, a good friend of Will's, ran over and hit Andy on the head with a club. Andy's eyes rolled back, he hit the ground, and he didn't wake up for an hour. Will, battered and bloody, said to hell with it all and stretched out beside Andy.

The men in the camp, with the exception of the nobility, who quickly retired to their tents and tied the flaps closed, fought until they were exhausted. Almost to the man, they fell down to the ground and lay there, chests heaving.

Finally, Bones, lying flat on his back in the grass, managed to gasp out to Lige, "What in the hell brought on all this, you igit?"

"Don't you be callin' me no igit, you low-life," said Lige, who was also stretched out on the cool grass. "And you know what brung it on."

"I don't neither!"

"Do too!"

"Don't!"

"Does!"

"I do not!"

"You think about it. You know!"

"I don't know! Why the hell do you think I'm askin'?"

Even though he wasn't a very smart man, that managed to get through to Lige. He thought about it for a moment. "You sent a feller over to our camp to see me and he said you said a lot of bad things about me."

"I never sent no feller over to see you! And I ain't said no bad things about you. I *thought* a bunch of bad things, but I never said 'em aloud."

Lige ruminated on that for another moment. He raised his bloody head and looked around. "Say, where is that feller anyways?"

"Back yonder at our camp, I reckon," Sutton said, holding a rag to his bloody mouth.

A tiny spark of suspicion entered Bones's head. He raised up on one elbow, the eye that wasn't blackening and closing because of a right cross from Lige's fist narrowed. "What did this here feller look like, Lige?"

"Wal, he were dressed in buckskins. Sorta tall and you could tell he was muscled up right good. He were clean shaven 'ceptin' for a moustache. And he moved real quiet like. Come to think of it, and I just thought of it, he had the coldest, meanest eyes I ever did see."

Bones flopped back on the ground. "You igit! That there was *Preacher!*"

"*Preacher?*" Lige hollered. "You mean the man we're a-huntin' come a-struttin' and a-sashshaying bold as brass right up into the big fat middle of our camp and tole me them lies?"

"Yeah." Bones heaved himself up to a sitting position. "Now you might git some idea of the type of man we're huntin'."

"Nervy ol' boy, ain't he?" Lige muttered around a swollen mouth.

"You could say that," Bones replied.

When Lige and company returned to camp, Lige found a note written on a scrap of paper and stuck on a tree limb. He laboriously read the missive.

"What do it say, Lige?" Fred Lasalle asked, peering over Lige's shoulder.

"It says, 'Git out of these mountins. I won't warn you agin. This here is yore only warnin'. Preacher?"

"The man must think he owns these here mountains!" Hugh Fuller said.

"Yeah!" a man called Billy said. "To hell with him."

A huge hulking monster of a man whose hands extended past his knees, giving him a distinct ape-like appearance, said, "I don't like this feller Preacher. I'm a-gonna tear his arms out when I find him and beat him to death with 'em."

"Way to go, Lucas," a much smaller man, only about five feet tall yelled. "That'll be fun to watch."

Lucas grinned at the man. What teeth had not rotted out were green and his breath could cause a buzzard to faint. "You and me, Willie. We'll catch this Preacher and be rich."

"All right, boys," Lige hollered. "Gather round. Come on, come on. I got things to say." When the camp had quieted down and the men gathered in a circle, Lige said, "At first light we start huntin' this murderin' no-count. And we'uns is gonna be workin' side by side with them ol' boys over yonder in the other camp. I think . . ."

"Hey!" a man hollered. "My powder horn's gone. Jeff, didn't you lay out a side of bacon to slice?"

"Yeah. Why?"

"Well, it's gone too."

The men all ran to their bedrolls and blankets and

tents. Soon, many of the men were cussing and stomping around.

"Preacher stole all the stuff," Bob Jones said. "He took enough powder to blow up half these mountains."

Preacher wasn't at all interested in blowing up the mountains. He had others things in mind.

The Cheyenne war chief called Bear Killer sat on his horse and looked down at the huge body of men in the valley below. He, along with representatives from the Ute, Arapaho, Kiowa-Apache, and the Southern Comanches were all traveling east, to make peace with each other. The location was about seventy-five miles east of Bent's Fort. The gathering of various tribes and the making of peace between them had been the idea of High Backed Wolf, a Cheyenne chief, a very famous warrior, and a man known for his diplomatic skills. He felt it was foolish to fight amongst themselves. After the historic meeting, which history only skims over very lightly, those tribes never again made war against the other.

Bear Killer looked down at the white men and shook his head. "Preacher cannot fight so many men and win. Perhaps we should wait until darkness comes and slip into the camp of the white men and help Preacher," he said to one of his warriors.

But the warrior shook his head. "No. Standing Bull said that Tall Man of the Arapaho told him that Preacher wants no help. This is a personal matter."

"Ummm. Yes. I remember. Preacher is indeed a brave warrior. I hope we never have to fight him again."

"Little Eagle told Stands Alone that the white men down there smell terrible. They do not wash their bodies and are very loud and vulgar. They kill animals and birds and leave them to rot on the ground. They do not dig proper places to dispose of their waste. They are not good people. They are wasteful and ignorant."

"I hope Preacher kills them all. If there are any left upon our return, we shall give Preacher some help in ridding our land of these worthless men. Without his knowledge, of course."

The Indians waited until the whites had passed and then rode on to their historical meeting on the Arkansas.

Several miles away, watching from near the timber line, Preacher could just make out the long double line of riders as they headed north. Preacher mounted up and headed south, staying in the timber far above the valley floor, no more than a shadow as he worked his way along.

He saw Bear Killer and his warriors and they saw him. The men passed within a few hundred yards of each other, lifted right hands, palms out, and rode on without speaking. Preacher picketed Thunder near water and began working his way toward the sprawling camp of the man-hunters. Using his spy glass, Preacher studied the camp. It was just about like he'd figured. Bones had left no guards behind. Only the cooks and servants were there, and Preacher wanted them gone. So far they had taken no part in the man-hunt, and Preacher held no animosity toward them. He spent the better part of an hour working his way up to the camp.

Preacher almost scared one of the servants out of his shoes when he suddenly rose up out of the grass about a yard from the man and said, "Howdy!"

The man dropped a load of tin plates he'd just washed and clutched at his chest, his mouth open and his eyes wide with fear. The others stood still and stared at Preacher. None of them made any move toward the rifles that had been placed around the camp in case of hostiles attacking.

"Relax," Preacher told the cooks and servants. "I ain't here to do none of you no harm. Y'all dish me up a plate of that good-smelling grub and a cup of coffee and we'll talk." Preacher sat down on the ground while a cook quickly served up a heaping plate of food.

Preacher thanked the man and said, "You boys reckon you could find your way out of these mountains?"

"Certainly," a man-servant replied. "I served in the British Army before gaining employment with the Duke. My experience with rugged terrain is vast."

"Is that a fact? Well, was I you boys, I'd busy myself packin' up and then I'd get the hell gone from here. Y'all ain't tooken no part in huntin' me, and I'm obliged to you for that. Your bosses is miles north of here, lookin' for me in all the wrong places, as usual. Now boys, when they do catch up with me, it's gonna get right nasty. Start packin'.'"

The servants and cooks exchanged glances. One said, "What about the savages?"

"They ain't gonna bother you none. They got themselves a big pow-wow down on the Arkansas. The four main tribes is gonna make peace with each other. 'Sides, they's enough of you and y'all's well armed. It would take a powerful big bunch of Injuns to attack you. When you get down to Bent's Fort, you ask around and hook up with supply wagons headin' back east and tag along with them for extree safety."

Several of the men turned and began packing. The others soon followed suit. One said, "The horses do not belong to us. There will be warrants issued for our arrest."

Preacher smiled. "There ain't nobody gonna be alive to issue no warrants, boys. There ain't none of that bunch gonna leave these mountains. Or damn few of them. So y'all take whatever you feel like takin'. Now, y'all seem like right nice fellers. So I'm gonna give you some advice. Y'all are all foreigners. You don't know nothin' about the West, and the men who has spent their lives out here. Look at me."

The cooks and servants stopped packing and looked.

Preacher patted the stock of his rifle. "This is the law out here, boys. No fancy robed judges or high-falutin' lawyers or badge-totin' lawmen. This is all there is. Now y'all hooked up with some mighty bad company. Maybe you didn't know what you was gettin' yourselves in for. I'll think that. 'Cause if you give me reason to think otherwise, I'd not look kindly upon you."

"We were told it was a hunting expedition," one said. "We had no reason to think it was anything else. We did not learn the truth until we were far from civilization back in Missouri—if civilization is the right word—and were in the middle of all that vastness."

"Pack and git!"

When the men had left, Preacher began gathering up all the blankets, tents, food, clothing, and medical supplies. He piled everything up and then went to the other camp and did the same. Then he set fire to the mess and began running across the valley floor to the slopes. When Bones and the gentry spotted the smoke, they'd come gallopin'. Preacher smiled as he ran effortlessly across the meadow. There was gonna be some mighty irritated folks when they saw what he'd done. Mighty irritated.

BOOK TWO

I can be pushed just so far.

Harry Leon Wilson

1

"The dirty, rotten, no good . . ." Bones went on a rampage, cussing and jumping up and down and throwing himself about like a spoiled child in the throes of a temper tantrum.

The men had managed to save quite a number of articles from the fires. But their tents were gone as were many of the blankets and spare clothing.

To heap insult upon injury, Preacher had left another note reading:

I WARNED YOU

A dozen men from Lige's bunch exchanged glances and without saying a word, mounted up and rode out. If they had any luck at all, they could catch up with the cooks and servants and ride back east with them. They wanted no more of Preacher.

Bones and Van Eaton and the royalty watched the men leave without comment. They were glad to be rid of them. Lige cussed the deserters and shook his fist at them and shouted dire threats until he was hoarse, but that was all he did.

Unbeknownst to Lige's people, at the orders of the

royalty, Bones, Van Eaton, and men had buried a great deal of supplies that were carefully wrapped in oilcloth and canvas.

"That was good thinkin'," Bones said to Sir Elmore after he had calmed down.

"Naturally," the Englishman replied.

No man among them had any way of knowing that a small group of settlers and a few missionaries had already left Bent's Fort, heading for the Rockies to establish a settlement and a church. The problem was, they were being guided by a man who was so inept he would have trouble finding the altar in a church.

"I am thrilled beyond words," Patience Comstock said to her sister, Prudence, as they bounced along in a wagon. "This is such a grand adventure. We'll be doing the work of the Lord by bringing God to the savages."

"Yes," Prudence agreed, tying her bonnet strap under her chin. "And won't Father and Mother be surprised to learn about that Preacher man they told us about back at the fort? Just think, Sister, a man of the Cloth so well-known and so devout, so . . . so, strong in his faith and loved by all that even the savages call him Preacher."

"Yes, sister. But I wonder why the Methodist Board of Missions didn't tell us about this man?"

"Well, he might be of another faith, dear."

"Of course. I'm sure that's it. No matter. We're all doing God's work." Patience tucked a few strands of auburn hair back under her bonnet. "I'm sure he's a fine gentleman."

"That dirty son!" Bones muttered, looking at the scorched boots he'd managed to pull from the smoldering mess. "I paid good money for these back in St. Louis." He tossed the ruined boots aside. "Preacher.

Preacher? How did a man like that ever get the name of Preacher?" he questioned with a snarl.

As it turns out, early on Preacher was captured by Indians and while they were mulling over whether to kill him outright or torture him to see how brave he was, the young man started preaching the gospel—sort of—to them. He preached for hours and hours and hours until the Indians finally reached the conclusion that he was crazy and turned him loose. Once the story got around, and that didn't take long, he was known as Preacher.

Preacher did nothing for several days except watch. He had been sure that once he burned the supplies of the man-hunters, they'd all give up and go home. He'd told the cooks and servants that he was going to kill all those after him just to get them moving. The truth was, Preacher's deep grief and hot anger over the death of Eddie and Wind Chaser had tempered somewhat. He could kill ten times the number of those men after him and that wouldn't bring the dead back to life.

He just wanted this over and to live his life in peace.

"Damn," Preacher said, lowering the spy glass. "What's it gonna take to discourage them fools down yonder?"

Some of the men were real woodsmen and frontiersmen. They'd been smoking fish and meat and making jerky and really eatin' pretty high on the hog. And Preacher had seen where a whole passel of supplies had been dug up. He had stung the man-hunters some, but that was about it.

Preacher didn't know it, but his troubles were only just beginning.

"Oh, sister," Patience said to her twin, Prudence. "Aren't they magnificent?"

"Breathtaking, sister."

They were gazing at the Rockies.

One of the settlers, a good solid, sturdy young man of German stock, named Otto Steiner, walked up to the twins' wagon. "Quite a sight, ja, ladies?"

"Oh, Mister Steiner, they are just beautiful!" Patience cooed.

"Ja, ja. All of that. Well, I just want to see those lovely rich valleys and lakes in those mountains where a man and his wife can raise kids and vegetables and have cows and fish and hunt. We go on now." He waved at the scout, who was now sober, having exhausted his supply of whiskey. "We go, man. Take us through the mountains."

The scout, known only as Wells, nodded his head and picked up the reins. "I ain't gar-enteein' nothin'. But we'll give it a shot."

"What do you mean, sir?" Patience demanded. "We were told back in Missouri that you knew this country."

"Wal, they lied. I ain't never been this far a-fore. And to tell you the truth, I ain't real thrilled about goin' no further, neither. So I don't think I will."

"What does that mean?" Otto asked.

"Means I quit." Without another word, he rode away, heading east. He did not look back.

The four wagons and eight people suddenly looked awfully tiny with the majestic mountains looming in front of them.

"Well now," Frank Collins said, walking up with his wife of only a few months with him. "This sort of leaves us in a pickle, doesn't it?"

"The Lord will see us through," Jane Collins said, smiling up at her husband.

Hanna Steiner joined the group, as did Paul and Sally Marks. "I didn't like that Wells person anyway," Hanna said bluntly. "He was a very untidy man who did not bathe enough and he cussed. I cannot abide a man who swears."

"Ja, Hanna," Otto said. "You are right about that, you surely are."

"Well!" Patience said, flouncing on the wagon seat. "We must press on." She picked up the reins. "The Lord is with us and surely He will hear our prayers this evening and send His man of faith in the wilderness, Preacher, to guide us through. I am certain of that. Onward, people. We'll lift our voices in Christian song as we travel through the wilderness." She popped the big rear mules on the butt with the reins and off they went, creaking and lurching and singing across the Plains, only a few miles from the Rockies. The faint sounds of song could be heard as the young pioneers headed bravely into the unknown.

The fare in the camp of Bones had decidedly gone downhill with their cooks leaving and much of their supplies destroyed. It was now mostly venison and beans. And not one sign of Preacher had been found by the daily patrols. It had been two weeks since the cooks and servants left and Preacher had burned their camp.

"I think the man has fled," Robert Tassin said.

"I concur," his countryman, Jon Louviere agreed.

Bones and Van Eaton, sitting on the ground a few yards away, listened but said nothing. It really made no difference to either man. The longer they stayed out, the more money they made. The rules and rates of the 'game' had changed. With the exception of Bones and Van Eaton, each man was being paid five dollars a day, a very princely sum for the time. Bones and Van Eaton were receiving substantially more. In addition, when, or if, Preacher was found, and the aristocracy killed him, each man in the group would receive a cash bonus. The entire group could have the reward money posted on Preacher's head. Literally. For the reward money could only be claimed by bringing Preacher's head back as proof. A carefully packed glass jug and pickling solution had been brought by the second group.

Up near the timber line, Preacher was getting bored. His hopes that the hunting party would go away and leave him alone had been dashed. On this clear and crisp mid-summer morning, just as dawn was lighting the horizon, Preacher reckoned it was time to open this ball and he was going to lead the band. He picked up two rifles and headed out.

Patience and Prudence and party had broken camp and were on the move. They were about eight miles away at dawn.

The camp of the man-hunters had shifted, the un-washed multitudes crawling out of their blankets, shaking out the fleas and various other bugs and headed for the creek for coffee water.

Bones was squatting by the fire, warming his hands and waiting for the water to boil. He was always surly in the mornings and this morning he was surlier than usual. Even Van Eaton did not dare to speak to him. The gentry were gathered together, as usual. They preferred their own company to that of the unwashed.

Bones reached for the coffee pot just as a rifle ball banged against the big iron kettle and ripped off, the flattened and ragged ricochet striking a man-hunter in the center of the forehead and dropping him dead on the ground. Bones kissed the earth, flattening out on his belly.

One of Bones's original group, Joey York, was a tad slow in reacting and Preacher's second shot ended his man-hunting days forever. The ball from the fancy hunting rifle punched a hole in Joey's chest and knocked him into a cookfire, setting his clothing and greasy hair ablaze. The ensuing smell was not exactly conducive to a good appetite.

"Did anybody spot the smoke?" Van Eaton yelled, from his position behind a tree near the creek.

"Do we ever?" Tom Evans called.

"Somebody pull Joey out the fire," Bones said. "The smell is makin' me ill."

One of the second party, a man called Stanley, jumped up and made it halfway to the smoldering body of Joey before Preacher nailed him, dusting the man from side to side. Stanley stumbled and fell dead without making a sound.

"He's got to be in that little stand of trees over yonder," Cal Johnson yelled, sticking his head up and peering over the log he was hiding behind. "But that's a good three hundred yards off. Man, he can *shoot!*"

Preacher's rifle boomed and Cal lost part of an ear. He fell back behind the log, squalling in pain as the blood poured. "Oh, God, he's kilt me!" Cal screamed.

Falcon glanced at him. "Naw. You'll live. But you gonna be wearin' yore hat funny from now on."

"Jesus!" Stan Law yelled. "Joey's stinkin' something fierce. Cain't nobody haul him outta there?"

"You want him out, you haul him out," Horace Haywood called. "I ain't movin'."

A man called Hoppy, because of the way he walked—one leg was shorter than the other—jumped up and hiphopped toward the fire. Preacher fired again and now Hoppy's left leg was equal to his right. The ball took off about half of his left foot. Hoppy flopped on the ground, screaming to high heaven.

"Charge, men!" Sir Elmore ordered. "Into the fray!"

"Charge yoresalf!" Derby Peel told him.

"By God I will!" Sir Elmore said. "Where's my saber?"

Baron Zaunbelcher quickly scurried away from Elmore.

"Stay down!" Bones yelled. "Don't be a fool. Preacher's got us cold."

"He's movin'!" Jimmie Cook yelled. "Headin' off to the south. If he makes the crick, he's gone for sure."

Sir Elmore jumped up, waving his saber. Baron

Zaunbelcher was keeping a good eye on the Englishman. "Now's our chance. Charge, men!" Elmore ran toward the creek, waving his saber. Burton Sullivan and Willy Steinwinder right behind him.

"Oh, Lord!" Bones said, crawling to his boots. "Come on, boys. We can't let nothing happen to them silly people."

En masse, the entire camp—those who were able— came to their feet, all running after Preacher, waving rifles and pistols and yelling and cussing. But Preacher had left the creek and was hiding among the trees that lined the bank. He caught sight of the sun flashing off of Elmore's blade and sighted in. The ball clanged against the polished steel and Elmore's entire body experienced the sensation of a railroad spike being hit with a sledge hammer. For a moment, before Burton hauled him down, Elmore looked like a man with a bad case of the twitches.

Using his second rifle, Preacher took aim and put a ball into a man's belly and the man tumbled to his knees and then slowly fell into the creek, face first. Two minutes later he had drowned. Preacher watched the entire running human wave hit the ground and he took off running, zigging and zagging through the grass and brush, heading for the ridges. Very quickly Preacher was out of rifle range and gone. He reached his horse and headed south.

Back at the camp of the man-hunters, they were busy patching up the wounded and seeing to the disposal of the dead. Elmore's right hand had stopped its twitching. He was looking sorrowfully at his slightly bent saber.

"Throw it away," Zaunbelcher urged.

"Indeed not! It's only bent a little. My father carried this sword during the War of 1812."

Baron Zaunbelcher almost said he now knew the reason the British lost, but thought better of it at the last second.

Preacher had put several miles behind him and the now scared, shook-up, and bloody band of man-hunters. He wasn't worried about them following him; not this soon anyway. He threaded his way through the timber, topped a ridge, and looked down into one of the prettiest valleys in this part of the country. He stared hard at the scene before him. He blinked. But the scene remained unchanged.

Four wagons, a half a dozen cows, one of which was probably a bull, and riding horses.

Four wagons? Here? Now?

Preacher rode down the grade and across the meadow just as the pilgrims were climbing down to the lush grass and flowers of the valley floor. Preacher had not had a bath in several days and it had been a couple of weeks since he'd shaved. His buckskins were stained and his hat had damn sure seen better days. He knew he looked rougher than a cob and meaner than a bear, but at the moment, he didn't much care. He rode right up to the wagons and got himself a jolt. Two of the finest-lookin' women he'd put eyes on in awhile stood side by side. Twins, with no difference he could spot in them at all.

"Howdy, folks!" Preacher called. "Y'all ain't got no drinkin' whiskey with you, now has you? I feel the need for a little Who Hit John."

"Sir!" one of the twins piped right up. "I'll have you know we are on a mission for God. We do not sanction with the partaking of strong drink."

"Do tell. Well, I'll be damned."

"And we do not hold with swearing, either!" Hanna said, standing with hands on hips. She was a trifle ample across the beam for Preacher's liking, but still a handsome woman.

"You don't say? Well . . . dip me in buffalo crap and call me stinky."

One of the twins stepped closer and stared at him. "Sir? Are you a mountain man?"

"I reckon. I been in these mountains ever since I was knee-high to a frog. What are you folks doin' out here all by your lonesome?"

Everybody started talking at once in a babble of

voices. Preacher dismounted and stood silently before them until they settled down. When quiet prevailed, Preacher said, "I was just kiddin' y'all 'bout that whiskey. I got me a couple of jugs stashed up in the brush that I stole from some guys."

"You . . . *stole* some whiskey?" Prudence asked.

"Yeah."

"Why?"

"So's I could drink it."

"There are other people close-by?" Otto asked.

"Oh, yeah. I'd guess near'bouts seventy or so about five miles yonder way." He pointed.

"*Seventy?*" Patience blurted.

"Yeah."

"What are they doing?"

"Doin' their best to kill me, ma'am."

"Kill you!" Sally shrieked. "Why?"

"'Cause I been killin' as many of them as I could, that's why."

The men and women all wore stunned looks on their faces. "You have been . . . killing them?" Frank Collins asked.

"Oh, yeah. I reckon up to the moment I've kilt . . . well, oh, fifteen or twenty, I reckon. But it's all right, 'cause they started it."

"You have personally killed fifteen or twenty men in your life?" Prudence asked, her face pale.

"Oh, no, ma'am. That's just in the last few weeks. I lost count on how many men I've kilt over the years. White men, that is."

"What . . . what is your name?" Patience asked.

"Preacher."

Patience paled.

"How many other men out here are called Preacher?" she asked in a tiny voice.

"Just me."

Patience fainted.

2

Otto caught the woman before she hit the ground and gently placed her in the shade of the wagon.

"What's the matter with her?" Preacher asked. "She comin' down with the vapors?"

Prudence glared up at him. "You . . . you . . . brute!"

"What did I do?" Preacher questioned, looking at the men and women.

Frank Collins said, "Really, nothing, sir. We all were under the impression that you were a man of God, that's why Patience fainted."

Preacher was clearly puzzled. Something was all out of whack here and he couldn't figure out what it was. "A man of God? I been called a lot of things over the years, but damned if I've ever been called that."

"Sir," Hanna said, looming menacingly before him. "I must insist that you refrain from swearing."

Preacher sighed. Before he could tell Hanna what was foremost on his mind, and after doing that would probably have to shoot her husband, Patience moaned and sat up.

"I had the most terrible dream," she said, her face flushed. "I dreamt that we were confronted by a horrible man who drank whiskey and ran around killing people."

Her eyes began to focus and they focused on Preacher. "Oh, my word! It wasn't a nightmare."

"Now, I have been called that a time or two," Preacher admitted. "Y'all splash some water on that female's face and get her up. I got to talk to y'all. This just ain't no place for pilgrims to be at any time, most especially right now." He looked at Hanna. "You make some coffee and put on some grub. I got a case of the hongries flung on me. I'm goin' over yonder to that crick and take me a wash and a shave. I'll be back."

"Well!" Hanna flounced about as Preacher turned his back to her and swung into the saddle.

"Do it," Otto told her. "I think that, if I understand correctly his quaint way of speaking, we are in trouble here. I want to hear what he has to say."

Prudence helped Patience to her feet and got her unflustered. Fifteen minutes later, Preacher reappeared. His buckskins were still stained, but he had taken a short bath and shaved the heavy growth of beard from his face.

"He really is a very handsome man," the women all silently concurred.

"He really is a very dangerous man," the men all silently concurred.

Preacher poured a cup of coffee and squatted down. The coffee was weak for his tastes, but he made no mention of that. "Now listen up, pilgrims. I got to tell you what's goin' on. Then you make up your own minds 'bout what kind of man I am. Not that your opinion means a damn to me. But I don't like to be judged wrongly."

While the bacon and fried potatoes were cooking, Preacher took it from the top, beginning with him and Eddie leaving civilization back east and the reasons why. When he finished telling about burying Eddie and his little paint pony, the only dry eye in the bunch was his. A couple of minutes later, he said, "Well, that's it, folks."

"I wonder why we heard nothing about the bounty on you?" Frank Collins asked.

"Prob'ly 'cause y'all don't frequent taverns and saloons and the like," Preacher told him. "Nor do you associate with them that does." He smiled. "Them mountain men back at the fort who told you I was a preacher of the gospel . . . you 'member any names?"

"Well," Hanna said. "There was this huge fellow called Horsehide Jack."

Preacher started grinning.

"Yes," Patience said. "And there was another gentleman with the unsightly name of Pistol Pete."

Preacher's grin spread.

"And one great bear of a man they called Papa Griz."

Preacher laughed. "Them ol' boys was havin' a high ol' time puttin' you folks on, was what they was doin'. Don't feel hard toward 'em. They didn't mean no harm. They was just funnin'. Humor gets sorta dark out here in the wilderness. 'Cause a lot of the time, they ain't a whole hel . . . heck of a lot to laugh about."

"I fear that because of my insistence that we press on," Patience said, "I have placed us all in great danger."

Preacher thought about that. "Maybe," he finally said. "But not if y'all will play along with a lie I'm dreamin' up right now."

"Whatever in the world do you mean, sir?" Prudence asked.

Preacher grinned and told her.

Preacher had carefully stashed the pilgrims and their livestock and wagons in a little canyon on the east side of the valley and told them not to light fires nor venture past the tree and brush lined entrance of the canyon. Then Preacher set out to find some man-hunters. Only this time he didn't have killing on his mind. Well, not much anyway

"Look!" Van Eaton cried out, pointing.

The small group of men looked at the man with a white handkerchief tied to the barrel of his rifle.

"By the Lord!" breathed Sir Elmore. "That's our quarry."

"He wants to talk," Bones said. "He's comin' under a white flag. We'll honor it."

The gentry with him looked at Bones as if he had gone mad. "You can't be serious, sir!" Robert Tassin said.

"I'm serious. A white flag is a white flag. We'll honor it."

Preacher rode slowly toward the six man team, stopping about ten yards from them. Bones and Elmore rode out to meet him. "You boys got another problem facin' you," Preacher said. "Not near 'bouts as dangerous as me, but a problem nonetheless."

"And what might that be, sir?" Elmore asked.

"The Methodist church sent out a flock of missionaries to bring the gospel to the heathens. They're holed up over yonder in a valley. I run into them some time back and told them what was goin' on here, 'tween us. The scouts that brung them in has gone back with a message to the church board and the President of the United States. They tooken all your names back on paper to give to important folks back east. Anything happens to them missionaries, and you'll all have federal warrants out on you. The war 'tween us is still on, but them Bible-shoutin' folks had best be left alone."

Sir Elmore Jerrold-Taylor's back straightened. "Sir, no harm shall come to those missionaries. I am a Christian myself and believe strongly in the Lord."

Preacher had no immediate comment on that, but his thoughts were grim. If this fool really believed himself a Christian person, then Preacher could pass for a duck. "Fine." He looked at Bones. "How about you boys?"

"They'll stay clear."

"Them missionaries, over my objections, has volunteered to set up a make-shift hospital and take care of the wounded. That all right with you?"

"Fine with me."

"That's wonderful," Sir Elmore said. "That's very gracious of them. But you destroyed all our medical supplies," he added with a pout. "That wasn't very sporting of you."

"Well, shame on me," Preacher said sarcastically. "My goodness! You just can't depend on nobody nowadays to be a good sport, can you?"

"Oh, quite true. Quite true."

Preacher shook his head at the Englishman's words. He couldn't figure out if the man was serious or just a teetotal damned fool. He backed Thunder up some twenty feet or so. "Now you boys do the same," he told the men. When they were about fifty feet apart, Preacher said, "Next time we see each other, you best start shootin'. 'Cause this is the last time I aim to be cordial with you."

"We'll do that, Preacher."

"Head on out," Preacher ordered.

"Don't you trust us?" Sir Elmore asked.

"Hell, no." He leveled his rifle. Bones and Elmore turned their horses, rejoined the group, and they all got gone.

"Do you trust these bounty hunters to keep their word, Preacher?" Otto asked.

Dark in the missionary's camp. The women had cooked up a fine meal and Preacher was laying back against his saddle, drinking coffee and smoking his pipe. "'Bout as far as I can pick up a grizzly bear and throw it."

"You said one of the nobility was called Zaunbelcher, is that correct?"

"Yeah. He's a baron. Whatever the hel . . . heck that means."

"It's a fine old family," Otto said. "But starting about a century back, they began marrying very closely. I'm afraid insanity is running in their blood now."

"I don't doubt that a bit. But you don't have to worry about that no more."

"Oh? Why?"

"'Cause I'm a-fixin' to stop his clock, that's why."

Paul Marks stared at Preacher across the fire. "You are going to fight seventy-odd men all by yourself?"

"They was close to a hundred or better when I started. And they'll be about ten less this time tomorrow."

"You say those deadly words so . . . casually." Patience said. "Doesn't human life mean anything to you?"

"Them folks huntin' me ain't human, Missy. You think about that."

A coyote pack started up, lifting their voices to the sky. The women shivered at the sound.

Preacher smiled. "The Injuns call them Song Dogs, ladies. They're sacred to some tribes. Coyote won't hurt you. Neither will a wolf if you leave the poor beast alone."

"Song Dogs?" Prudence questioned.

"Shore. Just listen to 'em. They's makin' pretty music. Just listen and enjoy it."

"You ever been married, Preacher?" Frank asked.

"The Injun way, yeah. I got kids. Y'all prob'ly frown on that, but that's the way it's done out here. And don't think Injuns take marriage lightly, 'cause they don't. Injuns is human people. Their ways is just different from ours, that's all. I don't agree with a lot of what they do, but then, I do agree with a lot they believe in and practice. When this little trouble of mine is all cleared up, I'll sit you down and try to convince you to head on back east. The Injuns don't want your religion, and they don't need it."

"Whatever in the world do you mean by that?" Patience cried. "They're poor unsaved heathens."

"They ain't no such of a damn thing, Missy. They worship the same God you do . . . in a way, that is. Their God has many names, but they all amount to the same thing. Man Above, Wakan Tanka, Grandfather Spirit, Great Mystery Power, Heammawihio—The Wise One Above. The God of the Pawnees is Tirawa, and they sacrifice a human to that God. And it's a terrible sacrifice, too. Now, I don't hold with that a-tall." Preacher picked up a handful of dirt and let it slowly dribble to the ground. "This is Grandmother Earth. The earth is life. The Injun respects the land and the critters on it.

"No, folks, the Injun has their own religion. When an Injun dies, his soul, tasoom, in Cheyenne, travels up the Hanging Road." Preacher smiled again. "That's the Milky Way to us. The Injun believes that after death everything is good; there is no reason to fear death. And that only those who take their own lives won't never rest in a peaceful village in the Land Beyond. Now as far as I'm concerned, that pretty much goes along with what's in the Good Book."

"But they must be baptized in the blood to be saved!" Patience said.

"I don't believe that, Missy. And I don't believe a person's got to congregate, neither. I think if a body accepts that there is a higher power over us all, and tries to live right, that person ain't gonna be denied entrance to the Land Beyond. You think there ain't gonna be no horses and dogs and cats and coyotes and wolves in Land Beyond? If that's the case, I don't want to go."

"You don't mean that, sir!" Hanna almost shouted the words.

"That's blasphemy!" Sally said.

"I just figure it's the truth," Preacher replied. "Be a mighty sorry damn place without critters to make friends with." He stood up and stretched. "Y'all sleep sound. I'll be around. But I'll be pullin' out 'fore dawn. Y'all might not see me for a few days." He walked off, quickly lost in the darkness.

"The man is either a simpleton and a fool, or a highly complex person," Frank Collins remarked.

"He's no fool," his wife said softly.

"He certainly is a very confident man," Paul Marks said.

"I . . . don't believe I have ever met a man quite like him," Patience admitted. "He is . . . delightful."

He was also gone when the pilgrims awakened the next morning. While they slept soundly, Preacher had built up the fire, made coffee for them, and left them a rather ominous note.

> YOU FOLKS BEST TAKE TO SLEPIN LIGHT.
> OR YOU GOIN TO WAKE UP
> SOME MORNIN AND BE DAID.

While Hanna, the self-appointed cook for the group, was slicing bacon, the sound of a single shot came faintly to the gathering of young men and women.

"Oh, dear," Patience said. "I hope nothing has happened to Mister Preacher."

Hanna looked at her and smiled.

Prudence looked at her and frowned.

The men glanced at one another and winked.

Their wives said to their husbands, "Now, you stop that!"

About three miles away, Bones squatted down in the brush and looked at the dead man. He was one of Lige's group who had gone into the woods to take care of his morning's business and instead got him a bullet in the head.

Bones was extra cautious this day as he crouched behind a tree, presenting no target at all. There had been something in Preacher's voice yesterday that told him game time was all over. The mountain man was through playing; from now on, it was going to be a deadly business.

"Is the wretch dead?" Duke Burton Sullivan yelled.

"Yeah."

"Oh, drat!"

Bones inched his way back to the edge of the camp he would have sworn was as secure as a fort. He knew damn well that Preacher, as soon as he fired, had changed position. He was probably on the other side of the camp now. Waiting as silently and as menacingly as a big puma. Watching through those cold hard eyes. It was not a real comfortable feeling.

"Everyone turn around," Bones said. "Until we're in a circle. Preacher'll have no choice but to stand and fight and die, or leave. Now move out."

But Preacher had already left the area. He had slipped in a ravine a few hundred yards from the enemy camp and snaked over the lip a hundred yards later. He'd had him a hunch that sooner or later Bones would wise up and do something smart for a change. It was about time for him to start using his noggin.

"Preacher!" a man shouted from the camp. "I know you ain't gonna answer me, but just listen. Me and two others want out. We're through. We quit."

"You yeller skunks!" Lige yelled.

"Call us whut you will, Lige. We're quitting this here hunt. Preacher! We're ridin' out. We're done. Don't shoot for God's sake."

God, Preacher thought. How come when the goin' gits tough, sorry low-lifes like them yonder start callin' on God when they never give Him a thought 'fore now? Preacher remained still and silent and waited.

The men took a chance that Preacher wouldn't shoot and quickly packed up, saddled up, and rode out.

Cuts it down some, Preacher thought, watching the three men until they were out of sight.

The men in the camp began their fanning out in an

ever broadening circle and Preacher pulled out. He figured they'd be looking for him all morning, and he had
some things he wanted to do. He began leaving a very
faint trail, knowing that some of those in Bones and
Lige's camp were real woodsmen and wouldn't fall for
too obvious a trail. He laid the trail winding out of the
valley and up into the mountains. He left a broken
branch here, a scar on bare ground there, as he left the
valley and headed for the high up. He'd already done all
the work for the surprise he had in mind. Now if Bones
and them would just come to the party.

3

"He's gettin' tired," Van Eaton said. "I tole you we'd wear him down after a time."

"I do believe you're right, old boy," Burton Sullivan said. "Come, come. Let's press on."

Not using his spy-glass for fear the sun would reflect off the lenses, Preacher squatted up near the tree line and watched the tiny, ant-like figures pause for a time, and then move on, following his faint trail. "That's right, boys. Just like the spider, I'm a-waitin'. So come on."

Preacher moved over to his already picked out and readied position and waited. Those below had sense enough to know they'd kill a horse trying to ride up, so they dismounted and were spread out, coming up in a single stretched-out line, about a thousand feet wide.

Preacher made himself comfortable and settled down for a time. He knew it would take the men below him thirty minutes or so to get where he wanted them.

"He slipped and cut himself here!" Tige shouted. "He's hurt and headin' for the high up, jist like a damn animal."

Bones and Van Eaton inspected the blood. And it was blood. Preacher had found where a big puma had killed a deer and hid the carcass after eating. He carefully looked around him, for the deer was still warm, and then put the heart and liver in a piece of the animal's hide and got the hell away from that place. He didn't want to have to fight no mountain lion . . . not just yet anyways.

"You mighty right about that," Bones admitted. "He's hurt bad, too. Look at all that blood. Come on, boys. We got him."

"Superb!" Jon Louviere said.

"The blood trail goes right up this grade," Falcon said. "I don't know how bad he's hurt, but he's leakin' some."

High above them, Preacher put his back against the rock wall behind him and both feet against a huge boulder. Once he got that rock rollin', it would pick up hundreds of other rocks and give Bones and them some grief . . . a lot of grief, Preacher hoped. While all the dust was fillin' the air, Preacher would shift over to another spot he'd inspected and rigged up, and supplied with a few goodies.

The men grew closer and Preacher smiled. "Bye, bye, boys," he whispered, and laid into the boulder.

There was no place to run. This high up, only a few scrub trees grew in their weird twisted shapes. They offered no protection against the tons of rocks coming down the grade at avalanche speeds.

One thing could be said about the nobility. They were all excellent mountain climbers and all had a healthy respect for the mountains. All were uneasy about this high-up, long, and ragged, rocky grade. They'd seen terrible accidents in the Alps, and this smelled like a tragedy about to happen. They lagged back and to one side.

Willy Steinwinder heard it first, and experienced the ground begin to tremble under his expensive hand-made boots. "Slide!" he yelled, and started running for safety, the others in his party right along with him.

The other men looked up, horror and fear in their eyes, their dirty and unshaven faces paling at the furious sight tumbling toward them.

A man from Tennessee glanced over at his friend,

Webber, just as a melon sized rock, traveling at great speed, slammed into Webber's face and took his head off. The blood spurted a good three feet into the air. The Tennessee man had about two seconds to scream before the rock slide buried him.

Bones ran soundlessly to one side, Van Eaton right beside him. They got clear of the major slide, but both were pelted with fist-sized rocks and both were bloodied and bruised.

Lige Watson lost his footing as a rock slammed into his head and sent him sprawling . . . but knocked him safely out of the major portion of the slide.

Jimmie Cook was flattened by a huge boulder and bloody bits and pieces of him were scattered all the way down to the valley floor.

Four men from Lige's group were pinned down and could do nothing except scream in fright and stare in horror and wait for death to clamp its cold hand around them, which it did, leaving no trace of the men behind.

The men were running for their lives, knowing it was hopeless; for many this was to be their last race. Behind them, shattered and bloody arms and legs were sticking grotesquely out of the dirt and rocks.

Preacher had shifted positions as soon as the dust began to rise from the tons of rocks tumbling down the grade, and was belly down, watching the massive slide snuff the life from the bounty-hunters.

It was over in less than a minute. But the dust was so thick it restricted visibility for several minutes. A man from Maryland known only as Teddy staggered out onto the now barren slope and stood dumbly for a moment. Preacher's rifle barked and Teddy began rolling down the grade, a big hole right in the center of his back.

"The dirty son!" George Winters cussed Preacher. "He ain't even givin' us time to tend to the dead and wounded."

Bones gave the man a disgusted look and said nothing.

Van Eaton looked at George. But like Bones, he kept his mouth shut.

Lige's bunch were the ones who had taken the real beating as far as loss of men. They had been so eager to trap and kill Preacher, they had forged ahead of the others and taken the brunt of the rock slide. Counting himself, Lige had about twenty men left. At least that's what he figured. Lige wasn't a very good counter.

High above them, Preacher's rifle cracked and Lige had about nineteen men left. A Delaware man dropped like a stone and began rolling down the grade. Several dozen horrified eyes watched the body slowly gain speed and finally land with a thud on the valley floor.

Bones, Van Eaton and his men, and the dusty and the now grime-faced nobility, knew better than to try to move. They all had witnessed Preacher's precision with a gun and knew that as long as it remained daylight, to move was to die.

"Stay down!" Rudi Kuhlmann yelled.

"I cain't take no more of this!" a man from Illinois screamed. "Spencer was kin of mine. I seen them rocks knock his brains out. Damn you, Preacher!" he shouted, standing up. "I'll kill you, Preacher. I'll . . ."

Die. Preacher's rifle sang its deadly song and the Illinois man slumped to the rocky grade, on his knees, a large stain appearing on the front of his shirt. The man had a very puzzled expression on his face. "No," he spoke for the last time. He finally fell over on his back, head pointed downward. He slid for a few yards, stopped, and was still.

"This is the way it's gonna be, boys," Preacher's faint shout reached the men. "You better face facts, you bird-brains. I know these mountains, you don't. I know ever' stream, ever' crick, ever' valley, ever' box canyon, and ever' cave. I could have kilt all of you a hundred times over, but I was hopin' you'd come to your senses and clear on out and leave me be. Now what's it gonna be?"

"I'm through, Preacher!" a man yelled. "You let me go and I'll never come back."

"Go on, then."

"Nelson," Van Eaton said.

"Let him go," Bones said. "More for us when the end comes."

"If we're alive when the end comes," Van Eaton replied.

"You and me got no choice in the matter. This is personal with Preacher, now."

"This ain't worth no five dollars a day," another man yelled. "I'm headin' out with Nelson."

"Fine," Preacher said.

"Sal," Van Eaton said.

"I've had it!" one of Lige's men shouted. "You hear me, Preacher? I'm haulin' my ashes back to New York State."

"Git gone, then."

"I'll see you in hell, Preacher!" another of Lige's men shouted. "But I don't want no more of this."

"Tell your mommy hello and stay close by her side," Preacher yelled. "I 'spect she'll be glad to see her wanderin' boy come home."

"You mighty right 'bout that."

"Anyone else?" Preacher questioned.

No one else chose to leave. Preacher knew that these staying behind were the hardcases. There would be no give in them and no quittin'. They were in this until the end.

Lige slowly counted his men. Near as he could figure it, counting himself, out of the original bunch, sixteen were all that was left. He shook his head. "I wouldn't have believed it possible," he muttered.

"Did you say something?" Wiley Steinwinder questioned the man.

"It just ain't reasonable that one man could do this much damage," Lige whispered.

"I will admit it is somewhat incredible," Sir Elmore

joined the conversation. "But this just makes it all the more exciting. Gads, what a formidable foe we face."

"Idiot," Van Eaton muttered. "I wish to God I'd never got mixed up with this pack of ninnies."

"You want to quit, Van?" Bones whispered.

"We cain't, Bones. Dark Hand is shore to have tole Preacher that you and me was in the bunch that tortured that kid. We got to see this thing through or elsest we'll be lookin' over our shoulders 'til the end of time."

That was the feeling among those of Bones's group who stayed. They had to finish this. For, to a man, they felt that Preacher would spend his life tracking them down. They were wrong. They could have left and Preacher would have gone on his way.

After a moment of silence, Preacher told them that. "Go on home, boys. If you say it's over, it's over. I mean that. They's been too much killin'. Let's stop it right now."

"He's lyin'," Bones told his people, having to shout across the barren slope, over the rocks and dirt that would forever cover many of his men.

"I ain't neither!" Preacher yelled. "I ain't never knowin'ly broke my word. Leave and don't come back and we'll call this even. You got my word on that."

"The hospital of the missionaries is safe ground for us all!" Bones yelled. "Any there is safe. You agree?"

"Does that include me?" Preacher hollered.

"Tell him yes and when he makes his appearance, we'll kill him," Sir Elmore urged.

"I agree to that," Tassin said.

But Bones shook his head. "No. Think about it. Maybe one of us will get wounded and have to go there for patchin' up. We'd be fair game."

"Unfortunately, he's right," Baron Zaunbelcher reluctantly said. "The camp of the missionaries must be declared neutral ground."

"All right, Preacher!" Bones yelled. "You got a deal."

"Let me hear the gentry say that. I want their word.

They claim their word is damn near holy, so let me see if they got the class to keep it."

That made the nobility angry. One by one they shouted their agreement to Preacher's terms.

"Pick up your wounded and tote 'em out of here," Preacher yelled. "Long as you don't make no funny moves, I'll hold my fire."

"Give us your word on that!" Juan Zapata shouted.

"You got my word on it."

The man-hunters cautiously left their hiding places and began seeing to the wounded. Preacher held his fire, content to watch. It took most of the afternoon to carry the bone-shattered men down the slope to the valley and get them in the saddle or on quickly made travois.

What they did not know was that Preacher had left the scene about fifteen minutes into the gathering and hauling off of the wounded. He packed up the supplies that he had cached and went over the top of the mountain.

Several miles from the slide area, Preacher stopped at a spring and washed the sweat and grime from his body and hair. Before the first wounded were on their long and painful way to the 'hospital,' Preacher rode into the neat little camp of the missionaries. They had rigged up several lean-tos as shelter for the wounded.

"Them rickety-lookin' things ain't near 'bout gonna be enough," Preacher told them, walking over to the fire and pouring a cup of coffee. "But I don't care if you lay 'em out on the ground for the varmints to chew on. Just 'member, y'all agreed to this scheme."

"We are sworn to serve our fellow man," Hanna said. "We follow the teachings of the Bible. Sometimes it is with an effort, and sometimes we fail, for we are mere mortals and therefore shall never attain perfection, but it is our duty."

"Mighty noble of y'all," Preacher said, sitting down with a sigh and relaxing. "Does my heart good to know they's people like y'all in the world. But if it's all right, I'll jist lay right here and watch y'all do all this good work."

"You are coming close to blasphemy, sir," Patience told him.

"I ain't neither. I'm tellin' the truth, that's all. Beats a lie, don't it?"

Patience flounced away, but not before stealing a flirtatious glance at Preacher.

Preacher ignored it.

He was dozing when Otto's frantic yell brought him awake and reaching for his rifle. He relaxed when he saw it was the wounded men from the slide.

Patience, Prudence, and the others in the group stared at Preacher in disbelief. "You . . . one man . . . did all *that?*" Frank Collins asked.

"And a heap more that's comin' up behind this first sorry-lookin' bunch," Preacher said, pouring himself a cup of coffee and stretching out. "And they's a goodly number of others all dead and buried under tons of rock and dirt. I done a purty neat job of it if you ask me."

"Incredible," Hanna said. "You behave as if you are proud of all the pain and suffering you have inflicted upon your fellow human beings."

"Oh, I am!"

"Disgusting!" Prudence said.

The first batch of wounded rode in and reined up. They stared at Preacher in wonderment and ill-disguised hate and hostility.

"Howdy, boys!" Preacher called cheerfully. "Looks like y'all run into some trouble, My goodness, what happened to y'all? Did you tangle with a whole passel of grizzly bar or get in the way of a buffalo stampede?"

"Very funny," Van Eaton said, painfully dismounting and limping back to the travois behind his horse.

"What's the matter with your head, Van Eaton?" Preacher asked. "How'd you git all them bumps on your noggin?"

Van Eaton lost his temper and reached for the pistol in his belt. A hard hand clamped down on his wrist and squeezed. Van Eaton thought for a second his wrist was going to be crushed. He looked into the broad peasant face of Otto Steiner.

"This is neutral ground, friend," Otto said. "But don't cause me to lose my temper. Back before I found Christ, four men came out of the darkness one night to rob me. I broke the back of one, the neck of another, and smashed the brains out of the other two. And I do not joke. I do not have much of a sense of humor."

"Neutral ground," Van Eaton hissed through clenched teeth, reeling from the pain in his wrist. "I give you my word. And I'll shoot any man who violates it."

Otto released his wrist and Preacher called out, "Have some coffee, Van Eaton. Supper'll be on in a few minutes. You best partake. It might be your last one."

4

Preacher had to hand it to the men and women who had wandered west to serve their God. They did a bang up job when it came to fixing up the wounded.

"We've all had medical training," Hanna told him.

Later, when Bones and Lige and most of their people had left, Preacher sat by the fire drinking coffee. He became conscious of eyes on him and looked up. Patience was staring at him.

"You think I enjoy all this killin', don't you?"

"Frankly, yes. I do."

"Well, you're wrong, Missy. 'Cause I shore don't. I've done given them ol' boys out yonder a dozen chances to back off and let me be. They could ride out of here tonight and I'd not give them another thought. Hell, Missy. I give them all another chance to leave this day, up on the slide."

"He ain't lyin' 'bout that, ma'am," a man with two busted legs spoke up. "He done it."

"More'un oncest," another wounded man said. "And I shore wish I'd a took his invite."

"And he's let some go," a third man offered up. "I tell you this, Preacher. When I can ride, you've seen the last of me."

Most of the bruised, banged-up, and broken men in the camp agreed, except for one loudmouth brute.

"Not me. I aim to kill you, mountain man. I'm gonna track you down and skin you alive. Then I'm gonna cut off your head, pickle it, and tote it back east to claim my reward."

"Why?" Patience asked him, a horrified look on her face.

Preacher smiled into his coffee cup and said, "That's Ed Crowe, ma'am. He's a murderer, a rapist, and a brigand through and through. But he claims to have repented his evil ways. Now he's a bonney-e-fied man-hunter workin' with Bones and Van Eaton. Two of the sorriest men on the face of the earth."

Ed cussed Preacher until Otto showed up and said, "If you do not stop that filthy language, I will gag you. If that doesn't stop your vulgar mouth, I just might rip out your tongue with my bare hands."

"Otto!" Hanna cried. "Please. Do remember who we are and what we represent."

"Be still," he told her. "There is a time and place for all things. Including violence."

Ed Crowe must have believed the big man, for he shut his mouth and after that, as long as he was in the camp of the missionaries, when he spoke, it was free of profanity.

"I . . . guess I've misjudged you, Preacher," Patience said. "I apologize for that."

Preacher waved it off. "I just wanted you to know that I ain't no heartless savage, Missy. And that I really didn't want all this killin' and did try to stop it." He stood up. "I best be goin'. Bones and Lige and the gentry and the rest of that pack of no-counts will be gunnin' for me at first light. I don't want no shootin' around this camp."

Before she could form a reply, Preacher had vanished into the night.

* * *

Bones and his bunch had pulled themselves into a tight little camp right next to a fast runnin', spring-fed stream. And there they stayed. They posted guards that stayed alert and were changed often. Each day, under a white flag, an unarmed man would ride to the camp of the missionaries to check on the wounded, and then ride back. Other than that, they did not leave camp. Preacher had no way of knowing what they were planning, only that it would probably be better than any previous plan. So far, everything they'd tried had failed miserably. For now, all he could do was wait and watch and see.

Preacher was determined that he would not start the next round of gunfire. He had given some thought to just picking up and moving on. But he knew the man-hunters would just come after him . . . after they did, God only knew what they would do to the missionaries, and Preacher had him a pretty good idea what they'd do to the women.

The mountain man felt that he was in between that much talked about "rock and a hard place."

He had not been back to the missionary's camp and make-shift hospital. He felt that would be just too dangerous for those good folks.

On the fifth day of inaction, Preacher got lucky. Just as dusk was spreading its first shadows all over the valley floor, Preacher sat in the brush on a slope viewing the scene below him through his spy glass. About a quarter of a mile from the camp of the man-hunters, a covey of birds suddenly shot up into the air.

"Now what's all that about?" Preacher muttered, shifting the glass and studying the area in question. But he could see nothing. Then he spotted a very slight movement in the tall grass. After studying the area for a moment, he collapsed the pirate's glass and smiled.

"Very good, Bones," he muttered. "Yes, indeed. You got more sense than I gave you credit for havin'." He picked up his rifle and moved out. Preacher thought it was a good thing he'd taken a long nap that afternoon, for it looked like it was shapin' up to be a long night.

The night was black and the air was heavy with moisture. A bad storm was building, and if a body has never been in the high-up country when a thunderstorm hit, you just can't imagine the sound and fury. The pounding of the thunder is unbelievable and the lightning so fierce it'll stand you hair up on end.

Preacher studied the sky and figured he had about an hour before the full brunt of the storm struck. He also figured he could do a lot of damage in an hour.

Mack Cornay froze like a rock when he felt the cold edge of a Bowie knife touch his throat. He started sweating in the coolness of the night air when Preacher said, "You just never learn, do you, boy?"

Mack was so scared he was afraid to reply. He remained stone-still as Preacher shucked his pistols out of his belt and laid them to one side.

"Are you gonna kill me?" Mack whispered, his voice a tremble in the darkness.

"I shore ought to. You would if you was in my moccasins, wouldn't you?"

"I reckon. Can we deal?"

"What do you have that I want?"

"Information."

"Talk."

"Me and Frenchy is on this slope. Cobb is about a quarter mile to the south. Pyle is acrost the valley with Hunter. Flores is closin' the box north and Percy is comin' out later this night to put the lid on to the south."

"That's right interestin' news. What is your name, boy?"

"Mack Cornay. Please don't kill me, Preacher. I'll git gone ifn you'll let me. I swear that on my mother's head."

Preacher thought about that. "How you figure on gettin' your horse away from the camp without bein' seen?"

Sweat was running down Mack's face. He thought hard for a moment. "I cain't. But I can slip into the missionary camp and take one of the wounded feller's horse. And I'll do it, too. You bet I will. For God's sake, Preacher. I'm beggin' for my life, man."

Preacher removed the razor sharp knife from Mack's throat and the man was so relieved he slumped face down on the cool earth. "Thank you, Jesus," Mack whispered. "I'm comin' home to see you, Mamma."

"Get gone, Mack," Preacher told him. "And you know what I'll do if I ever see you again."

"You'll kill me." Mack didn't put it as a question. He knew the answer.

"You got that right. Move! And be damn quiet in leavin'. You hear me?"

"Yes, sir, Mister Preacher. I'll be like a ghost."

"I ever see you again, you gonna be a ghost. Now get the hell gone from here."

Mack Cornay turned and looked at Preacher. "Thank you, Preacher."

"Take your rifle and pistols and clear out," Preacher told him.

Mack slipped quietly into the night. The odor of his fear-sweat lingered sourly for a few seconds and then the wind carried it away.

Preacher moved out. He would save Frenchy for last, for the man from Louisiana was known to be a bad one to tangle with. Preacher began working his way south. He'd heard some about Cobb, but nothing that impressed him.

Preacher laid a sturdy stick up 'side the head of Cobb and the man dropped like a stone into a well. Preacher trussed him up and waited for the man to come out of his addle.

"Oh, my dear sweet God!" Cobb said when he came to and his eyes began to focus.

"How come people like you always call on God or Jesus when you get in a tight?" Preacher questioned. "You damn shore don't pay no heed to His words 'til you do."

"I be good from now on," Cobb whispered, like he never heard Preacher's question. "Dear sweet Mamma, pray for me."

"Disgustin'," Preacher said. He popped Cobb across the face with a big hard hand. That got Cobb's attention. "Didn't your mamma whup you none whilst you was growin' up?"

"She beat me some."

"'Pears to me she didn't beat you enough. What am I gonna do with you, Cobb?"

"Turn me a-loose, I hope!"

"So's you can run tell Bones and them silly uppity folks what I'm doin' this night? Not likely."

"I wouldn't do that!"

"I think I'll just truss you up real good and let the bears eat you."

"Oh, Lord, Lord, please save me from this heathen!" Cobb cast his supplication to the heavens.

"Heathen? You call *me* a heathen?"

"I didn't mean it, Mister Preacher. I swear I didn't. You got me so bumfuzzled I ain't thinkin' straight."

"I tell you what I'm gonna do, Cobb. I'm gonna test you right good. I'm gonna see if you're a man of your word."

"I'm an honorable man, Preacher. You just ax anybody. They'll tell you."

"I bet they will," Preacher said drily. "I'd bet at least a penny on it. Cobb, I want you gone from these mountains. And I mean gone and stayed gone. I'm tired of all this fuss and bother. You know that ravine that cuts 'crost this valley?"

"Oh, yes, sir. I do for a fact. Runs all the way 'crost it. Comes within a few hun'red yards of the missionary camp. I know it real well. I bet I could . . ."

"Shut up an' listen. You beginnin' to babble. I want you to work your way down this slope and git in that ravine and over to the missionary camp. Then I want you to take one of them spare horses over yonder and git gone. I unloaded your weapons. So don't even think about pointin' any of 'em at me."

"I wouldn't. I swear it."

"Cobb, listen to me. I don't never want to see you again. You hear me?"

"Yes, sir. I do. I really do. And you ain't never gonna see me again."

"I better not ever see you again," Preacher said menacingly. "'Cause if I do, I'm gonna strip you buck-ass nekked and stake you out over an ant hill. Then I'm gonna pour honey all over your neck and head and sit back and watch whilst the ants gather and eat your eyes."

Cobb shuddered and crapped in his pants.

"Whew!" Preacher grimaced and fanned the air with a hand. "Git outta here!"

Preacher smiled as Cobb scurried away. Maybe he had missed his calling; he should have been an actor. He was sure convincing this night.

But he wasn't quite that lucky with Frenchy. Frenchy turned around when Preacher was about five feet away from him. Lightning flashed and Frenchy's eyes widened and his mouth dropped open. It took him about one second to recover and grab at the pistol behind his belt.

One second was the time Preacher needed. Preacher closed the gap and slugged Frenchy just as his hand closed around the butt of his pistol. Lightning flashed again and a cold rain began falling, slicking over the already treacherous footing on the rocky slope. Preacher lost his balance and fell down, dragging Frenchy with him. The two men hit the ground hard, with Preacher landing on top of Frenchy, knocking the wind from him. Preacher slammed a fist against the side of Frenchy's head, causing his hands to loosen their grip on Preacher's shirt. Preacher hit him again just as hard as he could and Frenchy's fingers lost their grip altogether, and his hands fell to the ground.

Preacher caught his breath and then quickly trussed

the man up. Already the Louisiana man was moaning and twitching. Preacher had just set the man up, his back to a rock, when Frenchy came to and opened his mouth to yell. Preacher jammed a handful of dirt into the man's mouth.

"You yell and I'll cut your throat," Preacher warned. "You understand?"

Frenchy believed him, for his eyes widened at the thought of that prospect and he nodded his head. Frenchy spat out the dirt and said, "What do you want, Preacher?"

"To give you a chance to get gone, Louisiana Man."

"You gittin' soft in your old age, Preacher?"

Preacher chuckled as the cold rain pelted them both. "You think I am, Frenchy?"

"No," Frenchy was quick to reply. "But you won't kill me while I'm tied like this."

Preacher hesitated. That was a fact and somehow Frenchy either knew it or had sensed it about the mountain man. "That's right, Frenchy. But what I can do is knock you silly, tote you up the mountain, strip you down to the buff, wedge you up under a run-off, and then let the weather do the rest. And I'll do that, boy—don't you doubt it for a second. I'm used to the high country. This cold rain don't bother me none. But you now, well, pneumonia'll kill you shore. Think about that."

Frenchy's eyes told Preacher he didn't doubt that at all. When he spoke, Preacher sensed he had won. Maybe. "All right, Preacher. You cut me a-loose and I'm gone."

Preacher freed the man's wrists and stepped back. "Frenchy, don't even think about makin' no funny moves or goin' back on your word. This will be the last chance you get. I mean that, boy. When I get done with this night's work, I aim to hallo Bones's camp in the mornin'. If they ain't packed up and pulled out by noon, the killin' starts."

Frenchy nodded his head. "You put Mack and Cobb on the run, didn't you?"

"Yeah, I did."

Frenchy shook his head.

"They was both weak sisters. I didn't figure they'd last this long. You won't put no more on the run, Preacher. You best know that now."

Preacher sensed then that he hadn't won this one. Frenchy was going to make his try. "Then they're fools, Frenchy. Don't you be one."

"Oh, I ain't no fool, Preacher. I just don't like you."

"That's your option, boy. But it ain't worth dyin' for. You best take heed to them words. I'm givin' you a chance to go on back to Louisiana. Take it, Frenchy. I been there. The women is pretty, the wine is sweet, and the food is the best there is. Hell, Frenchy, you don't even know me. I'm offerin' you your life. Think about it."

"What you say is true."

Frenchy stood up slowly, a strange smile on his lips. He faced Preacher. He didn't say a word as his hand flashed for his knife.

Preacher's right hand clamped around Frenchy's wrist just as the blade came free of the scabbard. Preacher twisted and shoved the big-bladed knife to the hilt in Frenchy's belly, just under his rib cage. Frenchy gasped in pain and staggered back. He stopped just as lightning flashed and looked down at the handle of his knife. He raised his head and looked into Preacher's eyes.

"No man has ever bested me with a blade. No man ever done that."

"They's always someone better, Frenchy. You should have had enough sense to know that."

Frenchy sank to his knees. He screamed just as thunder rolled and pealed and echoed around the mountains. His mouth filled with blood and he toppled over.

Preacher gathered up his weapons, powder, and shot. He looked down at the dead man and thought about his night's work so far. "Well, I reckon two out of three ain't all that bad."

5

Preacher took Frenchy's words to heart about there being no more who would quit and called it a night. He began carefully making his way back to his camp— a hidden cave-like overhang that nature had concealed so well Preacher doubted that any living being had ever before set a foot in the place. The storm was full-blown now, a real rip-snorter. Preacher built a small fire for coffee and food. He saw to Thunder and then stripped down to the buff and dried off, changing into another set of buckskins. He sat by the fire, deep in thought.

After tomorrow, when Preacher would tell those remaining man-hunters that if they didn't give up this foolishness and ride on out, it would be shoot-on-sight, he knew he would have to back up his threat with action. Problem was, he just didn't want to do that.

"What else can I do?" he muttered, as the bacon sizzled in the pan and the water started to boil for coffee.

The flames danced silently, offering him no answer to his question.

"Just do it, I reckon," Preacher said.

* * *

When the missionaries awakened, Preacher was sitting under the canvas over the cooking area, drinking coffee. It gave them only a slight start, since by now they had accepted that Preacher could move like a ghost.

"I hope y'all brought a whole bunch of medical supplies," Preacher said without looking up. "This here war is fixin' to get real nasty."

"How did you know we had awakened, sir?" Otto asked.

"I heard you open your eyes."

"That is ridiculous!" Prudence said.

Preacher shrugged.

"I believe him," one of the wounded men said.

"I suppose you left this lovely valley littered with dead and dying men last night," Hanna said.

"Just one. And I give him a chance to ride out 'fore I done the deed. Just like I'm a fixin' to give the rest of that pack of hyenas out yonder ample warnin'."

"And if they don't heed your warning?" Paul Marks asked.

Preacher turned his head and stared at the man. The look in the mountain man's eyes made Paul queasy in the stomach. Without realizing he had done so, he backed up a couple of steps.

"I'm tired of foolin' around with these people. I'm tired of bein' hunted. I'm just by God tired of it. And I ain't gonna put up with it no more. I can't just leave. I do that, you folks will be in for a real bad time of it. And I think you women know what I mean. And it ain't y'all's fault. You just happened to come along at a real bad time." He shook his head and poured more coffee. "I just don't see no other way out of this mess."

"There ain't no other way out, Mister Preacher," the man with broken legs spoke up. "I'd make a bet that you convinced Cobb and Mack to leave last night. If so, that's all that's leavin'. The rest will stay to the last man."

"You done some good guessin'," Preacher said. "I met

up with three last night. Frenchy decided to play his hand. His cards run out."

Ed Crowe opened his mouth. "I don't believe you kilt Frenchy, mountain man. I say you're lyin'."

Preacher glanced at the mouthy man. "When you get on you feet, Crowe, you and me is gonna go 'round and 'round. So you got that to look forward to."

"You don't scare me none!" Ed sneered.

"I'm real glad to hear that. Now shut up. Your whiny voice is gratin' on me."

Ed wanted to say something else. He wanted to pop off real bad. But the look in Preacher's eyes warned him silent. Ed dropped his gaze from Preacher's cold stare and shut up.

Patience and Prudence set about making breakfast—pan bread and bacon—and Preacher ate in silence until one of the wounded men called his name. He looked over at the man.

"You know them fancy gents is all 'bout half tiched in the head, don't you?"

"I figured it."

"Crazy as ever seen," another wounded man said. "And I've seen some crazies in my time."

"And both Bones and Lige has some real crazy folks ridin' with them," the first man continued. "Lucas and his buddy, Willie, they're 'bout two boards shy of a straight picket fence, if you know what I mean. But they're dangerous."

"They like to kill, you mean." Preacher did not put it as a question.

"Yeah. I believe so."

Preacher nodded his head. "'Preciate it." He rinsed out his plate and placed it on a table. "I'll see you folks later on. You best get some bandages ready. You gonna be needin' 'em."

He mounted up on one of the horses of the wounded men and rode out. Otto had told him about Cobb and

Cornay. The two men had staggered into the camp late the night before, both of them frightened out of their wits. They hadn't even paused for coffee. Just went straight to the picket line, saddled up, and rode out. They headed south. Said they were leaving the mountains and it would be a cold day in hell before they ever returned.

Otto had volunteered to ride over to the man-hunters' camp and tell them that Preacher wanted to speak to the men, all of the men. Preacher told him where to have the men meet him.

Preacher was sitting on a ledge overlooking the valley when the men rode up. En masse. He was taking a chance that one of them might take a shot at him, but it was a risk he was willing to take to put an end to this foolishness.

"All right, boys," Preacher called from the rock ledge. "Gather in close and perk your ears up good. By now you prob'ly found Frenchy and you know that Cobb and Cornay is gone. Here's the deal. Listen up, 'cause I ain't gonna say this but one time. You boys has wooled me around long enough. I'm done playin'. You can ride on out of here right now, and live to tell your grandkids about this stupid hunt. Or you can stay and die. If you ain't packed up and gone from here by mid-afternoon, I'm gonna start killin' you wherever and whenever I find you. No more deals after this one. That's all I got to say. Git the hell out of these mountains." Preacher turned and vanished from the sight of those below him.

The group of men sat their horses for a moment. No one spoke.

Tom Evans broke the silence. "You think he means all that, Bones?"

Bones thought for a moment and then nodded his head. "Yeah, I do, Tom. I think this hunt just took a bloody turn."

The royalty twisted in their saddles and looked the

men over. Sir Elmore called out, "Any of you men want to leave?"

Slowly, the men began shaking their heads. They were all making more money on this hunt than they could possibly make back where they came from. And they all stood a chance of making a small fortune. They weren't about to give that up.

"Preacher'll be on the prowl come the night," Van Eaton opined. "We best get back and get ready for him."

But Preacher had changed his tactics. He wasn't about to enter that valley after the man-hunters. They were going to have to come to him. He'd taken his pirate glass and studied the man-hunters' camp late that same afternoon. "Fools," he muttered. "Plain damn fools. You was warned, boys. Now you gonna learn these mountains is *mine!*"

A man named Jeff, from Lige's bunch, found that out the hard way the following afternoon. He decided he'd go kill him a deer, for they were all tired of smoked fish and jerky. He hadn't gotten five hundred feet off the valley floor when Preacher's rifle boomed. Jeff tumbled out of the saddle and hit the ground hard. When he opened his eyes, he was in a world of pain and looking up into the cold eyes of Preacher.

Those back at the camp had heard the single shot and exchanged wary glances. They all knew what it meant, and it didn't mean that Jeff would be bringing in any venison.

"Don't . . . leave me here to die alone!" Jeff gasped.

"Why not?" Preacher asked, a hard edge to his voice. "You come a-huntin' me, not the other way 'round."

"I got . . . information."

"Then you better talk fast, boy. 'Cause you ain't got long."

"Them down yonder is . . . gonna take you alive and . . . torture you. Then when they's had their fun . . . they's gonna turn you a-loose nekked and hunt you down."

Preacher shook his head in disgust. "How did you ever agree to go along with something like that?"

"It was my idee!"

Preacher could but stare at the man for a moment. "Anything else?" He asked wearily.

"Yeah. Them good-lookin' wimmin is gonna get used hard. After . . . we . . . them . . . is done with you. Pass 'em around 'til we git tarred of 'em. Kill the men slow to make 'em holler."

"Them fancy-pants foreigners go along with that plan?"

"Oh . . . yeah. They lookin' forward . . . to it." Jeff closed his eyes and died.

Preacher went through the man's pockets and found a handful of gold coins. He kicked a few rocks and leaves over the body and took Jeff's horse. He rode straight to the missionary camp. First thing he noticed was that Ed Crowe was gone. There were six men still out of action due to broken bones. Preacher gathered the men and women around him, within earshot of the wounded men, and laid it on the line for them. He was blunt and left nothing that Jeff said out.

"No, by God, they won't!" a man spoke up, his voice angry. "We would have died if it hadn't-ta-been for these good folks here. I done a lot of mean things in my life, but I ain't never put a hand on no good woman nor gentleman like these men is. We got our guns and ample powder and shot and patches. You go on and don't worry none about these folks. Bones and them will have to kill us to get to them. Right, boys?"

The three other men were very vocal in their defending the missionaries. Preacher eyeballed each of them, finally concluding that they meant it. It takes a sorry type of man to molest a woman, and these men were several cuts above that. No angels, mind you. But not gutterslime, either.

"You boys'll do," Preacher told them.

"You'll stay for food?" Patience asked Preacher.

The mountain man shook his head. "Too risky for y'all. By now, Ed Crowe's done told Bones and the others about these boys here talkin' hard aginst this hunt and their decision about not comin' back to their camp." Preacher held up a finger and thought for a moment. "But I tell you what I'll do to tip the balance some. I'll just wing me four or five tomorrow and then they can't do nothin' to y'all if some of their own men is here bein' taken care of by us. How's that sound to you?"

Patience stared up at him. Finally she found her voice. "Well, that certainly is an idea that none of us would have ever thought of."

"Good. Tomorrow I'll go bust some arms and legs and such and they'll have to bring them here. You make damn sure you get their guns from them and hide them good, you hear?"

"Whatever you say, Preacher."

"Y'all get ready for some new patients 'bout noon tomorrow." Preacher turned and left the camp.

That night, Preacher crept up close to the camp of the man-hunters and began taunting them. He cussed them loud and long and then he shifted locations, slowly circling the camp. He traced the ancestors of the nobility back to apes swinging from vines in the jungle and got them so mad they had to be physically restrained inside the camp.

"All of you is lower than a snake's belly!" Preacher shouted out of the darkness. "You couldn't whup a bunch of old women—none of you. I never seen such a bunch of yeller-livered cowards in all my borned days. Man-hunters, my butt! Ain't none of you ever fought a man 'til you come up on me. And you're all so skirred of me you can't sleep at night. I've bested ever' one of you so many times I'm feelin' plumb ashamed of it. I'm gonna go cut me a switch to use on you when I catch you. All of you act like a bunch of foolish children."

"Tomorrow you die!" Baron Zaunbelcher screamed out into the night.

"Stick it up your nose," Preacher told him. "You better leave these mountains, buzzard-breath. You best tuck your tail 'tween your legs and run on back to mommy and daddy in the castle and hide under the bed. That is, if you have enough sense to find the bed."

Zaunbelcher was so furious he was jumping up and down and screaming oaths.

Preacher then started in on the other gentry until the blue-bloods were livid.

Then Preacher started in on Lucas and his friend Willie, comparing them to an ape and a monkey. And that was the nice thing he said about the pair. Willie grabbed up weapons and fired blindly into the night while Lucas, trembling with rage, beat on the ground with his huge fists and roared out curses and threats until he was hoarse.

Preacher laughed and taunted the men until he had nearly the entire camp of man-hunters in an uproar of anger. Then he faded into the night. He had a hunch that come the morning, they'd be out looking for him.

"Damnit, it's a trick!" Bones said to the royalty. "Can't you see that? Preacher was tossin' insults at us to make us mad. He knows if we get mad we'll do somethin' stupid. And we can't afford to do nothin' stupid."

But his friend Van Eaton sided with the others. Preacher had been especially hard on Van Eaton, calling the man some terrible names.

"That mountain man dies tomorrow," Van Eaton said, pushing the words through clenched teeth. "That's it, Bones. He dies tomorrow."

But a lot of people had spoken words along the same lines. Preacher had buried them. If he felt like burying them, that is.

6

The man-hunters left ten guards at the camp, chosen by drawing lots, and the rest pulled out just after dawn. They were all angry to the core but most had tempered their wild anger down to a hot bed of coals. Bones had prevailed upon them to cool down: don't go after Preacher unless they had a clear head.

Preacher had laid down sign, albeit not too obvious, for he knew there were some real woodsmen in the bunch, and was waiting. He figured they'd come up on him sometime about mid-morning. He had chosen his spot with caution, taking pains to ensure himself several ways out. And he had made up his mind that if he got even the smallest opportunity, he was going to put a ball or two into some of those blue-blooded snooty-nosed gentry. Right in the butt, if he could. 'Cause that's what they'd become to Preacher: a royal pain in the butt.

Preacher was under no illusions. He knew he was in terrible danger. He knew that the slightest miscalculation on his part, and he'd be dead. Or worse, taken alive for torture. If anyone were watching, it would seem that he was taking this manhunt much like a game. They would be very wrong in that assumption. Preacher worked out in his mind every move in advance. He was confident, but only because he'd lived and survived by his wits and skill ever since he was a young boy.

Preacher waited.

Bones had spread his group out into teams, a good tracker with each team. He alone felt in his gut that Preacher was up to something. But he'd asked the trackers if the sign was too obvious and to a man they had agreed it was not.

"He ain't doin' this a-purpose," one had said.

"It's just that he ain't as good as he thinks he is," another one had opined.

But Bones still had his doubts. By now he had reached the conclusion that Preacher really wasn't as good as people said he was—he was *better!*

"I'm going over there to scout!" Prince Juan Zapata shouted, pointing toward a rise just at the edge of the valley, before the earth began to swell into mountains.

Before Bones could yell for him not to leave the group, the rich, spoiled Spaniard had spurred his mount and was gone at a gallop.

"Fool!" Bones muttered.

Juan topped the rise and dismounted to stretch his legs. He looked all around, and then bent over to pick a flower to place in his hat. Preacher's rifle boomed and the Prince took a heavy caliber ball right in one fleshy cheek of his royal butt.

Zapata jumped about three feet into the air and commenced to squalling loud enough to wake the dead.

Preacher had not been sure he could even make the shot because of the long distance, but he held high and was right on target. It surprised the hell out of the mountain man. Because of the distance, the ball had lost much of its power when it impacted with Zapata's regal ass, but it still had enough zip to imbed deeply in his rear end.

Preacher never in his life saw so many people leave so many saddles in that short a time.

"Sure a bunch of skittish folks," he muttered, reloading the fancy hand-made rifle that had once belonged to one of the Frenchmen. He tried not to remember which one it was. "Fine shootin' rifle. Be a damn shame to shoot a feller with his own rifle," he said with a grin.

He watched as the men began moving through the grass to the aid of the still-squalling Prince. Preacher took a chance that he might hit something and sighted it just ahead and above the head of a growing snake-like path in the tall valley grass. He gently squeezed off a round.

A man jumped up and grabbed at one leg. Preacher grinned. Looked like another one of those fancy-pants folks.

"My leg!" Duke Burton Sullivan screamed. "He shot me in the leg!" he yelled as he fell down to the ground.

"Smart, Preacher," Bones muttered, his face pressed against the coolness of earth. "Now I know why you done what you did last night. Fill up the hospital and we have to keep the missionaries alive to treat the wounded. You no-good, miserable . . ." He cussed for a moment, then added, "For an ignorant mountain man as I was told you was, you sure have a headful of smarts."

For reasons known only to him, Bates foolishly jumped up and made a run for the wounded Prince and Duke. He came close to making it.

"We'll sure give it a try," Preacher muttered, pulling his rifle to his shoulder.

The fancy hunting rifle banged and Bates had a leg knocked out from under him. He did a flip and hit the ground, hollering to the high heavens.

"Now that was a lucky shot," Bones muttered.

"You got lucky on that one, boy," Preacher muttered. "Let's get gone from here."

After five minutes or so had passed, Bones crawled to his knees. He sensed, more than knew, that Preacher had done his work and was gone. "All right, people. Let's gather up the wounded and get them to the gospel-shouters."

Bones looked over at Zapata, lying on his belly. "He can't ride, so some of you rig up a travios."

"This sorta knocks our plans in the head, don't it, Bones?" Van Eaton spoke softly.

"Yeah."

"And I was lookin' forward to dallyin' some with them women over yonder. I like 'em with some meat on their bones. That there Hanna hottens up my blood something fierce."

"Go find a cold crick and jump in it," Bones suggested.

"Hell, I took a bath last month!"

When the dejected and bloodied bunch of manhunters reached the site of the make-shift hospital in the middle of the wilderness, they were quick to note that not only were the missionary men armed, and armed well, so were the wounded. Even the women had shotguns strategically placed. Took Bones about one second to understand that if they made a try for the women, a lot of men were going to die, for several of the wounded were more than fit to travel. That meant they were staying behind deliberately to act as guards.

Bones cut his eyes to Van Eaton. His right hand man had picked up on it, too. He nodded his head slightly.

"I must have medical treatment!" Prince Zapata yelled. "I demand it."

"Put him over there," Otto said, pointing and trying to hide his smile. "I'll see to his wound."

"I demand you stop that smiling at me!" Zapata shouted. "I am seriously wounded."

"You don't demand anything from me," Otto bluntly told him. "And I never heard of anyone who died from being shot in der butt."

Bones, Van Eaton, and those who helped bring the wounded to the make-shift hospital took their leave and being careful to stay in the center of the long valley, made their way back to camp. It was a weary and dejected bunch of man-hunters. Even the shoulders of the nobility slumped a bit as they rode. Nothing had turned out the way they planned. But the thought of calling off the hunt was nowhere in their minds.

For the others, over coffee and hot food, the talk was, surprisingly, not of quitting, but of what to do next.

"Corner him and burn him out," Pyle suggested.

"Corner him?" Flores looked at the man. "How? Most of the time we don't even *see* him."

"I wish we had some cannons," Falcon wished aloud. "We could blow him out of the mountains."

No one chose to respond to that. But a few of the men did smile at the ridiculousness of the remark.

"I got an idea," Sam Provost said. "Let's do to him like he done to us. Let's insult him and make him mad. Then he'll lose his temper and do something stupid."

"He'd see through that charade," Jon Louviere said. "Whoever told you Preacher was a stupid man was very badly misinformed. He is very intelligent and cunning. Which makes this game all the more exciting."

Van Eaton looked at the man. "Game? This is a game to you?"

"But of course."

"Man," Van Eaton said, shaking his head, "I can't figure none of you all. We got people dead all over these mountains. That Preacher has put lead in near'bouts all of us at one time or the other. He's destroyed our camps, burned our supplies, stampeded our horses, ambushed us, caused rockslides, thrown snakes at us, made fools of us, and he ain't even got nicked one time. And you think it's a game?"

Bones poured more coffee and sat back down. "It's done got personal to me now. The money aside, it's a matter of honor. If we don't corner Preacher and bring his head back in that there jug, we're all done as bounty-hunters. We'll never be able to get another job. News of this will get out. You can just bet that them that quit and headed back east has done told the story to anyone who'll listen. Folks is laughin' at us all over the place. I can't have that. I won't tolerate it. I ain't leavin' these mountains 'til Preacher is dead and we got his head. I'll die first."

Bones had finally expressed what had been in the minds of the rest of the men; the constant thought that silently nagged and dug at their pride. One man was making fools of them all. That just wouldn't do. To a man, they couldn't allow it. The hunt had to go on. The men didn't have a choice, or so they thought.

"We got to leave the valley and take to the mountains," Tatman spoke up, raw hatred for Preacher burning in his eyes. "We got to stop thinkin' like this was back east and start thinkin' like a mountain man."

"By jove!" Sir Elmore piped up. "I think you've got it!"

"Maybe so," Bones said. "Maybe so. It's worth a try. We'll leave ten men behind to guard the horses and the camp, and we'll strike out on foot. We'll each take supplies for three days and fan out in the mountains." He looked at Tatman. "Good thinkin', Tatman. Real good thinkin'."

"What are them igits doin' now?" Preacher muttered, peering at the men through his pirate glass. "Looks like a bunch of ants scurryin' about down there." He studied the activity for a moment longer, then put away his glass and shook his head. "They're comin' after me on foot. They done lost what little sense they had left. They're comin' right at me, in my country, on foot. Lord have mercy!"

With a smile that would have caused a savage alarm, Preacher picked up his rifle and moved out. Now he'd show them how this game was really played. "Ants to a honey trap," Preacher muttered.

Tom Evans was the first to discover how far out of his class he was. Something smashed against the back of his head, dropping him into darkness. When he came slowly swimming out of unconsciousness, he thought for sure he was dead. He might as well have been. Preacher, and he was certain it was Preacher who'd hit him with something, had taken his shot bag and his powder. He'd busted Tom's rifle and pistols and snapped the blade off his fine knife. He had peeled him right down to the buff, and had even taken his boots. "Halp!" Tom hollered. "Somebody come halp me."

About a half a mile away, Homer Moore was waking up. He had a fearsome headache and a big lump on the side of his head that hurt like the devil when he gingerly fingered it. And he didn't have a stitch on. He looked wildly around him. His weapons were gone, as were his clothes. He was as defenseless as the day he'd been born. "Oh, Lord!" Homer said.

Cliff Wright heard a noise behind him and turned. He caught a rifle butt under his chin that knocked him cold. When he came around, he was hanging upside down from a tree limb by his bare ankles. Like the others, he had been left bare-butt nekked and could see where his weapons had been rendered useless by somebody. Preacher, he was sure. Cliff started hollering for help. He didn't know how he was gonna live this down. Come to think of it, he didn't know how he was going to *get* down. "Halp! Halp!" he yelled.

Tatman came charging through the brush and Preacher busted the man's right knee with the butt of Homer's rifle. He smashed the knee to pieces and Tatman was out of the game for a long time. The big man passed out from the pain. When he awakened, his weapons were gone. He began crawling for safety, moaning and cussing and dragging his knee-broken leg.

Derby Peel turned around about three times and got himself lost as a goose in the dense forest and underbrush. He panicked and began running and yelling. He fell into a ravine, landed on his rifle, busted the stock of his rifle and broke several of his own ribs in the process. He passed out from the pain in his side and chest.

The men were so widely separated, and the country so rough and heavily timbered and thick with brush, the cries of the totally embarrassed men could not be heard. It was only by accident that Derby Peel was found, lifted out of the ravine, and toted off to the missionary's hospital.

"The ignorant fool fell into the ravine and landed on his rifle," Lige remarked. "How damn clumsy can you get?" He turned around just as Preacher hurled a fist-sized rock that caught the big man in the center of his forehead and knocked him sprawling to the ground.

Jeremy King, one of Lige's bunch, whirled around, lifting his rifle. Preacher blew a hole in his chest and Jeremy landed on his back, dead eyes open and staring at nothing.

The woods erupted in wild gunfire, but Preacher had dropped to the ground an instant after he fired and the balls hit nothing except air, leaves, branches, and thudded harmlessly into the timber.

Tom Evans and Homer Moore, who had been wandering about trying to find their clothes, chose that time to blunder into the clearing . . . bare butt shining.

"My God!" Fred Lasalle blurted. "Them boys ain't got no clothes on."

"I always did wonder 'bout them two," Bob Jones said.

"What's all the shootin' about?" Tom asked.

"Git down, you fools!" Stan Law hollered. "It's Preacher up yonder."

"Don't get over here next to me," Bob warned.

Their worries were needless, for Preacher was a good quarter of a mile away, running through the timber. He spotted movement ahead and stopped, bellying down on the ground. He smiled when he recognized Van Eaton as one of the men.

Van Eaton moved just as Preacher squeezed off a shot. The ball slammed into a tree and Van Eaton got a face full of splinters that bloodied him and scared him. He dropped to the ground, sure that he'd been mortally wounded.

Preacher quickly reloaded and wriggled into a better spot. Sam Provost raised his head up and took the last look of his life. Preacher shot him between the eyes.

That was enough for Van Eaton. Leaving Sam's body behind, he and the other man with him, Horace Haywood, ran from the area. They'd gone about two thousand yards when they came up on Cliff Wright, dangling butt bare and all from a tree limb. One side of his face was bloody and scratched something awful. The men stood and stared in disbelief for a moment.

"Y'all want to stop that bug-eyed gawkin' and cut me down and find me something to wear!" Cliff hollered.

While Horace was cutting him down, Van Eaton asked, "What happened to your face? Did Preacher do that?"

"No!" Cliff snapped the word. "A big bear did. He come by about an hour ago and reared up two-three times a-sniffin' at me. Like to have scared me half outta my wits, let me tell you. Then he rared up on his back legs, reached up and slapped the pee outta me and just wandered off. I hate these mountains, Van Eaton. I mean, I really, *really* hate these mountains. I hate these mountains nearly 'bout as much as I hate that mountain man. And I *do* hate Preacher."

"All your guns is ruint," Horace told him. "And I can't find your clothes nowhere." He took off his jacket and handed it to Cliff. "Wrap that around you."

Van Eaton held up a hand. "Wait. Let's go back and peel the clothes offen Sam. He shore ain't got no more need for them. And his boots'll fit you too, Cliff."

"Suits me. I'll get his guns, too."

But Preacher had smashed Sam's guns, leaving them useless, and taken his powder and shot.

"Crap!" Van Eaton said, as Cliff removed the dead man's clothing. "Now I see what he's doing. If this keeps up we'll be throwin' rocks at him."

Lige and his dwindling bunch came cussing through the timber, dragging a moaning Derby Peel on a hastily made travois. Lige's head was bloody and there was a huge knot in the center of his forehead.

"What happened to you?" Van Eaton asked.

"Preacher," Lige said, a surly note to his voice. "He flung a rock at me."

Van Eaton sighed and muttered, "Now he's throwin' rocks at us. Good Lord Amighty." He pointed to Peel. "All right, all right. What about him?"

"He either fell into a ravine or Preacher throwed him into it. He's stove up pretty bad. Busted some ribs, I reckon," Homer said, red-faced. He was wearing Jeremy's jacket which wasn't quite long enough to cover his essentials, and Tom was wearing the dead man's pants.

"Where's your guns?"

"Busted up. Gone. I don't know. Preacher took all our powder and shot, too."

"Halp!" The shout came faintly to them. "Somebody come halp me. Over here."

"That's Tatman."

Van Eaton rubbed a hand over his unshaven face. "I hope to hell he's wearin' his britches. I done seen enough men's bare butts this day to last me a lifetime!"

7

The missionaries were amazed and somewhat amused that one man could inflict so much damage on so many. And to a person, they all realized something else about this legendary mountain man called Preacher. He could have easily killed all these men who now were straining their meager medical facilities and knowledge. But despite his tough talk and dire threats, he had elected to injure most and not kill.

If the missionaries were secretly amused, the man-hunters certainly were not. The nobility were livid with rage, and Bones and Van Eaton and Lige were so mad they could scarcely speak.

No plan they had conceived thus far had worked, and Preacher had made fools of them—again—toying with them as if they were little children.

"This is mighty fine venison you cooked up, ma'am," Tom Evans said to Patience. "One of your men shot this today, did he?"

"You might say that," she replied.

"Huh?" Tom said.

"Preacher brought it in about an hour before you gentlemen arrived," Prudence told him.

Tom's face turned beet-red and he almost choked on his food. He suddenly lost his appetite.

Duke Burton Sullivan was tempted to hurl his plate into the fire, but thought better of it. That would be very bad manners on his part. Prince Juan Zapata muttered some curses in his native tongue and laid his plate to one side. Derby Peel shook his bruised head and wished he had never left home. Tatman, his knee set and immobilized, was the first to admit—to himself—that the whole bunch of them were outclassed. None of the newly wounded men had any idea that Preacher was less than a hundred yards away, watching the scene through very amused eyes. After a time, Preacher picked up his rifle and slipped away. Bones and his men would not be expecting an attack on their main camp this soon after their fiasco in the mountains. Preacher thought he'd just go stir things up a bit.

Back at their own camp, Bones and Van Eaton sat to one side and looked over what was left of their group. It sure was a pitiful sight. Beat-up, bloodied, bruised, and embarrassed, the men were silent and sullen this late afternoon. But incredibly, almost to a man, there was no thought of giving up.

Joe Moss, one of Lige's group, got up from the ground to pour a cup of coffee. On his way to the fire, he paused to speak to Alan James, a man from his home state. Joe turned and Preacher's rifle boomed from the dusk and the shadows, the ball shattering Joe's left knee and knocking him screaming and thrashing about on the ground. Alan leaped for his rifle and brought it to bear. But there was no target. Only the darkness presented itself.

"Oh, Sweet Baby Jesus!" Moss hollered, jerking in pain. "I'm ruint for life."

Before the echo of the shot had faded, every man in camp had bellied down on the ground. Every man except Alan. He stood crouched, rifle at the ready.

Preacher's rifle boomed again, and Alan was spun around like a top, the big ball breaking his hip bone. He fell across Joe's shattered knee and Joe screamed and dropped into unconsciousness. All over the camp, men were cussing and casting about dire threats. But nobody got up to carry any of them out.

Preacher slipped across the valley and headed for his own camp. Somebody would be transporting the newly wounded over to the missionaries, and true to his word, Preacher would not ambush anyone doing that. He knew the man-hunters would not honor that if he was the one wounded, but that was their rock to mentally tote around. Preacher's conscience was clear and he planned on sleeping well that night.

The next morning, Sir Elmore, Baron Zaunbelcher, Willy Steinwinder, Bones, Van Eaton, and Lige rode over to the camp to see about their friends. They almost went into apoplexy when they saw Preacher, lounging comfortably and drinking coffee.

"Howdy, boys!" the mountain man called cheerfully. "Did y'all get a good night's sleep?"

"Just remember, this is a neutral zone," Frank Collins reminded the men.

"We'll honor it," Bones said. He looked at Preacher. "You got more than your share of nerve, Mountain Man."

"I reckon." He pointed to the several bouquets of wild flowers that now brightened the camp. "But I wanted to show the ladies how much I 'preciated them bein' here. So I picked them a bunch of flowers. Purty, ain't they?"

Willy Steinwinder's face became ugly and mottled with rage. When he got his anger under control, he said, "You . . . picked those flowers?"

"Well, they shore didn't leap out of the ground and

into my hand. I think y'all ain't bein' very gentlemanly 'bout this here situation."

"What do you mean, sir?" Baron Zaunbelcher demanded.

"Y'all didn't bring nothin' for the ladies, did you?"

Steinwinder turned his back to Preacher and looked up at the blue of the sky. He muttered darkly under his breath.

Preacher wouldn't let up. With a straight face, he said, "Here I am, havin' to hunt game so's the very men who was doin' their dead level best tryin' to kill me will have somethin' to eat. Now, that don't seem real fair to me. Seems like y'all would see fit to contribute somethin'."

The men stared at Preacher. A thousand thoughts were running through their heads but they were speechless. Stunned into silence. All of them.

Tatman hollered, "Kill him for me! Just hammer back and kill that smart-aleck for me!"

Bones found his voice. He looked at Preacher. "Took their guns, did you?"

"It seemed a smart move at the time, yeah."

Bones had also noticed that Preacher had a sawed-off shotgun lying across his lap. Bones knew what a sawed-off shotgun could do. He'd seen men cut in two with them. So he was very careful to keep his hands as far away as he could from his pistols. "So what now, Preacher?"

"Y'all can pull out and I'll forget all about this."

Van Eaton said, "You know can't none of us do that, Preacher. And you know why."

"Pride's a terrible thing sometimes, Van Eaton. You really figure it's worth dyin' for?"

"When you're in our line of work, yeah, I do."

"Maybe so. But y'all could change your line of work, you know?"

"My good man," Sir Elmore piped up. "I have a sporting proposition for you."

"I just bet you do. What is it?"

"Your mummy and daddy still living?"

"Yeah. My mum . . . mother and father is alive."

"Could they use ten thousand dollars?"

"Who couldn't?"

"Well . . . there are some of us who . . . never mind. My proposition is this: As soon as Juan and Burton are up to it, we shall put up bank notes worth ten thousand dollars. We'll, ah, let the good missionaries hold the notes. Then the eight of us hunt you. In an area that can be worked out. If we kill you, your parents are richer by ten thousand dollars. I mean, face facts man, we're going to kill you eventually. Why not make your parents' lives a bit easier?"

Preacher blinked, then blinked again. This fool really believed what he just spouted. Preacher chuckled softly. "No, mister high falutin' mucky muck. I think I'll pass. But I will take this time to try to get somethin' through your heads. I've tried before, but perhaps this time I can get through to you. You boys ain't gonna kill me. I may get bit by a rattler or a hydrophobia skunk; my horse might step in a hole and toss me and break my neck. I may get mauled by a puma or kilt by a grizzly. Some Injun might get lucky and do me in. All sorts of things can happen to a man out here in the Lonesome. But I'll tell you all what ain't gonna happen: you boys ain't gonna kill me. You best understand that."

"Oh, that's piffle!" Elmore said with a wave of his hand.

"No, it ain't neither piffle," Preacher said. "Whatever that means. It's pure fact. Now, boys, I mean what I say. This ain't fun and games. Whilst you're in this camp, you're safe. But out yonder," he pointed to the valley and beyond, "you're fair game to me."

Sir Elmore looked down his aristocratic nose at Preacher. "I must say, sir, that there is little distance between you and a fool."

Preacher smiled. "You mighty right about that. I figure five feet at best."

Before he left the missionary's camp, Preacher had asked if they had any kind of opiate to knock Tatman and a couple of others out. Otto assured him they did, and they most certainly would do just that.

Preacher left the camp feeling better. Otto was not a real trusting man when in the company of brigands and thugs. And the man was ox-strong. Had arms on him 'bout the size of Preacher's thighs. If Otto ever got his hands on a body, it would be all over 'ceptin for the buryin'. And Hanna wasn't no delicate bloomin' flower herself.

Preacher awakened in the wee hours of the morning. No sense of danger awoke him. It was the workings of his mind. For years Preacher had prowled the mountains and ridden the country in relative peace. He had run-ins with Indian and whites alike, all mountain men did. Indians who resented the coming of the white man and trashy whites who raided trap-lines and the like. Preacher had never been known as a trouble-hunter. And he tried to shy away from those who did want trouble. But the past two or three years had been rough on him. As his reputation grew, so did the people who came looking for him to make a name. Seemed to him the immigration of eastern folks heading for a new life out west had brought him nothing but headaches.

Preacher sighed and reached out to feel the coffee pot. The coffee was still warm enough to taste good. Without getting out of his blankets, he reached for the cup and poured it about half full. The coffee was just right. Black as sin and strong enough to bend nails. Good.

Preacher lay back, his saddle for a pillow, and tried to figure out the best thing he could do. If not for the mis-

sionaries, he thought he'd just pull out and hole up
'til winter.

But he couldn't do that with the gospel-shouters in the
valley. Bones and his men would have their way with the
women and the men. Preacher did not want to go
through life with that on his conscience.

So, he concluded, he had to see this fight to the end
whether he liked it or not. So all right. But he thought
he knew a way to do it without any more killing . . . or at
least keeping it to a minimum.

With that issue settled in his mind, he went back to
sleep.

8

The man fetched water from the creek, returned to the camp, and squatted down in the dim light of pre-dawn. He laid twigs on the coals, then added heavier sticks when the kindling burst into flames. He lifted the coffee pot and his right hand and arm went numb when a heavy caliber rifle ball punctured the pot and tore it from his hand. The early riser leaped for the safety of darkness and away from the campfire. The entire camp of man-hunters was awake and belly down on the cold ground. They watched through startled eyes as a fire arrow arched its fiery way through the air and landed on a pile of dirty, flea-infested blankets just vacated by Lige Watson. The blankets burst into flames and tall shadows lept around the murk of the camp. Another fire arrow landed inside the crude corral and the horses were spooked. They smashed through the flimsy barricade and spilled out into the valley, running wild.

Sutton leaped to his bare feet and Preacher cut him down with a ball in his leg.

Preacher had carried four rifles and his bow with him that morning, determined to put as many men out of action as possible, hopefully without killing any of them. If he could get enough of them wounded and unable to rude, he would take the missionaries and lead them away from this place and then maybe he could go on with his life and live in peace.

"Anybody see where he is?" Bones tossed out the question.

"No," Van Eaton replied from a few yards away. "It wouldn't make no difference no how. He moves as soon as he fires."

With the light increasing, Preacher ruined another big coffee pot, the big ball sending the pot flying.

"Two pots left," Tom Evans said sorrowfully. "And them horses are still runnin'."

"It'll take us the better part of two days to round them all up," Fred Lasalle said.

"You uncouth savage!" Jon Louviere yelled. "Stand up and fight like a man."

Bones shook his head and muttered, "I swear them people get dumber and dumber with each passin' day."

"I challenge you to a duel!" Sir Elmore screamed. "Meet me in honorable combat!"

"Sure he will," Van Eaton mumbled.

Another fire arrow soared gracefully through the air and landed in the grass behind the camp and flames began licking their way higher and higher. Bones had ordered the camp built inside a lazy half circle of the creek, so the flames had but one way to go—straight into the camp.

"We gotta put out that fire!" Bones yelled. "It'll burn ever'thing we got if we don't."

Hugh Fuller jumped up and grabbed a bucket of water. Preacher broke his arm with a ball. George Winters ran for his saddle and his sleeping blankets and Preacher cut his leg from under him. Preacher fired at another running man and missed him clean. Using his last loaded rifle, he shot Ray Wood in the side. Preacher gathered up all his empty rifles and began working his way around to the rear of the camp. The flames were leaping into the air and the smoke was thick.

"Stay on your belly and toss water or beat blankets on the ground in front of you!" Bones yelled. "Beat it out with your hands if you have to."

"Get shovels or use your blades to dig a break!" Van Eaton added, panic in his voice.

The smoke was so thick none of the man-hunters could see the single, odd-shaped arrow arch through the air and land in the middle of the flames. But they could all damn sure hear and feel the explosion as the bag of powder attached to the arrow blew, sending fire and sparks flying all over the place.

The concussion knocked one man down and stunned several others closest to the explosion. Another arrow landed and a second explosion rocked the smoky camp. Sir Elmore was only a few feet away from the second explosion and the explosion rendered him sillier than a happy lunatic for a few moments. He was wandering about the fire and smoke humming and playing patty-cake until Baron Zaunbelcher tackled him and brought him down.

Preacher figured he'd done a fair amount of damage and caused enough confusion for one morning. He ripped the hammers off three of the rifles, put them in his pocket and tossed the rifles aside. He took off at a run, circling the camp and heading in the direction of the running horses. He figured he'd have a good hour before any of the men came after him.

He managed to calm down and get hands on four of the trembling horses. He led them off into the mountains and turned them loose. They might return to the camp, and they might not. He left them on rich, belly high grass near water.

Several hours later, he watched from a distance as the wounded were taken to the already over-burdened, make-shift hospital. Near as he could figure, both groups combined had about thirty men still able to ride and fight. That was still too many for Preacher's liking.

He suddenly smiled. The deal was no shootin' or ambushin' whilst the wounded was taken to the hospital. There wasn't nothin' said about what might happen on the return trip.

"Now, that's sneaky, Preacher," he whispered. His smile widened. "Damn shore is!" he said aloud. "I'm proud I thought of it, too."

He counted the mounted men. Fifteen of them. They'd only managed to round up about a third of the horses.

He worked his way to the valley floor and made himself comfortable beside the creek bank. An hour later, common sense told him to abandon his plan. Bones had sent riders far ahead of the main group's return, riding on both sides of the creek bank with rifles at the ready. Preacher forded the creek, bellied down in the grass, and snaked his way clear. He smiled as he spotted the returning group. Bones was wising up. He'd split the group into two parties. One on the far side of the long valley and the other near the creek.

"You're learnin', boy," Preacher muttered. "But not fast enough to do you no good."

Preacher counted the men in the returning groups. He knew he'd wounded three, maybe four. He counted them again. One was missing. "Gettin' sneaky, aren't you, Bones?" Preacher whispered.

He stayed right where he was. Preacher could be more Indian than an Indian if he had to, and he figured this was a good time to do just that. He moved only his eyes. Birds soon became accustomed to the motionless presence and paid him no heed. It was a few minutes before dusk when Preacher sensed, more than heard, the man. Whoever he was, he was damn good. But Preacher knew there was no way the man could know where he was. What he had done was take a guess and it had proved out to be a good one.

The man, and it turned out to be a man Preacher had

heard called Bobby, came within twenty feet of Preacher. And Bobby was good. Real good. He moved as quiet as a mouse through a church. He moved so good that Preacher lost him. He couldn't see him, he couldn't hear him.

Preacher knew he was in trouble.

All right, Hoss, he thought. You played it smart and got yourself in trouble. Now what?

Bobby made the mistake of emitting a slight grunt when he jumped and that was the only thing that saved Preacher's life. He rolled to one side, leaving his rifle behind, and Bobby's tomahawk got buried in the dirt. Preacher kicked out, his foot catching Bobby on the knee and staggering him just long enough for Preacher to jump to his moccasins. Bobby immediately jerked a pistol out of this belt and Preacher's left hand shot out and clamped down on the man's wrist, preventing him from leveling the pistol. Locked together, the two men fought with fists. Preacher with his right, Bobby was his left.

Preacher slammed a big right fist again and again into Bobby's face, smashing his nose and pulping his lips. Bobby smashed a fist into Preacher's face and the blood from both men mingled in this death struggle. Bobby tried to back-heel Preacher but the mountain man had expected that and was ready.

Preacher heard the gun cock and finally managed to grab hold of his knife. He drove the blade into Bobby's side and twisted. The man-hunter screamed and pulled the trigger. Preacher felt a tremendous blow in his side and knew he'd been hit. How hard, he didn't know. But he knew it was bad. He jerked out the knife and cut Bobby from belly to backbone, then released the man.

Bobby fell to the ground. "At least I got lead in you," he gasped.

"You ain't gonna live long enough to enjoy it, though," Preacher spoke through gritted teeth against the throbbing pain in his side.

"I 'spect you be right about that, mountain man." That was the last thing Bobby said. He shuddered once, then closed his eyes and died.

Knowing the shot would bring man-hunters at a gallop, Preacher got gone from there.

"All right," Bones said, staring at the two distinct blood signs. He had inspected Bobby's pistol. "We lost Bobby, but he got lead into Preacher, and judgin' from the blood, it's a bad wound. And this time it's real."

"Let's proceed at once!" Sir Elmore said.

"No!" Bones snapped with adamance. "Not in the dark. Think about it. Preacher gonna be holed up like a hurt panther, lickin' his wounds. A wounded animal is the most dangerous. We go blunderin' out there now, some of us ain't gonna be returnin'."

"At least with Preacher hurt, we can all get a decent night's sleep," Van Eaton allowed.

Preacher was weak when he arrived at his mountain camp. Before leaving the valley floor he'd grabbed up enough makin's for several poultices and now he set about boiling water. He took off his shirt and inspected as best he could the wounds. And there were two, one in front, and the exit hole. Preacher had several bullet scars on his hide, and knew if the wound had been a killing one, he'd a been dead by now. But the bullet holes needed tendin', and the sooner the better. And he was already weak from the loss of blood. He made a broth from part of a venison haunch he'd hung up high and while that was simmerin' he cleaned out the wounds and applied the hot poultices. He added salt to the broth, for when you lose blood you crave salt. Then he drank two cups of the broth and felt a bit better. He put water on for coffee and lay back on his blankets to rest. Preacher was a realist, and he knew he was in real trouble. He was weak and in no shape for a fight. He'd heal quick—he always did. But he had to stay quiet for several days. As he lay warm by the fire, he reviewed his back trail. He'd left plenty of sign leavin' the scene of the death struggle, but he soon began erasin' his tracks. It wouldn't fool no Indian, but it might fool those with Bones. He had to have several days of rest. Preacher knew that wounds healed much quicker in the high up country . . . he didn't know why, but thought it probably had something to do with the cold, clean air.

He finally went to sleep just as the small fire was dying down to coals.

The trackers lost Preacher's sign less than two miles from the death scene in the valley. They started working in ever widening circles, but it didn't prove out. The mountain man had vanished without leaving a clue.

"They's got to be a drop of blood," Van Eaton insisted. "A broken twig, a bent leaf—something!"

"Look for yourself," Titus, the Kentucky man, said matter-of-factly. "Wounded he may be, but it didn't slacken none his ability to hide a trail."

At that moment, Preacher was less than a half mile from the man-hunters. But people who are unfamiliar with the mountains fail to realize that there are literally hundreds of places to hide without detection. Preacher had left his horses at the missionary camp and on foot, left practically no sign.

And in hiding, Preacher never disturbed the natural look of the landscape, using nature at its purest for concealment. Preacher rested while Bones and the nobility stomped all over the place and accomplished nothing except for the raising of blisters on their feet.

Finally, Bones called a halt to the search for Preacher and pulled everybody back to the main camp in the valley. There just wasn't any point in continuing. To the man-hunters, it seemed as though the mountain man had simply dropped off the face of the earth.

"Don't y'all be frettin' none about Preacher," Dirk, one of the newly converted men at the missionary camp told the women. "Hurt he may be, but that man is tough. And he knows ways to use what nature has provided to get hisself healed up."

"That's right," Will, another ex-man-hunter added. "That ol' boy is part wolf, part cougar, part bear, and all around mean when it comes to who flung the chunk. His kind is hard to kill. I seen a man up in the Blue Ridge one time take six balls in him and he still kept on comin'. He kilt them that was shootin' him and the last I heard, he was still alive and doin' right well, he was. There ain't no harder man in the world to stop than a feller who knows he's in the right and just keeps gettin' up and keeps on comin' at you."

Otto rode in and dismounted. "They've moved their camp," he told the group. "Over to the next valley west of here. This time they chose well. Preacher would be wise not to attempt any attack on this camp."

"If he's alive," Patience said, a gloomy note to her voice.

Otto smiled. "Oh, he's alive. I spoke with him not more than two hours ago."

Everyone started talking at once and Otto waited until the hubbub of voices had died down.

"He's still not a hundred percent, but very close to it. He's used Indian potions and poultices. We must learn those, people. Their healing powers are nothing short of miraculous. Preacher is fine."

Dirk gave Patience a friendly wink. "Told you," he said with a smile.

9

"We're just about out of everything," Van Eaton announced. "If we stretch coffee and beans and flour, we might last another ten days. No more."

"Them gospel-shouters has a-plenty," Dutch said. "I say we go take it and have our way with them women."

Three weeks had passed without any of the manhunters so much as glimpsing a track of Preacher. Preacher had moved very little. He had stayed alive by trapping rabbits, snaring mountain trout in fish-traps, and eating berries and tubers. After each rabbit, he would move the trap to a different location, sometimes no more than a few yards away. He was healed up and if anything, he was tougher and stronger than before. He was definitely leaner and meaner. He had killed a deer with bow and arrow and had passed the time by making himself a new pair of moccasins.

Now it was time to move.

Preacher had given up trying to understand the inner workings of the minds of those chasing him. He knew only that he was going to put an end to this hunt. He also knew that many of the men he had wounded would have by now left the missionary camp and rejoined

Bones and his bunch. So much for trying to limit the killing.

So, on a fine morning in late summer, Preacher made his way to a place the Indians called Echo Point, the summit rearing up just over fourteen thousand feet in the thin air. It was a place where a shout could be heard for miles in all directions.

"I am Preacher!" the mountain man shouted, the words bouncing from valley to valley. "I am called Ghost Walker. White Wolf. Killing Ghost."

His words reached every human ear within miles. The Indians smiled and looked at one another in satisfaction, and the white stiffened in shock.

"That's cocky! . . ." Bones hissed.

"Magnificent!" Otto said.

"To those who hunt me, your time has come. You will not leave these mountains. Your flesh will rot and your bones will bleach under the sun and be scattered by the critters. You've hunted me and shot me and done your best to kill me. But I live. I live! Now I hunt. Now you will know the fear of the hunted. I will stalk you during the day and cut your throats while you sleep at night. You . . . all . . . will . . . die!" Preacher thundered.

"Big blowhard!" Tatman said, hobbling about the camp on a crutch. His knee was far from healed, but it was just about as healed as it was going to get with the time he had left to him. He hobbled over to where Joe Moss sat on a log, his own busted knee wrapped securely and stuck out in front of him, and carefully sat down. "We owe that mountain man, don't we, Moss."

"In spades," the man said bitterly. He pulled out a knife and began sharpening the blade on a stone. "I want to skin him alive; keep him screamin' for a long time."

"Yeah, yeah! That's a good idee, for shore."

Derby Peel walked over, favoring his healing ribs, and agreed with what Moss had to say. "Just let me be there when you do it, boys. I owe him too."

"Least you can walk," Tatman said. "Me and Moss is crippled for life. It just ain't right what he done to us. It just ain't right. Cripplin' a man ain't no fair way to fight. It just by God ain't."

"Shore ain't," Moss agreed. "That man has condemned me to be a cripple for the rest of my days. There just ain't no justice in his world, that's for shore."

Bones and Van Eaton had heard the words and exchanged glances. "I ain't quittin'," Bones spoke softly. "I can't quit."

"I know," his friend replied. "I didn't say nothin' about quittin'. Just that we're soon gonna be out of supplies. Well," Van Eaton said with a sigh, "least we'll be together when the deed is done."

Bones gave him a sharp glance. "What the hell do you mean by that?"

"Aw, come on, Bones," Van Eaton whispered. "Look around you. Men all shot up an' limpin' an' crippled an' moanin' an' groanin'. One man done all that. One man, Bones. We ain't gonna beat that mountain man, Bones. And you know it well as me."

Bones made no reply. Just sat with his head down staring at his filthy hands.

Van Eaton stood up and put a hand on Bones's shoulder. "We been friends for nigh on thirty years, Bones. And we've made a right considerable sum of money chasin' wanted men. But I got me a feelin' in my guts that this here is our last run. Bones? We could always head west and change our names."

"No," Bones said firmly. "That mountain man ain't gonna make me turn tail like a whipped dog. Van Eaton?"

"Yeah?"

"You see me buried proper, all right?"

"All right. You do the same for me if I go first."

"You know I will."

On the other side of the camp, the nobility had listened to Preacher's words and promptly dismissed them as mere prattle. They had already discussed the matter of supplies and had decided that they'd give this hunt about ten more days and then head out of the mountains before winter. But they would return the next spring to resume the hunt. This had been the most exhilarating time of their spoiled, pampered lives.

Juan's butt had healed up well. Rudi's shoulder was a bit stiff but functioning. Burton's leg had healed up nicely as well.

They were ready for the hunt to resume.

Preacher strolled into the missionary's camp nonchalantly, as if he'd been gone for no more than an hour instead of three weeks. "Howdy, folks! Y'all got any vittles to eat?"

Everyone crowded around, inspecting him. Preacher looked to be better than he was the last time they'd seen him. Patience said so, speaking for all in the camp.

"It's the pure mountain air that done it. That and good clean Christian livin', of course," Preacher replied with a straight face. He looked around him. The area where they had housed the prisoners was empty. "What happened to all your patients?"

"Some died," John said. "They're buried in the meadow yonder. Most recovered and went back with Bones." He pointed to four clean-shaven and bathed men. "These four, Dirk, Simpson, Will, and Jim, have accepted Christ into their lives and are going to stay with us."

"Well, by golly, I think that's grand, boys." Preacher shook each newly converted hand and the former rouges and man-hunters grinned at him.

Dirk said, "You don't have to fret none about anything

happenin' to these folks, Preacher. Me and the boys would give our lives for these fine people."

Preacher stared hard at the man, and silently agreed that Dirk meant it. "I believe you. You're a good man."

His plate of food was ready and Preacher sat down and dug in. He ate that and then ate another full plate before he was full. He leaned back with his pipe and a cup of coffee and sighed. "Y'all got any medicines left?"

"Some," Prudence said. "But not a large amount. Why?"

"Y'all better get ready for some more patients. 'Cause after I finish this coffee and smoke, I'm fixin' to go huntin' me some no-counts."

Otto said, "We offered them salvation. They refused. Some even openly scoffed at us. Since that time we have posted guards out at night and none of us ever go without our weapons. The women have all had firearms training."

"That's good. 'Cause if y'all plan on stayin' out here, sooner or later you women will have to pick up a gun and kill you an Indian or a brigand. I just hope that when the time comes, you won't hesitate none in the pullin' of that trigger." He paused to puff on his pipe. "When I get done with my business, I want to set you folks down and talk to you 'bout your plans on settlin' in this country. It ain't the wisest choice you could have made. But that'll wait 'til another day."

"Our mission remains clear and our course is unalterable," Patience told him.

"Uh-huh," Preacher said. "We'll see."

"Preacher," Otto said, quickly changing the subject, "I've seen the man-hunters' new camp. It's a good one for defense. The best they've chosen."

Preacher smiled. "I've seen it too. And they couldn't have picked no worser place. I'm headin' over there now. I'll see you folks tomorrow or the next day. Bye."

* * *

Preacher lay in the rocks above the camp and studied it more closely through his glass. Bones couldn't have picked a worse spot if they'd all got together and held a stupid contest.

The camp had good water and there was graze for the horses, but the whole place was surrounded by timber. And Bones had built permanent watch shelters for the lookouts. Preacher memorized their locations and then stretched out for a nap. He planned on a busy evening.

Twice he'd lined up Tatman in his sights and twice Preacher had let the man live. He just couldn't pull the trigger. He just could not bring himself to shoot a man he'd made a cripple for the rest of his life. Preacher knew that if the conditions were reversed, Tatman would shoot him without blinking. . . . but maybe, he thought, that's one of the main things that separates us.

It would have seemed incredible to others, but for a moment, Preacher felt a twinge of pity for the group of man-hunters. He'd never seen a more beat-up and raggedy-lookin' bunch of men in all his days. They looked plumb pitiful. And he knew from the meager rations they were dishin' up that the bunch was nearly out of supplies.

From his position in the timber, Preacher counted the men. He shook his head. Way too many of them. The missionaries wouldn't stand a chance of beating them off if the man-hunters attacked in force. And if they ran out of supplies, they would attack and take what food the gospel-shouters had, and Preacher knew they had plenty.

Preacher experienced that old feeling of being "between a rock and a hard place" land on him again. Whatever he decided to do, he had to keep the safety of the missionaries foremost in his mind.

Damn! he thought.

He thought a lot worse than that when one of the men

stepped out of the campfire lit clearing and into the woods and came within a few feet of peeing on him.

I do get myself into some predicaments, Preacher thought sourly. The man finally closed up his britches and walked back into the clearing.

Preacher slowly backed away from the clearing, carefully avoiding the wet spot left by the man-hunter. He could have killed several of those chasing him—and he knew he probably should have—but for the time being, he left them live. He also felt he would probably regret that decision later on.

But Preacher wasn't going to leave the vicinity of the camp without first raising a little hell, letting the man-hunters know that he could move unseen among them any time he liked. He paused and gave that some thought. No, he concluded. No, he wouldn't do that. As much as he wanted to, he finally realized that wasn't such a good idea.

Preacher was torn with indecision. He just didn't' know what to do. He knew what he *should* do, but he couldn't bring himself to do it. For the hundredth time, he wished these people would just go away and leave him be.

Preacher had the same feeling now as when years back, his older brother had told him there wasn't no such thing as Santy Claus.

For two days, Preacher watched the man-hunter camp and waited for them to do something. But all they did was eat and sleep and lounge about and act like they didn't have a care in the world. But Preacher had some cares. He knew he had to get those missionaries out of there before the snows came. People who had never experienced a winter in the high country had no idea just how fearsome a thing it was. The temperature could fall to way below zero faster than anybody would believe possible. And the passes would be clogged with snow. A man who knew the country and was on a good horse could make it. A wagon? No way.

The next morning, early, Preacher was in the missionary camp. "Pack up," he told them bluntly.

"I beg your pardon, sir?" Prudence questioned.

"Are you hard of hearin', woman? I said pack up and harness up. I'm gettin' you people out of here."

"You don't understand, sir," Hanna said. "We . . ."

Preacher waved her silent. " I understand more than you do, lady. I know it's damn near autumn. And I know I can't allow you people to be trapped up here when the snow comes. All the signs—if you know how to read them, and I do—point to a fierce winter. Y'all just don't know what winter is like in the mountains. Folks, we're high up. Higher than you realize. You just can't imagine what it's like up here in a blizzard. I can't get it through your heads that once the snow comes, you're stuck. You can't get them wagons out. Personally, I don't see how you ever got 'em *in*. You think you've seen winters back in New York or Maryland or wherever the hell it is you come from? You ain't seen nothin' 'til you seen snows piled tree-top high and winds fifty mile an hour and temperatures thirty below and water froze so solid you can walk a horse acrost it. You'll die, people. And the ground will be froze so deep down, blastin' powder wouldn't even dent it and I'd have to wait 'til spring to dig your graves. Am I gettin' through to you? Good. Now pack up. We're leavin' and to hell with them foolish bounty-hunters. With any kind of luck we'll be gone two-three days 'fore they realize it. Now . . . move!"

10

"Gone!" Bob Jones yelled, jumping from his horse. "They're gone!"

"Who's gone?" Lige said, standing up.

"Them missionaries, that's who."

Everyone in the camp gathered around him. Bones grabbed him by the arm. "Are you sure?"

Bob gave him a dirty look. "Sure? Hell, yes, I'm sure. I just come from there. And the campfire ashes was so old and cold they didn't hold nary a spark."

"The ground around the ashes?" Van Eaton asked.

"Cold."

"Two days at least," Ed Crowe said. "How about tracks?"

"Plenty of them. Headin' south. I figure that's why ain't none of us heard nothin' from Preacher. He's leadin' them gospel-shouters out."

Bones was thoughtful for a moment standing amid the cussing and loud-talking group. The four men who had left his group to stay with the missionaries were seasoned fighters with no back-up in any of them. Otto Steiner, Frank Collins, and Paul Marks all looked to be capable and tough. And Bones had no doubts about the women being able to fight right alongside their men.

Add Preacher to that list and it made for a group who would stand tough and fight to the bitter end. True, Bones and company had them out-numbered about five to one, but sometimes numbers made little difference when the other men were fighting for their families and for God.

Sir Elmore Jerrold-Taylor had found his slightly bent sword and was waving it around. Zaunbelcher had moved quickly to the other side of the clearing. "Break camp, men!" Elmore shouted. "We follow and attack. To your steeds, men. Hurry."

No one paid the slightest bit of attention to him. By now the man-hunters had all come to the conclusion this his Lordsip was crazy as a bessie bug, and those with him weren't that far behind. Sir Elmore finally realized that no one was listening to him and walked off to pout.

"Well, we'll follow, for sure," Bones said. "But before we attack, I want to look this situation over."

"You mighty right about that," Van Eaton agreed. "Dirk and them others is no pilgrims. And them gospel-shouter men didn't look like no pushovers to me."

"I wonder where that damn Preacher is taking them?" Ligue Watson pondered about.

Preacher was taking the missionaries just as far away from the valley of the man-hunters as he could, driving them hard.

In two and a half days, Preacher had pushed the wagons over thirty miles. A phenomenal feat considering the country in which they were traveling. But there was just no way to hide the trail the wagons left in their wake.

Preacher wasn't too worried about any Indian attack, for the Indians would see he was taking the whites out of their territory, and that basically was what they wanted. But he was moving them out of Ute and Arapaho country and onto the edge of Cheyenne territory. Although Preacher had always gotten along fairly well with the Cheyenne, a body just never knew when a band of young bucks might happen along and take that moment to attack.

"Notional," Preacher told Otto as they rode side by side. "Injuns is notional people. I reckon I understand 'em 'bout as well as any white man, and I'll be the first to tell you even after all the years I spent out here I don't really know all that much. A man can ride into near'bouts any Indian village and get fed and put up for the night and treated right well. It's when you try to leave that it gets right testy. Don't ask me why they do that, 'cause I just don't know."

"Because they are savages," Otto said. "Uneducated, Godless savages."

"They're uneducated accordin' to the white man's point of view, yeah. Smart as a body can get in their own right. I done told y'all they ain't Godless."

Dirk rode up. The women were handling the reins to the teams, while the men ranged front and back and to the sides of the tiny train. Dirk had been lagging back about five miles. "No sign of Bones yet, Preacher."

"They'll be along. But I think I can get us down to the hot springs for a soak 'fore they catch up to us. The ladies is gonna enjoy these springs."

They sure did, and it was only with the greatest of effort that the men didn't try to sneak a peek at the ladies as they bathed and soaked and squealed and giggled in their birthday suits, splashing and playing in the hot water.

Dirk stuffed rags in his ears and wandered off to read the Bible. Simpson and Jim volunteered to stand watch about a mile from the springs, and Will rode off to see about shooting some game. When the ladies were done the men took turns washing off days of grime and soaking out the kinks and stiffness in weary muscles and joints. Upon their return from the hot waters, Prudence got to battin' her eyes something fierce at Dirk—who was a fine-lookin' man—and swishin' her bottom and sashshayin' about. Dirk got so flustered he walked into a tree and damn near knocked himself goofy. Preacher figured if he could get Dirk and Prudence together and toss a bucket of cold water on them, he'd have enough steam to run one of them big ugly and terrible soundin' locomotives he'd seen back east.

Preacher finally had to take off into the hills to get away from Patience. There was nothing he liked better than a good roll in the blankets with a fine-lookin' filly. But this was neither the time nor the place for a romantic tussle. However, he had learned a few years back that missionary women wasn't no different from other women when the candle got snuffed out and they got cozy. Loud, too. Preacher couldn't hear out the one ear for two days after a night with one particularly fine-lookin' gospel-shouter lady, a few hundred miles west and north of where they was right at the moment.

Preacher moved the pilgrims out the next morning. He'd heard tell of a tradin' post about four days from the springs and though he'd never been there, he decided to make a try for it. The missionaries were sorely in need of supplies. By this time, there were over a hundred and fifty trading posts scattered through the West. In two years trading posts had sprung up all over the place as more and more people were leaving their homes east of the Mississippi and heading west.

"Don't expect no fancy place like y'all seen in St. Louis," Preacher warned the ladies. "And the men there will likely ogle you gals from toes to nose. White women is scarce out here."

It was the most disreputable looking place the missionaries had ever seen. But it was a right busy post, doin' business with Indian and white alike. Preacher spoke with a couple of trappers he'd met over the years and knew slightly, then went inside to get a drink of whiskey.

Damned if the first person he spotted when he stepped up to the rough bar was a man who'd swore on his mother's eyes he'd someday kill Preacher.

Mean Pete Smith almost swallowed his chewing tobacco when he looked up and saw Preacher. His mouth dropped open and his eyes bugged out.

"Shut your mouth, Pete," Preacher told him. "Flies is uncommonly bad this year."

"You!" Mean Pete hollered.

"In the flesh."

Mean Pete stood up.

"Take your rough stuff outside," the owner of the post said. "I'll brook no trouble in here."

"Shut up," Mean Pete told him. "Me and this rooster here got things to settle 'tween us."

"Whiskey," Preacher told the man behind the planks, doing his best to ignore Mean Pete. "And don't gimmie none with no snake-heads in it."

The man looked hurt. "I serve only the finest of whiskey, sir."

"Right," Preacher said drily. "Aged a full two days at least. Put a jug out here."

The bar was separated from the mercantile part of the post by a log wall. A brightly colored blanket served as a door.

"You better enjoy that drink, Preacher," Mean Pete said. "'Cause it's gonna be the last'un you'll have."

Preacher poured and sipped and grimaced. "I was wrong. This here stuff was aged 'bout one day."

"Did you hear me?" Mean Pete roared.

"Oh, shut up, Pete," Preacher told him. "You said the same thing last time we hooked up and I left you on the floor. Now sit down and be quiet."

Mean Pete wasn't about to sit down and shut up. He had taken an immediate dislike to Preacher years back and challenged him to a fight. Preacher whipped him. For the last twenty or so years, every two or three years Mean Pete would come up on Preacher, challenge him to fight, and Preacher would tear his meat house down.

After gettin' his butt bounced off the floor six or eight times, Preacher figured Mean Pete was about the hard-headedest man he'd ever met. Now here he was again. Only now it seemed like he wanted gunplay. Preacher was tired of gunplay. Weary of it. And he didn't want to kill Mean Pete. He turned to face Pete.

Preacher asked, "Pete, where in the world did you ever get the name of Mean Pete?"

"Haw?"

"Your name. Who was the first to call you Mean Pete?"

"I disremember. What's that got to do with anything?"

"I was just curious. 'Cause I ain't never heard of no kick and gouge you ever won. And when them Kiowa come at us down on the Canadian that time all I 'member seeing from you was your big butt runnin' off. So how in the world can you be called Mean Pete?"

"Preacher," Mean Pete took a step closer, his hands balled into fists, "I just ain't a-gonna stand here and let you insult me. I'm a-fixin' to stomp your ugly face. And then I'm a-gonna shoot you."

"In that order?"

Mean Pete flushed and took another step. He was a couple of inches taller than Preacher, and maybe twenty five pounds heavier. Neither Preacher nor Mean Pete noticed when the blanket was drawn back and the missionaries all crowded into the opening, staring at the scene before them.

Mean Pete gave a whoop and a holler and jumped at Preacher. Preacher drew back and busted him smack in the face with the full jug of whiskey and Mean Pete hit the boards. Pete didn't even moan. He was cold out.

Preacher turned to the man behind the bar. "If the whiskey had been worth a damn, I wouldn't a-done that.

And if you want pay for that snake-head poison, get the money from him." He pointed to Mean Pete. "Now give me a good jug 'fore you make me mad."

Patience fanned herself vigorously. "My word!" she whispered to Prudence. "He is such a *forceful* man."

Patience and Prudence were awakened that night by Preacher's somewhat drunken singing. It was a ditty he'd learned from a boatman in St. Louis one time and it was about a Scottish lassie named Lou Ann MacGreagor and her red sweater. Seems she filled it out rather well. The ditty seemed harmless enough until Preacher got to the second half of the song. Those verses concerned themselves with Lou Ann's undies . . . or as it turned out in the next verse, her lack of them. Just as Preacher got all tuned up to sing a few more verses, each one raunchier than the other, Patience and Prudence immediately began singing hymns, loudly. As Preacher's singing became lustier, the other missionaries quickly joined in Christian voice.

By all accounts, it was a rather odd mixing of tunes. Somehow, between Preacher's bellering and the sweet harmonies of Patience and Prudence and the others, Lou Ann MacGreagor got to the promised land and got all mixed up with the prophets and everybody was girding their loins and dancing naked on the rock of ages with the angels and the meek.

A drunken Arapaho staggered out of the barn, where he'd been imbibing with some friends and joined in, singing in his own tongue about a lost love . . . which in this case was his horse.

Preacher woke up the next morning rather confused. He just could not remember ever hearing that ditty sung in quite that manner.

He finally put it off to bad whiskey. But he couldn't understand why Patience and Prudence and Hanna and Jane and Sally were all giving him such dirty looks.

* * *

By noon it appeared that Preacher had been forgiven for his night of drunkenness and people were once more speaking to him, not that it mattered one whit to Preacher whether they spoke or not. His head hurt anyway.

"That loutish fellow back there," Otto said, riding up beside Preacher. "Mean Pete. Will he be coming after you?"

"Naw," Preacher said. "He was drunk. He never does remember our fights . . . might be 'cause they're so short. The one thing he does remember is that he don't like me."

"Why?"

"I don't know. He took one look at me years back and decided he didn't like me. We been havin' these head-buttin's ever since. Mean Pete is kind of a strange feller."

"I'm sure he must have his good points."

"If he does, he sure keeps 'em hid right well."

"Where are you taking us, Preacher?"

"Bent's Fort."

"But, sir . . ."

Preacher shook his head. "Otto, you and the others is fine people. Good people, and you mean well. But ain't none of you needs to be out here in the wilderness. Come back in ten years. You want to save souls, practice on whites first, 'cause the Injuns don't want you. I told you the Injuns got their own religion and they're happy with it. You've told me time and again that you want to farm. Fine. Go to Arkansas or Louisiana or East Texas and farm. You and Hanna have kids and be happy. You can find heathens to convert anywhere. This whole country's gonna bust loose in a few years. The Injuns claim all this country as their own. They pretty much put up with us trappers 'cause I reckon we're all more Injun than white after all this time out here and we don't meddle in their affairs."

"But, sir . . ."

"Hush up an' listen to me. When we get to the fort, y'all hook up with wagons headin' back east and go. Now, damnit, Otto, you know in your heart and your brain that I'm right."

The man sat in his saddle in silence for a time. He slowly nodded his head. "Yes, you're right, Preacher." He smiled. "But it has been a grand adventure."

"Tell your grandkids about it. Write a book about it. And think kind thoughts of me."

"Patience will be disappointed. She, ah, likes you, Preacher."

"She'll get over it. She'll find her some fine Christian man and get hitched up and I'll be just a fadin' memory in her mind. Now go tell the others what we're doin', Otto."

Patience and Prudence both let out a howl at the news, but they soon settled down as Otto convinced them that they could better serve their church in a more civilized area. Now all Preacher had to worry about was getting the pilgrims to safety. He knew a place about two days away where mountain men tended to gather for a ride to Bent's Fort. If he could reach them before Bones and his bunch caught up with them, the missionaries would be safe, for Bones and his man-hunters would never attack a dozen or so mountain men. If they were foolish enough to do that, it would be the last time they ever attacked anyone.

Preacher's luck held and two days later, a few hours before dusk, he led the wagons into the encampment of mountain men.

"Wagh!" a huge bear of a man shouted, rising from the ground upon spotting Preacher. "It's Preacher, boys. With a whole passel of pilgrims."

"That's the man who told us you were a man of the cloth, Preacher," Otto said.

"Horsehide!" Preacher hollered. "You big ugly moose! Ho, Papa Griz. I brung you boys salvation. God knows you heathens need some."

"We was ridin' for the mountains to lend you a hand, Preacher," a man called.

"Hell, I don't need no help. But I'd like to prevail upon you boys to help these fine folks I got with me."

The mountain men took one look at Patience and Prudence and Preacher knew his worries were over. The missionaries would be safe. Preacher would resupply from his friends and then head back to confront and once and for all close the book on Bones and his manhunters. Preacher wasn't lookin' forward to it, but it was something that had to be done. He sat down by the fire and stretched his legs out with a contented sigh. Most of the wild and woolly and uncurried mountain men were gathered around the missionaries, unhookin' the teams, helping the ladies down from the seats and ogling Patience and Prudence, hopin' to catch a glimpse of a nicely shaped ankle. These men were as wild as the wind and just about as hard to handle, but they could be as protective as a mamma bear with her cubs.

Preacher took the cup of coffee handed him. "Word from the Injuns we've talked to is you've raised unholy hell with them ol' boys a-huntin' you, Preacher," a man known as De Quille said.

"Yeah? Well, I'm a-fixed to raise me some more hell with them."

"You want a couple of us to ride along with you?"

Preacher shook his head. "Naw. There ain't but about thirty or forty of 'em."

De Quille smiled. "Seems to me there was two bunches of about forty each started out after you, Preacher."

"I been whittlin' 'em down some."

"Do tell? I got news, Preacher. Them warrants on you has been lifted. There ain't no charges against you. It's all personal or both sidesnow, ain't it?"

Preacher looked at him and his eyes told the whole story. De Quille nodded his head. "That's what I figured," he said.

11

The next morning, Patience and Prudence held a short service before they pulled out. It was a strange, yet wonderful and moving scene. The rough and wild-looking mountain men standing with heads uncovered and bowed while the ladies sang sweetly and Otto said a short prayer. Fifteen minutes later, after the goodbyes, the wagons were rolling eastward.

Preacher sat by the fire, deep in thought, and finished the pot of coffee. He was trying to figure out a way to tell the men with Bones and those silly foreigners that all warrants against him had been lifted and if they killed him now, it would be murder. Then he wondered if that news would make any difference. Probably not, but he was going to try. Providing he could do so without getting his head shot off. One way or the other, he was going to end this man-hunt. If he could do it without spilling another drop that would be wonderful. But he had strong doubts. Like De Quille had said, and no matter how many excuses Preacher made, this was personal now.

Preacher made certain the fire was out, then he packed up and swung into the saddle. Might as well get this over with.

* * *

Bones and party had no knowledge of any trading post any closer than Bent's Fort, so they were riding straight south while Preacher was heading straight north. All of them heading straight toward canyon country. The only difference was, Bones and his bunch got lost in the maze of twists and turns and blind canyons. Preacher did not.

Preacher looped around the tortured maze of canyons, thinking even Bones would have more sense than to get all tangled up in there. He had stopped north of the canyons to rest and water his horse when the smell of death touched his nostrils . . . that sickly stench that he knew so well.

Preacher made no immediate move. Whatever it was out there was dead, and hurryin' wouldn't bring it—or them—back to life. And Preacher had him a hunch it was dead human bodies. Or what was left of them after the buzzards had feasted.

Preacher led Thunder, following the sink of death until he came to the scene. He ran around the scattered and torn-apart bodies, knockin' buzzards away until they finally got it into their pea-brains they were not welcome. It was something they were accustomed to, so they waddled off and waited with the patience of millions of years bred into them.

Preacher steeled himself and began trying to put body parts to the right body. What the buzzards hadn't worked on during the day, the critters had dined on at night. It was not a pretty sight; but one the mountain man had seen many times before. Buzzards will usually go for the belly, pullin' all the guts and soft organs out, the kidneys, and the eyes and mouth—diggin' for the tongue—first. Then they attack the rest of the body.

After a time, during which Preacher had to finally puke and get it over with, he finally concluded it had been a party of ten to twelve men, maybe as many as fifteen. And from the tracks, they'd each had them a pack horse or two. There was no sign of arrow or tomahawk, the men had not been scalped, so Preacher ruled out Indians. This was white man's work, and he had him a pretty good idea who'd done it. Bones and the scum with him. The men had been trappers, judging from what was left of their clothing. Their weapons and powder had been taken, along with their horses and all the supplies.

Preacher picketed Thunder and went prowling on foot until he found some sign. He recognized some of the hoofprints as horses being rode by Bones' bunch. He smiled. The fools was headin' straight into the maze. Odds were good they'd get lost, finally figure things out, and head right back this way. He would be waiting.

The bodies were, best as he could figure, 'bout two or three days old. He dragged the bodies and body parts into a natural ditch and worked the rest of the day covering them with rocks. Then he found a pointy rock and scratched into a huge boulder:

A PARTY OF ABOUT TWELVE MEN.
AMBUSSHED AND KILT BYBONES GIBSON
AND THE CRAP AND CRUD
THAT RODE WITH HIM. 1840. I THINK.

Preacher mounted up and rode for a couple of miles, then picketed Thunder on grass and took himself a long bath in a cold creek, usin' some soap that Hanna had given him. The soap was so strong it stung like the devil when he got it in his eyes, but it washed away the stink of the dead and got rid of a few fleas too, he was sure.

Dressed out in clothes that Frank and Paul had given him—he was airin' out his buckskins—Preacher put water on to boil and then tried to relax. He just didn't have an appetite at all for food—not yet anyways. The longer he sat and drank the hot, black, strong coffee and thought and brooded about the men he'd pieced together and then buried, the madder he got. He'd make a bet that he'd known some of those fellers. But the bodies had been so tore up there had been no way to tell. Those men had been ambushed, murdered, and then robbed of everything they had, right down to their britches and boots and jackets. They even took rings and amulets and such. Several of the men were missing fingers that had been hacked off.

Then, all of a sudden, it got real personal for Preacher. That body back yonder with no thumb on his left hand. Preacher had been with him when a Pawnee tomahawk had taken it off. Jon LeDoux was his name. And Jon had saved Preacher's bacon one time, too. Preacher's face tightened. Yeah. Up on Crow Crick, it had been. If it hadn't been for Jon, Preacher's bones would be rottin' under the ground. And Jon was never far from Ol' Burley Movant. Yeah. Bodies began to take shape now as Preacher could put missing fingers and scars and hair to faces. One of them back yonder had been Bill Swain, he was sure of it. And Bobby Gaudet had been a friend of Bill Swain. They'd all been down to the post to resupply and were headin' back into the Lonesome for the autumn season. Sure. That's why the wooden castoreum bottles had been left behind. Them ambushin' filth hadn't known what it was. Probably one of them uncorked a jug and seen how bad it smelled and left it. The grisly picture was beginning to take shape in Preacher's mind, and it was not a pretty one.

Now Preacher could, with almost dead accuracy, name every one of the men who'd been ambushed. He dug out a scrap of paper and a pencil and began writing down the names. Most of the men back yonder had kin, and they'd have to be notified. John Day had an Injun for a wife, but Preacher didn't have any idea where they'd chose to cabin in for the winter. Sam Curtis, on the other hand, didn't have anybody. He'd been an orphan when he ran off from the home and come west. Same with Onie. Preacher didn't even know Onie's last name or even if he had one. The others in the ambushed party would just have to lie in peace unknown, for Preacher couldn't put names to them.

But he could avenge them. And to hell with giving them murderin' ambushers any more chances.

"I found a way out," Jackson said, stepping down from the saddle and gratefully taking the offered canteen and drinking deeply. He wiped his mouth with the back of his hand. "But when we leave, stay bunched up; don't wander off. It's a twisted mess."

Actually, it wasn't that bad. It was just that these eastern men had never seen anything like the tortured and rocky canyons and it panicked them.

"Good work, Jackson," Bones said. "Get some rest. We'll pull out at first light."

"Preacher?" Van Eaton asked.

"God only knows where he is and what he's doing."

Preacher was waiting and watching about five miles inside the entrance to the canyons. He could see Jackson winding his way through the maze, lost as a goose and had been amused by the man's uncertain actions. Preacher had always found his part of the country rather pleasing; but it could be a mite hard on a man if he didn't know his way around.

While Bones and his party were resting that late afternoon, Preacher dislodged a few good-sized boulders and blocked the trail that Jackson had so carefully marked out with loads of rocks and dirt. He returned to his camp and fixed his supper, working with a cold and savage smile on his lips. Tomorrow should turn out to be right interesting, Preacher thought to himself.

"I thought you said this way was clear?" Lige asked Jackson, a surly expression on his unshaven face.

"It was, yesterday," Jackson replied. "Rock slides happen."

"Now what?" Bones asked.

"We either dig through all that piled up crap or take that other way through I told you about," Jackson said.

Those were the last words he ever spoke. Preacher's rifle boomed and the ball struck Jackson squarely in the center of his chest. He toppled off his horse and landed heavily on the sand.

Panic erupted on the canyon floor. Dozens of hooves churned up so much dust it blanketed the area like a thick, dirty fog. None of the man-hunters gave even a second thought to Jackson; not pausing long enough to see if he was dead or wounded. They just spurred their horses and ran for cover.

Preacher knew a dozen other ways out of the canyons, easier ways, for the area in which Bones thought he was trapped was really not that large. It just seemed that way to a man who was lost.

Preacher knew he was safe on the rim of the canyon. The sides were high and straight up. From where he sat, several hundred feet up, he could see two ways to leave this particular series of canyons. But he doubted those below would ever find them in time. He waited until the dust settled and the canyons were as silent as Jackson, sprawled on the sands.

"Bones," Preacher called. "I found them trappers you and your scum killed back yonder." He waited for denial. None came. "Some of them boys was friends of mine. And the worst one of them was worth more than the whole bunch of you. I been fightin' with my mind for days, tryin' to figure out if I should just go on and lose you crappy bunch of fools. Them you ambushed back yonder made up my mind. I can't let you people get back to civilization and kill more decent folks. I can't have nothin' like that on my conscience for the rest of my life. So y'all know what that means."

Preacher didn't expect any reply, and none came. "I just thought I'd let you know where you all stood," he called, then he began shifting locations, working his way around the edge of the rim, coming up, he hoped, behind Bones and his bunch.

"I warned you all repeatedly that we should have given those men a proper burial," Steinwinder chided all within the sound of his voice.

"Aw, shut up!" Sutton told him. "I'm tared of you and that flappin' mouth of yourn. Hell's far, boy. You was the one who wanted to scalp some of 'em."

He never got to say another word. Preacher's rifle boomed and Sutton took the ball through his head. He slumped against the now blood splattered, gray wall of the canyon.

"What a disgusting sight!" Steinwinder said, as he quickly moved to a more secure position, away from Sutton.

Preacher fired his second rifle and the big ball just missed Steinwinder's head, throwing sand in the man's eyes, and blinding him momentarily.

"I've been gravely wounded!" the Austrian hollered, stumbling to his feet. "Help me. I've been blinded."

Jon Louviere jerked him down and bathed his eyes with water.

Preacher was moving quickly, again angling for a better position. But the men had moved into the shadows of the canyon walls, and they were very difficult to spot. Preacher was all through playing games with the man-hunters. He wasn't interested in shots that only wounded. He wanted an end to this. And he hadn't been joking with Bones this time. Preacher was mad to the bone.

"We're trapped in here, Bones," Evans said. "Preacher'll just lay up yonder and pick us off one at a time."

"Maybe not. Jackson told me he'd found two ways out and marked both of them. Horace, you snake outta here and find that other pass."

"I'm gone," the man said, and began crawling out, staying in the shadows.

Up on the rim, Preacher passed up several shots that would have broken a leg or ankle or arm. He looked up at the sun. Nine o'clock, he guessed accurately. He had plenty of time.

Horace Haywood found the other exit, but it was narrow and dark and twisting and he didn't like the looks of it. But he liked it better than facing Preacher's shooting. He edged his way back to Bones.

"It's there, all right. But it ain't gonna be easy."

"Nothing has been on this trip," Bones said wearily. "Water the horses several times today. All that we can spare. Keep them fresh and in that pocket back yonder. Strip the saddles from them and rub them down good. Then tie down anything that'll rattle or make any kind of noise. That'll keep the boys busy for a time. And stay in the shadows and out of sight. Come full dark, we'll slip outta here."

Some of them wouldn't.

Flores mistook a round rock for Preacher's head. He slipped out of the shadows and lifted his rifle to his shoulder. Preacher's rifle sang its hot, smoky song and Flores was slammed back against the side of the canyon wall. "Mother of God," he whispered. "I am truly going to die in this horrible place."

"One place is as good as another," Prince Juan Zapata said, the Spanish penchant for fatalism surfacing at last in the man. "You are Catholic?"

"Si."

"I will pray for you."

"Gracias, amigo."

Zapata's dark, cold, and cruel eyes looked at the man. "Amigo?" He chuckled at the familiar usage from a man far beneath his royal class. "Well, why not? You know, Flores, up there on that rim is a better man than all of us."

"I know," Flores whispered, both hands holding his bloody stomach. "But we found out too late. Que hombre."

"Yes, he is. What a grand adventure this was going to be. Some adventure, right, Flores?"

Flores couldn't answer. He was dead. Zapata gently closed the man's eyes and lowered him full length to the sand.

"What were you discussing with that peasant, Juan?" Sir Elmore asked.

Zapata smiled. "You would never understand, Elmore. Not in a million years. I'm not sure I do."

12

Preacher had spotted the second way out of this series of canyons and left the rim above the man-hunters just after high noon. He'd seen Haywood crawling away and guessed correctly he was looking for another way out. Preacher had watched him return. From his vantage point, high above the group, Preacher would also see where the horses were being held and shortly after the man's return, had spotted unusual activity there. He figured accurately that Haywood had found the way out and the trapped men would try to slip away just after dark. That would be just fine and dandy. He could be waiting.

Preacher fired no more shots the remainder of that day. Just as the day began to cool and shadows were covering the entire canyon floor, Preacher heard several horses whining. Rifles loaded, he waited.

As the pass widened near where Preacher waited, the escaping men would be outlined faintly. Preacher would choose his targets with care, for he did not want to kill a horse. He also knew that if he got two this time, he would be lucky, for at the sound of the first shot, the man-hunters would put the spurs to their horses and leave the pass at a full gallop.

When the lead rider was faintly outlined, Preacher

sighted in and squeezed the trigger. The man tumbled from the saddle. Just as he'd predicted, the men behind the fallen man-hunter shouted and spurred their horses. Preacher grabbed up his second rifle and snapped off a shot. He saw the man jerk as the ball hit him, but the rider managed to stay in the saddle. Then the canyon was filled with dust and Preacher could see nothing. He reloaded his rifles and listened to the pound of hooves gradually fade into the early night. He wasn't worried; that many men would leave a trail anybody could follow. He'd pick it up come the morning. He made his way down to the canyon floor and stripped the saddle and bridle from the horse, turning the animal loose.

Preacher had been lucky, for the second man had been leading a packhorse. When the ball struck him, he lost the lead rope. Preacher smashed the weapons, rendering them useless, left the dead man where he was and took the packhorse back to his camp. The man probably had gold on him, but Preacher didn't want it. He relieved the animal of his burden and sat down to fix supper. He'd go through the newly found supplies at first light.

Over coffee, Preacher tried to put himself in the boots of the man-hunters. Where would they go? They were all eastern men, and most would want to get back to familiar territory. They did not know this country, and would probably elect to go back the same way they came. That was only a guess on Preacher's part, but he felt it was a good one.

Or was it? By now, the news of all those warrants against him being lifted would be common knowledge at Bent's Fort. Bones might not want to take the chance of running into any of Preacher's friends at the fort and risk gunplay. So the group might decide to head north and then cut east. Well, he'd know come the morning.

* * *

It was a silent bunch of men who finally reined in their weary horses and made camp. They had escaped the canyon but they all knew they had not escaped Preacher. The mountain man would be after them likes fleas to a dog.

They'd lost one packhorse, but still had supplies a-plenty to get them back to civilization. And to a man, that's where they wanted to go. They all agreed they wanted no more of the mountains and the mountain man called Preacher. Even the gentry agreed with that, albeit reluctantly.

"Preacher's gonna follow us if it takes him to hell," Van Eaton spoke softly to Bones. "We ain't never gonna be rid of that mountain man."

"I know," Bones said, weariness in his voice. Like the others, Bones was dirty and could smell the rancid stink from his body. His clothing was stiff with dirt and days-old sweat. "But I'm out of ideas."

"I got one," Van Eaton said. "We run like the devil his-self is after us."

"He is," Bones whispered. "He is."

Preacher had inspected the supplies, took what he needed, and turned the packhorse loose. Then he was on the trail of the man-hunters. He followed their tracks and found their now deserted camp. A dead man lay stiffening on the ground. Preacher figured it was the man he'd shot coming out of the canyon. Some of those with Bones had taken everything of value from the man, even taking his pants, jacket, and boots.

"You shore teamed up with a pack of lousy no-counts," Preacher said to the dead man. "But I reckon you wasn't no better than them so I ain't gonna waste my time plantin' you." He left the dead man and headed out, following the easy to see trail.

Bones was leading the men straight north. "You won't go north long, Bones," Preacher said. "You'll have to cut east in about three or four days. And I know where that'll be." He knew that Bones had some sort of a crude map, for one of the men who chose to remain with the missionaries had told him so.

"So I 'spect you'll be cuttin' some east today. Just about noon. I'll be a-waiting' for you, Bones. I'm gonna drive you back into the mountains, ol' son. You ain't gettin' out on the Plains. Not if I can help it. And I can help it." He lifted the reins. "Come on, Thunder. We got some hard travelin' to do."

"This ain't like Preacher," Bones said. "I don't believe for a second he's given up. So where is he?"

The nobility had been strangely silent for the past two days. They had finally begun to grasp the seriousness of it all. They had finally got it through their aristrocratic noggins that there was a very good chance they were going to die. Juan Zapata had sensed it first, back in the canyon. Robert Tassin had been next in line to understand the gravity of it all, and that feeling of doom had quickly spread to the others. They understood now that out here in the wilderness, their wealth and station in life meant nothing. They were in a situation where their money could not buy them out of it. And that knowledge was beginning to show on them. For the past two nights they had huddled together, speaking in low tones.

Bones knew the gentry was up to something. What, he didn't know. And he didn't care. He personally hoped they would break off and go it alone.

And that's exactly what they did.

The group had been traveling through a rough and dense part of the country, with each man having to concentrate on his own business. No one seemed to notice as the nobility began lagging behind . . . along with several other men. When Bones halted the group for food and rest at about noon, the gentry were gone, along with Dutch, Percy, Falcon, Hunter, and Bates.

"Hell with them," Van Eaton said. "I'm glad to be shut of the whole bunch."

"Yeah," Haywood said. "We got our money so who cares. Maybe Preacher will spend his time chasin' after them and leave us alone."

"But they took two of the mules and a lot of supplies," Lige pointed out.

Bones shrugged his shoulders. "I'm just glad they're gone. Good riddance."

Preacher studied the ground carefully. The bunch had separated here. Bones and his people were still headin' for the Plains, and twelve or thirteen others had continued on to the north. "Interestin'," Preacher muttered.

He had miscalculated where Bones would cut due east, and lost time in backtracking. But Bones had made a bad choice and had to travel through mighty rough country. Preacher figured he was only hours behind Bones. So he'd come up behind them. That was fine. He knew a short cut around this bushy tangle that Bones knew nothing about. And that might put him ahead of Bones. But it would be close. Real close.

"You seem to be the most capable among us, Mister, ah, Dutch," Sir Elmore Jerrold-Taylor said to the burly man. "So we have voted and you shall lead."

"Fine. First thing we got to do is get hid from Preacher. And I mean, hid good. When we get done restin' here, we'll take to that crick over yonder and stay in it long as we can. We'll leave it several times, but always come back to it. That'll cause Preacher to waste a lot of time huntin' for our tracks. We'll find us a place to hole up. Bet on it."

"Excellent thinking!" the duke exclaimed. "You get us through, and you shall receive a bonus."

Dutch nodded his head. "I want me a shot at Preacher. I owe that no-good. I really do."

"Perhaps you might think up a fine plan for an ambush, Dutch?" Baron Wilhelm Zaunbelcher suggested.

"I been thinkin' on one. I surely have."

Preacher beat Bones and his bunch by only a few minutes. But it was time enough for him to load up all his rifles and get into position. He would be shooting downhill, but the grade was a gentle one. And they had to come through, or try to come through, this pass, or else go miles out of their way. But Preacher wasn't going to allow them through . . . if he could help it.

Preacher let the first few riders enter the pass and then he emptied a saddle. Will Herdman was slammed out of his saddle, dead before he bounced on the rocky trail. Preacher grabbed up another rifle, but he was too late. Bones and crew were learning fast. Those who had entered the pass had left their horses and taken cover behind the huge boulders that littered the gap. Preacher reloaded and settled down for a long wait.

"Preacher!" Bones shouted from the mouth of the pass. "Listen to me, Preacher. The gentry is gone. They left us. We ain't got no more quarrel with you. This was a job of work, Preacher. That's all. You takin' this personal."

"You mighty right, I am," Preacher muttered. "You kilt Eddie, Wind Chaser, and his whole family and band. Then you kilt a dozen friends of mine. It's personal, all right."

"Preacher!" Bones shouted. "We're just a bunch of ol' boys tryin' to make a livin', that's all. And we didn't have nothing to do with killin' that boy or them trappers. That was all the work of the gentry."

"Sure," Preacher whispered. "Wonder how come it was that the supplies I took the other day still had a few traps amongst the other gear?"

"Look here, Preacher," Van Eaton shouted. "We made a mistake in comin' after you. But we're big enough men to admit it. Let's just call it quits and call it even. No hard feelin's, all right?"

Preacher had an idea. "I'll think on that for a minute," he shouted. He found a stick and put his battered old hat on one end. "All right, Bones. I'm comin' down and you and me, we can talk some. How 'bout it?"

"Get set to blow his head off," Bones told Van Eaton. "That's a good deal, Preacher," he shouted. "Ain't no reason at all why you and me can't be pards, now, is there?"

"Right," Preacher shouted back.

Preacher crawled on his belly for a few yards, and then slowly lifted the hat until the brim was even with the top of a large rock. A rifle cracked and the hat flew off. Preacher screamed as if in terrible pain and then fell silent. He quickly crawled back to his loaded rifles and waited. "You sorry . . ." He bit back the oath.

Preacher kicked at a rotting log and the log broke free and rolled a few yards, thudding against a rock. It sounded, he hoped, like a body falling.

"I believe we got him!" Lige shouted.

"I think we did," Van Eaton said, his words carrying up to Preacher.

"Good shootin', Van Eaton!" Evans said. "You finished the man for good this time."

"There's one I owe you, Van Eaton," Preacher muttered, sliding around into a better shooting position. "And you can bet I'll pay that debt."

Stan Law jumped up from his cover, a large knife in one hand. "I get to cut off his head!" he shouted. "Somebody bring the picklin' jar."

"No! I get to cut off his head!" Cantry shouted.

"We'll race to see who gets the head!" a thug called Billy yelled.

Preacher let them come, all of them, including Bones and Van Eaton, running up the grade, knives in hand, laughing and yelling and shouting and joking and racing to see who would get to cut off Preacher's head.

"Sorry, boys," Preacher said, then stood up. Holding two rifles like pistols, he fired, dropped those rifles, picked up two more, and emptied those. Then he grabbed for his pistols and really began uncorking the lead.

Billy went down, shot through the head. Cantry took a ball in the center of his chest and stopped abruptly, falling back against Bones and knocking him down, unknowingly saving the bounty-hunter's life. Stan Law took a ball through his stomach. The heavy ball, fired at such close range, tore out his back. Bob Jones stopped his running for a moment, and stared in horror at the growing carnage before him. He only had a moment to look before Preacher grabbed up his pistols. Bob took a double-shotted charge in the face and would have been unrecognizable even to his mother. Jose screamed in panic and turned around just as Preacher fired. The ball passed through his neck, just below the base of his skull. Paul Guy's bladder relaxed in fear and the last thing he would ever remember was that he had peed his pants.

Then the gang was running and rolling and falling and sliding down the grade, some of them losing rifles and knives and pistols in their haste to get away. When they reached the bottom, they didn't look back, just headed for their horses and galloped away.

Preacher glanced at the dead and dying sprawled grotesquely below him and without changing expression, began reloading.

"You a devil!" Stan gasped at him.

"I reckon I might have shoot hands with him a time or two," Precher acknowledged. "The difference between us is, I know when to turn loose."

13

The man-hunters ran their horses over rough country, straight west, for several miles before the exhausted animals could go no farther. Reason finally overcame fear and Bones halted the wild retreat before he and his men killed their horses.

Slumped on the ground, trembling from fear, exhaustion, and shame, Bones looked at what was left of his party of bounty-hunters. He'd come west with just over forty men. He was down to fifteen, counting himself. He looked over at Lige, sitting with what was left of his bunch. Counting himself, Lige had been reduced to six men.

Bones Gibson shook himself like a big dog and stood up, amazed that his legs would support him. He was ashamed of himself for running away like a scared cat from a pack of dogs. He looked at the discouraged and thoroughly filthy bunch of men. "All right, people, listen up. Look at me, damnit, you dirty pack of cowards!" That got their attention. They stared at him, some of them through fear-glazed eyes.

Bones said, "We're through runnin'. I mean it. This is the end of runnin' from that mountain man. We're gonna get out of this fix, in an orderly retreat. We're gonna operate like an army from now on. With captains and lieutenants and sergeants and the like. And I'm the captain of this company. Anybody don't like it, leave and do it right now."

No one moved. But new interest now took the place of hopelessness in many eyes.

"I'm fixin' to give you my first order. Here 'tis: We take shifts guardin' while the others take a bath in that creek over there. And I mean bathe. With soap. Then we shave close and give each other haircuts. And we wash our clothes and air out our blankets. When that's done, and we all look like human bein's again, instead of like a bunch of people who just crawled out of a cave, then we make our plans. Now move. Move!"

It was almost dark when Preacher hunkered down and watched the last one die. He rolled them all into a pile and tossed brush and limbs over them. He smashed their weapons and threw them aside. Then he went back to Thunder, saddled up, and rode out. He knew of a little spot that was ideal for a camp. He'd pick up the trail of the man-hunters come the morning. Right now, he wanted some hot food and a good night's sleep.

Miles to the north, Dutch had halted the men and made a very tight and secure camp. Dutch was under no illusions. He'd come to realize they were up against a first-class fighting man who possessed all the skills needed to not only survive in this godforsaken country, but to prosper in it. Dutch was going to call on all of his eastern woodsman skills to avoid Preacher. He did not want a fight with the man until the odds were all on his side. And he felt sure that would come, sooner or later. But for now, they had to stay alive.

The royalty had stopped their foolish antics, all of

them finally realizing this was not a game, not a sporting event. This was a life or death struggle against a very skilled and very determined fighter. And to a man, they had silently admitted they were out-classed by Preacher. And they had suddenly turned into the hunted.

It was not a feeling that any of them savored. Just the thought of it left their mouths experiencing the copper-like taste of fear.

Sound carries in the high country, and they had all heard the very faint sounds of gunfire to the south of them. They all wondered now many more men Preacher had killed.

"Canada," Sir Elmore said aloud.

"Beg pardon?" Dutch lifted his head and looked at the man.

"Canada," Elmore repeated. "We'll try for Canada. We'll be safe there."

"That's hundreds of miles away," Falcon said. "Up through the unknown. Winter's gonna be on us in a few weeks. We got to get out of these mountains."

"I concur," Zaunbelcher said. "I do not think any of us would live through a winter trapped in here."

Rudi Kuhlmann looked at the six men who had chosen to accompany the royalty. "Get us out of this alive, gentlemen, and none of you will ever have to worry about money again. And that is a promise."

"You got a deal," Dutch told him.

"We'll cut north in the morning," Bones told his group. "Head straight for Canada."

"Canada!" Lige blurted.

The men at least looked more or less human now that they had bathed and shaved and trimmed their hair. But their thoughts were still dark and savage when it came to Preacher. They had panicked back at the pass, and were ashamed of it. And each had silently promised nothing like that would ever happen again.

"That ain't a bad idea," Evans said. "I got some friends up there and they're doin' all right. They been up there for 'bout three years now. Huntin', fishin', trappin'. They're gettin' by, so's I hear."

"All right," Van Eaton said. "Canada it is. We'll pull out at first light."

"Now this is mighty interestin'," Preacher muttered, squatting down and studying the tracks. He had been following the tracks of Bones's bunch for two days. They had passed right by an easy way out of the Rockies and kept right on heading north. "Canada," Preacher whispered. "Canada? Now why did I think of that?" He didn't know, but the thought would not leave him. "Well, I ain't runnin' them ol' boys clear to Canada." He swung back into the saddle, curious now, and once more began his following the trail. He took his time, trying to figure out what in the world Bones had in mind this time.

Unbeknownst to either of the two groups, they were only about ten miles apart, and since Bones and his bunch were traveling faster, almost parallel to one another.

Preacher shared his supper with an old Indian and his wife who had stumbled onto his camp, and after eating, the men smoked and talked. The old man and his wife were of the Northern Ute, and both were not well. They were going back south to where they had first met, long ago, to build a lodge and die together.

The old Ute told him that there were two parties of white men, about eight or ten miles apart, both of them traveling north. He said he sensed evil in these men, and he and his woman had hidden both times. He said the men were not happy people; sullen and grim-faced. And they used bad language . . . at least it sounded bad to him.

The old man had heard of Ghost Walker, and was honored to be in the presence of such a fine and brave warrior. When Preacher awakened the next morning, he knew the old man and woman would be gone, and they were. Lying next to Preacher's blankets was a gift from the old Indian, one of the finest-made tomahawks Preacher had ever laid eyes on. Preacher hefted it and knew it was made to throw, and that was something he was a pretty fair hand at. He stowed it behind his sash.

As he rode, he smiled at the old Indian's news. So the gentry and the trash with them were only a few miles to the west of Bones's pack of hyenas. That was interesting.

"I believe we've shook him off," Fred Lasalle said, on the evening of the third day after the ambush in the pass.

"Maybe," Bones replied.

"I think we've lost Preacher," Percy said, at approximately the same time and sitting about six miles away from Bones's bunch.

"Maybe," Dutch said.

At that moment, Preacher was about four miles behind of both groups. He had cooked and eaten his supper, boiled his coffee, and then let his small fire burn down to only coals, just enough to keep his coffee hot. He sat with a blanket over his shoulders, drinking coffee and mentally fighting with himself.

He figured he'd more than avenged Eddie, Wind Chaser, and the trappers the man-hunters had killed and robbed. He ought to just give up this hunt and go on about his business.

Preacher had been fighting this mental battle for several days, and was no closer to a decision now than when he began. Even if there were some sort of law out here, he couldn't prove that Bones and his party had done anything. It would be his word against theirs. And if it came to that, Preacher might well be the one who ended up on the wrong end of the rope. Patience and Prudence and the others hadn't actually seen any of the man-hunters break any laws—and since everything had happened in so-called 'disputed territories,' he wasn't sure what country's laws applied where. Or even if there were any laws out here, was more like it. Preacher, like so many mountain men, was pretty much in contempt of the so-called laws of so-called 'civilized people.' Preacher felt that most of them were downright stupid.

Just before Preacher snuggled deeper into his blankets, for the nights were turning colder, he made up his mind to make no further contact with the man-hunters, other than continuing to push and follow them north. Well . . . he might accidentally hassle them a little bit. If the man-hunters started trouble, then he'd fight. But they would have to start it. He'd let Canada handle the man-hunters.

The weather grew colder, the days shorter, and the nights longer the farther north the men rode. Even though the two groups were only a few miles apart, neither group was aware of the other. But both knew that Preacher was still behind them, staying well back, but coming on.

Preacher had begun trailing one group for a day or so, and then swinging over and trailing the other. Both groups were aware of him. And the hunt became a game with the Indians. Word was passed from tribe to tribe and the Indians were amused by it all. If so many men were running away from just one man—even if that man was Ghost Walker—the fleeing men must surely be cowards and therefore not worth bothering with. They would not be brave under torture.

* * *

"What the hell is he doing?" Van Eaton threw out the question to anybody who might have an answer, although he knew no one in the group did.

"Following us," Bones said. "Driving us north. He's got something up his sleeve, for sure. And I think I know what it is."

"What?" Titus asked.

"I ain't got it all worked out yet in my mind. But I figure I'm close."

"Well, I'm gettin' right jumpy about him bein' back there," Tatman said. "It's gettin' hard to sleep at night, worryin' 'bout him slippin' into camp and cuttin' a throat or two. I say we ambush him."

"Maybe," Bones said. "Yeah, I been givin' that some thought, too."

Van Eaton said, "You don't reckon he's somehow got in touch with the Canadians and they're waitin' for us at the border?"

Bones smiled. "You always could read my mind, Van Eaton. Yeah. That's what I think he's done."

"How?" George Winters asked.

Bones shook his head. "I don't know."

"Preacher had the missionaries inform the Canadian authorities about us," Sir Elmore said, about the same time Bones's group was discussing what Preacher was doing.

What neither group knew was that there were no Canadian authorities within five hundred miles of where they planned on crossing the still ill-defined border. And what neither group knew was that they had crossed out of Ute country and were now in the territory of the Northern Cheyenne and Arapaho. Furthermore, neither the man-hunters nor Preacher was aware that they were all being carefully trailed by a band of Ute, who had some ideas of their own. For the moment, a rare event was happening: representatives of the Utes had met with chiefs of the Northern Cheyenne and Arapaho and agreed to a temporary peace. The Cheyenne and the Arapaho could fully sympathize with and understand what the Utes wanted, and they agreed to it, for the time being.

"I say we ambush Preacher," Zaunbelcher said. "If we plan it carefully, we can succeed. I am certain of that."

"Maybe," Dutch said. "And that's a big maybe. Preacher is a wily ol' curly wolf. The problem is, we don't never know just where he is. He disappears for days at a time."

"Wonder where Bones and them got off to?" Percy pondered.

"Who cares?" Dutch replied.

Preacher had felt eyes on him for the past two days. But it wasn't the kind of eyes that made the hair on the back of his neck stand up. It was more a curious feeling he felt. He circled and back-tracked, but he could not spot a soul.

It was Indians, he was sure, and probably Cheyenne or Arapaho, tribes that he got along well with. He was known to them, so why were they spying on him and not coming near his camp?

Preacher rode Thunder down into a creek, stayed with it for about a mile, and then exited on gravel. He tore up an old shirt and covered Thunder's hooves and walked him for about a mile. He picketed Thunder, climbed up on a bluff, and with his pirate glass in hand, bellied down, extended the glass, and began scanning the territory all around him.

It took a while, but his patience finally paid off. He smiled and put the glass away. "Well, I'll be damned," Preacher muttered. He knew the Ute riding in the lead. He was one of the big chiefs, Black Hawk. Then Preacher remembered something that caused his throat to tighten. He slowly shook his head. "You boys would have been far better off if you'd let me kill you back down south."

Then he noticed two Indians not five hundred yards away, below him. They were riding slow, studying the ground, trying to pick up Preacher's trail, and they looked frustrated because they had lost the trail and could not find it again.

Preacher watched them until they were out of sight. He made his way back to Thunder and then decided he'd just make his camp right where he was. There was water close-by, and plenty of dry wood. Besides, things were going to get real exciting in a very short time. Preacher decided he'd just stay out of sight.

After all, deep down, he was a peaceful sort of person.

14

"White Wolf has discovered us," Black Hawk was informed the next morning. "My scouts have found where he hid his trail and then watched through the long glass as we followed the two groups of men."

Black Hawk nodded his head solemnly. "And Ghost Walker did what?"

"Nothing. Returned to his camp, prepared his evening meal, and went to sleep."

Black Hawk smiled. "By doing so he has told us that whatever else happens to the evil men is in our hands. He will do nothing to interfere."

"How do you know that?" the man dared to ask.

Black Hawk shifted his obsidian eyes to the man, but did not take offense. "How I know is but one of the reasons I am chief of this tribe and you are not."

The man wisely nodded his head and backed away, knowing he had come dangerously close to overstepping that invisible line.

One of Black Hawk's closest friends and advisors chuckled in the misty morning air. "Good reply."

Black Hawk waggled one hand from side to side. "Not too bad for so early in the morning."

The two men laughed softly.

Black Hawk said, "We have gone far enough north. Today we begin taking a life for a life."

"Look!" Tom Evans cried, jumping to his feet and pointing to the east.

About a quarter of a mile away, on the crest of a hill, Preacher sat his horse and was staring at the camp of the man-hunters.

"What's he doing?" Derby Peel asked.

"He ain't doin' nothin'," Van Eaton said. "He's just starin' at us."

"There's a reason for it," Bones said, looking at Preacher. "Preacher don't do nothin' without thinkin' it through. But damned if I can figure out what it is."

The man-hunters turned at the sound of a thud. For a moment they were frozen where they stood, staring at the sight. Benny Atkins swayed on his feet, his eyes looking in horror at the arrow protruding from his belly. Then he screamed as the first waves of pain hit him. He sat down heavily on the ground, both hands holding onto the shaft of the arrow.

Clift Wright jumped for his rifle. He managed to bring the weapon to his shoulder just as an arrow entered the right side of his neck, the arrowhead ripping out the left side. His eyes widened in horror as blood filled his mouth.

Joe Moss, using a stick for a crutch, hobbled for his guns. He didn't make it. Two arrows tore their way into his flesh, one in his back and the other in his chest.

Preacher sat his horse and watched the scene without expression.

Ray Wood began yelling as mounted Indians charged the camp, seeming to come out of nowhere. Ray's yelling stopped abruptly as an Ute lance ran him through, pinning his flopping body on the cold ground.

Bones, Van Eaton, Lige Watson, and several more who

had already saddled their horses, left their supplies behind and fled the scene, riding hard. The other men were slaughtered. Some were taken alive . . . they were the less fortunate ones. Utes could be quite inventive with torture.

Ed Crowe died cursing Preacher. One of the attacking Ute, who spoke English, would wonder at that for the rest of his life. White men certainly did many strange things.

Alan James, Derby Peel, Fred Lasalle, Evans, Haywood, and Winters died in the camp. Tatman, Price, and Titus were taken alive.

With the blood lust running hot and high, one of the younger Utes galloped his horse toward Preacher, his lance-point level with Preacher's chest. A sharp shout from Black Hawk brought the brave to a halt just a few yards from Preacher. The young Ute stared hard at Preacher, then his eyes touched upon that terrible-looking pistol in Preacher's right hand.

"Back off," Preacher said in the Ute's own tongue. "I am not your enemy."

The young Ute lowered his lance and turned his pony's head. He rode back to the camp and jumped down, a scalping knife in his hand.

Preacher holstered his pistol and rode away.

Willie and Lucas, Lige Watson, Pierre, Homer, Calhoun, Van Eaton, and Bones made it out alive. The only supplies they had were what they had carried in their saddle bags.

"I can't believe no white man would just sit back and watch whilst red savages attacked other white men," Lige panted the words.

"What tribe was that?" Calhoun asked.

"Who knows?" Bones said. "They all look alike to me."

Homer fell to his knees and vomited up his fear, while

Willie and the giant, Lucas, clung to each other, both of them trembling in fright.

"Now we know why Preacher was layin' back," Pierre said. "He fixed it up with them savages to do us in. Damn his eyes!"

"Take anything we got and wrap them horses' hooves," Van Eaton said. "We got to hide our trail and find a place to hole up. It's the only chance we got. I'll make a wager them Injuns was from the same tribe as them we kilt in that valley. They ain't never gonna give up looking for us."

He turned and grunted as an arrow tore into his chest and penetrated his heart. Van Eaton had hunted his last man.

Lige Watson lost control of his senses and ran screaming from the shady glen. He ran right into the Ute lance. The Ute left him pinned to the ground. Lige would be a long time dying.

Pierre died on his knees, praying.

Homer was taken alive.

Calhoun ran blindly in panic, fighting the slashing branches and stumbling through the thick underbrush. He could not believe his eyes when he saw Preacher, sitting his horse about a hundred yards away.

"Help me!" Calhoun screamed, hearing the Utes coming up fast behind him.

"Man who needs help hadn't oughtta left home in the first place," Preacher told him.

"You'll burn in hell for this!" Calhoun screamed at the mountain man.

"I might," Preacher acknowledged. "But you'll be there afore me." He lifted the reins and rode away just as the avenging Utes reached the man.

Bones, Willie, and Lucas had lept into their saddles and whipped their near-exhausted horses into a run.

They didn't get far.

Bones and Lucas were taken alive, the Utes having known for days that Bones was the leader. His death would be most unpleasant. The Utes looked at the tiny Willie, trying to figure out exactly what sort of man he was. They'd never seen a dwarf. They finally decided it would be bad medicine to harm such a thing. They turned him loose.

Ignoring the screams, Black Hawk rode over to Preacher.

"Howdy," Preacher said.

Black Hawk studied the mountain man for a moment. "You know why we do this?"

"I know. All who are with you are family members of Wind Chaser's bunch."

In the Ute society, such offenses as stealing, adultery, and murder were private matters, the punishment left up to the family members.

"It ought to be that way in my society, too," Preacher added, knowing his words would please the chief.

"I have severely chastised the warrior who threatened you, Ghost Walker. But in battle the blood runs hot."

"I understand."

"Tell me about the other band of evil men."

Preacher hesitated, then said, "They are better mannered in the white man's way than the ones you just killed, but they are much worse in here." He pointed to his heart.

Black Hawk nodded his head at that. He understood perfectly. He turned his horse and rode back to the blood-spattered camp. Willie rode his horse over to Preacher. The little man was so scared he stank of it.

"What am I gonna do?" he asked.

"Stay just as far away from me as you can, Shorty. 'Cause I might take me a notion to kill you yet."

"You've got to help me. I can't survive alone out here!"

"That's your problem. You come a-huntin' me, to kill me. Now you want me to help you. No way. You'll survive. You know the way back. I got no sympathy for you a-tall. Now get movin'. Get clear out of my sight and do it fast. Git!"

Willie got.

Dutch was jumpy. He was all knotted up inside and couldn't keep his food down. Something was wrong. He had chosen this place to hide with great care, and felt they would be safe. But he hadn't heard a bird sing or a squirrel chatter all morning. The woods were as still as a graveyard.

"Something's awfully wrong around here, Dutch," Percy said, lumbering up, his big gut leading the way.

"Yeah. I feel it, too."

"I heard screamin' last night."

"You, too?"

"Yeah. It was faint, but I heard it. Like to have made me puke."

"I been told that Preacher is hell in any kind of fight—and we shore known that for a pure-dee fact now—but he don't go in for torture."

"Somebody was shore dyin' hard last night."

"Anybody else hear it?"

"Not that I know of. I was on guard. Give me goose bumps all over."

"Yeah. Me, too."

Percy looked toward the clearing and his eyes widened as if he'd seen a ghost. About four hundred yards away, there sat Preacher, just sitting in his saddle as big as you please, looking right at the camp. "Dutch!" Percy gasped. "I ain't a-believin' my eyes."

"What are you talkin' 'bout?"

"Preacher!"

"Preacher? Where?"

"Right there!" he pointed.

Dutch turned and as he did, his belly exploded in pain. He looked down at the shaft of the arrow that protruded from his gut. "Oh . . ." was all he managed to say before another arrow split his spinal cord and he dropped to the ground.

Percy shouted out the warning but it was too late, far too late. He took one step and went down with several arrows in his body.

The Utes were all over the camp a few silent seconds later and the fight was brutal and brief. The braves knew who to kill quickly, and who to take alive. They had been following the group for days, and after studying the men, Black Hawk had pointed out the gentry.

The royalty who had come to America to kill men for sport were no longer the haughty, sneering, arrogant bunch of several months back. They stood in a group, their hands bound cruelly behind them. They knew they were facing death, and they were not facing it well. They stank of fear and relaxed bladders and bowels. The sweat dripped from their faces and their legs shook so hard several had to be helped to stand as the stony-faced Utes stared at them, the contempt they felt for such fear showing only in their eyes. Preacher still sat on his horse out in the clearing, Black Hawk sitting on his horse beside Preacher.

"For the love of God, man!" Sir Elmore Jerrold-Taylor screamed at him. "Help us."

"For the love of God?" Preacher muttered. "For the love of *God?*"

"The white man calls upon his God to help him?" Black Hawk asked.

"Yes."

"Will this God of yours help them?"

"Well, now, I can't speak for God, but if I had to take a guess, I'd say no."

"Good. I would not like to fight a God."

Preacher held out a hand and the Ute solemnly took the offering and shook it. "I'll be goin' now, Black Hawk. You're welcome in my camp any time."

"And you in mine, Brother To The Wolf."

Preacher swung his horse and rode away. He wanted to put some distance between the Utes, their prisoners, and himself. He knew this bunch was going to die slow, long, and hard. And he knew why.

Black Hawk rode his horse into the center of the camp, his pony gingerly stepping around a sprawled out body.

"We have gold!" Burton Sullivan shouted at the chief. "We have money and jewels and all sorts of things we can give you."

"I will have them soon," Black Hawk said. "You have no more use for them."

"Filthy savage!" Baron Zaunbelcher screamed at the chief.

"Savage?" Black Hawk questioned. "You call me a savage? You are a very amusing person."

"Why?" Robert Tassin screamed at Black Hawk. "Why are you doing this to us?"

"I have done nothing to you. Yet. But I will."

"Why, damn you? Why?" Sir Elmore shouted.

Black Hawk smiled sadly. "Because Wind Chaser was my younger brother. I helped in his upbringing after our mother died. That's why."

EPILOGUE

Days later, Preacher holed up in a cabin he'd built some years back. He'd cleaned out the place, for pack rats and birds had been busy there, and then began cutting firewood for the winter ahead. He found his old scythe where he'd left it, sharpened it up with a stone, and worked for a solid week, from can see to can't see, cutting forage for his horses. He worked himself hard so he would not have time to think about what happened to the royalty, even though he knew perfectly well there was nothing he could have done to prevent it.

The entire Indian nation had put a death sentence on the heads of the man-hunters as soon as they learned of the massacre of Wind Chaser and his band. There was no way any of them would have been able to leave the mountains. And Preacher doubted that any of the men he'd sent packing had made it very far out. He didn't have a guilty conscience about what had happened, he just didn't want to think about it.

When his domestic chores were done, Preacher went hunting and started jerking and smoking the meat. He set out fish traps and began smoking his catch. He picked berries to make pemmican and dug up tubers and wild onions for the cellar. When he had done all he could do in preparation for winter, he relaxed. He hoped he wouldn't see a single solitary soul 'til spring. The past summer had given him a bellyful of people, both good and bad, but mostly bad. He occasionally thought of Patience and Prudence and those folks with them and wondered how they were. He knew they'd made it out of the wilderness safely, for a trapper friend of his told him that.

Preacher knew that the area west of the Mississippi was going to run red with blood very soon. As pioneer families began moving onto the land, the Indians were going to fight to preserve their way of life. It was going to be a terrible time for many years to come. But Preacher didn't know how he could do anything to prevent the blood from being spilled.

One fall afternoon Preacher sat on the porch, smoking his pipe and watching the sun go down. A family of wolves who were denned not far away had begun coming around and Preacher recognized both the male and his mate from a year or so back. They came around this evening to check on him.

"Howdy," he said to them, and then was amused in watching the young in their rough and tumble play. "Life's pretty good, ain't it?"

The wolves sat in front of the porch, cocked their heads to one side and looked at him.

"Yeah," Preacher said. "Life is pretty darned good. If a man just knows how to live it and rolls with the flow."

THE FIRST MOUNTAIN MAN: PREACHER'S PEACE

1

Under a bright blue sky, white snow was still glistening in the mountains, but new-growth green signaled the welcome arrival of spring in the lower elevations. A tall horseman rode through a narrow valley where the river meandered along a rocky bench, wooded by pines, willow, and aspen. The rider, dressed in buckskin, appeared and disappeared effortlessly as he blended in with nature.

The river splashed and babbled over rocks worn smooth by centuries of flowing water. From its depths, trout leaped into the air to snare flying insects that hovered over the sparkling surface. In the sunlit glades nearby, wildflowers bloomed in a profusion of color, scenting the air with their sweet fragrance.

The rider who came onto this scene was an impressive man, with a full mustache, square jaw, straight nose, and steel-gray eyes staring out from under a wide-brimmed hat. He sat his horse easily and was leading two mules, both packed to their maximum carrying capacity with beaver pelts. In a country where a man's deeds and character counted for more than his family name, this man who would someday be known as Preacher, was still known only by a single name, Art.

Art took a long pull from his canteen, corked it, and hooked it back on the pommel of his saddle, then shifted around to look at the two mules plodding along behind him. For some time now, he had been aware that two Indians were dogging him, riding parallel with him and, for the most part, staying out of sight. They were good, but Art was better. He was on to them as soon as they started shadowing his trail.

Art knew that the Blackfeet were denying white trappers access to the rivers and streams in the upper Yellowstone, but he was well out of their territory now. If these were Blackfeet, what were they doing this far down the Missouri River?

As soon as the stream rounded a bend, Art slipped his Hawken rifle from its saddle sheath, dismounted from his horse, and gave it a slap on the rump to keep it moving along. He wasn't concerned about the horse and mules getting away—they had been following the stream so rigidly that he was sure they would keep going in that direction, moving slowly and deliberately enough that he would be able to catch up with them again. Using the sharp bend in the stream as concealment, he quickly primed his weapons, cocked the hammers on his rifle and his pistol, and waited.

Art didn't want to kill them, whoever they were. He knew there were times when one had to kill and when those times came, there was no place for hesitancy. He had killed more times than he wanted to recall, starting with river pirates back on the Ohio River, English soldiers during the Battle of New Orleans, and Indians in various battles in between. And he knew he would kill again, but to the degree that he could, he made a compromise with grim reality. He would kill only when he had no other choice. It was the kind of man he was.

The Indians on his trail approached his position so

skillfully that he could barely hear them. Not one word was spoken, and the rocks that were disturbed by the horses' hooves moved lightly, as if they were dislodged by some wild creature.

Art watched; then as they came around the bend, he stood up suddenly, his Hawken pointed menacingly toward them.

"Ayiee!" one of the Indians exclaimed in a startled shout. His horse reared, and he had to fight to bring it under control. The other Indian raised his bow. The arrow was already fitted. He aimed without hesitation.

"No, don't!" Art shouted, but his shout had no effect. The Indian released the arrow and it whizzed by Art, coming so close that he could feel the air of its passing. Art pulled the trigger on his rifle; it roared and bucked and poured forth a cloud of smoke. The Indian who had shot at him tumbled from his saddle.

The other Indian, his horse now under control, knew that Art could fire the rifle only once. Realizing that he now had an advantage, he released an arrow toward Art, but missed. Dropping his rifle, Art raised his pistol and fired. The charge in the pistol exploded, sending a shudder through the shooter's powerful arm. The Indian's face disintegrated in a bloody red pulp as the ball struck him right between the eyes.

As the powerful echo of the last shot was still reverberating through the canyon, Art went over for a closer examination of the two Indians he had shot. As he suspected, both were dead, but something he didn't expect was to see that they were Arikara.

Why were the Arikara trailing him? As far as he knew, the Arikara were not causing any problems. Of course it might have nothing at all to do with any problems between the Arikara and the white trappers. These two could well be a couple of renegades just after his pelts. He knew that the load on his pack animals would tempt any thief, red or white.

Art recharged and reloaded both his weapons, then mounting one of the Indian ponies, galloped down the stream until he caught up with his animals. Letting the Indian pony go, he remounted his own horse and continued his journey.

Rendezvous at Clarks Fork

The smoke from hundreds of campfires could be seen from miles away. And if the smoke wasn't enough, there were also the smells, some pleasant, like the aromas of cooking meat, and others not quite so pleasant, such as the stench of hundreds of mountain men who had neither bathed nor changed their clothes for the entire winter. This was an important gathering place for trappers from the mountains, fur traders from the East, Indians of many tribes, explorers, mapmakers, merchants, whiskey drummers, card-sharks, whores, Indian squaws and their children by various fathers—some of whom might even be here.

For the trappers, this would be their first brush with civilization after a long winter of self-imposed exile in the mountains. It was the only encounter most would have, because they would sell their pelts to a furrier, trade for the few things needed to outfit them for the next year, then spend the rest of their money on whatever items the enterprising merchants would bring with them. Once their money was gone, they would disappear back into the mountains for another long year of solitude.

Though much younger than most of the other trappers, Art had grown to manhood in the mountains and knew the mountains and streams as well as the oldest and most experienced trapper present. He rode into the camp, sloping down a ridgeline leading his two mules.

"Art!" someone called. "Art, how are you, boy?"

The man who hailed Art was Clyde Barnes, a longtime

friend. Art waved at him, then, using his knees and a tug on the reins, headed his animals over toward him. Dismounting, he tied his horse to a sapling before looking around the sprawling, crowded encampment. The camp was alive with activity, like a giant beehive or anthill.

"Looks like quite a few of the men have made it down already," Art said.

"Yep, reckon you're one of the last ones to come in," Clyde said. He cut a chew off his plug of black tobacco and stuck it in his mouth. "But from the looks of your load there, I'd say you had reason to be late. Looks to me like you had a helluva good year, friend."

"It was a tolerable year," Art replied evenly. He was not given to overexaggeration, or much talk at all. He stared across his mule at Clyde as he busied himself unloading the furs.

"Uh-huh," Clyde said, smiling. "More'n tolerable, I'd say."

"I was sorry to hear about Pierre Garneau."

"Yeah," Clyde said. "I told him he had no damn business goin' back to New Orleans. He was a mountain man, through and through, not some New Orleans citified dandy-man. But he said that's where he come from, and that's where he wanted to die. Pretty definite about it. And that's what he done, by gar. He died of the swamp fever."

Art credited Clyde and Pierre Garneau with saving his life. Nearly ten years earlier, Art had been found in the mountains, more dead than alive, by the two men who were then trapping partners. They nursed Art back to health that year, and shared their take with him. They didn't have cause to help him, could have left him to die all alone out there. Although Art had long ago gone his own way, and sometimes even went for an entire year without seeing either one of them, he had always counted Pierre and Clyde as close friends.

Then, two years ago, Pierre had decided he was too

old to spend another bitter winter in the mountains. They threw a memorable going-away party for him at Rendezvous that year.

"You sold your plews yet?" Art asked. "Plew" was another word for *pelt*.

"Yeah," Clyde answered. He spat out a dark, evil stream of tobacco juice. "Got me a dollar and a half a pelt for 'em, I'll tell you."

Art looked up in surprise. "A dollar and a half apiece? We got two and half last year. Did the market drop on furs?"

"Not as much competition this year," Clyde replied. "Ashley ain't sent anyone out."

William Ashley, who had his office in St. Louis, was the leading furrier, the best known and most respected, and his presence always ensured a fair price.

"He get out of the business?"

"Not from what I've heard. He's still buying furs back in St. Louie. But like the man says, we ain't in St. Louie." Clyde gestured around the encampment and wrinkled his nose.

"I reckon not," Art said. He ground-staked his animals, free of their burden after their long journey, and found a seat on a fallen tree trunk. The weight and tension of hundreds of hard miles melted from his shoulders. Rendezvous was like home to him, maybe the best home he'd had since he was a boy. God, that seemed so long ago, when he had left his ma and paw and the other kids to seek adventure . . .

"Say, did you hear about the big battle last summer?" Clyde asked, working another chew in his mouth.

"What battle was that?"

"Twixt the soldiers and the Indians. The soldiers belonged to an outfit called the Missouri Legion."

Art shook his head and shrugged his wide shoulders. "Didn't hear anything about it."

"Well, wasn't that much of a battle the way I he'ered it

told," Clyde said. "More shoutin' than shootin'. Couple of white men killed, maybe as many as fifteen or twenty Arikaras. Then the Arikaras run away and that was the end of it."

"The Arikaras? Not the Blackfeet?"

"Arikaras," Clyde said.

"Well, then, that might explain it."

"Explain what?"

Art told Clyde of his encounter with the two Indians on the way down to Rendezvous. He was still bothered by the fact that he'd had to kill them both.

"I thought maybe they were just a couple of renegades," Art said. "Never thought we'd have any trouble with the Arikara."

"Yeah, that's what I thought too. I mean, the Arikaras can be dealt with. It's the Blackfeet that would as soon scalp you as look at you."

"What do you reckon got into their craw?" Art asked.

"From what I he'ered, a couple of Ashley's men traded them some bad whiskey for good plews. Once the Indians sobered up, they realized they had gotten the raw end of the deal. They got even by stealing nearly all of Ashley's supplies. One thing led to another; next thing you know, there was an army of soldiers and trappers here to teach the Indians a lesson."

"Doesn't sound to me like that was any too smart." In fact, it sounded downright stupid and wrong to Art. "The Blackfeet already keep us out of their country. Sounds like the Arikara are going to be doin' the same thing. So, with Ashley not here, who's doin' the tradin'?"

"Fitzhugh from Cincinnati and Peabody from Philadelphia."

"Neither one of them's paying more'n a dollar and a half?" Art asked.

Clyde shook his head. "No. The bastards got together on it, I'm sure of it. Mr. Ashley never would do that. He knows that without us, he's got no trade. And if we can't make a decent livin', then he won't have us."

"That's the long and short of it," Art agreed. It was the way of trapping and trading, the way he had learned over the years of back-breaking, dangerous life in the mountains.

"You know what they say he's payin', back in St. Louie?" Clyde asked.

"What?"

"Five dollars apiece."

"Five dollars?"

"Yep," Clyde said. He glanced at the two carrying racks Art had unloaded. "If you could get those plews to him back in St. Louie, why, you'd make yourself a fortune."

Art examined his pelts for a moment, absorbing the idea of a better, fairer payment. Made sense to him. "Yeah," he finally said. "Yeah, I would, wouldn't I?"

"Course, to get that kind of money, you got to take 'em to Ashley. Might as well have to take 'em to China, far as I'm concerned."

"Five dollars?" Art scratched at his jawline, feeling the need for a bath and a bedroll, but adding up the dollars in his mind.

Clyde stared at his young friend. "Art, don't tell me you're really thinkin' 'bout doin' that." He brought another foul chew up to the front of his mouth, ready to fire it like a minié ball.

"Five dollars apiece is a lot of money," Art said emphatically.

"So it is, but what do you need all that money for anyway? What you going to spend it on out here?"

Art smiled. "There's always things to spend your money on," he said. "And five dollars is a lot of money."

"Yeah, you keep sayin' that. And I keep hearin' you say it. But Ashley is in St. Louie and you are here. Like as not, if you started out today, you'd be two, maybe three months getting there, and that's only if everything went like it's supposed to. You could lose all your pelts along the way. Fact is, you could lose your scalp along the way."

"Maybe," Art said. He knew the risks, but was calculating the return in his mind.

"I'll be damned. You're going to try it, aren't you?"

After only the slightest hesitation, Art nodded. "You want to come along?"

Clyde shook his head. "I done sold my catch."

"Buy 'em back."

"I done spent all my money."

"I'll tell you what. If you'll come with me, help me get my plews back to St. Louis, I'll give you a quarter of them."

"A quarter of them? How many is that?"

"Forty-five," Art answered. "At five dollars apiece, that would be two hundred and twenty-five dollars."

"Two hundred twenty-five dollars?" Clyde gasped, almost choking on his own saliva and 'bacca juices. "That's more'n I made here for a whole winter's trapping."

"What do you say? Want to come with me?"

"Hell, yes, I'll come," Clyde said, smiling broadly, exposing a jagged row of black and yellow teeth. He ran his hand across the top of his head and spat violently. "I may wind up losin' my scalp over it, but I reckon it's a chance worth takin'. Anyhow, it's been quite a while since I seen me a real town. I might just enjoy that."

"First thing we've got to do is sell off our animals and get us a boat," Art proposed.

"A boat? Wait a minute, you plannin' on goin' all the way to St. Louie by boat?"

"Sure, why not?"

"Why not? 'Cause I don't feel like paddling all the way to St. Louie, that's why."

"You don't have to worry about that, Clyde. It's purely downstream all the way, which means the river will take us. All we have to do is put the boat in and keep it in the center of the river. Like slicing a pie."

"There's another thing," Clyde said sheepishly, his eyes squinting. "I can't swim. Besides which, maybe you don't have to paddle, but I can't believe you can just put a boat in the water and expect it to float you there. You gotta know what you're doin' and where you're goin'."

"I do know what I'm doing," Art said. "I've been on flatboats before. I know the river."

Clyde stroked his chin as he examined his young friend. "You're crazy, you know that."

"You still going with me?"

Clyde laughed. "Yeah," he said. "I'm still going with you. I reckon I'm crazy too."

Arikara Village, Sunday, May 23, 1824

In a place not too far from where the two Indians had attacked Art, several Indian warriors were sitting in a large council circle engaged in the ritual smoking of an ornately carved and feathered ceremonial pipe. The council had been called when the bodies of two of their warriors were brought back to the village. Now the women were weeping, while the men of the village were trying to decide what should be done to answer this outrage. Their honor and the honor of the dead were at stake.

"They were killed by a white man who takes beaver," one of the council elders said.

The leader of the council, whose name was Buffalo Robe but was called The Peacemaker, held out his hand, and the others looked at him, awaiting his words.

"I know that the blood runs hot in our young men," he began. "And there are those who would seek revenge." He put his hand over his heart. "My heart demands revenge as well"—he moved his hand to his head—"but my head tells me this would not be a wise thing."

"No, no, we must have revenge!" one of the younger warriors declared.

Again, The Peacemaker held out his hand. "I have listened to the words of your heart. But those are words of passion, not words of wisdom. Here is what my head says. Have you forgotten that the white man sent an army against us? Have you forgotten that they had many guns and we had few, and they killed many of our brothers, while we killed but few of them? If we go to war, we will have more weeping among our women, and more of our tepees will be empty."

"What of Red Hawk and Mean to His Horses?"

"Does the sign not show that Red Hawk and Mean to His Horses attacked the white man? If this is so, they wanted to do battle, and they lost. I say no more war."

One of the men sitting in the circle was Standing Bear. Standing Bear's Indian name was Wak Tha Go, and that was the name he used. At six feet six inches, Wak Tha Go towered over every other man in the village, in fact over most men throughout the country. He got his height, unusual for an Indian, from the very tall French trapper who had raped his mother. Now, as the pipe was passed to him, he took a puff into his lungs, then fanned the smoke from the bowl into his face. A medicine man of the Arikara, Wak Tha Go belonged to the Bear Society, and was now wearing a bearskin robe as a symbol of his station. When he stood, wearing his robe, he could frighten those who didn't know him, for with the robe and his size, he was very much like the bear he emulated. He was a strong, courageous warrior who had proved himself in many battles.

"What does the medicine man-warrior Wak Tha Go say?" the warrior who had been speaking with The Peacemaker asked. He turned to Wak Tha Go. "Do you who stand as tall as the tallest bear counsel peace as well?"

"If you kill the cub of a rabbit, the rabbit's mother will

turn and run. If you kill the cub of a bear, the bear's mother will turn and fight." Wak Tha Go looked at The Peacemaker. "The Peacemaker would have us be rabbits." He fingered the bearskin robe he was wearing, then lifted it with one hand high above his shoulder. "I belong to the Bear Society. I am not a rabbit!" he said resolutely.

"Aiii yi, yi, yi!" the others in the council shouted, for they realized that Wak Tha Go had just made his decision to take revenge.

"Wak Tha Go! Will you lead us?"

"Yes."

"The trappers are gathering for their Rendezvous," The Peacemaker said quietly, and the others were silent and listened. "There are more trappers there than there are arrows in all our quivers. Would you lead our men to slaughter?"

"We will fight like a bear," Wak Tha Go said in reply, looking at each man in turn around the council circle. "But we will be smart like a fox. We will not attack them in Rendezvous."

Upper Missouri River, Wednesday, May 26, 1824

Johnny Swale, Billy Harper, and Eddie Meeks had left Rendezvous two days earlier and were now headed back into the mountains. They had enjoyed a successful trapping season, and the same pack animals that had taken their furs down to be sold were now loaded with supplies they had bought to see them through until next season. Included in the packs was an especially precious cargo: several jugs of whiskey.

Although the whiskey was meant to be a year's supply, the men had broken out one jug already, and were passing it back and forth even in the first miles of their journey.

"Hey, Billy, you know that little ol' Indian gal of Dempsey's?" Johnny shouted. Johnny was riding in front, Billy all the way to the rear.

"Yeah, I know her. What about her?" Billy called back.

"You think she's worth a hundred plews?"

"What do you mean, is she worth a hundred plews?"

"I mean a hundred beaver pelts. You think she's worth that?"

"I don't know," Billy answered blankly. "Why do you ask?"

"'Cause Dempsey lost all his trappin' money in a poker game and he was lookin' to sell her. Quiet Stream, he said her name was. She was some good-lookin' for an Indian. Fact is, if I hadn't already sold my furs, I mighta took him up on it."

"What would you do with some Indian girl?"

"Ha! I'd keep her to warm my bed on those cold winter nights," Johnny said. "That's what I'd do with her."

"You're full of it, Johnny. You . . ." That was as far as he got before there was a too-close whooshing sound, then a thump. "Ughhh!" Billy grunted. It was the last sound that ever came from his mouth.

Hearing the unusual sound behind him, Eddie turned, just in time to see Billy tumble from his horse, an arrow sticking out from between his shoulder blades.

"Indians!" Eddie shouted, before he himself was cut down by three arrows.

Johnny didn't wait to check on the fate of his friends. Instead, he slapped his legs against the side of his horse and urged it into a gallop.

"Ayiee!" Wak Tha Go shouted, urging his own horse into a gallop after the white trapper.

If Johnny had released the rope leading to his pack mule, he might have gotten away. But that mule was carrying nearly everything he owned. He thought, once, about dropping the line, but couldn't make himself do it.

Because Johnny was slowed by his burden, Wak Tha Go was able to come right up on him. When he looked over toward his attacker, poor Johnny couldn't believe his eyes. It looked as if a bear was riding a horse! He pointed his pistol and pulled the trigger, but the gun wasn't primed so it didn't fire. He cursed and began to weep. The last thing he saw on earth was the hideous grin on the giant bear-man's face as he brought his war club down on Johnny's head.

St. Louis, Wednesday, May 26, 1864

W.C. Philbin nodded his rather large, baldish head and made a few appropriate comments in order to prove to Mrs. Abernathy that he was listening to her. In fact, he was having a hard time paying attention because he knew she would only be repeating the same thing she had been harping on for the last two years.

Philbin was the director of the St. Louis Home for Orphaned Boys and Girls. The orphanage was located in a large two-story building that had been left to the city in the will of Mason Pierpont, Mrs. Abernathy's father. It was left with the stipulation that it would be used to provide a "safe, clean, and moral home for the unfortunate children of the city."

W.C. Philbin believed he was doing that, exactly as dictated by the will. But Mrs. Abernathy had recently learned that a rather significant portion of the money that was needed to run the home was being donated on a monthly basis by a woman known only as Jennie.

"I cannot bring myself to believe that you accept her money," Mrs. Abernathy said.

"Why shouldn't I accept it? Her money spends as well as anyone else's money."

"I shouldn't have to explain the why of it to you, Mr. Philbin. My dear, late father specifically stated in his will that this fine old home would go to the city, provided it is used to house our poor, unfortunate orphan children in a place that is safe, clean, and moral." Mrs. Abernathy sternly held up her finger. "Morals, Mr. Philbin, morals. *Her* house, the so-called House of Flowers? It is nothing but a whorehouse. I need hardly explain to you that the conduct of that woman is anything but normal, let alone clean or moral. She is a common prostitute. Filthy, filthy!"

"She may be a prostitute, Mrs. Abernathy, but I assure you, she does not ply her trade in the St. Louis orphanage. And there is nothing common about her. Her monthly contribution makes up almost fifty percent of the operating budget. Why, without her, I don't think we would even be able to keep the doors open."

"Nevertheless, I want you to stop accepting donations from that woman," Mrs. Abernathy insisted. She sniffed as if to acknowledge a foul odor in the air.

"If we do that, Mrs. Abernathy, we will have to start looking for emergency homes for all our children."

"Are you telling me you won't turn her away?"

"I'm telling you I can't," Philbin said. "Not turn her money away and survive. You seem not to understand. . . ."

"Very well. I can see right now that I will have to find some other way to keep that woman from polluting the morals of our dear, precious children." Mrs. Abernathy stood up then to her full majestic height and matronly girth, and started toward the door. Before she reached the door, she turned back toward the upset orphanage director.

"I never thought I would see the day when I would go to court to try and overturn the will of my father, but I'm convinced that had he known a low-life prostitute would be frequenting this place, giving you her filthy sin money, he would never have left our home to your care."

"And I am equally convinced he intended this home to be used for the good of the children," Philbin said.

"And to that end, I will accept money from whatever source I can, as long as it is not illegal."

"Good day to you, Mr. Philbin," Mrs. Abernathy said haughtily. She slammed the door behind her as she left.

As Mrs. Abernathy was leaving, Jennie was just arriving, having been brought to the orphanage by carriage, driven by an old, white-haired black man who wore a beaver hat. The contrast between the two women was quite pronounced. Jennie was young, slender, and very pretty. Mrs. Abernathy was in her late forties to early fifties, very stout, and plain-looking, to put it kindly. When she saw Jennie, a scowl crossed the society lady's face, making her even less attractive.

"Wait here, Ben," Jennie said to her driver.

"Yes'm," Ben said.

"Hello, Mrs. Abernathy," Jennie said, smiling broadly. "Isn't this a lovely day?"

"Hrumph," Mrs. Abernathy grunted, pointedly turning away from the young woman.

Jennie was still looking back over her shoulder when she stepped into the orphanage.

"Good morning, Mr. Philbin," she said when Philbin came to meet her. "I've brought my contribution."

Philbin held up his hands, as if about to refuse the money. "Miss Jennie, I . . ." he started, then paused.

"Yes?"

Philbin let out a big sigh, then reached for the money. "I thank you," he said.

2

Art and his friend Clyde Barnes experienced a few anxious moments when they first saw the Indians, but realized quickly that the handful of men and women who had come down to the bank to wave them ashore were Mandans who wanted only to trade.

"Do you think we should put in?" Clyde asked.

"No point in being unfriendly," Art replied, turning the tiller to land the boat. When they got close enough, Art tossed a rope to the Indians and, by sign, indicated they should make the boat fast by looping the rope around a tree. The Indians complied easily, and in so doing, pulled the boat ashore.

There were a total of eight Mandan Indians in the party, six men and two women. Two of the men were old and gray, while one of the others looked to be still in his teens. The remaining men and women were probably of middle-adult years. One of the older men pointed to his chest.

"I am Tetonka," he said.

"I am Artoor," Art said, using the pronunciation of his name that the Shawnee had used when he lived with them, seemingly many years ago. From them he had learned many of the ways of the Indian peoples.

"Do you want to trade, Artoor?" Tetonka asked.

"What do you have to trade?"

Tetonka spoke to the others, and they began to display their wares, from rawhide shirts to moccasins, pipes, and rattles. One of the items was a very pretty dress of white doeskin, finely worked with red, green, and blue dyed quills. Clyde pointed to the dress.

"I'd like that," he said.

"What do you want with that?" Art asked.

"Who knows?" Clyde said. "When we get to St. Louie, I might just give it to a pretty girl."

Art laughed, and Clyde began bargaining with the Indians. One of them pointed to a frying pan.

"Art, you have a frying pan, don't you?" Clyde asked.

"Yes."

"I thought so. We don't need two, and I can always get myself another one with all the money I'm goin' to make." He handed the frying pan over, then took the dress.

During the course of the trading Art got three rabbits, three combs of honey, and some wild greens. The trading ended to the mutual satisfaction of all. As Art was untying the boat, Tetonka came over to speak to him.

"You are good men," the old Indian said. "My heart will be sad when you are killed."

"What are you talking about? We aren't going to be killed," Art said.

Tetonka nodded his head sadly. "Yes, you will be killed soon." He signed as he spoke, making a slashing motion across his throat when he said *killed*. "There are many Arikara who want to kill all white men. Yes. When they see you, they will kill you."

Art knew that Tetonka wasn't lauding the fact, but was giving Art a warning of the danger ahead. Art's only question now was if this was a warning against the Arikara tribe in general, or a specific warning.

"Have you seen the Arikara?" Art asked.

Tetonka nodded again, and held up seven fingers. Seven was a very precise number, which had to mean that this was a specific warning about a particular war party.

"Where are they?" Art asked.

Tetonka pointed downriver. "Where river does this," he said, signing a curving motion with his hand. "There is big rock over the river. They wait on rock."

Art put his hand on Tetonka's shoulder. "Thank you, my friend," he said. Neither he nor the Indian smiled, but both felt the friendship between them.

"What was the big parlay with the old chief about?" Clyde asked as he finished carefully packing his loot.

"We've got trouble ahead," Art said.

"What kind of trouble?"

"Arikara."

"Damn," Clyde said, understanding the severity of the warning. "So what do we do now?"

"We'll position the load so that we're in between the bundles," Art suggested. "That should be good enough to stop any arrows they might shoot at us from ashore."

It was about another mile downstream before the river curved again. At the bend in the river Art saw a large rock, part of which hung out over the water. "There it is," he said.

"Yeah," Clyde replied nervously. "I see it."

Between them they had two rifles and two pistols, all charged, loaded, and primed. In addition they took their powder horns and lead-shot with them as they squeezed in between the two rows of bundles. They were ready when the boat drew even with the rock.

"There's one," Clyde said, drawing a bead on an Indian ashore.

Art stuck his hand out to keep Clyde from shooting. "No," he said. "Let's not shoot unless they shoot first."

Clyde eased the hammer back down. "If you say so," he said.

When Two Ponies saw the boat coming downriver, he signaled Wak Tha Go. Wak Tha Go then passed the signal on to the warriors who waited in canoes. This would be the third time Wak Tha Go and his war party had encountered white trappers since leaving the village. On the two previous encounters, they had killed the trappers, but gotten little for their efforts. But this boat was laden with pelts and supplies, and would be a great coup, one that the village would sing about around the campfires. The women and the elders, as well as the warriors, would be pleased.

Armed with one of the rifles they took from the trappers they had attacked earlier, Wak Tha Go ran across the cape to be on the other side of the river bend. From there he would have an excellent, unobscured view of the boat as it approached, and of the attack of his warriors.

On board the boat Art watched the Indian closely until they slipped by, unchallenged. He was about to breathe a sigh of relief when, ahead, he saw two canoes coming swiftly toward them.

"Art!" Clyde called.

"Yes, I see them," Art replied evenly, betraying no emotion, no fear. "Get ready."

There were at least four men in each canoe, and they were paddling hard to close the distance. One man in each canoe launched an arrow toward the boat. Because Art had been expecting an attack from the riverbank, he and Clyde had moved everything to provide protection from the sides. While that protected them from any attack from the riverbank, it left them exposed to a frontal attack. As a result, both arrows came dangerously close: The first stuck in one of the bundles; another stuck in the deck of the boat.

"Take the one on the right!" Art shouted.

The canoe on the right was the closest. Art shot at the canoe on the left, and had the satisfaction of seeing the Indian in front tumble out, along with his oar. And as the Indian fell, he also upset the canoe, which was exactly what Art had hoped would happen.

"Damn!" Clyde shouted in disgust when the bullet he fired missed its mark and made a splash in the water near the pursuing canoe.

Clyde then pulled his pistol and started to shoot it.

"No!" Art shouted. "You reload! I'll do the shooting for both of us!"

"Good idea," Clyde agreed, handing his loaded pistol to Art.

Art held his shot, waiting for the canoe to come much closer. During that brief period, the Indians shot several more arrows, many of them coming uncomfortably close. Finally, the canoe drew within pistol range. Art aimed and fired. He hit the lead paddler, but unlike the man in the first canoe, this one fell back, and the canoe did not swamp.

In the meantime, the other canoe had been righted, and the Indians had climbed back aboard and resumed the chase.

Art killed a second man in the canoe on the right, and because two of their number had now been killed, they started paddling back down the river in order to join up with the other canoe. Doing so put them out of pistol range.

Clyde handed Art a loaded rifle. "Here," he said. "And the other one is loaded too."

"Thanks," Art said. One of the Indians seemed to be giving instructions to the others, so he was the one Art selected as his target. Raising the rifle to his shoulder, he took careful aim, then pulled the trigger. The talkative Indian fell into the river and began to float away, face down in the water.

That left only two Indians in each canoe. When the Indians saw that the odds were now much less favorable to them, they turned and began paddling hard for the bank.

"Ha, ha, ha!" Clyde shouted, standing up and moving to the edge of the boat. "Run, you cowardly bastards, run!" he shouted.

On shore, Wak Tha Go watched with disbelief as his men were shot down, one by one. What he had thought would be an easy killing raid had turned into a disaster. Who was this trapper who killed almost every time he fired his rifle?

Wak Tha Go raised his own rifle. He wanted to kill the white man who was so deadly with his own shooting, but he could not get a good shot at him. The other man, though, the one who had been loading the rifles, was within easy range.

"If I cannot kill you, white man, I will kill your friend," Wak Tha Go said under his breath.

Just as Wak Tha Go was about to pull the trigger, Art happened to catch him out of the corner of his eye.

"Clyde! Get down!" Art shouted.

"What for?" Clyde asked, turning toward Art with a big grin on his face. "They're skedaddling like pups. Why, I . . ."

That was as far as Clyde got. There was an angry buzz in the air, followed by a distant explosion, then a thump as the bullet plowed into Clyde's back and exited through his chest.

"What?" he asked in surprise as he tumbled back

against the plew bales, then slid to the deck in a seated position. He put his hand on his chest, then pulled it away to examine the blood that had pooled in his cupped palm. "I'll be damned," he said, more out of almost childish curiosity than anything else.

Art grabbed the rifle that Clyde had just loaded. He looked toward the riverbank, hoping to get a bead on the Indian who had shot Clyde, but the Indian was nowhere in sight.

"Damn!" Art said in frustration.

"Did he skedaddle?" Clyde asked with a strained, lopsided grin on his stupid face.

"Yes," Art said, squatting beside his friend.

"That means we run them all off, didn't we?"

"Yes," Art said.

"Ha! I reckon we showed them not to tangle with the likes of us," Clyde said. Clyde coughed, and as he did so, flecks of blood came from his mouth. "Oh," Clyde said. "Oh, that's bad, ain't it?"

"I won't lie to you, Clyde," Art said. "You're not goin' to make it."

"I'm not? You want know a funny thing? It ain't hurtin' all that much," Clyde said.

"Can I get you something? A chew of tobacco? A drink of whiskey?"

"Some whiskey maybe," Clyde said.

Art pulled the cork on a whiskey jug, poured some into a cup, then held the cup up to Clyde's mouth. Clyde took a couple of deep swallows, then chuckled.

"What is it?" Art asked.

"I was just wonderin' what ol' St. Peter is goin' to say when I show up at them pearly gates with liquor on my breath."

"I don't reckon he'll say much of anything, given the way things are," Art said. He wanted to strangle his friend for his stupidity. He wanted to save his life, but knew it was finished.

"Wonder if ol' Pierre is there . . ."

"Sure, he is. I expect he'll be standing there to meet you himself," Art said. "He'll probably fix you some of that crawfish pie he was always talking about."

"I'd rather have some beaver tail. Never knew anyone who could cook beaver tail like Pierre."

"It was good," Art said, remembering it from the many times Pierre had cooked it for him as well.

"Art?"

"Yes?"

"I want you to do somethin' for me."

"What's that?"

"You know that purty dress I bought? Well, once you get to St. Louie, I want you to give it to a purty girl."

"Do you have someone in mind?"

"No," Clyde answered. He coughed again, struggling to smile as the color drained from his hard-weathered face. "You pick one out for me. I was just goin' to give it to the first purty girl I seen who would take it."

"I'll find someone," Art promised.

"You know, it's beginnin' to hurt now. Fact is, it's hurtin' somethin' fierce."

"Want some more whiskey?"

"I don't reckon," Clyde replied. "Ol' St. Peter might close an eye to me havin' whiskey on my breath, but don't know how he'd take to me bein' drunk."

Clyde closed his eyes and was silent for a long time. Art bent over to see if he could hear his friend breathing, but he couldn't. He was going to have to put ashore in order to bury him, but he didn't want to do it yet. He needed to make certain he was far enough downriver to be away from the Indians who had attacked them.

Then Clyde surprised Art by speaking one more time. "Lord, I sure would've loved to see me a purty girl in that purty dress," he rasped. Those were his last words.

* * *

Art didn't come ashore until after dark. By that time he had drifted far enough downriver that he was sure there were no more Arikara bucks around. He also figured that the darkness would offer some protection and allow him to bury his friend safely and in peace.

Art dug a grave about one hundred feet from the river's edge, then lowered Clyde into the hole and covered him up. He gathered stones to cover the grave in a primitive sort of cairn, a sort of civilized gesture that would have been unfamiliar to the man buried beneath the cold earth. Afterward, he stood alongside the freshly dug grave, took off his own hat, and held it across his heart.

"Lord, this fella's name I'm sendin' to you is Clyde Barnes. He probably drank too much, cussed too much, and gambled too much. That's the way it is with mountain men, but you, knowin' everything like you do, probably already know that. But that means you also know what was in his heart, and Lord, when you look into his heart you'll see Clyde was about as fine a man as there could be.

"Clyde has some friends up there, and I'd like for you to arrange to have them come meet him, take him under their wing, and show him around. I've got a special reason for asking this, Lord, because truth to tell, it was Clyde and Pierre who took me in when I first come to the mountains. They were good men, both of 'em, and once you get 'em up there and give 'em a chance, why, I think you'll see that too.

"I know there's probably some proper way to end prayers, but I can't think of any way of endin' this one except to just end it. Amen."

* * *

St. Louis, Wednesday, June 2, 1824

When Theodore Epson, the chief of tellers of the River Bank of St. Louis, passed by the boardroom of the bank, he saw that it was filled with women, all of whom seemed to be talking at once. Smiling, he shook his head and walked on by. Women . . . strange creatures all.

Making such a meeting room available to the public had been Epson's idea, and he'd convinced the board of directors that it would be very good business for the bank. The board had accepted his proposal, and today was a good example of how it was being put to use. The ladies all belonged to the Women's Auxiliary of the St. Louis Betterment League, and its president was Sybil Abernathy, wife of Duane Abernathy, the chairman of the bank's board of directors.

As he closed the door between the front and back of the bank, Theodore Epson heard Mrs. Abernathy banging her gavel to call for quiet.

"Ladies, ladies, may I have your attention please?" Mrs. Abernathy said.

Most of the conversation halted, though there was one woman in the back who continued to hold court with the three or four who were gathered around her.

"Mrs. Peabody!" Mrs. Abernathy called. "Would you please take your seat now?" When she got no response, she shouted. "Mrs. Peabody, would you *please* take your seat now?"

"All right, all right," Mrs. Peabody answered. "You don't have to shout. I'm not deaf, you know."

In fact, Mrs. Peabody was quite deaf, so deaf that she didn't even hear the other ladies laugh at her patently absurd declaration.

When all were quiet and seated, Mrs. Abernathy began the meeting.

"Ladies, I called this special meeting today because I am deeply concerned about the state of morals of our city, more specifically the lack of morals in our fair metropolis. I have heard it said that the people back East sometimes refer to St. Louis as Sodom and Gomorrah on the Mississippi. If we are to build a decent society here, if we are to be recognized by our Eastern cousins as a civilized city, then we must take action immediately to stop this moral decay."

"What moral decay are you talking about, Sybil?" one of the ladies asked.

"What moral decay? Well, I'm talking about this . . . this Jennie woman, who doesn't even have a last name, and the house of prostitution she operates right under our very noses."

"Has she done something?" another asked.

"Of course she has done something. She is operating a house of prostitution," Sybil Abernathy said in exasperation. "Didn't you hear what I just said?"

"Well, yes, but there have always been houses of prostitution, and there always will be. You know how the men are, or at least some of them, none of *our* husbands or brothers, I'm sure. The way I look at it, better to have someplace like that where you know where it is, than to have women of the evening roaming our streets."

"And we don't have that, Sybil," another pointed out.

Mrs. Abernathy was obviously surprised by the reaction she was getting. She had expected overwhelming support for her campaign to rid St. Louis of Jennie and the ones who worked for her in the House of Flowers. Instead, she was getting resistance.

"Sin is sin, and immorality is immorality, no matter where it occurs," Mrs. Abernathy said.

"Of course it is, and I'm not justifying what she does," one of the women said. "It's just that she is discreet and she does stay out of everyone's way. I guess I never considered it as much of a problem."

"What about the orphanage?" Mrs. Abernathy asked.

"What about it?"

"Perhaps you didn't know that she donates a rather healthy sum of money to the orphanage every week."

"Why, I would think that to be a good civic-minded thing to do," one of the women said.

"Would you think it to be a good thing if you knew that she recruits her prostitutes from among the children of that orphanage?"

"What?" several of the ladies shouted.

"You don't mean that she actually uses the children?"

Mrs. Abernathy smiled with sly satisfaction. Now, at last, she had gotten them into the proper frame of mind to consider this grave matter that was affecting the city they claimed to care about so deeply.

"As far as I know, she doesn't use the very young children," Mrs. Abernathy said. "But two of her prostitutes are former residents of the orphanage home."

"Oh, my, but that is terrible!" someone said.

"We must do something about this!" another added.

Mrs. Abernathy nodded in triumph. "And do something we shall," she said.

Arikara Village, Wednesday, June 2, 1824

When Wak Tha Go returned to the village, it wasn't in the triumphant manner that he had envisioned, but rather in disfavor. His adventure had cost the lives of four of his eager young warriors, and the widows and families of the slain wept bitter tears of grief. All turned their back on him, blaming him for the deaths.

Wak Tha Go went from tepee to tepee to plead his case, but none would hear him. When council met that evening, Wak Tha Go was not invited to sit in the first circle. Angry at being ostracized, he hung back in the darkness, watching the others as they sat around the fire, mourning and listening to ageless stories and songs.

Wak Tha Go felt they should be telling stories and singing songs of his great deeds. After all, he had personally killed one of the white men who had killed the three warriors. And before this, there had been other encounters with the white trappers in which the Indians emerged victorious, killing the trappers while not losing even one of their own. They had taken booty and scalps, counted many coups. In any war, there was bound to be loss. Why could the others in the village not see this?

The Peacemaker was a chief, but not an all-powerful, autocratic chief. He ruled by persuasion and counsel, and always with advice and assistance from the other elders in the tribe. There was a difference between leading during peacetime and leading during battle, however. War chiefs were neither appointed nor elected. A war chief assumed a position of authority, and if others chose to follow him his authority was validated. Peace chiefs and war chiefs usually coexisted and supported each other—but these were extraordinary times.

In the case of Wak Tha Go, his authority as a warrior chief had lasted only as long as he was successful. Now his rank within the tribe was no higher than anyone else's.

"Grandfather, tell us a story," one young boy asked of The Peacemaker.

"Yes, Grandfather, tell us of Buffalo Cow Woman," another said.

The Peacemaker was not their blood grandfather, but was addressed as such by many of the young. Not only was this a token of respect for The Peacemaker; it also, by implication, included the young person in The Peacemaker's family. Elders, whether they held the status of chief or not, were automatically respected by younger people.

"Buffalo Cow Woman?" The Peacemaker said. "You want to hear of the mother of us all?"

"Yes! Yes!"

"Then gather close so that your ears do not fail to hear the words I speak, for I must speak them quietly." He held his finger to his lips in a shushing motion. "If Buffalo Cow Woman hears us speaking of her, she may get very angry. And if she gets very angry, she will gallop through the village, trampling every tepee, and putting out all the fires. She will cause the meat to go bad and hide the honey and take away the rain. If she does that, we will all . . ." He paused for a long moment, looking directly into the faces of all the children who were now hanging on every word. "Die!" he barked.

The younger children began to whimper in fear. Even the older children shivered, but they were older and braver, and did not cry.

Wak Tha Go had been just on the periphery of the council circle, listening to everything that was being said. When he saw the council circle dissolve and saw the children move toward the center, and heard The Peacemaker start his story about Buffalo Cow Woman, he snorted and walked away.

"Buffalo Cow Woman," he said under his breath, scoffing at the name. Everyone in the village was listening to children's stories when they should be listening to stories about his great exploits and even greater plans for the future. Let them listen now, he thought. He would leave this village and go to join the Blackfeet. The Blackfeet were warriors, not old women like The Peacemaker and the cowards who listened to him.

3

On the Missouri River, Monday, June 21, 1824

After Art put into shore and secured the boat, he carved a mark in the railing. He had no idea what the date was, though he figured it to be sometime in mid-June or later. If he had remembered to find out the date before he left Rendezvous, he would know now, because he had carved a notch for every day since he left. He had been on the river now for thirty days. The days had been long and lonely since Clyde's death.

Once he made camp, Art took his rifle out into the woods, and less than half an hour later was back with a rabbit. He skinned the rabbit, salted it well, skewered it on a green willow branch, then put it over a fire, suspended between two Y-shaped sticks. Within minutes the rich aroma of roasted rabbit filled the air.

Art had never gone down the Missouri, so he really had no idea how far it was to St. Louis, nor how long it would take him to get there. He was sure that the river didn't go in a straight line. In fact, what with all the twists and turns, he would be surprised if the river route didn't double the distance a crow flies. But he had neither horses nor mules, and floating down the river—even if it was longer—was certainly superior to walking.

Shortly after nightfall, as Art was laying out his bedroll, he became aware of eyes staring at him from the dark. With the hair on the back of his neck standing up, he slipped his pistol from his belt and stared into the black maw that surrounded his camp.

"Who's there?" he called.

There was no response.

"Who's there?" he called again, and this time he augmented his call with the deadly click of his pistol being cocked.

A low, frightening growl came from the darkness.

"Are you a wolf?" Art called. Thinking to lure the animal from the darkness, he took a piece of rabbit and held it up. "Come on in, boy. Come get this meat."

Tossing the meat about ten feet in front of him, he raised his pistol, ready to shoot the moment the wolf showed itself.

It wasn't a wolf, at least not a full-blooded wolf, though the dog clearly had many of the markings and features of a wolf. The animal walked into pistol range, growling, its eyes locked on the mountain man while it was moving toward the proffered morsel.

Art lowered his pistol and watched the big dog use its powerful jaws to pull the meat away from the bone. The dog fascinated him, not only by its size and power, but also by the way it carried itself. It clearly showed no fear of him.

When the dog finished the first piece of meat, Art threw another piece out—this one closer than the first. The dog came for it. By the time he threw the last piece of meat, the dog was quite close—close enough for Art to touch, and he did so, rubbing the dog behind its ears.

"How'd you get way out here in the middle of nowhere?" Art asked.

Though the dog didn't snuggle against Art's hand, it was friendly enough to be nonthreatening; the growling had ceased.

The dog slept near Art that night. When Art got ready to leave the next day, the dog jumped onto the boat with him.

"Shoo," Art said, waving his hand. "Get off."

The dog walked to the front of the boat and sat there, staring at Art with penetrating eyes.

"What are you doing? You can't go with me."

The dog made no effort to leave.

As a young boy, Art had once owned a dog. He remembered that Rover would go fishing and hunting with him, and he smiled.

"I guess you would be good company at that. All right, you can stay," Art said.

The dog came much closer.

"So, what shall I call you? How about Rover? I used to have a dog named Rover."

The dog growled.

"You don't like Rover? How about Skip? That's a good dog name."

The dog growled again.

"All right, suppose I just call you Dog and be done with it. If you even are a dog . . ."

The dog made a few circles on the deck of the boat, lay down with his nose between his paws, and closed his eyes. Art laughed. "All right, you seem to like that name, so Dog it is."

Over the next several days, Dog proved to be more than just good company. One night, as Art was making camp, Dog disappeared. Art thought that he had run away, but a short while later Dog returned to camp, carrying a rabbit in his mouth. He dropped it at Art's feet, providing them with their dinner for the night.

* * *

House of Flowers, St. Louis, Tuesday, June 22, 1824

Jennie was in the kitchen, taking inventory of her food items. She had to keep a well-stocked kitchen because most of her girls not only worked there, they slept and ate there as well. She was measuring the flour, trying to determine how much she would need, when a girl came in.

"Miss Jennie?"

Turning, Jennie saw Carla. Though Carla lived there, she wasn't really one of Jennie's girls, in that she wasn't a prostitute. She worked as a waitress at LaBarge's Tavern, and paid for her room and board at the house, though Jennie charged her far less than the going rate.

"Yes, Carla?"

"Deputy Constable Gordon is here to see you."

"Thank you, Carla. Would you tell him I'll be just a minute?"

"Yes, ma'am. Or if you want to, you can go talk to him and I'll put things away in here."

"Would you, Carla? That's sweet of you," Jennie said. Taking off her apron and making a quick adjustment to her hair, Jennie went into the parlor. Deputy Constable John Gordon was standing in the foyer, rolling his hat in his hands. Jennie smiled broadly as she approached him.

"Why, John, I didn't expect to see you here this time of day," she said. "You don't usually come until it's quite late."

"Uh, sorry, Miss Jennie, but this ain't exactly a business call."

"John, you know I don't like to treat my callers as customers. I would hope that all of your calls are more social than business."

"Yes, ma'am, but, well, this ain't social either."

"Oh?" Jennie replied, her face registering her curiosity. "If it isn't business nor social, what is it?"

"Sort of duty, you might say," Deputy Constable

Gordon said. "The chief constable would like to see you down at his office. He asked me to come get you."

"All right, John. Just let me get my portmanteau and I'll be right with you."

Because he had ridden a horse down to Jennie's, Deputy Constable Gordon waited for Jennie's driver, Ben, to bring her carriage around. He rode alongside the carriage as Ben drove Jennie to the chief constable's office.

"Shall I wait here, Miss Jennie?" Ben asked.

"Yes, Ben, if you would, please," Jennie said.

Jennie had no idea what the visit was about until she stepped into the office. There, she saw Mrs. Abernathy and two other women, all of whom greeted her with sour expressions.

"Miss Jennie," the chief constable started.

"Do you feel it is necessary to address a colored woman as *Miss?*" Sybil Abernathy said. "Because I certainly don't."

In surprise, Jennie jerked her head toward Mrs. Abernathy.

"Don't look at me, girl, like you don't know what I'm talking about," Mrs. Abernathy said. "Are you going to deny that you are a colored slave girl?"

"Now, Mrs. Abernathy, if that is true, who does she belong to?"

"She belonged to a man named Bruce Eby," Mrs. Abernathy said.

Surprised to hear the name of the man who had once owned her, Jennie looked down toward the floor.

"Is that true, Miss, uh, Jennie?"

"I used to belong to him. I'm a free woman now," Jennie said.

The constable stroked his chin. "Then, you *are* colored?" He shook his head. "You sure don't look colored to me."

"I'm Creole," Jennie said.

"Creole, colored, it's all the same," Mrs. Abernathy insisted. "The point is, she was the legal property of one Bruce Eby."

"Was?" the constable said, looking at Mrs. Abernathy. "Even you are saying she was, and not is, the property of this man, Eby. Where is he anyway? Why isn't he making a claim?"

"He can't claim her because he is dead," Mrs. Abernathy said. She pointed to Jennie. "And she killed him."

"What?" the constable replied. He looked sharply at Jennie. "Is she telling the truth? Did you kill your master?"

"No, sir, I did not kill him," Jennie said.

"If she didn't kill him, she was the cause of his being killed," Mrs. Abernathy said.

"Is that right? Was he killed because of you?"

"In a way, I suppose that's right."

"When did this happen? And where?"

"It happened several years ago," Jennie said. "At Rendezvous on the Missouri River."

"And you were his slave?"

"Not when he was killed. Another man won me, just before the killing. And he's the one that set me free."

"Can you prove that you were set free, and don't belong to the estate of the man you say was killed?"

"I can," Jennie said. "I have a letter of manumission, given to me by the man who had just won me, fair and square, and signed by two witnesses."

"Where is this letter of manumission?" the constable asked.

"I keep it . . ." Jennie started, then she glanced over toward Mrs. Abernathy. "I'd rather not tell you where I keep it."

"Ha!" Mrs. Abernathy said. "You won't tell us where you keep it, because it doesn't exist. You don't have a letter of manumission. You are a runaway slave."

"I am not a runaway slave! I am a free woman!" Jennie insisted.

"Can you get that letter, Miss Jennie, and show it to me?"

"Yes, I can do that."

"Please do so."

"Arrest her, Constable. Arrest her and put her in jail," Mrs. Abernathy demanded.

"I can't do that, Mrs. Abernathy."

"What do you mean you can't do that? You heard her confess that her master was killed because of her."

"Maybe he was killed because of her, and maybe he wasn't. But that doesn't give me any cause to arrest her. In fact, even if she killed him and it happened at Rendezvous on the Missouri, I still couldn't arrest her, because that would put it way out of my jurisdiction."

"Am I free to go?" Jennie asked.

"Yes, I can think of no reason to hold you."

"Wait!" Mrs. Abernathy said. "What about the fact that she is using girls from the orphanage in the House of Flowers?"

"What?" Jennie and the constable asked in unison.

"You heard me. Some of the girls who work for her now came from the orphanage house. Isn't there some law that would deal with that? Because if there isn't, there should be."

"Some girls? What girls?" the constable asked.

"Carla Thomas is one," Mrs. Abernathy said. To Mrs. Abernathy's surprise, both the constable and the deputy constable laughed.

"What is it? What's wrong?" Mrs. Abernathy asked. "Do you find that funny?"

"Yes," the constable said. "Mrs. Abernathy, everyone knows that Carla Thomas just lives in the House of Flowers. She's not a prostitute."

"Nevertheless, to even have a young girl living there is wrong."

"She's nineteen years old," the constable said. "And I reckon she's old enough to live anywhere she wants. I don't see as I have any right to tell her she can't stay there."

Mrs. Abernathy glared at the constable, deputy constable, and Jennie for a long moment before she spoke.

"I can see now that you aren't going to do anything to rid us of this . . . this blight on our city, are you? You are going to allow this whore, and the whores who work with her, to continue to corrupt the morals of our young men."

"We have no laws on the books against keeping a bawdy house, Mrs. Abernathy," the constable explained. "The only law we have is one that prohibits women from plying their trade on the street. And as far as I know, neither Miss Jennie—"

"Miss Jennie? Why are you calling a colored woman Miss? Even if she was freed, she is still colored, and certainly doesn't deserve being addressed as Miss."

Constable Billings sighed. "As I was about to say, neither *Miss* Jennie"—he came down hard on the word *Miss*—"nor any of her girls have ever violated that particular law. So, to answer your question, Mrs. Abernathy, no, I don't intend to put her in jail, run her out of town, or even close her establishment. Now, if you ladies will excuse me, I have work to do."

Mrs. Abernathy pulled herself up to her full height, then looked at the two women she had brought along for moral support.

"Come, ladies," she said. "It is clear that we can expect no support from Constable Billings." She stared at Billings. "Don't forget, Constable, we have a federal marshal in St. Louis. Since you refuse to do your duty, I will go to him."

The constable looked back at Jennie. "Miss Jennie, you're sure you can find the paper that proves you're free?"

"Yes, sir, I'm sure."

"You'd better go get it and bring it to me as quickly as you can."

"Yes, sir."

"I assure you, this isn't over," Mrs. Abernathy hissed. "I am a determined woman and I will find a way to rid our city of this filth."

The House of Flowers

Back in her room, Jennie opened the chest that sat at the foot of her bed. In the bottom of the chest, under a quilt, there was a locked tin box. Opening the box, she removed a little packet, bound by a red ribbon. When she untied the ribbon, she saw what she was looking for: the all-important letter of manumission.

Holding the letter in her hand, she let her mind drift back to the day it was signed, some six years earlier.

Bighorn Mountains, Spring of 1814

Jennie was tired. It was more than the bone-weary, back-sore tired that comes from working; it was the kind of deep-down tired that begins to tell on a person who has been through several years of "being on the line," selling her body to trappers and tradesmen, soldiers, scouts, and anyone else Bruce Eby offered her services to. Furthermore, it was a tired that wasn't ameliorated by any money she might earn. For Jennie was not only a prostitute, she was property—a slave owned body and soul by Bruce Eby.

Eby had brought Jenny to Rendezvous, a seasonal gathering of fur trappers, mountain men, and traders, because he could sell her services for three times what the market would bear in a city. But even with the increased cost, Jennie—an exceptionally pretty young woman of nineteen—had been doing a brisk business. For three days and nights, the line outside her tent was unabated, interrupted only when Eby reluctantly gave her a couple of hours to sleep.

Now, however, because of the excitement of an upcoming shooting match, Jennie was able to find a respite from her activities. Taking advantage of the break, she stood just in front of her tent, looking toward the gathering crowd of shooters who were preparing for the upcoming match.

Some of the shooters were cleaning their guns, others were sighting down the barrels of their rifles at the targets they would be using. Some shooters just stood by calmly. In that group of quietly confident men, she saw and recognized a young man she had known from before—when he was a boy and she was still a young girl. No, she reminded herself. Art may have been a boy then, but she hadn't been a young girl. She had never been a young girl.

"Art?" she called. "Art, do you remember me?"

Startled to hear his name spoken by a woman, Art turned to see who had called him. He saw a young woman between eighteen and twenty, with coal-black hair, dark eyes, and olive skin. For a moment Jennie could see the confusion in his eyes; then she saw that he recognized her.

"Jennie? Jennie, is that you?" he asked.

She smiled at him. "You remembered," she said.

"Yes, of course I remember."

Spontaneously, Jennie hugged him. He hugged her back.

"Here, now, that's goin' to cost you, mister," a gruff voice said. "I ain't in the habit of lettin' my girls give away anything for free."

Quickly, Jennie pulled away from Art, an expression of fear and resignation in her face.

"If'n you want to spend a little time with her, all you got to do is pay me five dollars," the man said.

"You are Bruce Eby," Art said.

Eby screwed his face up in confusion. "Do I know you, mister?"

"No," Art answered. "But I know you. What have you got to do with Jennie?"

"Ahh, you know Jennie, do you? Then you know she's the kind that can please any man."

Art looked at Jennie, who glanced toward the ground. "He owns me," she said.

"What about it, mister?" Eby said. "Do you want her, or not?"

"Yeah," Art said. "I want her."

Eby smiled. "That'll be five dollars."

"No," Art said. "I don't want her five dollars' worth. I want to buy her from you."

Jennie's heart skipped a beat. Art wanted to buy her? Could he? Oh, please, Lord, that it be so, she prayed quickly.

Eby took in a deep breath, then let it out in a long sigh. "Well, now, I don't know nothin' 'bout that. She's made me a lot of money. I don't know if I could sell her or not."

"You bought her, didn't you?"

"Yes, I bought her."

"Then you can sell her. How much?"

"One thousand dollars," Eby said without blinking an eye.

"One thousand dollars?" Art gasped.

Eby chuckled. "Well, if you can't afford her, maybe you'd better just take five dollars' worth."

"No," Art said. "I reckon not."

"On the other hand, you could come back next year. I 'spec she'll be a lot older and a lot uglier then. You might be able to afford her next year."

Jennie looked at Art. For just a moment there had

been a look of anticipation and joy in her face. Then, when she realized that her salvation was not to be, the joy had left.

"I'm sorry, Jennie," he said.

"I am too," Jennie replied. She fought hard to hold back the tears.

"Shooters, to your marks!" someone called.

Looking away from Jennie, Art picked up his rifle and walked over to the line behind which the shooters were told to stand. Jennie went over as well.

Jennie stood in the crowd with those who weren't in the shooting contest to watch. There were a few favorites, men who had participated in previous shooting contests, and the onlookers began placing bets on them.

The first three rounds eliminated all but the more serious of the shooters. Now there were only ten participants left, and many were surprised to see the new young man still there. Even Jennie was pleasantly surprised to see that Art was still in contention, and privately she began pulling for him, hoping and praying that he would do well.

"All right, boys, from now on it gets serious," the organizer said. "I'm putting a row of bottles on that cart there, then moving it down another one hundred yards. The bottles will be your target, but you got to call the one you're a-shootin' at before you make your shot."

As Jennie looked up and down the line of competitors remaining, she saw that one of them was her master, Bruce Eby. Eby had the first shot. "Third from the right," he said. He aimed, fired, and the third bottle from the right exploded in a shower of glass.

This round of shooting eliminated four competitors; the following round eliminated two, and the round after that eliminated two more. Now only Art and Eby remained. A series of shots left them tied.

"Move the targets back another one hundred yards,"

the organizer ordered, and two men repositioned the cart.

By now all other activity in Rendezvous had come to a complete halt. Everyone had come to see the shooting demonstration. Only two bottles were put up, and Eby had the first shot.

"The one on the left," Eby said quietly. He lifted the rifle to his shoulder, aimed, and fired. The bottle was cut in two by the bullet, the neck of it collapsing onto the rubble.

"All right, boy, it's your turn," the organizer said.

Art raised his rifle and aimed.

"Boy, before you shoot, how 'bout a little bet?" Eby said.

Art lowered his rifle. "What sort of bet?"

"I'll bet you five hundred dollars you miss."

Jennie saw Art contemplating the offer. She didn't know if he had that much money or not. And if he did, she didn't know if he was confident enough in his shooting to take Eby up on his offer.

"Ahh, go ahead and shoot," Eby said. "I'll be content with just beating you."

"I'll take the bet," Art said.

"Let's see the color of your money."

Art took the money from his pocket, then held it until Eby also took out a sum of money. Both men handed their money over to the organizer, who counted and verified that both had put in the requisite amount.

"It's all here," the organizer said.

"All right, boy, it's all up to you now," Eby said.

Once again, Art raised his rifle and took aim. He took a breath, let half of it out . . .

"Don't get nervous now," Eby said, purposely trying to make him nervous.

"No fair, Eby. Let the boy shoot without your blathering," someone said.

Art let the breath out, lowered his rifle, looked over at

Eby, then raised the rifle and aimed again. There was a moment of silence; then Art squeezed the trigger. There was a flash in the pan, a puff of smoke from the end of the rifle, and a loud boom. The bottle that was his target shattered. Like the other bottle, the neck remained, though only about half as much of this neck remained as had been left behind from the first bottle.

"Yes!" Jennie shouted in pleased excitement. Quickly, she covered her mouth before Eby looked toward her. He wouldn't go easy on her if he knew she had been cheering for his opponent. Fortunately, the applause and cheers of the crowd covered up Jennie's response.

The organizer handed the money over to Art. "Looks like you won your bet," he said, "but the outcome of the shooting match is still undecided. Gentlemen, shall we go on? Or shall we declare it a tie?"

"We go on," Eby said angrily. "Put two more bottles up."

"Wait," Art said.

Eby smiled. "Givin' up, are you?"

"No," Art said. He pointed toward the cart. "We didn't finish them off. The necks of both bottles are still standing. I say we use them as our targets."

"Are you crazy?" Eby asked. "You can barely see them from here. How are we going to shoot at them?"

"I don't know about you, but I plan to use my rifle," Art said.

The others laughed, and their laughter further incensed Eby.

"What about it, Eby?" the organizer asked. "Shall we go on?"

Once more, Eby looked toward the cart. Then he saw that the neck from his bottle was considerably higher than the neck from Art's bottle. He nodded. "All right," he said. He raised his rifle, paused, then lowered it. "Only this time he goes first."

Art nodded, and raised his own rifle. "The one on the right," he said.

"No!" Eby shouted quickly. "You have to finish off the target you started. You have to shoot at the one on the left."

"I thought we could call our own targets," Art replied.

"You can. And you already did. Like you said, we didn't finish them off. You called the bottle on the left, that's the one you've got to finish."

"I think Eby's right," one of the spectators said.

"All right," the organizer agreed. "Your target is what remains of the bottle on the left."

"A hunnert dollars he don't do it," someone said.

"Who you goin' to get to take that bet?" another asked. "Ain't no way he can do it."

"What about you, mister?" Eby asked. "You want to bet whether or not you hit it?"

"No, I'll keep my money," Art said.

"Tell you what. You wanted the girl a while ago. I'll bet her against a thousand dollars you don't hit it."

Jennie felt a sudden flash of hope, followed by a feeling of guilt. If Art could hit the target and win her, she would be free of Bruce Eby. On the other hand, if he missed—and this target was very small—then he would lose the one thousand dollars, which was, in all likelihood, every cent he had. Part of her begged him to accept the wager, and yet she prayed that he would not.

Art looked over at Jennie and she saw that he was going to take the bet. She took a deep breath and held it. Could he hit the target? It was mighty small, and it was a long way off.

"What do you say, mister?" Eby taunted. "Is it a bet, or isn't it?"

"I don't want the girl to come to me."

Jennie felt a sudden draining of all the blood from her face. She had allowed herself to think that he might win her from Eby; now that hope was dashed.

"You don't want the girl? Then what do you want?" Eby asked.

"If I win, I want you to set Jennie free."

Jennie gasped, and her knees went weak. Could this be? Could it really be that for the first time in her entire life, she would be free?

"All right, boy, you hit that sawed-off piece of a bottle neck on the left there, and I'll set her free," Eby promised.

Art nodded. "You've got a bet."

Everyone expected to wait for a long moment while Art aimed, but to their surprise he lifted the rifle, aimed, and fired in one smooth, continuous motion. The bottle neck shattered. The reaction from the crowd was spontaneous.

"Did you see that?"

"Hurrah for the boy!"

"Who woulda thought . . ."

Jennie saw Eby raising his rifle, aiming it at Art. "Art! Look out!" she screamed.

Almost on top of Jennie's shouted warning, there was a loud bang, followed by a cloud of smoke. When the smoke rolled away, Eby was lying on his back with a large bullet wound in his chest. Turning quickly, Jennie saw another mountain man standing there with a smoking rifle. He had shot Eby.

"Clyde Barnes! Where did you come from?" Art asked.

"I decided to come on in early as well," Clyde said as he held his still-smoking rifle. "I couldn't let you have all the fun."

"Ever'one seen it," the organizer of the shooting match said. "Eby was about to shoot the boy when this fella shot him. We ain't got no judge nor law out here, but I say it was justifiable homicide."

"Hear, hear!" another shouted.

"Anyone say any different?"

There were no dissenters.

"Then let's get this piece of trash buried and get on with the Rendezvous. Oh, by the way," the organizer said, looking over toward Jennie. "I reckon we also heard the bet. Girl, you're free."

"Wait, you can't do it like that," someone else shouted.

Once again, Jennie felt a sinking sensation in her stomach. Was this all to be a cruel hoax? Was she destined to remain a slave? But if so, who would be her master? Eby was dead.

"What do you mean you don't do it like this?"

"Someone is going to have to draw up a letter of manumission."

"Manumission? What is that?"

"It's a letter that says this here girl has been given her freedom."

"Who signs the letter?"

"We all heard Eby wager the girl to this young fella. That means she belongs to him, until he gives her freedom. I reckon he'll have to sign it. Can you write your name, mister?"

"Yes," Art said. "I can write my name."

The man stuck out his hand. "The name is P. Edward Kane. I've done some lawyerin'. I can fix up the letter for you for two dollars."

Art took two dollars from his pocket and handed it to the man. "Here's my two dollars," he said.

"It'll need two witnesses," Kane said.

"I'll be one of the witnesses," the man who had shot Eby said. "The name is Clyde Barnes."

"And I'll be the other," another trapper said. "The name is Pierre Garneau."

The House of Flowers, St. Louis, Tuesday, June 22, 1824

Jennie held the precious paper in her hand. Showing this to Constable Billings would validate her claim to be a free woman. She held the paper to her breast and thanked the Lord for her freedom. Then, opening the paper up, she studied the three signatures: Clyde Barnes, Pierre Garneau, and the most important one of all, Art. Only Art. Even in this document, he had used the only name she knew him by. She thanked the Lord for Art too, for the man who had made her freedom, her new life possible.

The man she knew, she thought. She smiled. She knew him, all right; she knew him that night in what is sometimes referred to as the biblical sense. For that night, she had made a man of the boy, and he had made a woman of her, touching her soul for the first and only time in her entire life.

4

It was just after midnight, about six weeks since Art
had begun his trek from Rendezvous, and the campfire
was now little more than a scattering of orange-glowing
coals. Both Art and Dog were sleeping nearby. Art had
made his encampment in a meadow at the river's edge,
about one hundred yards from the edge of a thick forest.
A full moon illuminated the scene in shades of silver and
black.

The night had come alive with the sounds of nature:
the whispering river, wind sighing through the trees, and
night creatures from frogs to cicadas. Two men emerged
from the trees, interrupting this peaceful scene.

"There it is, Cally! I see the boat!"

"Well, why don't you just shout it out, Angus?" Cally
replied.

"I see the boat," Angus said again, much quieter this
time.

"I see it too."

"What you think he's got on that boat?"

"I seen 'im from the ridge just afore he landed. Don't

know for sure what he's a-carryin', but my guess would be beaver pelts."

"Beaver pelts?" Angus said. "When you ask me to come along with you, I thought maybe we was goin' to rob a trader, carryin' whiskey and the like. What do we want with beaver pelts?"

"Beaver pelts is the same as gold back in St. Louis."

"How we goin' to get 'em to St. Louis?"

"Same way he was doin' it. We're not only goin' to take his pelts, we're goin' to take his boat. Get your gun out, make sure it's loaded."

"It's loaded, all right," Angus said as he pulled his pistol from his belt.

Dog growled quietly, then sat up, fully alert. The sudden movement awakened Art. Opening his eyes, he saw two men moving awkwardly across the open field, clearly illuminated in the moonlight. Dog growled again, standing with his back arched menacingly.

"I see them, Dog," Art said. Slowly he reached for his rifle and pulled it toward him, cocking it at the same time.

Dog stood up, but as yet made no move toward the men.

"Wait," Art said under his breath. Without moving, Art lay as if he were asleep, all the while watching the two men approach. When they got within twenty yards, Art suddenly sat up. "Now!" he said.

Dog leaped forward as if he were on springs. Within ten feet of the two men, he hunkered down on his hind legs, ready to pounce again. He growled, baring his fangs.

"You two boys better hold it right there," Art said. He did not have to shout, but spoke as if he were chatting with them in a parlor. "If you move again, Dog will rip open your throats."

"He—he can't get both of us," Cally said.

"What makes you think he can't? How long do you think it would take for him to rip out your windpipe?"

Still growling, Dog inched even closer. He had their scents now, something his wolf-brain would never forget. They were as good as dead if he felt they posed a deadly danger to Art.

"No!" Angus said. "Call off your dog, mister. Call him off!"

"Put your guns down on the ground," Art ordered calmly. By now he was on his feet, walking forward, pointing his rifle at them.

"Suppose we just put our guns back in our belts and walk away," Cally said.

"Put them on the ground," Art repeated. "Only, do it real slow. You don't want to upset Dog now, do you?"

"No, no, we don't want to upset him," Cally said. "Do what he says, Angus."

Holding their guns, they started to bend down.

"Turn the guns around," Art said. "Hold them by the ends of the barrels."

"Mister, these things is loaded and charged," Cally said. "We'd be fools to hold them by the ends of the barrels."

"You'll be dead if you don't," Art said, moving his rifle menacingly to cover Cally.

"All right, all right," Cally said. First Cally, and then Angus, turned their pistols around so they were holding them by the ends of the barrels. Then, bending over, they put their guns down, all under the watchful eyes of Dog and Art.

"It's after midnight. Seems to me that's a little late to be making a sociable visit on a man's camp. So, what are you boys doing here?" Art asked.

"Nothing," Cally replied. "We just seen the boat tied up and was sort of wonderin' who you was and what you was doin' here."

"Who I am is none of your business," Art said. "And as to what I'm doing here, I was trying to get a little rest."

"What are you carryin' on that boat of your'n?"

"That's none of your business either," Art said. He made a waving motion with his rifle. "I expect you two boys better get on now."

"What about our guns?"

"Leave 'em."

"Them guns cost money, mister. We can't just leave 'em here."

"Come back for them in the mornin'. I'll leave 'em in the river."

"By the river?"

"In the river."

"They'll get all rusted."

"Clean them. Now, get." Art made another wave with his rifle, and the two men, with one final look at Dog, turned and started walking quickly back across the meadow. By the time they reached the tree line, they were both running.

Art laughed, then rubbed Dog behind the ears. "Well, now, Dog," he said. "You're turnin' into a pretty good partner to a man."

Blackfoot Village, Upper Missouri River,
Monday, July 5, 1824

Because Wak Tha Go had a sister who was married to a Blackfoot Indian, he was welcomed in the village of the Blackfeet. This was good, because he was no longer welcome in the village of the Arikara. Four young men who had followed him when he led the war party on an adventure had been killed. The wives and mothers, the sisters and brothers of those who were killed were angry with Wak Tha Go.

In this way Wak Tha Go was eating dinner in the lodge of his sister when her husband, Yellow Dog, came to him.

"Crazy Wolf is holding a council now, and he wants you to come," Yellow Dog said.

"I will come," Wak Tha Go said. He finished the last of the piece of meat he was eating. Wiping his fingers on his chest, he followed the husband of his sister through the village and to the circle where the council was meeting.

They were seated around the fire. Wak Tha Go sat in the outer ring of the circle. If he sat in the inner circle, and had been asked to move back, it would have brought him dishonor. By sitting in the outer circle, it would bring him honor to be invited to move closer to the fire, which he fully expected to happen.

"Wak Tha Go," Crazy Wolf said. "Come, sit in the inner circle with the elders of this band."

There were a few grunts of recognition and respect as Wak Tha Go, his presence now honored by Crazy Wolf's invitation, moved to the inner circle.

"I will tell a story," Crazy Wolf said simply once Wak Tha Go was seated.

"During the geese-flying time, white soldiers made war on the Arikara people. They came in the night, while the people slept, and they killed many and set fire to the tepees and burned food and blankets. They also stole many horses, but Wak Tha Go, who is a brave warrior, did not forget what the white soldiers did, and he made war against them. But now the Arikara want war no more, and The Peacemaker has said that he will make peace with the white soldiers. But Wak Tha Go will not make peace with the white soldiers, so he has come to us, the Blackfoot people. So I say, from this day until there are no more days, Wak Tha Go will be a Blackfoot."

Crazy Wolf pointed to Wak Tha Go as he spoke, and the others smiled and congratulated him for making war against the white soldiers, and for coming to join them.

"Wak Tha Go, will you speak now?" Crazy Wolf said.

Nodding, Wak Tha Go stood, then turned to face the other Indians.

"I have heard that the Blackfeet turn away the white trappers who come to your land to hunt the beaver.

"I have heard that the warriors of the Blackfeet have fought bravely and well against the trappers while other villages and nations surrender to the white trappers.

"I have heard that there is no warrior more fierce than a warrior of the Blackfeet."

"Ai, yi, yi, yieee!!!" the others cheered.

"What would you have of us, Wak Tha Go?" Crazy Wolf asked. "You have abandoned your people because the Arikara want to make peace with the whites? Have you come to bring the word of peace from your people?"

"No," Wak Tha Go answered resolutely. "I have come to the Blackfeet because only the Blackfeet will make war. The Arikara are no longer my people. They are more rabbits than people. I belong to the Piegan Blackfeet."

"Show us that you are deserving," Crazy Wolf said. "Become a leader of our warriors."

"I will," Wak Tha Go answered, and his response was greeted by more cheering.

The council was not yet over, but Wak Tha Go left. He knew that it was better to leave while they wanted him to stay than it was to stay when they wanted him to go.

He would lead a war party of Blackfeet warriors, and he would count many coups and he would steal many things. But what he wanted to do more than anything else was to kill Artoor, the white man he had seen on the boat. Wak Tha Go had learned Artoor's name from Tetonka, the Mandan who had traded with him.

* * *

St. Louis, Wednesday, July 21, 1824

He put in at LaClede's Landing in St. Louis after two months on the river. Even from the river, he could see that the city had changed a lot since he was last here many years before. Missouri was a state in the Union of States now, and St. Louis had grown from a frontier town to a bustling, prosperous city of nearly ten thousand people. That was a lot of people—too many people for someone like Art who had grown accustomed to life in the wilderness and going for days or weeks without seeing another human soul.

A friendly hand ashore took the rope Art tossed to him, and made the boat secure.

"You'll be wantin' to sell them furs, I reckon," the man said.

"You buying?" Art asked.

"No, Mr. Ashley does the buying. I just work for him."

"That would be William Ashley?"

"Yes, sir. You know him, I expect."

"I know of him. If he's the one buying, I'm selling."

"Very good, sir. If you'll permit me, I'll get the plews loaded and down to Ashley's office."

"I'd appreciate that," Art said, surprised to find someone so helpful upon his arrival. He hoped for his sake that the man was honest as well.

Fifteen minutes later the pelts were loaded onto an oxcart and hauled down to Ashley's office. Art sat with his fur bundles, his legs dangling over the back as the cart rolled up Market Street. Dog followed along behind the cart, seeming not to mind the people and the traffic everywhere. Of course, the people gave Dog a wide berth.

St. Louis was a vibrant city, alive with the pulse of commerce and enterprise: the scream of a steam-powered sawmill, the sound of steamboat whistles from the river, the hiss and boom of the boats' engines, and the clatter of wagons rolling across cobblestone streets. To someone used to solitude so quiet that he could hear the flutter of a bird's wings, the noise of civilization was almost unbearable.

The cart stopped in front of a two-story building. A neatly painted sign out front read: FURS BOUGHT AND SOLD, WILLIAM ASHLEY, PROP.

Even before Art dismounted, a dignified-looking man, wearing mustard-colored trousers and a blue jacket, came out of the building and began looking Art's load over. The man's whiskers were neatly trimmed, his hands clean, his eyes bright and direct.

"You've got some good-looking plews here," he said.

"Would you be Ashley?" Art asked.

"Indeed that is who I am, sir. William Ashley, at your service." He bowed slightly, politely, but not in servility.

"Then you're the man Clyde told me to look up."

"Clyde?"

"Clyde Barnes."

"Ah, yes," Ashley said, smiling. "I know of Mr. Barnes. How is he?"

"He's dead. Killed by Indians on our way downriver."

"I'm sincerely sorry to hear that. Blackfeet?"

"Arikara."

"I see. Well, the Blackfeet have always been hostile to our fur-trading enterprise, but the problem with the Arikara is more recent."

"Is it true that a couple of your men traded bad whiskey to the Arikara for pelts?"

"Word does get around, doesn't it?" Ashley said. "Yes, unfortunately it is true. The men were working for me. But the idea of trading whiskey for plews was their own. I don't do business that way, never have, and never will. Believe me, Mr. McDill and Mr. Caviness were severely reprimanded."

"Reprimanded? What does that mean?"

"It means I gave them a good scolding."

"People have gotten killed over that, and more people are likely to get killed, and all you did was give them a scolding?"

"I have no authority to do anything more to them," Ashley said. "I'm not the law."

"I reckon not."

"What's your name, sir?" Ashley asked.

"Art," the young trapper said simply.

"Art? Art what?"

"Just Art."

"Well, I reckon if Art is enough for you, it's enough for me," Ashley said.

Since leaving home at an early age, Art had made a point of never using his last name. This way, he figured, he would never do anything that would bring dishonor to his family back in Ohio. He needn't have worried about such a thing, for so far in his young life, he had been the epitome of honorable conduct. It was the way of the man that the onetime runaway boy had become.

"That your animal?" Mr. Ashley asked, pointing to Dog, who stood at alert between the cart and Art.

"Not mine, but we have traveled a piece together."

"Tell you what, Art. Give me a day to get your plews counted and graded. Come on back tomorrow morning and I'll have your money."

"All right," Art agreed. He started to leave, then caught himself and turned back. "Do you suppose I could have twenty dollars now?" he asked.

Ashley chuckled knowingly. He had dealt with mountain men for a long time. "Want to take advantage of the big city, do you? Yes, of course you can. You can have much more than that, if you need it."

"Twenty is enough."

"Come on inside."

Art followed Ashley into his storehouse. As the door opened, a little bell attached to the top of the door rang. Surprised, Art looked up at it.

Ashley chuckled. "If I'm in the back, that little bell lets me know when someone comes in," he explained.

The back of the store that Ashley mentioned was his counting and grading room. A counter separated the front of the store from the back, and through a door that led into the back, Art could see several long tables around which men were working.

Ashley went around behind the counter, took twenty dollars from a strongbox, then opened a ledger book and wrote Art's name in it. Beside Art's name he wrote, "Twenty dollars on advance." He turned the book around and handed the quill pen to Art. "Make your mark here," he said.

"I can read and write," Art said.

"A mountain man who can read and write? I'm impressed."

"Mr. Ashley, do you know a man by the name of Seamus O'Connor?"

"Seamus O'Connor? It doesn't ring a bell with me."

"He owned a place called the Irish Tavern. I used to have friends who spent time there: a man named Tony, another named James O'Leary."

"Ah, yes, I remember them. O'Leary was a big strapping fellow. And the other—Tony, you say? They worked for Ed Gordon down at the wagon-freight yard."

"Yes!" Art said, smiling broadly. "That's them. Do you know where I can find them?"

Ashley shook his head sadly. "They're dead, son. Both of them."

"What? How?"

"They were unloading a riverboat when the boiler exploded. Killed Gordon and six of his men, including your two friends Tony and James."

"Oh."

"Sorry to have to be the one to tell you."

"That's all right," Art said. "Those things happen." He held up the silver coins. "Thanks for the advance."

With Dog alongside, Art left the store and walked on up Market Street, looking for the Irish Tavern. It was no more. In its place was something called the Joseph LaBarge Tavern. Art was standing in front of it, looking it over, when he heard a woman's voice call out from just inside the building.

"No, please, don't! It was an accident!"

"You bitch! I'll teach you to be clumsy around me!" a harsh voice said. The voice was followed by a smacking sound and as Art looked up, he saw a young woman propelled backward through the open front door. She fell on the porch, and a large, gross-looking man stomped out of the saloon behind her.

"Please," the young woman begged. "I didn't mean to spill the beer on you." She tried to get up, but as she did so, the big ugly man hit her again, knocking her back down onto the porch. She rolled over onto her hands and knees and tried to escape him that way, but he followed after her and kicked her. She cried out in pain.

Art stepped up onto the porch behind the man.

"I'll learn you to spill beer on me, you worthless whore. I'll kick your ass clear into Illinois," the man growled at the young woman, who was still cowering on the wooden planks of the porch.

"Sir?" Art said from just behind the man.

"What do you . . ." the man started to ask, but he was unable to finish his question because as soon as he turned toward Art, the young mountain man brought the butt of his rifle up in a smashing blow to the man's face. The blow knocked out two of the man's teeth, broke his nose, and sent a stream of blood gushing down across his mouth and into his beard. If he hadn't been ugly before, he certainly was now. His eyes rolled up into his head, and he dropped heavily to the porch.

The young woman, now on her knees, looked on in shock and fear as Art reached his hand for her.

"Ma'am, may I help you up?" he asked.

The woman made no effort to take his hand.

"Don't be afraid. No one's going to hurt you any-more," Art said. His hand was still extended toward her.

Hesitantly, the woman took his hand, and Art pulled her to her feet.

"I—I didn't mean to spill the beer," she said. "But he grabbed me as I walked by. I was startled. I couldn't help it. I tried to explain and apologize, but he wouldn't listen."

"Ma'am, you don't owe an explanation or an apology to anyone," Art said reassuringly. "Least of all to a pig like him. Why don't you come back inside and sit down until you feel better."

"Thank you," the young woman said.

Art led her back toward the front door of the saloon, which was still open, and now crowded with many patrons who, drawn by the commotion out front, had come to the door to see what was going on. They made way for Art, the woman, and Dog.

"Hey!" the man behind the bar called. "You can't bring your dog in here."

"He's not my dog, and I'm not bringing him anywhere, he's just with me."

"Get him out of here."

"You get him out," Art said.

"You two, get him out," the man behind the bar said, pointing to a couple of the patrons. The two men started toward Dog, but he bared his wolflike fangs at them and growled. They stopped in their tracks.

"Get him yourself, LaBarge," one of them said.

LaBarge came out from behind the bar, looked at Dog, then shrugged. "He can stay if he don't cause no trouble," he said.

The others laughed.

Art walked all the way to the rear of the saloon, then chose a chair that put his back to the wall and gave him a good view of the entire room. Dog trotted along with him, then curled up alongside. Art was sitting next to an iron stove. The stove was cold and empty now, but still smelled of smoke and charcoal from its winter use. Once again, the proprietor, LaBarge, came out from behind the bar.

"Carla, I expect you'd better get back to work now," LaBarge said.

"Yes, Mr. LaBarge."

"Give her a chance to catch her breath," Art said.

"You paying her wages, mister?" LaBarge asked.

"No."

"I am. So she'll do what I say. Get back to work, Carla. And be more careful 'bout spilling beer on the customers."

"Yes, sir," Carla said. Looking at Art, she smiled. "What can I get you?"

"A beer."

"It's on the house," LaBarge said.

"Thanks."

"I reckon you done what you thought was right, hittin' Shardeen like that. But it's goin' to get you kilt. Shardeen ain't a man you want to mess with."

A moment later Carla brought Art his beer and, smiling shyly, set it in front of him. From the folds of her dress, she removed a couple of boiled eggs, wet from the brine in which they were stored. "These here two hen's eggs is from me," she said.

"Thank you, Carla," Art said, smiling up at her.

Carla walked away, and had just returned to the bar when the front door burst open and the man Art had encountered, the one LaBarge had called Shardeen, rushed inside. He was carrying two charged pistols, one in either hand.

"Where is that son of a bitch!" he yelled angrily. His nose was flattened almost beyond recognition, his eyes were black and shiny, and his beard was matted with blood.

When Shardeen entered, everyone else in the saloon scattered, moving so quickly that chairs tumbled over and tables were pushed out of the way. Art's rifle was leaning against the wall behind him. It was loaded, but not primed, so even if he could get to it, it wouldn't do him any good at this moment.

Seeing Art in the back of the saloon, Shardeen let out a loud bellow and shot at him. There was a flash of fire and a puff of smoke. The bullet crashed into the smoke-stack of the stove, sending out a puff of soot. With a shout of frustrated anger over his miss, Shardeen raised his other pistol and fired it as well. This one slammed into the wall behind Art. Art had not moved a muscle since the big man had entered the tavern.

Dog jumped up and growled at Shardeen.

"No, Dog," Art said quietly. "I'd better handle this myself."

With both pistols empty, Shardeen pulled his knife and, with an angry roar, rushed across the room toward Art. Now Art moved. He pulled his own knife and waited for him. At the last moment, Art danced to one side, rather like a bullfighter avoiding a charge, and like a bullfighter, thrust toward Shardeen. His knife went in smoothly, just under Shardeen's rib cage. With a grunt, Shardeen stopped, then staggered and fell. Art twisted his knife so that, as Shardeen went down, the brute's own weight caused the blade to open him up, spilling blood and steaming intestines. Art pulled the knife out. Shardeen fell face down on the floor, flopped a couple of times like a fish out of water, and then was still.

"Is he dead?" Carla asked. She had fled, in terror, to the back corner of the room, but peeked out.

"I reckon he is," Art said, pouring beer on his hand to rinse away the blood.

"Get him out of here," LaBarge said.

"Hold it!" a voice called from the front. The order came from a member of the St. Louis Constabulary, the militia group that Mayor Lane depended upon to maintain order in the city. "You people just leave him right where he is until I find out what happened here."

"Shardeen got hisself kilt, that's what happened," LaBarge said. "And if truth be told, there ain't nobody in St. Louis likely to shed a tear over the sonofabitch."

"I agree that if anybody in this town needed killin' it was Shardeen," the constable said. "But just bein' downright mean don't give someone the right to kill him. Who did it?"

"I did," Art said.

"And who might you be?"

"Art."

"Art? Art what?"

"Art's enough."

"No it ain't enough, mister. Not when murder's concerned."

"Oh hell, John," LaBarge said to the constable. "Art didn't murder Shardeen. He killed him in self-defense. Ever'one in here will testify to that."

"That's right, Constable," one of the customers said. "Shardeen come in here a-blazin' away at this young fella."

"Who are you?"

"The name is Matthews. Joe Matthews."

"You're saying Shardeen shot first?"

"He didn't shoot first," Matthews started, but he was interrupted by the constable.

"Well if Shardeen didn't shoot first, how can it be self-defense?"

"You didn't let me finish. He didn't shoot first. He was the only one who shot."

"That's right," LaBarge said. "And if you'll take a look over there, you'll see where them two bullets went. One into the wall and the other one into my stovepipe.

Which, incidentally, I'm going to have to replace before next winter, so if ol' Shardeen has any money in his pocket, by rights it should come to me."

"How'd you kill him if you didn't shoot him?"

"With a knife," Art replied.

"After Shardeen come at him with a knife," Matthews added quickly.

"All right, maybe you'd better come with me," the constable said. As the constable started toward Art, LaBarge put his hand out to stop him.

"Now, hold on there, John. I done told you it was self-defense, and there ain't a man present but won't back me up. You got no call to be takin' him in."

"Hear, hear!" some of the others shouted.

"I got Mayor Lane to worry about," the constable said. "I've got to answer to him."

"All you got to do is tell him that you investigated it and found it to be self-defense, pure and simple," LaBarge said. "Besides which, the mayor is so tied up with this here General Lafayette fella comin' to town, that he don't want to be bothered with somethin' like this, and you damn well know it."

The constable stroked his jaw for a moment as he considered LaBarge's words. Everyone in the saloon stared at him, waiting for his answer. Finally, he nodded in resignation.

"I reckon you're right," he said. "A jury is sure to find him innocent, so why go to the bother? Ain't goin' to be no charge here."

Every patron in the saloon erupted in a loud cheer.

"Now," LaBarge said, pointing to Shardeen's body. "Someone get this trash out of here."

5

After leaving LaBarge's Tavern, Art passed by Chardonnay's, a restaurant that advertised itself as "St. Louis's finest dining establishment." It had been a long time since he had eaten a meal he didn't cook himself, and even longer than that since he had eaten in a restaurant, let alone a fancy "establishment" like this one. Opening the door just a crack, he took a sniff. Whatever they were cooking smelled awfully good to him.

"Dog, I expect you'd better not go in here with me," he said. This place was very different than LaBarge's, for sure.

Dog looked up at him as if challenging him.

"Don't look at me like that. This just isn't a place for dogs, that's all. Why don't you just wait for me over there, and I'll bring you something to eat."

Shaking himself in a way that caused his loose skin to make a flapping sound, Dog walked over to the corner of the porch, made a few quick turns, then settled down. His eyes were closed even before Art went inside.

A well-dressed, dignified-looking man came to his table. "May I take your order, sir?" he asked in an affected, cultured voice.

"What's good?" Art asked as he looked at the menu.

"Sir, I assure you everything on our menu is without parallel."

"That means it's good?" Art asked.

"Indeed it does, sir."

"All right then, I'll have pork chops, fried potatoes, and a half-dozen hen's eggs."

The waiter looked chagrined. "I beg your pardon, sir. Did you say pork chops, fried potatoes, and eggs?" he asked.

"Yes."

"Excuse my asking, sir, but why would you come here to order such pedestrian fare? We have rack of lamb, pork tenderloin, coq au vin, and many other viands not served by any other restaurant in the city. You can get what you just ordered at any cheap hotel in town."

"You do have pork chops, potatoes, and eggs, don't you? Hen's eggs now, not those nasty things from a guinea."

"Yes, of course we have those things, but . . ."

"And biscuits?"

"Our bread is baked fresh daily."

"Biscuits?" Art repeated.

"Yes, sir. We can prepare biscuits."

"Good. I'll have biscuits. And pie. Do you have any pie?"

"Apple and pecan."

"All right."

"All right?" the waiter asked, confused by his answer.

"All right, I'll have apple and pecan."

"Sir, you do understand, do you not, that by apple and pecan, I'm referring to two separate pies. I don't mean something like apple-pecan pie."

"Yes, I want one of each."

"Very good, sir."

"I'll have beer with my dinner, and coffee with my pie," Art concluded.

"Yes, sir," the waiter said. "I must say, sir, your appetite is quite prodigious."

"That's all right. I don't reckon it's catchin'," Art said. He wasn't sure whether he was having fun, but he knew that the waiter wasn't.

"Indeed, sir," the waiter replied without a smile.

Art watched the waiter until he disappeared into the kitchen. Out of the corner of his eye, he saw someone standing just inside the front door, looking at him. It was a woman.

"Art?" the woman said.

At first, Art couldn't see her features clearly, because she was standing in silhouette. He put his hand up to shield his eyes. Realizing that she wasn't clearly visible, the woman moved out of the bright light.

"Do you recognize me now?" she asked. The woman was quite pretty, with dark, almost black hair, brown eyes, and a clear, olive complexion.

"Jennie?" Art said, recognizing someone from his past. "Jennie, is that you?"

With a happy little laugh, Jennie hurried to him. Art stood and they embraced.

"Yes, it's me. I thought I would never see you again," Jennie said.

"Sit down, sit down," Art told her. "Have dinner with me."

"Oh, I don't know," Jennie demurred. "I've never been in here before. This is a pretty fancy place. I'm not sure I would be welcome."

"You're welcome anywhere I'm welcome," Art said.

Hesitantly, and looking around as if expecting to be tossed out at any moment, Jennie sat at the table with Art.

"When Carla described the person who came to her rescue, I thought of you. Then when she said that the only name you gave the deputy was Art, I knew it was you. So I checked with Mr. Ashley, and he said he saw you come into Chardonnay's. I just had to come in here to see for myself."

"I'm glad you did," Art said. "I'm really happy to see you, Jennie. How are you doing? What are you doing in St. Louie?"

"I own my own whorehouse," Jennie said proudly and without irony. "Carla, the girl you helped, is one of my boarders."

"I thought she worked for LaBarge."

"She does. She just works for me part-time—but not as a, well . . . you know what I mean, I think. What are *you* doing in St. Louis?"

"I brought in my winter's trapping," Art said. "I could have sold it at Rendezvous, but I decided to bring the plews in myself this time."

"Rendezvous," Jennie said. "Oh, I remember those. They were always exciting, and could have been fun if I hadn't been hauled around as Eby's slave."

At that moment the officious waiter came out of the kitchen carrying Art's order on a tray. Seeing Jennie, he stopped. "What are you doing here?" he asked.

"She is with me," Art said. "She would like to order. I've invited her to eat with me."

"No," the waiter said. "Absolutely not. I do not allow her kind in here."

"*You* do not allow?" Art asked. "I thought you were just the waiter. What does the owner say?"

The waiter smiled. "The owner is my father-in-law. He would say exactly what I am saying. Prostitutes are not allowed in here."

Jennie reached her hand across the table and put it on Art's hand.

"It's all right, Art," Jennie said. "I told you that I wouldn't be welcome. I'll leave now. I don't want to make any trouble."

"Oh, there's no trouble," Art said easily. He stood. "I'll leave with you."

"But sir, you aren't being asked to leave," the waiter said.

"As far as I'm concerned, I was," Art said. "I told you the lady was my friend."

"But what about your food?" the waiter said.

"You eat it."

The waiter looked at the pork chops, fried potatoes, and half-dozen eggs.

"Oh, sir, I couldn't possibly eat . . . this," he said, screwing his mouth up distastefully.

"Then feed it to the pigs," Art said. "Come, Jennie." He started toward the front door with her.

"But you haven't paid for your meal," the waiter called to him.

"What meal? You don't expect me to pay for a meal I haven't eaten, do you?" Art called back.

Jennie laughed. "Why don't you come with me?" she asked. "I'll fix you the best meal you've ever eaten."

"Miss Jennie, I'll just take you up on that," Art said.

As they stepped out the front door of the restaurant, Dog stood up and started toward them.

"Oh!" Jennie said, recoiling back against Art.

Art chuckled. "Relax, he won't hurt you."

"What is that? A wolf?"

"No, Dog is a dog."

"Dog is a dog?"

"Yes. His name is Dog."

"Why would you name him something like that?"

"That's the name he picked out for himself," Art said without further explanation.

"Well, I certainly don't understand men—or dogs, in this case," she said with a slight laugh.

Art finally got his pork chops, fried potatoes, eggs, biscuits, and gravy, and he was positive the meal was better here than it would ever have been at that fancy restaurant.

Jennie not only cooked his supper for him, it was obvious that she enjoyed doing it.

"It's nice having someone to cook for," Jennie said as she took a steaming apple pie from the oven.

"It's nice having someone to cook for me," Art said.

"Is it?"

"Yes, of course it is." He looked into her dark eyes and liked what he saw there. He remembered every moment he had been in her presence, everything that had happened to them together.

"Dog seems to be enjoying his meal," Jennie said. Dog was eating from a plate she had put on the floor for him. "You, me, Dog, it's almost like a family, isn't it? I mean we could . . ." Jennie stopped in mid-thought and looked at Art with a wistful smile. Her eyes were deep and pensive and Art looked directly into them. Then he turned away quickly, as if ashamed of the fact that he had gotten a momentary glimpse of her unguarded soul.

Realizing that she had gone further than she intended, she changed the subject. "Uh, do you want some more coffee?"

Art held out his cup. "Yes, I'd love some," he said. "Thank you."

Art ate ravenously, enjoying the meal as much as any he had ever eaten, appreciating it as much for Jennie's company as for the food itself. Her voice, her laugh washed over him like a rain shower. And the food was delicious.

"Oh," he said after he had put away his third piece of pie. "I have something for you."

Jennie looked surprised. "You have something for me? But how could that be? Did you know you were going to see me here?"

"No," Art said. He smiled. "Finding you here was a very happy accident."

"Then I don't understand. What do you mean you have something for me?"

"It's something that a friend of mine bought," he said.

"And his last wish was that I give it to a pretty girl. Well, you are the prettiest girl I know."

"Why, thank you, Art," Jennie said, beaming over the compliment. "But what do you mean, his last wish?"

He told Jennie about Clyde, how Clyde was one of the two men who had rescued him many years ago, and how Clyde had been coming to St. Louis with him. He told also of the Indian attack that had cost Clyde his life.

"I know who Clyde is," Jennie said, wiping away a tear. "He is the one who saved your life by shooting Bruce Eby. His name is also on my letter of manumission. He was one of the witnesses, along with Pierre Garneau."

"They were good men, both of them," Art said. He pulled the dress from his pack and showed it to her.

"Oh, Art!" Jennie said. "It is beautiful!" She reached for it. "Can I?"

"Of course. It's yours."

Jennie held it up to herself. "I don't think I've ever seen anything as beautiful," she said. She held up her finger. "Wait, I'll be back."

Jennie disappeared for a few minutes, then returned, wearing the dress. She had removed her heavy "professional" makeup. Now, in the simple and beautiful Indian dress of white doeskin, Art could see her for what she really was—the girl he remembered her to have been some dozen years before. He felt a catch in his breath.

"Jennie," he said quietly, the words almost caught in his throat. "You look like a queen."

Jennie laughed, then did a pirouette and a curtsy. "Why, thank you, kind sir," she said. "And thank you for this dress. I will treasure it, always."

Thursday, July 22, 1824

St. Louis was too noisy. It seemed to Art that there had been something going on all night long, from boat whistles, to bells, to people laughing and yelling in the saloons and dram shops. Then, shortly after sunrise, the sawmill started again, its terrible screech filling the morning air. Though he had barely managed to sleep through all the other noise, this one woke him up.

Art, bare from the waist up, stood at the second-floor window, looking out on the busy street below. Across the street, a shopkeeper was sweeping his front porch, the broom making a scratching sound against the planking. A fully packed wagon clattered by while, somewhere nearby, a carpenter was hammering vigorously.

"Good morning," Jennie said. Coming up behind him, she put her arms around him and leaned into his back. By that action, Art realized that she was naked. "Do you want some breakfast?" she asked.

"Uh, maybe later," Art said, turning toward her.

With her now-familiar happy little laugh, Jennie led him back to the bed they had shared the night before. Dog, lying curled up over in the corner, didn't even open his eyes.

"I never knew anyone who could eat as many eggs as you can," Jennie said with a laugh as she put two more onto Art's breakfast plate.

"I like hen's eggs," Art said. "And there aren't that many chickens in the mountains, so anytime I get into town, I eat as many as I can."

"It's a good thing you don't live in town. You'd keep a whole henhouse busy just laying eggs for you."

Art broke the egg, then sopped up the yellow with a biscuit.

"No chance of me ever living in town," Art said. "I couldn't stand the noise. And as for hens . . ." He just grinned.

"Most folks who live here just sort of blank it out of

their minds," Jennie said. "It gets to where you don't even hear it anymore."

"For you maybe, not for me."

"How long are you going to stay in town?"

"Only another day or two," Art replied. "I'll need to get supplies and some livestock and start back for this winter's trapping."

"So, you're going to go back into the mountains all alone?"

"Yes. That is, I'll be alone unless Dog comes with me."

"Is Dog going with you?" she asked pointedly.

Art looked over at Dog, who, having eaten his own breakfast, was lying on the floor with his chin resting on his two front paws. "I don't know, that's up to Dog."

"You say you couldn't live in the city because of the noise. I don't know how you can spend an entire winter in the mountains all by yourself. I know I certainly couldn't."

"It's nice up there," Art said. "The stars are so big and bright that you get the feeling you could reach up and pull one down. And the silence is wonderful. After the first snow, it is so quiet that you can hear the wind singing through pine boughs half a mile away."

"You can keep your silence. I prefer civilization."

"Well, I reckon that's why God didn't make everything the same color," Art said. Finishing his eggs, he stood up. "I'd better see to my supplies."

"You don't have to leave, you know," Jennie said. "You could stay here in St. Louis. Or we could go somewhere else, down to New Orleans maybe."

Art looked at Jennie for a long time before he opened his mouth. Just as he started to speak, Jennie put out her hand to stop him.

"No, don't," she said. She shook her head and bit her bottom lip.

"Don't what?"

"Don't say what you were going to say."

"How do you know what I was going to say?"

"I just know, that's all. You were going to tell me that there could never be anything between us."

Art took Jennie's hand in his.

"I wasn't going to say that, Jennie. There is something between us, and there always will be. But I can't live in the city, and you wouldn't survive in the mountains. The Indians have a saying. A fish and a bird might fall in love, but where would they live?"

Jennie's eyes flooded, then a tear slid down each cheek. She forced a smile through the tears.

"Which one of us is the fish?" she asked. "And which is the bird?"

"You're the bird," Art said. "A beautiful bird." He raised Jennie's hand to her own cheek and caught each of the tears with the tips of her fingers. Then he moved those fingers to his lips, where he kissed them.

Jennie nodded, struggled to speak. "Art, will you come back? Will I see you again?"

"I'm sure of it," Art said.

Jennie said, "I think you will be back too. And until you do return, I will always have last night to remember you—to remember us by."

The strange small doorbell jingled as Art stepped into William Ashley's furrier establishment. Ashley came from the back of the building. He was as dapper and precise as he had been at their first meeting.

"Well, if it isn't my friend with no last name," Ashley greeted. "Come for your money, I suppose?"

"Yes, sir."

"Well, I've got it right here," Ashley said. He opened a ledger book and ran his finger down the column until he came to what he was looking for. "They were nearly all top-quality plews, by the way. Out of one hundred eighty-three, only thirty-seven were less than first-class.

That leaves one hundred forty-six at five dollars and ten cents each, coming to seven hundred forty-four dollars and sixty cents; thirty-seven at three and a half dollars each, for one hundred twenty-nine dollars and fifty cents, minus the twenty-dollar advance brings it to a grand total of eight hundred fifty-four dollars and ten cents. How do you want that, in cash, credit, or a bank draft?"

"Credit?"

"That means I'll keep it on the books for you until you leave. That way you won't be carrying so much money around."

"Oh," Art said. He stroked his jaw as he studied Ashley for a long moment.

Ashley chuckled. "Look, if you're worried about me cheating you out of the money, why don't I just give it to you now."

"Oh, I'm not worried about you cheating me," Art said. "I think I could convince you to give me what is mine."

This time Ashley's chuckle was an out-and-out laugh. "I reckon you could, Art, I reckon you could. I heard about the little fracas between you and Shardeen down at LaBarge's Tavern yesterday. Fact is, the whole town has heard of it in gruesome detail. You don't strike me as the kind of person a man would want to cross."

"I wouldn't take too kindly to it," Art agreed. "I tell you what, give me another twenty dollars. I'll collect the rest later."

Ashley counted out twenty more silver dollar coins, made another entry in the book, then handed them over to Art.

"Now don't spend that all in one place," he quipped.

"Why not?" Art replied, not understanding the joke that was tired even in those days.

Ashley laughed, shook his head, and held up his

hand. "Never mind. It's your money, you can spend it any way you want to, with my hearty congratulations."

When Art left Ashley, he saw quite a crowd gathered down by the waterfront and, wondering what it was, walked down to see.

"It's the Marquis de Lafayette," someone told him. "You know, the French hero who helped us gain our independence from England?"

"I've heard of him," Art said. "But I didn't know he was still alive."

"He's sixty-seven years old," Art's informant told him. "I read about him in the newspaper."

"What's he doing in St. Louis?"

"He's touring America. From here, he is going to go downriver to New Orleans."

Nine carriages were waiting at the riverfront to carry the Marquis de Lafayette and his party of dignitaries to the home of Major Pierre Chouteau, where Mayor William Carr Lane would present the great Revolutionary War hero and confidant of George Washington with the ceremonial keys to the city. Lafayette's boat had been spotted downriver, and a fast rider had brought the news to St. Louis. As a result of the early warning, not only the carriages of the official party were on hand, but so were a couple thousand St. Louis citizens, resulting in the crowd Art had encountered.

A preacher, wearing a long black coat and a stovepipe hat, was working the crowd. He had a hooked nose and a protruding chin so that it wasn't too hard to imagine the chin and nose actually touching each other. He was rail-thin. As he spoke, he stabbed at the air with a bony finger.

"Hell and damnation, eternal perdition waits for every one of you. This is a city of sin and debauchery, a den of iniquity! Turn your backs on temptation, order Satan to get behind you. For if you fail to do this, if you close the door to God's holy word, worms will eat your rotting body and maggots will gnaw at your innards."

The preacher delivered his sermon in a loud, singsong voice, pausing between every sentence for an audible gasp of air.

"I am the way and the life, says the Lord, and only by me will you be saved!"

The sound of an approaching boat whistle could be heard over the preacher's sermon.

"Here he comes!" someone shouted.

Everyone rushed down to the wharf, including those who had been listening to the preacher, but the preacher was undaunted. He continued his delivery with as much zeal as he had displayed when he was surrounded by a large audience.

Art joined the others who had gathered to watch the arrival of the Frenchman who had come to help the Americans during the Revolutionary War. Lafayette was old, with a shock of bright-silver hair, but he stood erect and moved with a sprightly step down the gangplank and onto the riverbank. He was met by Mayor Lane, who escorted him to the first in the line of carriages.

"Thank you, General!" someone in the crowd called, and all, including Art, began to applaud.

Lafayette waved at the crowd as his carriage departed. The team of matched white horses pranced saucily, making hollow clops on the cobblestone street.

As the crowd began to dissipate, Art decided to go check on his furs. The preacher was still going strong, renewed and invigorated by the fact that he had regained much of his audience.

6

Art spent the better part of the day just wandering around town, finding some parts of St. Louis that were familiar to him, and marveling at the tremendous growth of the city since he was last here. Mid-afternoon found him back down by the riverfront, where he saw the same preacher he had seen in the morning. The preacher was still going strong, railing loudly against all the sins of man and underscoring those sins with very vivid descriptions of them.

Art stayed to listen for a few minutes, marveling at the strength of the preacher's voice, then turned away to continue his survey of the town. That was when he heard it.

KABOOM!

The explosion was so loud that it shattered windows all over St. Louis. The shock wave rolled through the town, and Art could feel it in his stomach.

"What was that?" someone called.

"It come from Dunnigan's store. Look down there!" another said.

When Art looked in the direction pointed, he saw a huge cloud of smoke billowing up from one of the buildings. Fire was leaping from the roof.

"We better get down there. Those folks are going to need help," another shouted.

A crowd gathered quickly around Dunnigan's store, and Art went with them, watching as the building burned furiously. From up the street he heard the sound of a clanging bell and galloping horses.

"Here comes the fire engine!" someone shouted.

"Ain't nothin' left they can do," another said.

The team pulling the fire wagon came to a halt in front of the burning building. The driver and his assistant jumped down from the wagon seat and began playing out the hoses.

"You men . . . get on the pumps!" the driver shouted and a half-dozen men, three on each side, began pumping the handles to build up the pressure. Within a shorter time than Art would have imagined, a powerful stream of water gushed from the hose toward the fire. Others present grabbed buckets and began replacing the water in the tank that was pumped out by the men on the pump handles.

After several minutes of diligent application of the water, the men gained control of the fire. The flames drew down, then disappeared altogether. After several more minutes, even the large billows of smoke were gone, replaced by a few smoldering embers. The building was totally destroyed, but quick action had prevented the fire from spreading to the adjacent buildings.

In LaBarge's Tavern that evening, Art learned that, in addition to the storeowner, Danny Dunnigan, four other men had lost their lives in the explosion and fire.

"One of 'em must've been smokin' a pipe," someone said. "You'd think a fella would have better sense than to smoke a pipe while he was workin' around gunpowder."

"McDill, I done seen you smokin' around gunpowder lots of times," someone said.

At the mention of the name, Art looked up to see who McDill was. McDill, he knew, was one of the two men who had created the problem with the Arikara.

McDill was a big man with a flat nose and a scar that hooked down across his left eye, causing a deformation of the eyelid before it disappeared into a bushy, red beard.

"Well, I'll tell you this," McDill said. "I got me enough sense to know how to do it without gettin' my fool head blowed off, which is more than you can say for Thompson now, ain't it?"

"Thompson was one of the men killed?" another patron asked. "George Thompson?"

"One and the same."

"Why, Thompson was supposed to lead Ashley's trading party, wasn't he?"

"He was supposed to," McDill said. He chuckled. "But I don't reckon he'll be doin' that now."

"Who you think Ashley will get to lead the party, now that Thompson's got hisself killed?"

"Well, I reckon it'll either be me, or Ben Caviness there," McDill said. He pointed to one of the men who was sharing his table. That man was nearly as big as McDill, but dark-haired and clean-shaven. "Either one of us could do the job all right."

"Better'n all right," Caviness said, his massive arms crossed against his chest.

Ben Caviness, Art knew, was the other man who had traded whiskey to the Arikara. The damage he and McDill had done had set back relations between the Indians and the whites, possibly for good. At least it would take some sincere talking and trading to win back the trust of the tribes who had once been friendly to the white fur trappers.

"Percy McDill, there ain't no way in hell William Ashley is goin' to let either one of you lead that party," a patron said. "Ever'body knows you two is the ones that caused all the troubles with the Indians last year."

"'Twas a misunderstandin' is all," McDill said. "There wa'nt nothin' wrong with that whiskey. Only mistake we made was in givin' whiskey in the first place. Indians can't handle whiskey. I know that now."

"Yeah, you know it now, but it took a war for you to learn your lesson."

"Wasn't that much of a war," McDill said. "And in the long run, it was probably a good thing."

"How can a war be a good thing?"

"It taught the Indians better than to mess with us," McDill insisted. "They's slow learners anyhow, seein's they ain't got no proper schools and such. So they need to be teached proper."

"Yeah, well, that ain't the way I look at it, and I don't think that's the way Ashley looks at it either. You notice, he didn't send nobody out to Northwest to buy furs this year. Like I say, there's no way he's goin' to make you head of his trapping party."

"I'd like to know just who it would be then, if not me or Caviness," McDill said. "Who? Matthews? Montgomery? Hoffman?" McDill snorted what may have been a laugh. "Them three is greener than a spring sapling. Couldn't none of 'em find their way up the river and back. Me 'n Caviness is the only ones that's made the trip more'n one time."

"I'm afraid McDill may be right," another said. "I reckon when it comes right down to it, Ashley won't have no choice but to put one of the two of 'em in charge."

Caviness laughed, speaking at greater length than he had in a long time. "Why so glum? You gotta find the furs if you want to make any money, and best way to do that is go with someone that knows what he's a-doin'. Very few of us around anymore, what with Injuns murderin' and accidents a-happenin'. Come on, boys, me 'n McDill will set all of you up to a drink."

After that oration, several crowded up to the bar to get a refill.

Art, who was sitting by the stove that still had Shardeen's bullet hole in the pipe, watched the whole thing with little interest. He noticed, however, that the two men sitting at the table next to him made no effort to join the others at the bar. One of the two men was the one who had spoken up for him yesterday, when the constable was investigating the incident with Shardeen. His name, Art remembered, was Joe Matthews. The other man at the table with Matthews was the one who had challenged McDill when McDill suggested that he or Caviness would lead the trapping party.

"I'll say this," Matthews said, speaking quietly to his table companion. "There ain't no way I'd go up the river with either one of them no-count bastards in the lead. Ain't neither one of them worth a bucket of warm piss."

"Yeah," the other agreed. "If they didn't get you lost, they'd more'n likely get you kilt by Indians. Besides which, they're goin' to make life miserable for anybody that's under them."

"Still, McDill is right. There's no one else in St. Louis, right now that Ashley can get to lead the party. The good ones has already left."

"Gents," Art said. "Since you two aren't drinking with McDill and Caviness, maybe you'd let me buy you a beer. Least I can do, in thanks for your speaking out for me," he added to Matthews.

"Well, that's very generous of you, mister," Matthews said.

"I remember your name is Matthews," Art said. He looked at the man with Matthews.

"The name is Montgomery," he said. "Don Montgomery."

Art signaled to Carla and she brought three beers to the table.

"I take it you men aren't too fond of McDill and Caviness," Art said as they began drinking.

"Fond of them? I doubt their own mothers are fond of those two. Do you know them?"

Art shook his head. "No. But I had a run-in with a couple of Arikara because of them."

"You're lucky you still have your scalp," Matthews said.

"Was the fella right when he said Mr. Ashley wouldn't have any choice but to make one of them two the head of his party?" Art asked.

"Yeah," Matthews said disgustedly. "I'm afraid he was. All the good ones have left already."

"Too bad," Art said. He sat in silence for a couple of minutes, then finished his drink. "It's been nice talking to you," he said. The two men watched him leave, then fell to talking between themselves again.

Departing the tavern, Art walked back down to William Ashley's fur trading post. Seemed he couldn't stay away from the place. Again, the little tinkling bell over the doorway announced his entrance.

Almost instantly, William Ashley appeared from the back room where he had been working. He smiled at Art, as if he were genuinely glad to see him.

"Well, if it isn't the man called Art."

"Hello, Mr. Ashley," Art said.

"What can I do for you, Art?"

"It's time for me to get my supplies laid in for the winter," Art said. "But . . ."

"But what?"

Art made a motion in the general direction of the burned-out store. "Dunnigan's store got burned down. And Dunnigan was killed in the fire. Don't know where I can get outfitted now."

"I can outfit you, Art. I have all the things you'll need right here. Including livestock."

"Is that a fact? Well, I may just have to take you up on that." Art frowned and frankly eyed the successful fur trader. "Though I reckon, now that Dunnigan's place is gone, you'll be wantin' to charge a body an arm and his leg to do business with you."

"Well, a fella has a right to make a reasonable profit," Ashley said. "But I won't hold you up none, I promise you that." He opened the ledger book and took a quill pen from the inkwell. "You just tell me what you need and I'll . . ." Ashley stopped in mid-sentence, then closed the ledger book and stared at Art for a long moment. "On second thought, I've got a proposition for you. I won't charge you anything at all if you'll do a favor for me."

"What kind of favor?"

"I want you to lead the trapping party upriver," Ashley said.

Art chuckled. "The way they're talking over in the tavern, you'll be asking McDill or Caviness to lead the party."

"Well, truth to tell, I figured I was goin' to have to ask one or the other. What with Thompson dead, they're near 'bout the only ones left in town that could find their way upriver and back without wearing a quiver of arrows in their backs. But they are a couple of the biggest no-accounts that ever drew a breath, and I hate the thought of putting either one of them in charge."

"Why would you ask me to lead the party?" Art asked. "You don't know anything about me."

"I know you brought in the largest catch of any single man this season," Ashley said. "And they were all fine pelts too. I've been through 'em all. Most folks will try and pass off ten or twenty bad pelts, but you culled them out, had all the lower-quality plews together. That's plumb unusual in my experience. Why'd you do that, Art?"

"I figure if a man wants honest treatment, then he needs to be honest." The young mountain man had remembered the lessons taught to him by his father and mother, and even some of the preaching he had heard in church of a Sunday many years ago.

"That's a good policy. But it's not just the pelts you brought back that makes me think you would be a good man. I checked around on you, Art. There's some fellas in town say they remember you from the war. They say you was at New Orleans with Andy Jackson."

"That I was." It was the experience of a lifetime, and Art had been but a boy, fighting in a man's war. He drank up knowledge of men and weapons like a sponge, which had stood him in good stead in the later years.

"And they say you was made a lieutenant even though you was only fifteen years old."

Art chuckled. "I don't know that I was a real lieutenant," he said. "I think they may have just done that to be nice."

"Well, real or not, everyone who's ever heard of you has nothin' but good things to say about you. Plus, there's no denying that you can handle yourself if it comes down to it. Your run-in with Shardeen yesterday proved that. That's all I need to know that I'd like you to lead my trading party upriver."

"I'd like to do it for you, Mr. Ashley," Art said. "But I work alone." It was truer than Ashley or any man could ever know, just how alone a man he was. Except maybe now that he had Dog in his life . . .

"Oh, don't misunderstand me, Art. I'm not asking you to trap with the team. You can still work alone. All I want you to do is to lead my party upriver and"—he paused for a moment before he continued—"make peace with the Indians."

"I beg your pardon?"

Ashley stroked his jaw. He could see he had the mountain man's interest, but he needed to convince him that only he was the right man for this job. "You see, Art, that's the whole of it. Truth to tell, McDill or Caviness either one could lead the party upriver, but because of what happened with the Arikara last year, there's likely to be even more Indians now that don't want us comin' into their territory. I need somebody that can parlay with them, work out a way that our men can trap in their country without getting their scalp lifted. I sure can't count on McDill or Caviness for that."

"I don't know," Art said, considering every angle of this proposition, and not liking it much. "There's a lot of Indians up that way: Poncas, Sioux, Cheyennes, Mandans, even the Arikaras that I could probably deal with. But there's also Blackfeet, and they are about the goldarned orneriest people there are in creation."

"Do this for me, Art, and I'll outfit you for free. A horse and two mules, food, gunpowder, lead, matches— anything and everything you need, I'll furnish. And I'll let you pick out your own livestock. Then, once you get the party upriver and make peace with the Indians, why, you can go off on your own. And because I'm giving you your personal outfit free, every pelt you bring back will be pure profit for you."

"Same price as you're payin' now?"

"No guarantees—don't know what the market will bear—but I can assure you I won't cheat you, never would."

"If I agree, when do we leave?"

"Leave whenever you want to. You'll be in charge," Ashley said.

"All right. Have your party gathered up, ready to go by sunrise tomorrow morning."

Ashley smiled broadly, then extended his hand. "Thanks," he said. "I'll start getting your supplies together."

"Mr. Ashley, you're a respected businessman in St. Louis. I expect you know just about everyone and everything about the town, don't you?"

"You mean, am I a busybody who sticks his nose into everyone's business?"

"No, I didn't mean that."

Ashley chuckled. He took a pipe from a collection he kept on his desk, and began to fill it with fragrant tobacco. "I know you didn't. I was just funnin' with you, that's all. Yes, I know quite a bit about what is going on in this ragamuffin town that some people call a city. Why do you ask? Do you have a question about someone?"

"There's a girl here in town . . ."

"My, you work fast," Ashley said, interrupting Art. Clearly he was impressed with the young man. "You've only been here a few days and you've already met a girl?"

"Well, the fact is, I've known her for a long time," Art said. "I would just like to know how she's getting along."

"I'll tell you if I know. What's her name?"

"Jennie."

"Jennie? What's her last name?"

"She doesn't have a last name."

Ashley laughed again. "Art, what is it about you and last names? You don't have a last name, now you're asking me about a young woman who also doesn't have a last name. Jennie, you say? Well, there must be a dozen women and girls in this town named Jennie."

"This Jennie lives in a big white house over on Chestnut Street."

"Well, that narrows it down a bit," Ashley said. The smile left his face. "Wait a minute, a big white house on Chestnut, you say? Are you talking about the House of Flowers?"

"I dunno. The House of Flowers?"

"The House of Flowers is a big white house on Chestnut Street run by a girl named Jennie. But it's a . . . uh—"

"Whorehouse?" Art asked.

"Well, I wasn't going to say that exactly, but yes. It is. Is that the one you mean?"

"Well, yes, that's the one I mean. Didn't know it was called that. How does the town treat her?"

"She's a whore. How is the town supposed to treat her?"

"She's a good woman," Art said. Before Ashley could reply, Art held up his hand to stop him. "I know she's a whore, but she didn't have much choice in that. But inside, she's got a good soul, and I wouldn't want to see her hurt in any way."

"Well, as far as I can tell, she isn't being mistreated," Ashley said. "She sort of minds her own business, so the only people who ever take note of her are the people who are her customers."

"She must be doing pretty well to own that big house," Art said.

"Yes, well, that's another matter. There are some who say she might have bitten off more than she could chew when she bought that house. You see, she couldn't buy it outright, so the bank holds the paper on it. And from what I understand, some of our . . . so-called decent folk . . ." Ashley just about choked on the word "decent." He went on. "Well, the good citizens of the city of St. Louis are trying to get the bank to foreclose."

"Why?"

"Why? Well, because St. Louis is becoming a very important city, and there are those who feel that having something like the House of Flowers is bad."

"Who are the ones that say this?"

"Well, one name that comes to mind is Mrs. Sybil Abernathy. She is President of the Women's Auxiliary of the St. Louis Betterment League. Betterment League," he snorted. "A genuine bunch of busybodies is what they are. Put me to shame in that department." He tried to make light of an unpleasant situation.

"Is Jennie behind in her payments?" Art persisted.

"Oh, I'm sure she isn't. Duane Abernathy, Sybil's husband, is chairman of the board of directors of the bank. Believe me, if Jennie was late in her payments, he wouldn't hesitate to throw her out on her you-know-what."

"Then I don't see how anyone can do anything against her."

"One would think so," Ashley replied. He looked at the younger man and saw the naïve kid who still resided inside the tall, strong, weathered exterior. Still, it made Art that much more likable and trustworthy. "But there is a clause in her contract that would allow the bank to call in the note at any time."

"Can a bank do that? I mean if you are paying on time?"

"Yes, as long as that clause is in the contract. And that clause is put into many loans that the bank considers at risk. Whorehouses are considered at risk. Though why they are, I don't know. They always seem to do a brisk business."

"How much does Jennie owe, do you know?"

"I think it's around five hundred dollars or so."

"Pay it off," Art said.

"I beg your pardon?"

"I want you to take five hundred dollars, or however much it takes, from my account here, and pay off Miss Jennie's loan."

"Art, that's a helluva lot of money. Are you sure you want to do that?"

"Yes."

"Well, if you are going to do that, why don't you just take the money yourself and give it to her?"

Art shook his head emphatically. No question in his mind about this. "No," he said. "I'd rather do it this way. That is, if you will do it for me. And I don't want her to know that the money came from me."

Ashley paused for a moment; then he nodded in complete understanding. "Yes, of course I'll do it for you," he said. "You are a rare man, Art. A rare man indeed. And the rest of the money in your account?"

"I'd like for you to just keep it on your books."

"You mean you want me to act as a bank for you?"

"Yes, if you don't mind."

Ashley smiled. "I don't mind at all. Fact is, I do run

sort of a bank here. You won't be the only one to leave your money on the books."

"Thanks," Art said. "I appreciate that, Mr. Ashley."

The two men shook hands, and without another word Art left Ashley's place and wandered back down to the waterfront, where again the same talkative preacher was holding court. Dog, who had trailed Art at a close distance throughout the entire day, stayed with him every step. Art always kept him within sight from the corner of his eye, but didn't seek him out or pet him or feed him. Dog was a survivor, for sure. Now, Art stopped to listen for a few minutes to the longest nonstop sermon he had ever heard—and he remembered a few from his childhood.

"These here new-fangled steamboats is an abomination to the Lord!" the preacher said in his singsong voice. "I say now that all God-fearin' people should rise up against them, for surely they will mean the end of us all.

"Steam wilts the grass, so the horses and cattle cannot feed. The noise of those infernal engines keeps the chickens from layin', puts the pigs off'n their feed, and makes our womenfolk barren."

He held up a Bible and pointed to it.

"And it also poisons the water, for listen to this." The preacher opened the Bible and began to read. "From the Book of Revelation, 9:11. 'The waters became wormwood, and many men died of the waters because they were made bitter.'"

He slammed the Bible shut, then stabbed at the air with a long, bony finger. "Hear the word of the Lord!" he shouted.

Chuckling quietly and shaking his head, Art walked away. The preacher was still railing behind him.

Returning to LaBarge's Tavern, Art took the table that had become his during his time in St. Louis. He was eating a supper of beans and bacon when a shadow fell across his table. Looking up, he saw McDill and Caviness staring down at him.

"Something I can do for you gentlemen?" he asked.

"I'm told you plan to lead the fur-trapping party out of here in the morning," McDill said.

"That's right."

"Well, you ain't goin' to do it."

"Oh? Why not?"

"'Cause by rights that job belongs to me 'n my partner here," McDill said. "So if I was you, mister, I'd just get on out of town tonight and forget about the fur trapping party."

"Sorry. I've already given my word to Mr. Ashley," Art said easily. The more he saw of these two, the less he liked.

"Maybe you don't understand what I'm tellin' you, boy. I'm tellin' you you ain't goin' to lead no fur-trapping party."

"McDill, why don't you and Caviness back away and leave that fella alone?" someone asked. "If Mr. Ashley chose him, it's good enough for me."

"Yeah, me too," another said.

"That goes for all of us," another added.

"Matthews, Montgomery, Hoffman," McDill said, scoffing. He pointed at them. "Once we start up the river tomorrow with me 'n Caviness in charge, I'm goin' to remember your sassy mouths."

Each of the three men took a step back.

"What's your name, mister?" Caviness asked.

"My name is Art. Oh, and this is Dog."

So far, Dog had not raised his head.

"Art? That's all? Your name is just Art?"

"That's enough for me."

McDill snorted what might have been a laugh. "Art and Dog," he said. He looked at Caviness. "Hey, Ben, which one of these two is a real dog?" he asked. He and Caviness laughed at his joke. McDill hiked up his trousers as if he were about to do something—but he didn't make his move yet.

"You know what I think?" Caviness chimed in. "I think we ought to just whup old Art here, just to show him who his master is. Don't think he's very smart."

"Yeah," McDill said. "What do you say, Art? Shall we show you who your master is?"

"There are two of you," Art said.

McDill flashed an evil smile. "Well, then, we'll just take turns with you. First one of us will whup you, then the other. How does that sound?"

"That sounds fair enough. Who is going to be first?" Art asked easily.

"Who is going to be first? What difference does that make?" Caviness asked.

Art smiled up at them. "Oh, it makes a lot of difference," he said. "You see, under this table, I'm holding a charged pistol. I intend to shoot whoever is going to be first, then I'll let Dog deal with the other one. Dog," he called sharply.

Dog woke up, sat up, and seeing that Art was being confronted by two men, let out a low intense growl.

"Wait a minute now," McDill said, taking half a step backward.

"Come on, gentlemen, make up your mind. Who is going to be first?"

"You . . . you ain't got no charged pistol under that table," Caviness challenged. He had held his ground, but stood there with some uncertainty, looking back and forth between McDill and Art.

"Try me," Art said. He moved not a muscle, kept both men within his range of vision. Only his jaw clenched, and his enemies could see that.

"McDill? Caviness?" LaBarge called from behind the bar.

"You stay out of this, LaBarge. This here ain't none of your concern," McDill said in as blustery a voice as he could manage.

LaBarge laughed. "Oh, I ain't plannin' on getting into

it," he said. "But I was just wonderin' if you had any last wishes. I mean, after he and Dog kill the two of you, is there anyone you want me to write?"

Matthews laughed. "Are you joking, LaBarge? There ain't nobody who will miss either one of them after they're dead."

"You're probably right," LaBarge said. "I just wanted to give them a chance." He took a wet towel and began to damp down the bar surface, but kept an experienced tavern keep's eye on the situation.

"I don't believe he's holdin' no charged pistol under that table," McDill said.

"I don't either," Caviness said, though not quite as forcefully as before.

"You go first," McDill said.

"Me go first?" Caviness replied. "Hell, no, I'm not going first. You go first."

The two men stood there for a long moment, staring at Art, who was looking, without wavering, back into their eyes. By now the rest of the tavern realized that a potential life-or-death confrontation was reaching some sort of climax. A few chairs scraped along the rough-planked floor as men prepared to evacuate the battlefield if need be.

"I seen him yesterday," a voice said. "He was cool as a cucumber while Shardeen emptied both his pistols at him. Then, when Shardeen come at him with a roar, that fella never flinched. He just stood there waiting, and the next thing you know ol' Shardeen was deader'n a polecat in a wagon rut."

Caviness began to sweat, and McDill licked his lips nervously.

"Ah," McDill said with a dismissive wave of his hand. He tried to force a smile. "We was only funnin' with you, Art," he said. "If you're goin' to be leadin' us tomorrow, we just wanted to know that you've got the makin's, that's all. We didn't mean nothin', did we, Caviness?"

"No," Caviness said. "We didn't mean nothin'. Uh, would you call your dog off now?"

"He's not my dog," Art said. He looked over at Dog and nodded. Dog eyed Art, then the two bullies, and gave up his threat position; he lay down again with one eye shut, the other open wide.

"If you're planning on going on this trip, be in front of Ashley's at sunrise tomorrow," Art said.

"Yeah, yeah, we'll be there. You, uh, can put away your pistol now," McDill said.

"Oh, yeah," Art replied. With a smile, he brought his hand up from under the table. He was holding a fork. "As it turns out, you were right. I wasn't holding a pistol."

Everyone in the tavern began to laugh then, as much from a release of tension as from the humor of the situation. LaBarge unthinkingly used the soiled towel to mop his own brow.

"Why you . . ." McDill sputtered.

"Come on, McDill, Caviness," Hoffman said. "He got you, that's all."

"Yeah," Montgomery added. "He got you good."

Scowling, McDill and Caviness turned and marched out of the tavern, chased by laughter, whistles, and cat-calls.

Art, the mountain man, returned to his meal, using the fork-pistol to shovel in the food that would be his last city meal for a long time to come.

7

It was just before sunrise, and in the east the sky was pearl-gray, laced with streaks of pink. The Mississippi River was glowing a silver-blue, as if it had its own internal source of light. Roosters were crowing, and in the backyard of a nearby house a cow bawled to be milked.

Although Art had told everyone to be in front of Ashley's place by sunup, they all arrived even before the sun rose. Art, who had picked out his livestock the night before, now saddled his horse, then checked the harness on his pack mules. Neither of his mules was heavily loaded now, as they were carrying only the supplies he would need for the winter, as well as some trading material for the Indians. Ashley had furnished a goodly amount of trade goods, so much that these items were equally distributed among all the mules in the party.

After Art checked his own animals, he went down the line looking at the others, and meeting the men who would be traveling with him.

"What's Ashley doing, giving the Indians all this stuff?" McDill asked as he worked on his animals. "We give them all this stuff this time, they're going to expect it every time. And if we show up empty-handed, there's going to be hell to pay."

"Yeah," Caviness replied. He too was working on the loads of his mules. "If we had any kind of leader, he'd tell Ashley what a fool he's makin' of himself."

Art knew that McDill and Caviness were talking for his benefit, but he paid no attention to them. Instead, he just looked over the harness and the load. The loads were skillfully packed, evidence that McDill and Caviness knew the business. Art hoped he would have no more trouble with them.

Third in line was Don Montgomery, followed by Joe Matthews. Montgomery and Matthews were first cousins, about twenty-two years old. They were a little green, but they seemed willing enough. Last was Herman Hoffman. Hoffman was a big Hessian, and at fifty, the oldest of the group. Hoffman had fought in the Napoleonic Wars, and any misgivings Art might have had about whether or not Hoffman would follow a much younger man were dispelled when Hoffman spoke. Hoffman was a military man, used to the structure of command, and in his mind, Art was his commander, pure and simple.

"Have you been trapping before?" Art asked.

"Nein," Hoffman said. He held out his large, rough hands. "But I am strong and good worker. I will do what you tell me and I think all will be fine."

Art smiled. "I think all will be fine as well."

Looking down the street, Art saw William Ashley moving toward them, having walked up from his home. Although the sun had not yet risen, there was enough light for Art to recognize him from some distance away. Reaching the group, Ashley lit his pipe before he spoke.

"Well, Art, you have your party together, I see. Have you met all of them?"

"Yes. McDill, Caviness, and the others."

Ashley chuckled. "Yes, I heard about your little run-in with those two last night. But from what I hear, you handled it very well. I don't think you'll be having any more trouble from those two. And they are good trappers. I probably would have had one of them lead the group if you had refused. It's just that they . . . well, you saw how they are last night. And this is as much a peacemaking trip as anything else. After what happened last winter, I don't think I could trust either one of them to make a lasting peace with the Indians."

"No, I wouldn't think that very likely," Art agreed.

Ashley took a letter from his pocket and handed it to Art. "This is a letter to Joe Walker," he explained. "Joe is in command of a fort built by the American Fur Company. We may be competitors in business, but they'll have as much an interest in having peace with the Indians as we do, so I reckon Joe will treat you all right when you get there. Also, if you need to replenish any of your supplies, this letter promises that I'll make it good to them."

"Thanks," Art said, taking the letter and putting it into his saddle pouch.

By now several early-rising St. Louis citizens had turned out to watch the departure. While this was neither the first, nor would it be the last fur-trapping party to leave the city, it was the largest and it was being sent out by William Ashley, the most important fur trader in St. Louis.

"Sun's up," Art said, looking across the river. "I expect we'd best be going."

"Good luck to you, Art," Ashley said, reaching out to shake Art's hand. Then he called to the others. "Good luck, good trapping, all you men!"

"Mount up!" Art commanded as he swung into his saddle. Twisting around, he waited until Hoffman, the last man, was mounted. "All right, let's go!" He waved the party forward.

The convoy of eighteen horses, six men, and one dog stretched out for nearly a block as Art led them forward.

He planned to go north to the Missouri River, then turn and follow that river all the way to its head.

From her bedroom window on the second floor of her house, Jennie watched Art and the others leave. She had thought he might come to her again last night, hoped that he would, and purposely turned away customers so she would be ready for him. But he didn't show.

When she finally realized, well after midnight, that Art wasn't going to come see her again, she was angry and hurt. But as she considered it, the anger and hurt left, to be replaced by a terrible sense of sorrow and longing for what she knew could never be.

"Oh, Art," she said quietly. "Why couldn't we have met at another time and another place—you a farmer, and I an innocent young girl?"

"Miss Jennie?" one of her working girls called from downstairs. "Miss Jennie, will you be coming down to breakfast?"

"Yes, Lily, I'll be right there," Jennie called back. Before she turned away from the window, she kissed her fingers and blew the kiss toward Art, who was now so far up the street that she could barely see him.

"Go with God, dear Art," she said quietly.

The River Bank of St. Louis had assets of nearly one million dollars, and that figure was proudly displayed on the front window of the building. In keeping with its success, the bank occupied one of the most substantial buildings in St. Louis. Built of brick and stone and iron grillwork, it sat squarely on the corner of Fourth and Market.

Although the bank was owned by a consortium of St. Louis businessmen, it was managed by its chief teller, Theodore Epson, a New Yorker who had been hired by the Board when the bank was opened. Epson arrived every morning exactly one hour before the bank opened. During that quiet hour, he would go over all the transactions from the day before, often finding a mistake one of his tellers had made.

Epson enjoyed finding mistakes, because it gave him an opportunity to berate the hapless teller who made it. It also gave him a sense of self-satisfaction and reinforced his personal belief that, without him, the bank would fall into insolvency.

One of the most difficult tasks Epson had was in controlling the loans granted by the bank. It seemed that every board member had a close, personal friend who had fallen into financial difficulty and could survive if only they could secure a loan. Epson tried to explain to the board member concerned that the bank was not in the business of lending money to help people, but was in the business of lending money to make more money.

On the other hand, a few of the board members were after him to deny some of the more solvent loans. One example was the mortgage note the bank held on the House of Flowers. Mrs. Abernathy and her Women's Auxiliary League for the Betterment of St. Louis had done their job well, and now there were many St. Louis citizens protesting against Jennie and her House of Flowers. There were many who wanted Jennie's note called and her loan terminated, because they considered her business to be unsavory.

"Unsavory it might be," Epson told them. "But it is certainly a profitable business. Would that all our accounts paid as promptly as the House of Flowers."

Closing the book of yesterday's transactions, Epson checked the Terry clock that stood against the wall, and saw that it was less than a half minute until time to open. He walked over to the front door, raised the shade, and saw several people standing just outside the door. The man first in line expected Epson to open the door at that precise moment, but it wasn't yet time. Epson remained standing behind the glass, staring at the clock.

"Let us in, Epson! It's time to open the door!" someone shouted.

Holding up his finger, Epson shook his head, indicating that it was not yet time. As the crowd grew more frustrated, Epson continued to stare at the clock. The moment the minute hand reached the twelve, the clock began to chime. Then, and only then, did Epson reach for the door.

"Well, it's about time!" one of the customers said, his irritation clear in the tone of his voice.

"You know the hours, Mr. Warren," Epson said. "Our bank opens its doors promptly at nine o'clock. Not one minute sooner and not one minute later."

The customers poured into the bank, then hurried to the two teller cages. Epson watched with a sense of smug satisfaction, then returned to his desk. He had been there for no more than five minutes when William Ashley arrived. Stepping inside the bank, Ashley looked around for a moment, then came straight to Epson's desk.

"Mr. Epson, I wonder if I might have a word with you?" Ashley said.

"Certainly, Mr. Ashley," Epson replied, standing to greet him. "It is always a pleasure to greet one of our fair city's most powerful businessmen. How are you doing, sir?"

"I'm doing fine, Epson," Ashley said.

Epson's eyes squinted and he continued the conversation in a somewhat more guarded tone. "I must say I'm a little surprised to see you, though. I've been given to understand that you have started your own bank for the fur trappers."

Ashley shook his head in the negative. "Not at all," he said. "All I'm doing is keeping some of my trappers' earned income on the books for them."

"Isn't that what a bank does?"

"I suppose. But I'm only doing it as a favor for my trappers. Most of them don't like to carry any more money than they need."

"Nobody does," Epson said. "That's what banks are for. You could steer some of your accounts our way, you know."

"Yes, I know," Ashley replied. "And I fully intend to, over a period of time."

"Really?" Epson asked, brightening. "So, have you brought me a deposit today?"

"Not a deposit, but a payment."

"A payment? I don't understand. A payment for what? You don't have a loan here."

"It isn't for me. It is for one of your customers. It's more than a payment, actually. I intend to pay off the entire mortgage."

"Why would you pay off someone else's mortgage?" Epson asked. He frowned. "Wait a minute. Have you made the loan yourself? That's it, isn't it? You're paying off the loan because you have made it yourself. You *are* going into banking."

"No. All I'm doing is paying off the loan on behalf of an interested party."

"I see. And what loan are you paying off?"

"I'm paying off the loan on the House of Flowers."

"You are paying off the whore's loan?"

"Yes."

"I don't understand. Why would you do such a thing?"

"I assure you, sir, I am not paying the loan from my own funds. I am doing so on behalf of an interested party. He doesn't want this Miss Jennie to know that he is doing it."

Epson stroked his jaw as he studied Ashley. "Are you saying that she doesn't know her loan is being paid off?"

"That's right."

"I am curious. Who is her benefactor? Some business-man in town?"

"I don't believe I'm at liberty to say who it is," Ashley

said. "I wasn't told that I couldn't tell, but I wasn't given permission to tell either. Therefore I feel ethically bound to keep his identity a secret."

"Ha!" Espson said. "I was right, wasn't I? It is some local businessman. And of course he would come through someone else, if he wanted it kept secret. Like as not, it's one of the same men who, in public, call for that house to be closed, while in private, are her biggest supporters. Who is it? The mayor?"

"I told you . . . I don't believe I'm at liberty to say. It doesn't matter anyway. All I intend to do is pay off the note. Now, are you going to accept the money, or what?"

"Yes, yes, of course I'll accept the money."

Later that same afternoon, Jennie herself called at the bank. Seeing her the moment she stepped through the door, Epson went over to meet her.

"Yes, Miss Jennie," he said. "Is there something I can do for you?"

"I wonder if we could speak in private for a few moments?" Jennie asked.

"Yes, of course we can. Come over here to my desk. We can talk there without being overheard."

There were no other women in the bank, but there were several men customers, most of whom knew who Jennie was, many of whom had been paying customers at the House of Flowers. It would have been easy to pick out the ones who were the customers, for while the others stared at Jennie in unabashed curiosity, her customers looked away pointedly, pretending as if they didn't even see her.

Epson led Jenny through the gate of the small, fenced-in area that surrounded his desk. He offered her a chair, then sat as well.

"Now, Miss Jennie, what is it that we can only discuss in private?"

"Recently, some people have been attempting to close down my business," Jennie said.

Epson scratched his cheek with his forefinger. "Ah, yes," he said. "You would be talking about the Women's Auxiliary of the St. Louis Betterment League."

"You know about it?"

"Yes."

"Then you also know that chief among these women is Mrs. Abernathy."

Epson nodded. "Sybil Abernathy, yes."

"Doesn't her husband have something to do with this bank?"

"Yes indeed, he is the chairman of the board of directors of the bank."

"I thought as much." Jennie opened her portmanteau and fished out a piece of paper. "According to the contract, even if I am not in arrears, the bank can call in the remainder of my loan at any time. Is that right?"

"Yes, but . . ."

"That's what I thought. That's why I want to pay off the entire loan today. That way there will be no chance for the bank to foreclose." Jennie began writing a bank draft. "I believe the amount is four hundred and seventy-five dollars."

Epson was silent for a long moment, and Jennie looked up at him questioningly. "Am I not right?" she asked.

Epson wondered what he should do. He had accepted the money from William Ashley to pay off her debt, but was instructed not to tell Jennie.

"Mr. Epson, is four hundred and seventy-five dollars correct?"

"Uh, yes," Epson said. He would take the money now, and decide later what to do.

Jennie wrote the draft and handed it to him.

"I'll, uh, take care of this for you," Epson said.

Jennie smiled at him. "Thank you," she said. "I may be

worried for no reason at all, but Mrs. Abernathy seems to be quite a determined woman, and I fear she may convince her husband to exercise the foreclosure clause in the contract. I would rather just own the house free and clear so that there is no question."

Epson nodded again. "Yes, I'm sure you are doing the right thing," he said. He picked up the draft and put it in his pocket. "I'll have the title delivered to you."

"Thank you again," Jennie said, getting up from her chair. Epson stood quickly, then walked with her to the door. He stood in the door and watched as Ben helped her climb into her carriage. Then he returned to his desk and sat there for a long moment, contemplating what he should do.

Opening one drawer of his desk, he removed a letter he had received from a bank back in Philadelphia.

"So, in conclusion, Mr. Epson," the letter read, "our bank is prepared to offer you a rather substantial salary should you accept the offer to become our chief of tellers. Please let us know, soonest, should you be interested."

Epson studied the letter for a long moment before he returned it to the desk drawer.

"Mr. Epson?"

Looking up, Epson was startled to see one of his tellers standing there. He had not noticed the teller's approach.

"Yes, Mr. Franklin?"

"I noticed the lady customer with you. Is there some business transaction you would like me to take care of?"

"Uh, no," Epson said. "Nothing at all. She just had a few questions she wanted answered. Please return to your teller's cage."

"Very good, sir," Franklin said.

By nightfall Art and his party were already fifty miles upriver. They were still in the settled part of Missouri, and when they made camp that night, they were within sight of a farmhouse.

"After it's dark, me'n Caviness will go down there and get us some eggs," McDill offered.

"Why would you wait until after dark?" Art asked.

"What do you mean, why? Wouldn't you love to have some fresh hen's eggs with your breakfast come mornin'?"

"That would be good," Art agreed.

"Me too, but I don't want to get shot in the ass by some farmer for stealin' 'em," McDill replied, as if he were explaining something to a child.

"I see," Art said, masking his disgust. "You were planning on stealing the eggs."

"Of course I was planning on stealing them. You don't think he's goin' to just give them to us, do you?"

"No," Art said. "But he may sell us some."

"Sell us some? You mean you want to buy eggs?"

"Yes."

McDill and Caviness laughed. "This here will be my seventh trip up the river," McDill said. "And I ain't yet bought a hen's egg, or a chicken."

"Well, we're going to buy them this time," Art insisted.

"Huh. I reckon next thing you'll have us doin' is sayin' our prayers and singin' church hymns," Caviness said.

"A few prayers and hymns wouldn't hurt either one of you," Art replied. "But you'll not be getting them from me. All right, I'll go down and buy us some eggs. Who wants them?"

"I do," Montgomery said. Matthews and Hoffman also wanted some.

"I reckon a fip apiece will be enough to buy us a couple dozen."

"A fip? You ain't gettin' no five cents from me," McDill announced.

"Fine," Art replied. "You aren't getting any eggs."

Art collected from Montgomery, Matthews, and Hoffman.

"Uh, I'd like some eggs," Caviness said, pulling a coin from his pocket.

"You, Ben?" McDill asked.

"Well, five cents ain't that much, Percy. And I be damned if I'm goin' to sit here in the morning watching everyone else eat eggs while I don't have none."

McDill waited for a moment, then sighed. "All right, all right," he said, handing a coin to Art. "I'll go along with it. But I'll be damned if I don't think this is about the dumbest thing I've ever seen, payin' good money for eggs when they're that easy to steal."

With the money collected from the others, plus his own, Art saddled his horse. Dog came over, ready to go with him.

"Dog, I'll be back soon. You stay here and watch my things," Art said.

When Art swung into the saddle, Dog stayed behind and watched him. Not until Art was out of sight, did Dog go over to where Art had made his own camp. Dog did a couple of circles on the bedroll, then lay down.

"The way this fella is acting, he's prob'ly going to say we have to pay the Indians for whatever beaver we trap," McDill complained.

"My pa is a farmer," Matthews said. "It's hard, honest work. I don't think he would appreciate someone stealing from his henhouse. Besides, five cents isn't too much to pay."

"I agree," Montgomery added. "Buyin' eggs is better'n getting shot for stealin' 'em."

"What about you, Hoffman? Everyone else is putting in their two cents' worth. What do you think?"

"I think Art is our leader," Hoffman said. "We signed on to obey, we should obey."

"Ahh, he's got all of you buffaloed," McDill said with a dismissive wave of his hand. He looked over toward Art's bedroll and packs. "Wonder what he's brought with him."

McDill started toward Art's packs.

"What are you doing?" Matthews asked.

"I'm going to look through his packs."

"You got no right to do that."

"You going to stop me?" McDill challenged.

Matthews shook his head.

"I didn't think so."

Matthews grinned. "I don't have to stop you. He will."
He pointed to Dog.

"Ha. That dog's not going to do anything. He knows
me now. Don't you, Dog?" McDill said as he started
toward Art's packs.

Dog stood up and watched him.

"See, he's not going to . . ."

That was as far as McDill got before Dog darted quickly
to intercept McDill. Putting himself between McDill and
Art's packs, Dog bared his fangs and growled.

Matthews and the others laughed.

"You still want to mess with Art's things?" Matthews
asked.

"I wasn't goin' to do nothin' but see what all he was
carryin'," McDill said.

"I think maybe you should go back to your own
bedroll now," Hoffman suggested.

"Come on, Percy," Caviness said. "If that dog decides
to go after you, he'll have your windpipe pulled out
before we can stop him."

"Ha, what do you mean before we can stop him?"
Montgomery asked. "I don't intend to even try to stop
him."

"All right," McDill said. He pointed at Dog. "But me
and you's goin' to have an accountin' one of these days."

When Art approached the farmhouse he saw a tall,
bearded man standing on the front porch. The man was
dressed in homespun and holding a rifle.

"Somethin' I can do you for, mister?" the farmer asked.

"I'd like to buy a couple dozen eggs, if you've got any for sale," Art said.

The farmer looked surprised. "Did you say you wanted to *buy* eggs?"

"Yes, sir, I did. If they're not too dear, that is."

The farmer stroked his beard for a moment. "You a fur trapper, are you?" he asked.

"I am."

"Uh-huh, I thought so. They been comin' through here right regular over the last few weeks. You're the first one asked to buy eggs, though. The others tried to steal 'em."

"Tried?"

"They's one of 'em buried over there," the farmer said. "I yelled at him to get out of here an' leave my hens alone, but he turned and shot at me. So I shot back. It's a fearsome thing, killin' one of God's own, but I didn't have no choice in the matter."

"It doesn't sound like you did."

"So, you're wantin' to buy yourself a couple dozen eggs, are you?"

"Yes, sir, if you have any to sell."

"I got 'em. What about twenty cents for two dozen eggs?"

Art thought of the money he had collected. He didn't know how he would divide ten cents up among six men. He could keep the money and no one would be the wiser, but he didn't want to do that. "What about three dozen for thirty cents?" he asked.

The farmer nodded. "I reckon I can do that," he said. "Come around back with me, you can help me gather 'em. But you better stay close to me."

"Stay close to you?"

"Over there," the farmer said, nodding. When Art looked in the direction the farmer had indicated, he saw two dogs, both of them bigger than Dog. Though they weren't growling, they were looking at him with dark, intense eyes. "If'n you had tried to come in here without me, them dogs woulda been on you."

"They look mighty fierce."

"They are fierce," the farmer said. "That's why they ain't nobody got away with any of my eggs yet."

"I can see that," Art said. "I've got a dog that's been followin' me around lately. He's come in handy a time or two."

"Dogs is good things for a body to have," the farmer said. He gathered up the eggs, wrapped them in a cloth bundle, then, held his hand out palm up.

"Here you are," Art said. "Thirty cents." He dropped the coins into the man's palm. The farmer wrapped his hand around the coins, then handed the eggs to Art.

Carrying the three dozen eggs carefully in a cloth bundle, Art returned to the campsite.

"Three dozen for thirty cents?" Montgomery asked. "You made a pretty good bargain."

"Ha," McDill said. "I could've gotten 'em for nothin'. You should've let me do it my way."

Art smiled. "Yes," he said. "Now that I think about it, I should have let you try."

Junction of Platte and Missouri Rivers,
Saturday, August 14, 1824

There were so many people gathered at the junction of the Platte and Missouri Rivers that it resembled a small town. Tents and temporary shelters had been erected, some of which were made of logs, chinked with mud, to take on a more permanent look. Several keelboats were tied up, or pulled ashore, awaiting future employment. There were even a few squaws and children of some of the mountain men, thus giving the encampment even more of the look, feel, and sound of a nearly civilized city.

The more substantial structures belonged to employees of the Eastern fur dealers. These men would buy the pelts here, at a reduced price, then boat the pelts back downriver next spring. Until such time as there were furs to buy, though, they supplemented their income by providing liquor and goods from stores they had brought with them.

Most of the goods the mountain men bought weren't paid for at the time of purchase, but were put on an account. The account was settled when the trappers brought in their winter's catch. The representatives of the fur dealers would merely deduct from the pelt count so that, while a trapper might bring in fifty pelts, his indebtedness could cause him to be credited with only twenty-five or less.

As Art led his party into the encampment, he was greeted by hellos from dozens of other mountain men.

Art returned the greetings, then swung down from his horse. He looked back toward the ones who had come in with him. "Get your horses unsaddled, and take the load off your mules," he called. "We're going to be here for a while."

"How long are we going to be here?" McDill asked.

"Two, maybe three days," Art answered.

"If I was leadin' this outfit, we wouldn't spend no more'n a day here. I think we should get on up into the mountains, get us a head start on the others."

"You want to go ahead on your own, McDill, go ahead," Art said. "I'm not keeping you." Art had already unsaddled and ground-staked his horse, and was now quickly and skillfully relieving his mules of their burden.

"I didn't say nothin' 'bout goin' on by myself," McDill replied.

Art walked over to a fallen tree trunk where a couple of men were sitting. A small campfire blazed in front of the downed tree, and one of the men tossed a few cut-up branches into the fire. McDill and the others were still working with their loads. Dog went with him.

"Hello, Art," the older of the two said. This was Jeb

Law. Before Art went out on his own, Jeb had wintered in once with Art, Pierre, and Clyde.

"Hello, Jeb," Art replied. "Ed," he said, nodding to the younger of the two.

When Art sat, Dog settled down in front of him.

"How'd you come by the wolf?" Jeb asked.

"I didn't come by him, he come by me," Art said. "He just sort of attached himself to me."

"You gotta watch makin' pets of wolves. They don't ever get over their wild."

"I figure he's at least as much dog as he is wolf, and the dog part is pretty smart."

"Say, where at's ol' Clyde?" Jeb asked. "Did he decide to stay back in St. Louie?"

Art shook his head. "Clyde didn't make it," he said. "We was jumped by some Arikara. Clyde was killed."

"Oh," Jeb said. "That's a damn shame. Clyde was a good man."

"Yes, he was."

Jeb picked up a jug of whiskey from behind the log, and offered it to Art. Art pulled the cork, hefted it to his shoulder, and took a couple of drinks. When he brought the jug back down, he opened his mouth to suck in some air.

"Whooee," he said. "Where did you come by that poison?"

"McGhee's sellin' it," Jeb said, speaking of one of the furrier agents. "It's not so bad, once you get used to it. I think he puts a little mule piss in it to add to the flavor."

"That explains its kick, then," Art said.

Jeb laughed out loud. "Its kick. Hey, that's a pretty good one."

"You get your furs sold in St. Louis?" Ed asked.

"Yes. I sold them to William Ashley."

"I figured you'd go to him. Get a good price, did you?" Ed asked.

"I did."

"Might think on doin' that myself this year."

"It's not an easy journey," Art said.

"No, I reckon not, what with it getting Clyde killed and all," Ed replied. "Still, it might be worth it for the higher price."

Jeb nodded toward the men who had ridden in with Art. "So, what's with these men?"

"I made a deal with Ashley to lead these fellas up to the head of the Missouri. I will also be making peace with the Indian tribes."

"Makin' peace with the Indians, huh? Well, I reckon if anyone should try and make peace it's Ashley. It was his men got 'em all riled up in the first place."

"It was a couple of men who were working for him," Art said. "But it wasn't none of Ashley's doin'."

"A couple of men workin' for him, huh? Well, I'd like to get my hands on them two, let 'em know what I think of 'em."

Art chuckled. "If you're serious 'bout getting your hands on them, there they are." He pointed to McDill and Caviness.

"What? You mean that's them?"

"Yep."

"Well, all I can say is, they got some brass comin' out here now, after all the trouble they caused. Was they part of the deal you made with Ashley?"

"Yes," Art answered. He told Jeb and Ed of the arrangement he'd made with William Ashley, in which he would lead Ashley's trapping party up to the headwaters of the Missouri, and would also parley with the Indians in an attempt to make peace.

"Why would you agree to such a thing?" Jeb asked.

"Well, if we don't have peace with the Indians, we're going to wind up spendin' so much time lookin' back over our shoulders that we won't get any trapping done," Art explained. "I don't want to see any more of my friends get killed. And Ashley agreed to outfit me, including livestock, if I would do it. So, here I am."

Jeb nodded, then pulled a pipe from his pocket. He stuck a long stick into the fire, captured a flame, and lit the fire. "Well, I don't blame you none, I reckon. Sounds like a pretty good deal to me." Jeb took several puffs from his pipe. Not until the bowl was smoking did he continue. "Parleying with the Indians might be a little harder than you think, though."

"Why's that?"

"According to the squaws, a good number of the Arikara has gone to live with the Mandan. And you know how Indians is. The enemies of their friends are also their enemies."

"What about the other tribes? The Ponca, the Sioux?"

"Haven't heard anything from them. They might open their lodges to you. On the other hand, they may scalp you as soon as they see you. You're up here now. If I was you, I'd just forget about the rest of the deal you made with Ashley, and cut them boys loose to go on their own."

Art shook his head. "Can't do that," he said.

"Why not?"

"Because, for one thing, I gave my word to Ashley. And I'm not one to go back on my word. And for another, if I cut 'em loose now, McDill and Caviness will take over."

"The ones who started all this trouble in the first place?" Jeb asked. "Why would they take over?"

"That's just the way of it. And I'd hate to turn them loose on Matthews, Montgomery, and Hoffman."

"That's the other three?"

"Yes, and they're green as grass. Wouldn't take much for McDill and Caviness to prod them into doing about anything they ordered."

"Who's the big fella?" Ed asked.

"That's Herman Hoffman. He's a Hessian."

"He looks like he could take care of hisself pretty good," Ed said.

"I expect he can. Only trouble is, he's a man who believes in authority, and if he figures that McDill or Caviness are giving the orders, he'll follow them."

"You don't plan to trap with those men, do you?" Jeb asked.

Art shook his head. "No. Soon as I make peace with the Indians, I'll go out on my own. Thought I might head up toward Wind River."

"Ought to be some good pickin's up there this winter," Jeb agreed.

"Fight, fight!" someone shouted.

Looking around, Art saw several people running toward the center of the camp area.

"Art, it's Percy McDill!" Matthews said, hurrying to find him.

"Damn, it didn't take him very long to get into trouble," Art said, getting up from the fallen tree trunk. By the time he reached the center of the commotion, he saw that the fight was over. McDill was sprawled on his back, and the man he had been fighting with was standing over him.

"You want 'ny more?" the man asked McDill.

"No," McDill replied sullenly. He had his hand on his chin, moving it back and forth as if testing to see if his jaw was broken.

"I reckon that'll teach you to mess with my squaw," the victorious brawler said, brushing his hands together as he turned his back to McDill and started walking away.

The man shouldn't have turned his back because McDill leaped to his feet with his knife in his hand.

"Dog!" Art shouted.

Dog leaped up and clamped his jaws down on the wrist of McDill's knife hand. With a roar of pain and surprise, McDill dropped his knife.

"Get away!" he shouted. "Get away from me!"

"Dog," Art said again, and at this command, Dog let go. McDill stood there, rubbing his wrist.

"What the hell?" McDill said. "What did he do that for?"

"Because I told him to," Art said.

"What's going on here?" McDill's adversary asked, turning around at the commotion.

Realizing that he had lost his advantage now, and not wanting to press the issue any further, McDill waved his hand in irritation.

"Nothing," he growled. "Nothing's going on. Just go on about your business."

"Yeah, I'll do that," the other man said. He pointed at McDill. "So long as you stay away from my squaw."

"He won't be bothering your squaw anymore," Art said. "I can promise you that. Come on, McDill, I expect you better keep yourself out of trouble until we leave here."

"I don't understand you, mister," McDill growled in anger as they walked away from the confrontation. "I mean, we come out here together. I figured that should make us pards, of a sort. And pards is supposed to look out for one another."

"I was looking out for you, McDill. The fella you braced is one of the best-liked trappers out here. If I had let you kill him, you would be hanging from a tree limb by nightfall."

8

A beautiful cabriolet carriage, pulled by a team of matching white horses, stopped on Chestnut Street in front of the House of Flowers. Duane Abernathy, well turned out in a gaberdine suit with silver-buttoned vest, beaver hat, and white gloves, was the lone passenger in the magnificent carriage, as befitting his elevated station in St. Louis.

Constable Billings, mounted, had ridden alongside the carriage, eating its dust. When they stopped, he looked over at Abernathy.

"Are you sure you want to do this, Mr. Abernathy?"

"I'm sure, never surer of anything in my life as a man of business," Abernathy said. "Before he left, Mr. Epson disclosed to me that the occupant of this house was in arrears on her payment. Serve the warrant, Constable. I want her, and all the trollops who work with her, out of the house by noon today. Serve the blessed warrant, my man."

"Perhaps if you would give her an opportunity to pay off the loan in one payment," Billings suggested. He had pleaded with the banker before, when he had first learned of Miss Jennie's financial problem.

"She cannot pay off the loan," Abernathy said. "I have reviewed her bank account. It is nearly depleted. In fact, she recently withdrew an amount of money exactly equal to what she owes my bank. One who was seriously trying to avoid arrears would have used that money to clear the debt. Do your duty, Constable. Serve the warrant, I say again." Abernathy sat back in his comfortable carriage seat and pulled his hat more snugly onto his head. He called to the driver to take him back to the bank.

With a sigh, Constable Billings tied off his horse at one of the several wrought-iron hitching posts in front of the fine white-painted house, then went inside. Jennie met him in the foyer.

"Constable," she said, greeting him with a genuine smile.

Constable Billings removed his hat and rolled it in his hands for a moment before he spoke. He had never been in such an uncomfortable situation in his life. His heart was bleeding.

"Miss Jennie, I hate being the one to do this, but I've been asked to serve a warrant of eviction."

"Eviction?"

"Yes, ma'am," Billings said. By now, several of Jennie's girls had gathered in the foyer as well, to see what was going on. They could see this wasn't good.

"But I don't understand. How can I be evicted from my own house?" Jennie asked. Her dark eyes were wide with question and disbelief.

"Well, ma'am, that's just it," Billings replied. "This isn't your house anymore. According to the loan contract at the bank, it can be foreclosed at any time if a payment is late. And you are late."

Jennie shook her head vigorously. "But that's not true, Constable. I don't even have a loan at the bank anymore. I paid it off—in full."

Billings's eyes opened wide in surprise. "You paid the loan off? When?"

"Why, back in July," Jennie said. "I wrote a bank draft for the full amount to Mr. Epson."

"Miss Jennie, would you come with me?" Billings asked. "Perhaps if we went to the bank, we could get to the bottom of this."

"Yes, I would be glad to come with you," Jennie said.

Constable Billings, Duane Abernathy, and Logan Mc-Murtry, the new chief of tellers, stood in the little fenced-off area that was the office of the chief of tellers. His mahogany desk was covered with correspondence, bank papers, and open ledger books. Several inkwells held inks of black, blue, and red.

"As you can see, Constable Billings," Abernathy said, taking in the papers and open ledgers with a sweep of his hand, "her loan is still outstanding."

"But how can that be?" Jennie asked, incredulous. She was trying not to be intimidated by these men and the situation. "I have paid off the loan."

"By bank draft, you say?" Billings asked.

"Yes, four hundred and seventy-five dollars," Jennie said. "I'm sure if you check the ledger, you will see where I issued an instrument of that precise amount."

"Oh, I agree, you wrote a draft for four hundred and seventy-five dollars," Abernathy said. "For here is the entry, made on July twenty-third, in the year of our Lord, eighteen hundred and twenty-four. But, according to this entry, the funds were given directly to you. You'll see as much right here." He hefted the ledger to show her.

"What? No," Jennie said. "They were to repay the loan."

"Miss Jennie, do you have anything to prove that?" Billings asked. "A receipt, a letter, something to show that the loan was paid?"

Jennie shook her head. She now regretted not asking Epson for a payment note and the title on the very

morning she had paid him. "No, I don't. Mr. Epson said
he would take care of it for me, and I assumed that he
would. Perhaps it was delayed by his departure to
Philadelphia."

"You say you gave the money to Epson?" Billings
asked.

"Yes."

"Well, if you gave it to him, but there is no record of it,
what do you think happened to the money?"

"I'm sure I don't know," Jennie said. Although inside,
she now had deep suspicions, and she was almost sick
with fear and regret.

"Oh, I'm sure you do know," Abernathy said. "You
kept it for yourself."

"No, I didn't, I can assure you. I gave the money directly to Mr. Epson."

"And yet, clearly, there is no entry to that fact, your as-
surances notwithstanding," McMurtry said, pointing
with an ink-stained finger to the ledger book.

"I wish there was some way we could talk to Mr. Epson.
He would be able to clear this up, I'm sure." Jennie
looked from McMurtry to Abernathy, but saw no sympathy in either man.

"I did talk to Mr. Epson," Abernathy said. "Before he
left, he informed me that if the bank received no more
money from you by the next payment date, you would be
in arrears."

"Mr. Epson told you that?" Jennie asked in surprise.

"He did."

"But that's not true. He knows that's not true."

"Why, then, would he tell me such a thing?" Abernathy asked.

"I hate to say this but, if he didn't apply the money to
my loan as I assumed he would, the only thing that could
have happened to it is that he took it."

"You are saying that Theodore Epson stole your
money?" Abernathy asked.

"That's the only conclusion I can come to," Jennie replied.

Abernathy let out a long, disgusted sigh, then shook his head. "You know what I think, Constable?" he asked, turning to address Billings. "I think that when this woman learned that Mr. Epson had left our bank to take employment back East, she figured that would be the perfect opportunity to make such a spurious claim. She seeks to defraud the bank at the expense of the reputation of as fine a young man as has ever graced our fair city. I wish there was more we could do to her besides confiscate the house. I wish we could throw her in jail for libel and slander and throw away the key!"

"But I'm telling the truth," Jennie pleaded. "I swear I'm telling the truth! I gave the money to Mr. Epson."

"Do your duty, Constable," Abernathy said. "Evict this woman from my house."

"I'm sorry, Miss Jennie," Billings said, and the tone and expression in his voice gave truth to the fact that he really was carrying out his duty under duress. "I'm afraid I'm going to have to ask you, and your girls, to leave the house."

"But, please, Mr. Abernathy. If you turn us all out, where will my girls go?" For the first time in a very long time, Jennie felt desperate. It reminded her of her days as a slave, when she had absolutely no control over her own destiny, the days before the mountain man had purchased her freedom and given her a chance at a new, independent life.

"Where you and your girls go is none of my concern," Abernathy replied coldly. "However, I would remind you that, while St. Louis has no ordinance prohibiting a bawdy house, we do have a law against street solicitation for immoral purposes. And I intend to see that Constable Billings and his men uphold that law. So, I wouldn't go out on the street if I were any of you."

"I'm sorry, Miss Jennie," Billings said.

Jennie sighed, and with her eyes brimming with tears, reached out to put her hand on Billings's arm. "I know this isn't your fault," she said. "You are just doing your duty."

"Yes, ma'am," Billings agreed. He pulled his arm from her gently, embarrassed at her gesture in front of the bank men. "I'm glad you see it that way." He was caught in a bind, and hated what he now had to do.

Philadelphia, Pennsylvania, Monday, August 16, 1824

Theodore Epson sat across the desk from Joel Fontaine, the president of the Trust Bank of Philadelphia. They were in Fontaine's office, and as a measure of the size of the Trust Bank, Fontaine's office alone was as large as the entire River Bank of St. Louis.

"I've never been to the teeming metropolis of St. Louis," Fontaine said. "But I would dearly like to visit there sometime. How did you find it during your time there?"

Epson shook his head in disgust and disappointment. "I assure you, Mr. Fontaine, you would not like it. St. Louis is a dirty, lawless, and barely civilized town. Its streets are filled with trappers and fur dealers who are little more than wild savages. Prostitutes conduct their business without fear of the law, though I am pleased to say that I put into motion a means whereby the most notorious of all the brothels will, no doubt, be closed very soon."

"Oh? And, how did you do that?" Fontaine asked with genuine curiosity.

"I denied them access to their ill-gotten gains."

"Good for you," Fontaine said. "I'm sure the city of St. Louis was sorry to see such an upstanding citizen as yourself leave its precincts."

"No doubt," Epson replied. "But I assure you, sir, that

feeling was not reciprocated. I can't tell you how happy I was to get your offer so I could leave that Godforsaken place."

Fontaine looked down at a piece of paper that lay on his desk. "And I see that you have just opened your own personal account for nine hundred dollars," he said. "That is an impressive amount of money, so you must've done well by yourself while you were in St. Louis."

"Yes, I, uh, was quite frugal during my stay," Epson said, pulling his heavily starched shirt collar away from his neck. Epson had kept the money given him in confidence by William Ashley, and he had executed the draft given him by Jennie, keeping that money as well. Even after the expense of moving from St. Louis to Philadelphia, he still had over nine hundred dollars left. All in all, a profitable enterprise—albeit with other people's money.

Some might consider what he did as dishonest, but Epson was convinced that he had performed a service for the city of St. Louis. It was clear that a majority of the citizens there wanted the whorehouse to be closed, and this would give them a way to eliminate it. He justified keeping the money from Jennie because it was obviously obtained as a result of her immoral and indecent operation. He also didn't feel guilty about keeping the money given him by William Ashley because he was certain this money came from some businessman. The way he looked at it, everyone benefited from his action except for the two people: the whore, and her mysterious benefactor, who was obviously a hypocritical businessman. And no one would feel sympathy for them.

"Mr. Epson?" Fontaine said.

Epson had drifted away with his self-satisfied thoughts, and it wasn't until then that he realized that Fontaine was talking to him.

"I'm sorry," Epson said. "You were saying?"

"I was just saying, on behalf of the bank, welcome to

Philadelphia," Fontaine said, sticking his hand across the desk.

"Thank you, sir," Epson said, accepting the handshake. He smiled. "I am very glad to be here—in fact, more than you'll ever know."

House of Flowers, St. Louis, Monday, August 16, 1824

There were tears, sobs, and expressions of concern for their immediate future as Jennie called all her girls together. She informed them silently that they were being forced out of the house.

"But why, Miss Jennie? What have we done to anyone?" one of the girls asked.

"We have committed no offense," Jennie replied. "It's just that there are some people who are all proper on the outside, but just plain mean on the inside. I fear we have made enemies of such a person."

"But how can they throw us out of the house? I thought you had paid the bank everything you owed them," Carla said.

"I *have* paid the bank what I owe them," Jennie said. "But it would seem that Mr. Epson was not as honest as he appeared. He ran away with the money."

One by one, the girls came to Jennie, hugged her, then went back to their rooms to pack their few belongings. Jennie lingered in the foyer for a moment longer, allowing her hand to pass over the banister and looking at the crown molding around the room. She realized, with a pang of regret, how beautiful the house was, and how much she was going to miss it.

Slowly, as if by delaying each step she could stave off the inevitable, Jennie climbed the stairs to the second floor and went into the bedroom. This was the same bedroom where, for many years, she had dreamed and fantasized about Art. Recently, as if a fantasy realized, Art had appeared out of nowhere. When she awakened the next morning she saw that it wasn't a dream . . . he was still there. Now, after a glorious reunion, Art had gone back West, returning to the mountains. What if he came back looking for her? Without this house, he might not find her.

Unable to control her tears, Jennie began packing her clothes.

It was more than a loss of livelihood, or even the loss of a roof over her head, that made Jennie cry. The House of Flowers was the closest thing to a real home Jennie had ever had in her life. It had been her plan to make enough money to someday leave the prostitution business. Then the House of Flowers truly would have been a home. Perhaps even a home to which Art might some day come to live.

Deep in her soul, she knew that it was very unlikely that Art would ever settle down in a city, but fantasies of such a future had occupied her thoughts for a long time.

When Jennie came down to the foyer a while later, all five of her girls were gathered in the foyer with all their belongings, waiting for some direction from the woman who had taken care of them for so long.

"What do we do now, Miss Jennie?" Sue Ellen asked.

Jennie shook her head sadly. "I wish I could tell you," she said. "I wish I knew what *I* was going to do."

"I know what I would do if I were a man," Carla said. "If I were a man, I would leave St. Louis."

"Leave St. Louis and go where?" Lisa asked.

"I don't know. West maybe," Carla said. "Yes, I'd go West."

At that moment, the front door opened and a white-haired old black man came into the house.

"Miss Jennie," Ben said, "I got the carriage drawed up out front. You want me to put your luggage in?"

"Yes, I suppose . . ." Jennie said. Then she looked at

the other girls and suddenly smiled. "West?" she said to Carla. "You would go West?"

"Yes."

Jennie laughed out loud. "What a great idea!" she said. She grabbed Carla, hugging her as she danced around the foyer

"Miss Jennie, are you all right?" Millie asked.

"All right? I've never been more all right," Jennie answered, gathering herself and putting on her best face for the girls. "Ben?" she said to her driver.

"Yes, ma'am?" Ben replied, as confused by Jennie's antics as were the girls.

"Do you think you can find someone who would trade us a good, sturdy wagon for the carriage?"

"Miss Jennie, I 'specs you could get two fine wagons for this carriage. This is a fine carriage."

"Even better. Get two wagons, and four mules."

"Mules, Miss Jennie?"

"Yes, mules," Jennie said. She looked again at her girls. "Sue Ellen, Cindy, Lisa, Millie, Carla, we're going West!"

Ponca Village, Upper Missouri, Tuesday, August 31, 1824

The Indians of the Ponca tribe went all out to welcome Artoor and his fellow travelers. The women made Indian fry bread and roasted game, the men performed dances, and Artoor was invited to join them in the inner circle of the council fire. When McDill started to sit in the inner circle as well, without being invited, a couple of warriors stood in his way.

"Art, tell these ignorant savages to stand aside and let me sit down," McDill said.

"You can sit anywhere you want, McDill, except in the front circle," Art said.

"What do you mean I can't sit in the front circle? I'll sit any damn where I please."

Art, who was already seated, turned to look back toward McDill. "You can sit anywhere you want, McDill, except in the front circle."

"You're sitting there."

"I was invited."

"Why wasn't I invited?"

"Perhaps it is because you presumed to sit there before you were invited."

"That makes no sense. If they were going to invite me anyway, why not just let me sit there now?"

"It is the Indian way," Art said without any further explanation. His patience had long since begun to wear thin.

Grumbling, McDill sat further back, joining the other trappers.

Spotted Pony held his arms forward, spread shoulder-width apart, palms up. A shaman placed a lit ceremonial pipe into his hands, parallel with Spotted Pony's shoulders. Gingerly, Spotted Pony lifted the pipe above his head and mouthed a prayer. Bringing the pipe back down, he turned it very carefully, pushing the bowl forward with his right hand, bringing the mouthpiece back with his left. He took a puff on the pipe, then used his right hand to wave some of the escaping smoke back into his face. Afterward, he held the pipe out toward Art, inviting him to smoke as well.

Art smoked the pipe with Spotted Pony, being very careful to follow the same prescribed ritual. Art then passed the pipe around to the others in the inner circle, and only after all had smoked did the conversation begin. He wasn't a regular user of tobacco, but he understood the importance of the pipe to the Indians.

"You are the one called Artoor?" Spotted Pony asked.

"Yes."

"You have killed many Indians, Artoor."

"Yes. I have killed many Indians, and I have killed

white men. But I have only killed those who were trying to kill me."

A very old and wrinkled man leaned over to say something to Spotted Pony. This was the shaman, the medicine man who'd lit the pipe and placed it so carefully in Spotted Pony's hands when the ritual began. The shaman spoke in a mixed guttural, singsong voice, nodding his head often as he spoke.

Spotted Pony nodded as well, as the other spoke.

"He Who Sees says that your heart is pure and your words are true, Artoor," Spotted Pony said. "You have killed only those who try to kill you."

He Who Sees spoke again.

"You and another were riding on a big canoe on the water when Arikara attacked you. They killed the one with you, but they did not kill you."

Art nodded, wondering how the old man knew. "They killed my friend, Clyde Barnes."

"You killed many of them." It wasn't a question, it was a statement, and Art saw no reason to reply.

The shaman spoke again.

"But you have made an enemy of Wak Tha Go," Spotted Pony continued.

Art looked confused. "I do not know Wak Tha Go," he said.

"Wak Tha Go is the warrior who killed your friend," Spotted Pony explained. "You killed many of his warriors and now, because the tepees of many were empty when he returned to the village, Wak Tha Go is no longer welcome among the Arikara, his own people. He is not welcome by the Ponca, the Mandan, the Sioux, or the Crow. The heart of Wak Tha Go is very hot, and cannot be cooled. He wants only to kill you."

"I hope to make peace with the Arikara, as I hope to make peace with the Ponca, Mandan, Sioux, Crow, and Blackfeet. I would even make peace with Wak Tha Go, if he would cool his heart."

"You have brought gifts for the Ponca?" Spotted Pony asked.

Art smiled, grateful that Mr. Ashley had provided for this moment. "Yes. The fur chief who lives in St. Louis has sent many good gifts to show his appreciation for allowing trappers to take beaver."

"It is good that we should have peace," Spotted Pony said.

From each village, an Indian messenger was sent ahead to the next, telling of the peace mission of the trapper known as Artoor. Because the messengers were sent ahead, every village turned out to welcome Art, and soon he had negotiated peace treaties with nearly all the Indians along the Missouri: the Poncas, Sioux, Cheyennes, Hidatsas, Mandans, and even the Arikara. The Indians all acknowledged the rights of the trappers and fur traders to take beaver on their land, and Art promised fair treatment to the Indians on all future trades.

"No more will our people trade bad whiskey for good pelts," Art promised with all sincerity.

For his part, the Arikara chief known as The Peacemaker promised that the Arikara would make no more war, but, he also warned that Wak Tha Go, who had made his own personal war against Artoor, had left the Arikara and now lived with the Blackfeet, and called himself a Blackfoot.

"I think Wak Tha Go and the Blackfeet will not make peace with you," The Peacemaker said.

"I will try to make peace with him," Art replied. "I have lived with the Indian and I consider the Indian to be my brother. I have no wish to kill my brothers."

At the mouth of the Yellowstone, Art sent word to the Blackfeet, Assiniboin, and Crow, inviting them to come talk peace. Only the Crow could be coaxed in, and their chiefs came to the meeting arrayed in their finest blankets and robes.

The meeting, designed to discuss peace, nearly started a war. Art displayed the gifts he intended to give the Indians in exchange for their promise not to make war on the white fur trappers. When one of the chiefs reached for the gifts before he was invited to do so, McDill clubbed him over the head with his pistol butt. Angry, the other chiefs threw off their robes and raised their war clubs, forcing Art and the others to wade into the fray, swinging their muskets. Within a few moments, all five Indians were on the ground and it was obvious to Art that McDill was about to kill one of them.

"No, McDill!" Art shouted.

McDill was on the ground with his knife at an Indian chief's throat. The Indian was staring up at him defiantly, unable to defend himself, but unwilling to show fear.

McDill held the knife there for a long moment, until Art pointed his rifle at McDill.

"I said no. Leave him be," Art said.

"Whose side are you on?" McDill asked. "The man or the redskin?"

"I'm on *my* side," Art said. He desperately tried to hold his anger in check. "If you kill him we'll have the entire Crow nation on our backs."

McDill made no effort to release the Indian chief.

"Let him up—now," Art said, cocking his rifle. "If you don't, I will kill you."

The other Indians, who by now had regained their feet, looked on with wide eyes at the drama playing out between the white men. They had never seen such enmity between these fur trappers before.

"You'd kill one of your own?" McDill asked.

"You aren't one of my own, McDill," Art said flatly

McDill let out a long sigh, then stood up and put his knife away.

"Sure, Art, I was just funnin' with him anyway," he said.

Warily, the chief regained his feet and looked over at Art.

"Help yourself," Art said, pointing to the gifts.

The Indian hesitated.

"Here," Art said. He picked up a fine bone-handled knife and handed it to the chief. "This is for you."

Smiling, the Indian held the knife out and looked at it.

"Here, for you. For all of you," Art said with an inviting swipe of his hand.

"Wait," McDill said. "Not all them gifts is for the Crow. We still got the Assiniboin and the Blackfeet to worry about."

"That's a fact," Art said. He nodded toward the remaining chiefs, who were now gathering up the presents. "But the time may come up here when we need some allies. And these Indians may just be what we need, provided you don't try any more dumb-fool stunts like the one you just pulled."

When the Crow left the encampment an hour or so later, they were laden with every gift Art's little party had remaining. Now, if the trappers encountered the Blackfeet, or any other hostile tribe up here, they might be able to count on the Crow for help. In fact, just before the Crow left, one of them, the one who had nearly been killed by McDill, approached Art.

"You would have killed your own to save me?" he asked, speaking English quite well. Art was surprised because, until this moment, they had communicated only in sign language.

"Yes," he said.

"How are you called?" the Indian asked.

"I am called Artoor."

The Indian nodded. "I have heard of you, Artoor. I am Red Tail." Red Tail put his right hand on Art's left shoulder, and Art did the same to him.

"And I have heard of you," Art said.

"It is good that you would kill one of your own to save the life of a Crow. Because you would do that, we will throw out all that has passed behind us. The Crow will be the friend of Artoor."

"And you will not make war with the trappers and fur traders?"

"We will make no war," Red Tail said. Abruptly he turned and joined the others. Mounting, they rode away quickly, yipping and howling as they proudly displayed their gifts.

9

Perched high on the end of a bluff that protruded over the water, stood a fort constructed of palisade logs. There were two projecting blockhouses on corners opposite each other from which the guards would not only have a view of the river approach and surrounding countryside, but could also cover, by rifle fire, the outside walls of the fort itself. The American flag fluttered from a wooden pole atop the nearest blockhouse.

Although the structure had all the appearances of a U.S. Army fort, it was actually the trading post Ashley had told Art about. It had been established by the American Fur Company, and was ably commanded by Joe Walker, the head of the trading garrison.

The front gate to the fort was closed tight when Art and his entourage arrived. Art looked toward the blockhouse that had a view of the gate; it appeared to be empty.

"Maybe there's nobody here," McDill suggested.

"Someone is here," Art said. "The gate has to be closed from the inside."

"Is not good military sense to leave blockhouse empty," Hoffman said.

Dog barked, and a face appeared over the balustrade of the blockhouse.

Art laughed. "Dog had the right idea," he said. "All we had to do is knock."

The man in the blockhouse pointed a rifle down toward them, more than a bit unsteadily.

"Who are you, and what do you want?" he called.

"The name is Art, and we've got a letter for Joe Walker," Art said, holding up the letter. "From Mr. William Ashley in St. Louis."

The man in the blockhouse stared at them for a long, silent moment. His face was screwed up, as if he had been eating lemons.

"For God's sake, man, do we look like Indians to you?" McDill called up to him.

The guard called down to the inside of the fort. "Open the gate."

A moment later the gate creaked open and Art and his group rode inside. Just inside the gate in the middle of the open area, which resembled a small parade ground, sat a cannon. A dog came running toward them, his fangs bared. Dog hunkered down toward the ground and growled. The canine who had approached stopped, barked a quick, ribbony yap at Dog, then turned and ran away. A man came up to meet them.

"You the one the Indians called Artoor?" he asked.

"Yes," Art replied.

"We heard you were coming. Come on in, Mr. Walker is waiting for you."

"How did you hear we were coming?"

"Word spreads upriver faster than people do," the man said.

Joe Walker was only two inches over five feet tall, and nearly as big around. He had a bald head and a full brown beard, and he scratched at his bushy whiskers as he read the letter Art presented to him.

"How are things back in St. Louie?" he asked.

"Noisy," Art replied.

Walker laughed. "Noisy indeed," he said. "Yes, I would say the city is noisy, all right. I miss it, though, all the people—and especially women . . . not many women out here, except the Indian gals, who are nice but don't palaver the American language much."

Art said, "Some people talk too much as it is."

"You and your men must join me for dinner. I am anxious to hear more about your trip."

Art's party actually cleaned themselves up a little before they sat down with Joe Walker in his quarters for a sumptuous meal.

"How goes your peacemaking mission?" Walker asked over the meal of fried trout and baked potatoes.

"How did you know of our mission?" Art asked.

"Word has come from the friendly tribes downriver," Walker explained.

"So far it has gone well. We have made peace with the Arikara and they were on the warpath last year."

"But you have not made peace with the Blackfeet."

"No."

"Nor will you," Walker said. "The Blackfeet are why we built this fort. Such savages are they that even their own kind will have little to do with them. However, I wish you good luck in your effort. Were peace to be made with them, it would make our task much easier."

"Well, we sure want to make your life easier," McDill said. The Hessian, Hoffman, shot him a hard look. But McDill was unaware of his own stupidity. "What did I say?" he asked when there was only silence after his remark.

Walker went on. "We are here to improve the business prospects of the American Fur Company, and we appreciate the efforts you gentlemen have exerted to ensure our success."

"Glad to be of service," McDill muttered under his breath so that only Caviness could hear him.

After the meal, Art and Walker talked on long into the night about the goings-on in the territory, swapping information. Art was determined to know as much as he could about what lay ahead for him and his men.

In the Blackfoot Village

Wak Tha Go got up with the sun and walked through the quiet village. The fire of last night's council had been reduced to a pile of white ash that gave off only a tiny amount of smoke.

The Blackfeet were aware that Artoor was making peace with all the other nations, and they held council to decide whether or not they would accept his peace offer. There were some who counseled peace. Chief among the peacemakers was a man named Running Elk, who was the oldest and wisest shaman of the village.

Wak Tha Go was very much against making peace. And though Wak Tha Go was a recent émigré to the Blackfoot Nation, he had been totally accepted as one of them. This was in part because of his reputation as a fierce warrior, and in part because he was a member of the Bear Society, one of the most honored of the war societies. Wak Tha Go proposed that, instead of making peace with Artoor, they send out a war party to find him and kill him. Wak Tha Go even offered himself as leader of the war party.

The discussion was heated on each side of the issue, but by the end of the evening no real decision had been made. As far as Wak Tha Go was concerned, "no decision" was just as effective as a decision in favor of war. That was because it effectively kept the current policy in place. And the current policy of the Blackfeet was belligerence with the white trappers and hunters.

Still thinking about the council of the night before, Wak Tha Go left the tepees and the smoldering campfires, then climbed to the top of the one-hundred-foot promontory that jutted out over the Yellowstone River. From there he could see the sun, now a glowing orange ball poised just over the distant horizon. As the sun rose higher in the sky, it began to spread pools of brilliantly shining gold and silver across the surface of the water. Then, when it became so bright that it started to hurt his eyes, Wak Tha Go turned to look back at the village he had just left.

Here and there wisps of smoke curled up from holes in the tops of the tepees, evidence that the people of the village were just beginning to rise. Then, quite unexpectedly, the rising hackles on the back of his neck told Wak Tha Go that he was not alone. He spun around quickly and was shocked to see Running Elk behind him.

Wak Tha Go had not heard Running Elk approach, indeed would not have thought him capable of even climbing the hill, and yet there the old man was, sitting cross-legged on the ground, looking at Wak Tha Go with a gaze that seemed to penetrate to his very soul.

"How did you get here?" Wak Tha Go asked.

No answer.

"What are you doing here?"

When Running Elk still didn't answer, Wak Tha Go went on, speaking to cover the awkwardness of the moment.

"If you have come to speak again of making peace with the white man, you may as well shout your words into the wind, for my ears are closed," Wak Tha Go said.

Running Elk remained silent.

"Why do you not speak?"

The old man stared with eyes that were so penetrating as to be almost frightening. Wak Tha Go had never seen such intensity in anyone's eyes before.

Running Elk was wearing a red shirt, trimmed in

yellow. This was not the kind of clothes one wore on ordinary occasions, and Wak Tha Go wondered about that. He also noticed that Running Elk's knife, bow and quiver of arrows, his war club, and his pipe all lay on the ground beside him.

"How did you get by me?" Wak Tha Go asked. "And why are you wearing your finest clothes and carrying your most prized possessions?"

Wak Tha Go was very uncomfortable now, and the more he tried to cover his embarrassment, the more obvious his embarrassment became. "Are you making a journey?"

"Yes," Running Elk replied, speaking for the first time. "I am making a journey."

"Where are you going?"

"Where I go is not important," Running Elk said. "I have come to tell you of things to come."

"You will tell me of things to come?" Wak Tha Go scoffed. "Are you one who can see into the future?"

"I am a man of knowledge," Running Elk said.

"So, you are a man of knowledge, are you? Then tell me of my future."

"You have two futures."

Wak Tha Go laughed. "How can one man have two futures?"

"You have two futures, but can only choose one. One is the future of peace. One is the future of war."

"I will not ask you which future I should choose, for I know what you will say. You would have me choose the future of peace."

"I cannot choose for you."

"Then I choose the future of war."

"You choose war so you can have revenge against one white man."

"Yes."

"You are a brave and ferocious warrior. But you have not chosen wisely. Many of my people will be killed."

"I don't care how many are killed as long as I kill the one called Artoor."

Running Elk shook his head. "Artoor will not be killed."

"He will be killed, and I will kill him," Wak Tha Go insisted.

Running Elk held up his hand to silence Wak Tha Go. "I do not have much time," he said. "Hear my words so that you know what I speak is true."

"I will listen," Wak Tha Go said.

"The time will come when the one called Artoor will visit our village, and while he is here his tongue will speak without ceasing from sun to sun. The people will not understand his words, but they will feel his power and the one called Artoor will be given a new name."

"One cannot be given a new name unless one does a great deed," Wak Tha Go said. "What great deed will Artoor do, that he will be given a new name?"

"He will do not one great deed, but many great deeds. He will live long and become a man of the past and the future," Running Elk explained. "Among the Indians of all nations, songs of Artoor's deeds will be sung in councils and around campfires. White men will tell stories of him in the places where they gather, and they will write of him in their books. He will be remembered by the grandchildren of the grandchildren of their grandchildren."

"And what is this new name to be?"

"He will be called Preacher."

Wak Tha Go laughed. "Preacher? Preacher is what white men call the teachers of their religion. It is not the name of a great warrior."

"He will make it the name of a great warrior."

"How is it that you know all these things, Running Elk? Do you have the gift of seeing into the future?"

"I do not see the future, I am the future," Running Elk said.

"You speak in riddles, old man," Wak Tha Go said. He

turned away from Running Elk and looked back out over the village. The pearlgray of early morning was sharpening in tone and tint, and the tepees took on definition from the bright light of day. He saw three women in mourning dress approaching one of the tepees. "And if I kill Artoor, what will happen to the future you see?"

Running Elk did not answer, but Wak Tha Go didn't repeat the question. He was too interested in what was going on in the village below. He saw that one of the three women was carrying a deerskin. She stopped just outside the tepee, laid the skin down, unrolled it, then took out a red and yellow shirt, a knife, a bow and quiver of arrows, a pipe, and a war club. It wasn't until then that he realized what was going on. The three women were part of a funeral.

"Look, someone has died," Wak Tha Go said. He pointed. "The women of his family have come to prepare the body." Wak Tha Go looked more closely at the women. "Wait, I do not understand what I see. Those are the women of your family," he said. "Your wife, your daughter, and the wife of your son. Running Elk, what are they doing?" Wak Tha Go turned around to ask his question, but Running Elk was gone.

"Running Elk?" Wak Tha Go called. Running Elk was nowhere around. Wak Tha Go wondered where the old Indian had gone, and how he had gotten away without being seen.

Wak Tha Go turned back toward the village and saw that the women had gone into the tepee. Suddenly he felt a strange, tingling sensation, and his body convulsed as if he had had a chill.

"No!" he shouted. "No, this cannot be!" He hurried down the side of the hill, running so hard that he was panting for breath when he reached the tepee. Pushing open the flap, he went inside. The oldest of the three women looked around at him, and Wak Tha Go saw that her eyes were filled with tears.

"What has happened?" Wak Tha Go asked.

"My husband has died," she said.

Looking beyond the women, he saw the body of Running Elk, lying on a bed of furs.

"When . . . when did he die?" Wak Tha Go asked in a strained voice.

"Last night, after the council," the woman answered.

"But no, this can't be," Wak Tha Go said.

The women misunderstood his reaction.

"It is good to see that you are saddened," said Running Elk's daughter. "You spoke against him in council. I am glad he is not your enemy."

Wak Tha Go realized then that he would have to accept a fundamental truth. The person who had come to speak with him this morning was not Running Elk, but Running Elk's spirit. He turned and walked away from the tepee, thinking about the things Running Elk had told him. Wak Tha Go felt privileged to have been visited by Running Elk's spirit, for only those warriors with great medicine were given such visions. But he couldn't tell anyone about it, because Running Elk had come to him to advise the path of peace, when he wanted to . . . suddenly Wak Tha Go had an idea.

He would tell everyone of the visit of Running Elk's spirit. And when they would ask him why Running Elk came to him, he would tell them it was because Running Elk had changed his mind and now wished to say that the Blackfeet should make war against the trapper named Artoor.

Outside St. Louis, Missouri

Jennie and Carla rode in the wagon bed as old Ben, Jennie's longtime driver, handled the reins and gently slapped the horses forward. They were heading West. Four other girls rode in the second wagon, and they would share the driving duties, following Ben's lead. The only problem was, they weren't sure exactly where they were going, other than West. There was precious little in the way of civilization out there beyond St. Louis, and all of them were more than a bit scared at the prospect of leaving behind the place and the people who were so familiar to them. But they sympathized with Jennie's plight and wanted to support her—and they trusted her to take care of them.

Her mind, though, was occupied with thoughts of Art and where he might be, and whether she would ever see him again. . . .

She remembered when they met, how Art had been such a boy, and how he had tried to be her friend. He didn't know how the world worked then. He didn't know about slavery and the evil things that men do to each other. He'd found out quickly enough—those were dark days when Jennie had been owned as property, and used as property by her masters and other men. Lucas Younger had been one such owner. Art had joined up with the Younger party one time, and he and Jennie had become friends.

One day they talked as she sat in the back of the moving wagon. Art was riding close behind to be with her and try to comfort her.

"Why do you call your pa Mr. Younger?" he had said. He didn't know any better.

Jennie looked at Art, surprised, shocked even at his naïveté. She said: "He ain't my pa."

"Oh, I see. He's your step-pa then? He married your ma, is that it?"

At that, Jennie shook her head. "Mrs. Younger ain't my ma."

"They ain't your ma and pa?"

"No. They're my owners."

"Owners? What do you mean, owners?"

"I'm their slave girl. I thought you knowed that."

"No, I didn't know that," Art said. "Fact is, I don't know as I've ever knowed a white slave girl."

"I ain't exactly white," Jennie said quietly.

"You're not?"

"I'm a Creole. My grandma was black."

"But how can you be their slave? You don't do no work for 'em," Art said. "I mean . . . no offense meant, but I ain't never seen you do nothin' like get water or firewood, or help out Mrs. Younger with the cookin'."

"No," Jennie said quietly. "But gathering firewood, or helping in the kitchen, ain't the only way of workin'. There's other ways . . . ways that"—she stopped talking for a moment—"ways that I won't trouble you with."

"You mean, like what you was doin' with all them men last night?"

At that moment, Jennie cut a quick glance toward him. The expression on her face was one of total mortification. "You . . . you seen what I was doin'?"

"No, I didn't really see nothin' more'n a bunch of men linin' up at the back of the wagon. Even when I went to bed, I couldn't see what was goin' on on the other side of the tarp."

"Do you . . . do you know what I was doing in there?"

Art shook his head. "Not really," he said. "I got me an idea that you was doin' what painted ladies do. Only thing is, I don't rightly know what that is."

Jennie looked at him in surprise for a moment; then her face changed and she laughed.

"What is it? What's so funny?" Art asked.

"You are," she said. "You are still just a boy after all."

"I ain't no boy," Art said resolutely. "I done killed me a man. I reckon that's made me man enough."

The smile left Jennie's face, and she put her hand on his shoulder. "I reckon it does at that," she said.

"You don't like doin' what Younger is makin' you do, do you?"

"No. I hate it," Jennie said resolutely. "It's—it's the worst thing you can imagine."

"Then why don't you leave?"

"I can't. I belong to 'em. Besides, if'n I left, where would I go? What would I do? I'd starve to death if I didn't have someone lookin' out for me."

"I don't know," Art said. "But seems to me like anything would be better than this."

"What about you? Are you going to stay with the Youngers?"

"Only as long as it takes to get to St. Louis," Art replied. "Then I'll go out on my own."

"Have you ever been to St. Louis?" Jennie asked.

"No, have you?"

Jennie shook her head. "No, I haven't. Mr. Younger says it's a big and fearsome place, though."

"I'll bet you could find a way to get on there," Art said. "I'll bet you could find work. The kind of work that wouldn't make you have to paint yourself up and be with men."

"I'd be afraid. If I try to get away, Mr. Younger will send the slave catchers after me."

"Slave catchers? What are slave catchers?"

"They are fearsome men who hunt down runaway slaves. They are paid to find the runaways, and bring 'em back to their masters. They say that the slave hunters always find who they are lookin' for. And most of the time they give 'em a whippin' before they bring 'em back. I ain't never been whipped."

"I can see where a colored runaway might be easy to find. But you don't look colored. How would they find you? Don't be afraid. I'll help you get away."

"How would you do that?"

"Easy," Art said with more confidence than he really felt. "I aim to leave the Youngers soon's we get to St. Louis. When I go, I'll just take you with me, that's all. You bein' white and all, you could pass for my sister. No one's goin' to take you for a runaway. Why, I'll bet you could fine a job real easy."

"Maybe I could get on with someone looking after their children," Jennie suggested. "I'm real good at looking after children. You really will help me?"

"Yes," Art replied. He spat in the palm of his hand, then held it out toward Jennie.

"What . . . what is that?" Jennie asked, recoiling from his proffered hand.

"It's a spit promise," Art said. "That's about the most solemn promise there is."

Smiling, Jennie spat in her own hand as well, then reached out to take Art's hand in hers. They shook on the deal.

Now Jennie was on the move again. She had achieved her dream of living in St. Louis, but had seen the dream shattered by evil men and women who hated her for her race and her profession. Had the world changed at all since that day she and Art had made their spit promise? How she wished she could see him here by the side of this wagon as she headed West again.

How many times had she been bought and sold since she was a young girl—the girl Art saw when they first met? Both of them had been sold as slaves after that, but he had escaped and fled into the mountains, become a man whom other men respected. Well, in the last decade she had become a successful businesswoman. No one had owned her. Respect was harder to come by, though, for a beautiful Creole woman who lived by her wits and her body.

Yet she knew one thing. She would never be a slave again. She would die first. That much was certain.

10

Upper Missouri

Art's party of trappers rode west along the upper
reaches of the wide and wild Missouri. All were alert to
the danger that they knew lurked behind every stand of
trees and every hill. They kept to the lowest point everywhere they went, and on the third day out from the fort
Art led them onto an old Indian trail that looked well
traveled. It took them up to a shallow tributary of the
Missouri River and into a wide ravine that gave them
shelter and hid them from view throughout most of the
day's travel.

The floor of the ravine was wide, and most of it was the
streambed, nearly two hundred yards across, sandy and
rocky. Along each side of the river were low bluffs,
almost black in color from the dark earth and the shadows when the sun did not strike them directly. As the
ravine opened to the high plain ahead, there was a small
island, only about fifty yards long and thirty yards wide.
It was dense with willow, alder, and a few tall cottonwoods standing proudly. It took Art's men the remainder of the day to reach the little island.

"We'll camp there tonight," Art said, pointing to the

island. He turned his horse into the cold stream. Dog followed, then ran ahead, leaping from the water that wasn't even chest-high to him onto the dry, brushy shore of the island. He immediately went to explore its length and breadth.

"Yes, sir," Herman Hoffman said unthinkingly, the first words he had spoken for the entire day. He was dependable, though Art wondered what kind of trapper he would make. Still, it was none of his concern.

McDill and Caviness grumbled something about Art's decision, but they were wise enough not to share it with the rest of the party. The cousins, Montgomery and Matthews, willingly led their pack animals across the wide, shallow stream onto the island, without a word of protest. Green they might be, but they knew enough to follow their leader's orders for their own safety.

They all ate a light, cold supper. Art and Hoffman, along with Dog, took the first watch after dark, followed by McDill and Caviness. The youngsters took the final watch, which would last until breakfast time.

They kept the horses together in a tight circle at the center of the island, tethered to the strong cottonwood trees. Art had insisted on this, even though McDill had laughed at such seemingly needless precautions.

Wak Tha Go had formed a party of twelve men, including himself, from the Blackfoot village. He had hoped for more, since he had announced Running Elk's "prophecy" that the white trappers would be annihilated by the Blackfeet. But he thought he would have more than enough strength, outnumbering the whites two-to-one—in country familiar to the Indians and strange to the trappers.

He was dressed in full war costume, wearing buckskin leggings and moccasins elaborately trimmed with beads and feathers, with a single eagle feather fastened in his scalp lock. He wore a white buffalo robe, which was very rare, tanned and soft, over his otherwise-naked torso. And his face was painted in lines of red and black, which gave him a fierce, menacing appearance to anyone who might meet him in battle.

The others were similarly dressed. Each warrior carried a rifle or musket, as well as arrows and a hand ax for close-up, hand-to-hand fighting and scalping. The war party rode out from the village before dawn, heading southwest to where their scouts had said the white men were camped on an island in the river.

As their leader, Wak Tha Go rode about two horse lengths ahead of his men, so they could admire his courage and fierce appearance. The enemy, too, would be cowed by his warrior's paint and regalia, he knew.

He had told the braves his strategy the night before, when one of the scouts had returned with word that the whites were making camp. "We will ride up to their camp in the early morning and attack before they leave, while they are unprepared." He planned to approach from the east, with the rising sun at their backs. It was a simple attack plan that should work easily.

Nothing would give him greater satisfaction than wiping out the white trappers and counting coup on their property. They could use the horses and rifles too. It was going to be a good day to have a fight.

Art rose before sunup and folded his bedroll neatly and began packing his horse. He did not light a fire. Something told him that they should not this morning. He didn't know why, but he had learned to follow his instincts on such things.

Dog was patrolling the island, sniffing and snooping around in the underbrush. He also kept an eye on the horses, which whickered nervously whenever he was close by. He seemed to enjoy making them nervous, Art thought.

"Come here, boy," he said, tearing a piece of jerky in half and tossing it toward Dog. He chewed on the other half himself. He was hungry, but he had learned to live with hunger as a fact of life in the wilderness. Dog too, being half wolf, instinctively knew to eat when it was available because he could not know the next time there might be an opportunity.

The other men began to get up to face the new day on the trail. Art watched them. There had been plenty of time for him to form judgments of these men. And there was no question that, other than McDill and Caviness, he liked them; in fact, he respected all of them, even the two hostile ones, for their trail sense and ability to adapt to new, sometimes dangerous conditions away from the city. He only wished there was more of a chance for peace with the Indian tribes—then all of his party would have better prospects for survival and profit from pelts, as would Mr. Ashley himself.

But Art couldn't take on the whole world by himself. He had to have friends and allies to change the ways of the frontier. It was a daunting task. How could you change men? Take McDill, a born bully and a bad man. Still, in a fight he would be a valuable man to have on your side. The Hessian, Hoffman, was another case: a good heart and fiercely loyal to his leader. The others too were fighters with whom Art could trust his life. If it ever came to that . . .

Just then he heard the war shrieks coming from the other side of the riverbed, from atop the bluffs there to the northeast of the camp. He jumped upright and snatched up his rifle, checked the load.

"Everybody up! We've got trouble!" he called to the men.

From a slow, deliberate waking, they all leaped to their feet, guns in hand.

"What the hell?" McDill sputtered.

Again the war whoops arose, high-pitched and threatening.

"We're being attacked," Art said simply. "And we better be prepared to defend ourselves. They're coming in from over there," he said, pointing across the flat, shallow river. The rising sun lit the black bluff from behind, and skylined atop the ridge there were several Indians on horseback, brandishing their war spears.

They knew better than to stay there. After a minute to show themselves and, they hoped, to scare the white men on the island, they rode down to the other side—all but one. That one, a tall man with a single feather on his head and his face painted, remained visible and defiant, as if he were challenging them to take a shot at him.

Art was tempted to do just that, but until he knew how many of them there were and where they were coming from, he held off shooting anybody.

He turned to the others. "McDill and Hoffman, you two take the rear and see if any of them are attacking from the other side of the river. I doubt it, but we just don't know for sure." Those two turned and went to their positions.

To the others, he said, "Caviness and Montgomery, take the left—over there by those trees—and Matthews and I will take the right. If the Indians split up their party to attack from two ways, we'll be covered. If we see them coming from just one direction, we'll regroup to face them there. Okay?"

"Yes, Boss," Montgomery said, and saluted smartly.

Caviness grumbled something about how they were likely to die today, all because of Art—or something like that.

Art paid no attention to the grumbling. He and Matthews turned, moved over to some tall scrub to their right, and hunkered down there, rifles at the ready, powder and shot close at hand for reloading.

He had divided up the men to put one quick loader

with one slower man. He was the quicker between Matthews and himself. McDill was quicker than the Hessian, and Montgomery was lightning-fast on the reload, while Caviness was slow as molasses. Art could only hope for the best, hope that each man and each pair would hold position. The trouble was, how many Indians were about to attack?

The men could only wait. Then the attack came. From atop the bluff the tall Indian, who certainly was the leader of the raid, rode straight down the side of the bluff, his horse kicking up black dirt and rocks as he came. He gave out a high-pitched war cry that was answered by the others.

To the left, from where Art's men were, a column of attackers came around the bluff, brandishing guns and spears.

"McDill, any sign back there?" Art called out loudly, trying to be heard above the sound of the attackers' war whoops.

"Nobody—not yet!" came the reply. "I don't think they're coming from here!"

Art had to make a quick judgment. He had no way of knowing whether the Indians had ten or a hundred men in their war party, or some number in between. He would have to go with his gut instinct on this. His own men's lives were in his hands now—just like his own.

"All right, move up, cover Caviness and Montgomery, but don't bunch up too tight. We've got to present a wide front."

He had learned some about military tactics during his brief time with Jackson's army and in talking with old soldiers over the years at Rendezvous. But he was mainly following common sense in the situation at hand. His ears were splitting from the Indians' whooping and shouting, but he tried not to let that scare him or distract him. He had to stay in control and get these men through this situation.

Matthews said, "What should we do?"

Art said, "Stay put for just a second. Look, they're listening to the chief. I count a total of twelve. That's not a lot, but twice as many as us. At least that's how many we can see right now."

It looked pretty bad for Art's men. He counted again: twelve, including the chief. "They look like Blackfeet," Art surmised aloud.

"Yeah," Matthews said. "All painted up for war." He tried not to sound as scared as he felt.

Earlier, Wak Tha Go had risen before dawn and said his prayers to the Spirit to guide him in his holy purpose, to wipe out these evil intruders on the sacred land of the red people.

His purpose was simple: to kill them all. He would achieve this by a swift surprise attack at dawn. He outnumbered them two-to-one, and each of his braves had the fighting heart of five men! It would be a simple task to wipe them out long before the sun reached its zenith in the sky.

He urged his followers to keep their horses quiet as they first approached the bluff that overlooked the enemy's camp. They rode closely together and arrived at their destination in good time. In near-silence they all rode up to the top of the bluff, Wak Tha Go in the lead. He indicated that they should line up so they would be visible to the men below against the pink and red morning sky.

When all were in place, Wak Tha Go let loose a long, loud war yell: "Yee-yee-iii-haa! Yee-yee-ii-haa!"

The other warriors followed with their own shrieking cries that were meant to terrorize the enemy, who was presumably still in his bedroll. They smiled and laughed to each other. A good day for a raid! Too bad there were so few white trappers; they would have to fight each other for their scalps.

"Go now," Wak Tha Go ordered them, according to his plan of attack.

He remained alone on the very top of the bluff, looking down into the camp of the enemy. He could see the forms of the men as they scrambled from their bedrolls. One in particular moved slowly, was not in a panic. It was hard to tell from this distance, but he appeared to be a young white man, tall, and there was a dog near him. This man looked up at Wak Tha Go. Did their eyes meet? Wak Tha Go was not sure, but he did know that he had sent a message of fear into this man's heart—and into the hearts of the others as well.

Wak Tha Go smiled to himself. Then he unleashed another powerful yell, which was the signal to his braves to move down the slope and around to the riverbed. He pulled his own horse around and reluctantly moved away from the ridge top, where he had been skylined to those below. He would meet them face-to-face now, not from above. . . .

He was proud of these men who had stepped forward to go on this raid. They were the bravest of the brave from among the Blackfoot village where he had found refuge and purpose. He would proudly lead them into battle this day.

When he got to the bottom of the bluff, he wheeled his pony around and went to the head of the column of warriors, then rode with them onto the sandy shoreline of the river. Again, he looked across to take measure of the men who would die today, his enemy. They did not look like much. They were armed, seemingly ready to meet the attackers. The dog was still there, pacing back and forth, prowling like a wolf, not barking.

The fierce Indian leader raised his own spear and lifted his voice in a shout. The others followed suit, raising a huge, eerie war cry. Wak Tha Go kneed his mount into action and plunged into the river. His men did like-wise, their horses kicking up the shallow water.

As he charged, Wak Tha Go threw his spear toward the man he thought was the leader of the whites. It missed. The Indian took up a rifle that had been loaded and primed and lay across the horse's neck. He held it high, to keep it dry, and pushed his mount forward into the gunfire from the men on the island.

Art shouted to his men to hold their fire until the at-tackers came closer. He watched the tall, fierce warrior who led the party. The man's spear came whistling toward him, and he ducked beneath the rock and scrub for cover. The spear missed. He lifted his rifle and took aim. When the charging leader was within about ten yards, he fired. He missed.

The Indian whooped and the other defenders started to fire their guns. Art quickly reloaded and primed his weapon and lifted it again.

In the first fusillade, one of the Indians was shot from his pony and fell into the shallow river. They kept yelling and kept coming. They released their spears, which flew just over the defenders' heads.

"Keep shooting!" McDill shouted from his position, the sound of panic in his voice.

The young mountain man, Art, didn't feel panic or fear. He knew what had to be done. He didn't shout, just carefully aimed his rifle at another of the Indian riders and slowly squeezed the trigger. The weapon kicked him back and black smoke exploded from the barrel. The at-tacker, about the sixth along the line, fell from his horse. There were two down.

Now the Indian leader wheeled his horse to the right, and just missed getting shot by Montgomery, who had been trying to get a bead on him. Montgomery's gun roared and the ball shot past Wak Tha Go's shoulder.

The big Indian turned and smiled, as if to say, "You can't hurt me!" He pulled his horse to the rear of the attacking party, then turned to charge again.

The Indians kept coming, and now they had their own rifles and bows at the ready. Arrows thunked into the earth by Caviness, Matthews, and Hoffman. McDill frantically reloaded and lifted his gun, just in time for a ball from one of the Indians to whiz past his head, missing him by just a few inches.

In a huge explosion of gunpowder and shot, the island defenders fired almost simultaneously, causing the Indians' horses to rear and wheel madly, splashing and snorting. Another man fell. The trappers were cutting down the odds with each passing minute.

The braves circled and fell in behind their leader and charged again. The arrows flew and buzzed. One arrow struck Hoffman in his right arm, just below the shoulder. It passed through his flesh and left a bloody pulp. But he barely flinched as he reloaded his rifle, ramming a ball into the barrel.

Art saw the blood streaming down the German's arm, but couldn't stop to respond. He fired again at the attackers, missing his target as the Indian weaved out of harm's way.

In the melee, a couple of the Blackfeet had managed to pull the bodies of the fallen braves from the river and put them on the riverbank, so they wouldn't be trampled by the repeated charge against the island. All the whites could see was the splashing and the oncoming arrows as the Indians kept up the attack, even in the face of strong gunfire.

It was a miracle that Art had not lost a single man yet. He looked around and saw that his men were fiercely concentrated on doing their best to fire, reload, fire, and reload—again and again, almost like machines. He was proud of them, but there was no time for sentiment. He focused on his own job, and was able to get off another shot. This time he hit one of the horses, which went down in a violent, trumpeting death. The rider leaped off in time, and ran back to the other side of the river.

Wak Tha Go was unhappy at this turn of events. He had expected to wipe out the whites with the surprise attack, but instead he had lost three men and the whites none. He called to his men to take the three fallen braves away, back to the far side of the bluff where they had come from in the morning. He cursed the white men who had killed the Blackfoot warriors.

Secretly, he wondered if he had done something to offend the Great Spirit of Breath who protected his people. What had he done wrong? The bullets of the whites had cut down three brave Blackfeet. This was not the way it should be.

He left two men to watch the defenders so that they would not escape. Then he led the others, with the bodies of the fallen braves, to a camp about a quarter mile away, in a tree-sheltered area where they could re-group and plan the next attack.

One of his men came to Wak Tha Go and said, "Why have we lost these warriors, my chief? Were we not sup-posed to kill the evil white ones? Instead, they have killed our men."

"This I know, my brother, and I will pray for an answer to your question. I do not know what is in the mind of the Spirit who guides and gives life to all His creation."

The brave rode ahead with his head down, leading a horse with one of the corpses draped over it. There would be sadness back in the village when they returned with the dead.

Wak Tha Go knew that his grandiose promises must be fulfilled. He must wipe out these men on the island, or else he would lose face with the village, and with his own men. Hatred and vengeance flared up inside his soul like a roaring campfire. He must go and pray and think about what to do.

He rode off away from the other men after instructing them to make camp and prepare the bodies of the dead for eventual burial by their families and the other people of the village.

He was gone for several hours. At dusk he returned. The warriors awaited him. They had kept up their watch on the island. The whites were hunkered down in their defensive positions, expecting another attack. But the warriors couldn't move without Wak Tha Go to lead them, so they had stayed in camp and mourned their dead. They all jumped up and greeted him when they saw him riding in.

When he had dismounted, he said to them: "Tomorrow we will attack again. The Spirit has told me that victory is ours. We will avenge our dead brothers with the scalps of the evil men."

Clouds covered the moon. Art was grateful for this as he sneaked out of the island camp at the far end of the island from where the Indian sentries watched through the night. He had blackened his face with charcoal and dirt to take off the pale shine that could be seen by a sharp-eyed watcher.

He carried only his knife and had pulled his hat low over his eyes. He half-crabbed, half-swam to a stand of cottonwoods on the bank about a hundred yards upstream from the scene of the day's fighting. He moved slowly but steadily so that he would not create any unusual movement in the water and so that he could blend into the night shadows.

Dog watched him with one eye, seeming to understand that he had to go out alone.

He had not told the others what he was going to do. They did not even know he had sneaked away. Caviness

and Hoffman were standing watch, and he had success-
fully eluded even them. That idea didn't make him very
happy, but he put it aside and kept moving, stealthily,
until he came to a point where he could cross over the
river and step onto the rocky bank.

Once on dry land, he darted toward a sheltering rock
and then circled around in a wide arc through some
trees to the other side of the black bluff, careful that he
didn't make a sound as he moved through grass and underbrush. His moccasins trod over the earth like feathers and carried him to within about fifty yards of the
Indians' encampment.

There he waited. The moon eventually fell lower in
the sky, below the treetops that ringed the quiet camp.
The horses were tethered nearby, and Art avoided them,
staying downwind as much as he could.

He knew what he had to do, but it would be the most
difficult thing he had ever done in his life. He must kill
the Indians' war chief and end their siege of the island.
The cool night wind blew over his still-wet body, and he
clenched his teeth so that they would not chatter in the
surprising cold. He was reminded how winter could
come down fast and hard in this high country, even in
August or early September. He had even known it to
snow at this time of year.

He waited. He was armed only with his knife, which
never left his side. The steel blade was clean, extremely
sharp, ready to do its killing work. He measured his
breathing so that it was smooth and soundless. He
waited some more.

After he had been in place for more than two hours,
the young mountain man moved. Very slowly he crabbed
forward until he was within fifty feet of the camp. He surveyed the sleeping forms of the enemy to determine
which was the leader—the one farthest from the three
bodies of the dead Blackfeet, separated a few feet from

the others. It was a calculated risk, but he would take it. He trusted his own instinct on this.

Keeping his breathing as shallow as a snake's, he got on his belly and crawled forward. Now there was no moon, no light, just the wind. He remained downwind from the camp, knowing that the slightest scent or movement would betray him and that would be the end of his life.

The smell of the dry summer grass filled his nostrils. It was like being in a dream, and suddenly he remembered the same smell from when he was a boy. He had always spent his time outdoors, away from his family's home, exploring and hunting and sleeping out under the stars. He had always felt comfortable in the grass, or propped up against a tree. Those days were long past, and he was no longer a boy. Now he was a man on a killing mission.

He was forty feet from his target. He stopped. Waited. Then he moved again, pulling himself forward with powerful arms, his belly sliding against the cold dry earth.

When he got within twenty feet of Wak Tha Go, he removed his knife from the sheath at his belt. He held it in his right hand. The handle, wood covered with leather, warmed in his hand. Sweat beaded his palms.

He crawled closer. Art almost stopped breathing now. Any sound would betray him. He was within fifteen feet. With agonizing slowness, he got within about ten feet. He pushed himself. Sweat covered his brow and his entire body, making him nearly as wet as he had been after coming out of the river. He stopped blinking his eyes as he got even closer.

Then there was a sound! He held himself completely, utterly still. What was it? It wasn't the wind or any animal movement—it sounded human. Then he realized what it was: the war chief's sleep-breathing! He was close enough now that he could almost feel the breeze of the man's breath.

Art's hat formed a tent at the top of his vision. It was

completely dark now, and as if by magic he had been transported to this spot, within five feet—almost striking distance—of Wak Tha Go. He did not know the man other than as an enemy.

Wak Tha Go expelled a long, loud breath. Then he turned slightly in his sleep. Art froze. He waited nearly ten minutes, then crept closer, using his toes now to propel him forward. Five feet. Four feet. Three feet. Truly, he felt like a snake slithering toward its prey. Eyes unblinking.

Now he made a bold move. He brought himself parallel to the sleeping man's body. He rolled himself over one time until he was nearly face-to-face with the enemy. With a swift movement he clamped his left hand down over Wak Tha Go's nose and mouth.

The shock startled the Indian awake. His eyes opened wide and he saw Art for an instant. Art felt him start to struggle, to fight off his attacker. But it was too late.

With a blindingly powerful swing, Art brought his knife up, then down, plunging it directly into the Indian's heart. He had to push Wak Tha Go's head down, stifle his cry. It took every ounce of strength the young man had to hold the powerful Indian's mouth and nose and push the long steel blade as far as possible into the chest. Then he withdrew the knife.

Blood bubbled up out of the deep, deadly wound in the chest cavity. Art smelled it, felt it on his hands and arms. It was warm and wet. Still trying to be absolutely silent, he wiped his hands in the grass and started to turn to make his way out of the camp without being detected by the others.

He stopped himself. If he wanted to end the siege of the island, he must send an unmistakable signal to the Indians. They had lost three men in the battle, now their chief to a killer in the night. But how would they know who had done it?

Art removed his hat. He hated to lose it, for a hat was

a part of a man on the trail, as necessary as a gun, though for vastly different reasons. He placed the hat on Wak Tha Go's upper chest. Then he reached around and found Wak Tha Go's own knife. In the brief struggle before his life had ended, the Indian had groped for the knife and his dead hand was close by.

The mountain man took the knife and plunged it through the brim of the hat, pinning it to the dead warrior's chest.

What would they say to that? he wondered. He hoped it would spook them enough to call off another attack. Pushing himself away, he crawled for several yards before he got to his feet and ran quietly away into the night.

The next day came and the Indians did not attack. None of the men on the island knew why—except Art himself. As they packed and prepared to leave, he told them.

11

The party was somber, glad to have survived the siege of the little unnamed island, grateful that Art had put a knife in their enemy's chest. Even McDill and Caviness were quiet for the first two or three days out, after such a close call. Dog held back, but followed the party off the island.

The man who would one day be called Preacher, leader of this column, rode out one morning to scout the forward area west of the Missouri River, which rolled wide and shallow around boulders and over rocks up in this north country. He rode about five miles out, ahead of the other trappers.

From the day he had left his family in Ohio, Art had been a fiercely independent man. He remembered to this day the letter, just a brief note really, that he had left behind. It said, simply:

Ma and Pa
   Don't look for me for I have went away. I am near a man now and I want to be on my own. Love, your son, Arthur.

He was on his own, all right, and had been for more than twelve years as he grew into manhood among the Indians and mountain men of the West. He had known more adventures than he could have ever dreamed up back in Ohio. . . . As he breathed in the Missouri bad-lands air untainted by man, he said a silent prayer of thanksgiving to the only God he knew, the Creator of this land of savage beauty. He was not much given to introspection, and had never been a churchgoing man, but sometimes he just felt that he had to look up and say thanks.

He was almost unaware of the men he had left behind. Ahead lay a thicket that stretched out like a green island on the brown land. He kneed his mount in that direction. Maybe this was a place where his party and their horses could rest for a while at midday, out of the sun that was already beginning to beat down hard on them. There hadn't been rain here for at least two weeks, and the ground was sere and hard-packed, stony even away from the river.

Art dismounted when he was about twenty yards outside the thicket, leading his horse forward, alert to sounds and smells out of the ordinary that would signal danger. He cradled his trusted rifle after he had loaded and primed it, then hobbled the horse when he got to the edge of the thicket.

Moving through the underbrush, he peered into the shadowy area beneath the trees, measuring each step with as much silence and stealth as he could manage. He entered an opening that must have been about ten yards by twenty yards, enough space for a house and garden, he thought—though it was unlikely that any white settler would ever come to this remote part of the world to build such a house. Dog, who had followed him, yowled.

Then, with a suddenness that nearly took his breath away, he saw it: a grizzly bear with its long black-brown back turned to him. The animal became still, then sensed Art's presence, then turned toward him and stood at its full height. As the bear turned, he could see three smaller animals—cubs. This was a mother, a griz-

zly sow, who was tending her young. She was as dangerous as ten men. He knew this when he heard her roar,
an earsplitting howl of anger and defiance.

The huge, dark bear stood nearly ten feet tall on her
hind feet. Her giant clawed paws slashed at the air as the
cubs, not knowing what was happening, scurried over
each other to stand behind their aroused mother.

Her black eyes locked on Art, who stood stock-still at
the edge of the opening beneath the trees. He took one
step forward, toward the grizzly that was ready to attack.
This was unexpected, and the bear cocked her head,
then opened her mouth again, baring yellow teeth and
fangs. The sow trumpeted a warning to the approaching
man and to the wolf-dog.

Art had never seen anything like it: this monster with
black eyes towering over him. Deliberately, he raised
his rifle and aimed, held steady. With almost lightning
speed, the grizzly attacked.

The mountain man fired his rifle, sending a ball directly into the chest of the advancing bear. She shuddered as she took the impact of the lead in the center of
her huge body. But it did not stop her. The grizzly came
on, flailing her razor-claws, roaring in pain. With im-
mense speed and power the wounded sow pounced, her
arms extended.

Art reacted just as quickly, ducking first as the bear-
talons swept the air where his head had been. He felt the
wind of her violent swipe. He dropped his rifle, useless
now, and ran toward a nearby tree. He scrambled to get
a foothold in a low branch, and had to jump up to reach
for a higher branch. He slipped, jumped again, and took
hold this time.

The bear spun almost a full circle with the momentum
of her attack. Her back was to the man. The ball in her
chest was the source of incredible pain, and blood
leaked from the entry wound. She turned, spotted Art as
he tried to clamber up the tree.

She shook her gigantic head, mouth open, and saliva sprayed all around her. In two steps she was at the tree where Art hung, trying to gain a footing. As she grabbed for him, he swung out of her reach and pulled himself up higher into the tree.

He thought if he could hold out and not let the grizzly get him for just another minute, she would die from the wound he had inflicted. But she showed no sign of dying. The cubs watched from the side of the clearing as their mother attacked yet again.

This time she stood at her full height and reached for Art, clawing him across the back with one paw, pummeling him with the other. Art felt the deep cuts in his back and the blow to his left shoulder, shaking him from his precarious perch in the tree. He wanted to howl in pain himself, but did not. He had to hold on, had to try. . . .

The great grizzly sow seized her prey then, holding both of Art's legs and pulling him off the tree. Dog yapped at the bear's legs, but she ignored him.

He tumbled to the earth, falling with a hard thud and wincing at the pain. His back was in shreds and he felt the warm blood from the razor wounds there. He rolled away from the attacking bear, but was not quick enough.

With an ear-shattering roar, the grizzly went after him again. She reached down and swiped, this time slicing into his arm with her claws. He wanted to scream, but did not. His only thought was escape—but there was nowhere to go. He struggled unsteadily to his knees. He pulled free his hunting knife from its sheath at his belt. With his good arm he pushed the knife toward the mad animal, found his target.

As he stabbed the blade into the wounded grizzly's chest, he felt it scrape against the giant's ribs. The foamy spittle at the gaping mouth became pink, then red. The bear's black eyes locked on Art, who could barely breathe as he was caught in a savage tent made by the huge animal's body.

Then it closed in on him and fell on top of him. Art was crushed beneath the thousand-pound weight of the grizzly sow.

It was only an hour, but it seemed like days to Art, who drifted in and out of consciousness. His men found him lying beneath the carcass of the bear he had killed. It took all five of them another hour to figure out how to lever the dead body off the man. The bear's blood mingled with Art's, leaving him a bloody, pulpy mess. He fought through the pain to remain alert.

"She-bear . . ." he gasped. His eyes sought the three cubs who had sniffed around their mother before Art's party arrived.

McDill looked around, cursed, and shot at the nearby cubs, who scattered out of sight. There was little hope for them now. They would soon join their mother in death.

Hoffman, ignoring his own injury, and the others knelt beside their leader. He lay on his back more dead than alive. He bled from claw wounds in his face, chest, back, shoulder, and thighs. One leg and several ribs were broken. His face was a red mask of blood, and he had to spit to keep it out of his mouth as he breathed.

"He's tore damn near to pieces," Don Montgomery said. Matthews turned away and got sick. "Aw, Joe, come back here and help him."

"He should be dead," McDill muttered, standing over Art.

"Maybe we should put him out of his misery," Caviness suggested.

"By God!" Hoffman, the big German, leapt to his feet and pushed his face against Caviness's. "You will not kill our captain as you say! You will die if you try to hurt him, because I will kill you!"

It was the longest speech any of them had ever heard

the Hessian give. His face was red from heat and anger. Caviness took one step backward.

"I was just saying maybe it would be the merciful thing to do, that's all." Caviness looked around at the others, but no one came to his defense. He had not won any friends on this journey, and even McDill looked away.

"All right, all right, I'm sorry," he said finally.

"It is good," Hoffman said, then went back to tend to Art.

All of them had thought it, but only Caviness had said it. As they looked at the tall young mountain man lying in a pool of red-black blood, none of them thought he could survive the day. But carefully they cared for him, washed his wounds, and bandaged him. McDill tended to his horse, then fetched his bedroll, which they laid out in a semi-sheltered spot by a tree. Hoffman went to the stream close by and filled Art's canteen with fresh water.

He brought it back and propped it up next to his wounded friend. "Here is water for you," he said.

"He's a regular orator," McDill commented to Caviness as they built a cook fire.

No point in riding farther today. They would camp here for the night and start out in the morning. As the others ate, Art listened to their palaver, drifting in and out of consciousness.

"We should rig up a travois," Matthews said. "Maybe we could get him back to the fort for medical help." He looked at the others, sitting around the fire. "We can't leave him here."

"He's gonna die," McDill spat.

"We don't know that," Matthews said angrily. "He's our leader. We've got to stay with him."

"He can't lead us nowhere now." McDill was relentless, couldn't let go of his hatred for Art and his need to take over the expedition and prove himself.

Montgomery and the German knelt by the severely injured man, and helped him drink some water from a canteen. For all they knew the water, like his blood, would leak out of puncture holes in his body. But they had to do something. Art couldn't eat anything in his condition, and he was barely conscious enough to move his lips to drink. The two men looked at each other in despair.

"Damn," Montgomery said simply. He was not a man of words.

Hoffman too was sad and angry at the grizzly sow who had nearly killed his friend—and angry at the disloyalty shown by McDill and Caviness. "We must keep an eye on those men," he told Montgomery in a low voice. "I do not trust them."

"Hell, no," Montgomery hissed. "They's a pair of snakes if there ever was, damn their souls to hell."

That night the members of the party slept fitfully. All were exhausted but full of uncertainty about their mission. Without their designated leader there was nothing to hold them together. They stood watch in three shifts through the night, but there was no sound, no threat from man or beast. The dawn came suddenly.

Art drifted between sleep and unconsciousness, his injuries stabbing him with pain in nearly every part of his body. At sunup, when the camp began to stir, he was aware of the activity, heard the men's voices and smelled the morning cook fire, but his eyes remained closed.

The wound in his throat was especially painful, and he could feel the copious dried blood on the bandage there. He was more than half-certain that he was going to die.

"So I'm in charge now," McDill announced to the others as the men drank their morning coffee.

"The hell you are," Matthews said, glaring at McDill and Caviness.

"Maybe it's hell for you," Caviness said, "but McDill here is the only one with the experience to do it. So you just shut up and listen to him. He'll get us out of here in one piece, like Art there can't do just now."

"Besides," said McDill, "those Blackfeet are liable to attack again. You want us to sit here and wait for them to gather their forces and come wipe us out?" McDill tossed his coffee dregs onto the ground and glared at Matthews and the other men.

For a minute no one said anything, then the Hessian, Hoffman, said to McDill, "You will leave Art here to die?"

"You want to stay here and die with him?"

"He might live if we can care for him."

"Look at it this way. Do you think he would endanger the whole group if you were injured and going to die?"

Again, the men were silent. It was hard to stand up to McDill when he was like this, at his bullying worst. He stood there like a big mule, his fists clenched, scowling at them all.

"Well—what do you say? You want to be women and stay here and watch him die and likely get killed yourselves?"

Caviness added, "And probably a lot worse than poor old Art here—scalped and gutted like a deer by them Blackfeet."

"It ain't right to just leave him," Montgomery muttered.

"What's that? Speak up," McDill demanded.

Hoffman said, "He means we got to do something. We cannot just leave the man here to die."

"All right, you want to do something, you can leave him some food and water. Maybe he'll want to eat something— if he can. I'm not saying we shouldn't do anything for the poor soul." His words were sympathetic, but McDill turned and gave a wink to Caviness that the others couldn't see.

That seemed to satisfy Art's friends. They settled in for a quick breakfast, saying nothing among themselves and watching McDill and Caviness with suspicion.

The men changed that bloody neck bandage after they had eaten. Matthews cleaned and loaded Art's rifle, and the others put a full canteen and a supply of food beside the wounded man. Caviness stood to one side and watched. But McDill helped, brought Art's horse around after he had watered it, and ground-tethered it nearby.

All the while, Dog, the young mountain man's faithful sentry, walked around Art's still form, occasionally licking at his wounds, eyeing the other members of the party who approached. He growled at McDill, who kept a safe distance at all times, spitting and cursing at the animal. Dog didn't interfere with the others who were trying to help Art.

"C'mon, let's get movin'," McDill said finally. He swung into the saddle alongside Caviness, who was already mounted.

"Good-bye, friend," the Hessian said as he stood stiffly above the unmoving injury-wracked body.

Matthews and Montgomery put a blanket over the long-legged mountain man, who lay with his eyes closed, breathing raggedly. They looked over at Dog, who sat at the alert just a few yards away. "Take care of him," Matthews muttered beneath his breath so that McDill couldn't hear him.

"I said time to move out!" the new leader of the group barked. "It'll be noon before we know it and you women won't be too happy then, believe me." He reined his horse around and started off.

The others mounted and rode away without looking back at their gravely wounded leader.

Percy McDill had worked out a plan with his pal Ben Caviness. When the party had ridden about three miles he suddenly pulled up and halted their advance.

"Damn it all!" he cursed. "I left my spare canteen back at the campsite."

"Since when did you carry a spare canteen?" Matthews

piped up. He was very observant and hadn't noticed that McDill was so extra-prepared.

"Since none of your damn business," McDill said. "But I'm not going to leave it there to rust when we may need it on the trip."

"Art could use it," Matthews suggested.

"He's got a canteen full of water. He don't need no extra. I do. Ben, you'll be in charge of this outfit until I get back. I'll push hard and catch up with you in a couple of hours. I won't hold anybody up." McDill wheeled his horse around and started off at a brisk pace.

Caviness said, "All right, you heard him. Let's ride."

McDill pushed his horse pretty hard, and made it back to the campsite in a short time. He had never carried a second canteen, never even thought of it until he and Caviness hatched this scheme for him to return and finish off Art once and for all.

Nothing was different: The young man lay there like a corpse, except that his chest moved up and down in shallow breaths. And Dog was not there!

Good, McDill thought. That damn wolf-dog won't stop me from doing what I have to do. First he took Art's canteen and food cache from beside him and put everything in a saddlebag. The rifle he concealed as best he could in a makeshift saddle holster that he had rigged the previous night so the others wouldn't see that he had stolen the soon-to-be-dead man's gun. Then he went back to the injured man. He moved as swiftly as he could, to get the job done and get back to his companions.

The others had cleaned Art's deadly knife and left it in his belt holster. McDill bent to retrieve the knife. He'd then slit the younger man's throat and be off. . . .

A low, intense growl shattered McDill's concentration and made him stiffen and stand up straight.

There stood Dog, fangs bared, eyes black with anger and hatred for Art's enemy. It seemed that the animal knew exactly what McDill was up to. But Dog wasn't going to let it happen. He'd kill the man first, before he touched the knife. The canine growled again, threateningly, an evil sound from deep within its gut.

McDill froze. His eyes grew wide as saucers and he took a tentative half step back from Art. Dog's growls increased in volume with each move McDill made. The man had to think quickly. He looked over and saw Art's horse just a couple of yards to his right. Dog was still about eight or nine yards away. Almost without thinking, McDill took two quick steps until he had put the horse between himself and the wolf-dog.

Then he whistled quietly, and his own horse ambled over toward him. Using the second horse as a shield, he was able to mount his own and, holding the reins of Art's horse, start moving back from Art's body. He wanted to take out his rifle and shoot the vicious guard dog to death, but he couldn't and still keep a hand on the reins of each horse. Slowly, he backed both horses away from the campsite. Art had not moved or given any indication that he knew what was going on.

Dog was frustrated. He walked closer to the badly injured man, growling all the while but powerless to attack McDill.

The man smiled, showing yellow teeth. "So, you think you're tough, you dad-blasted devil," he said aloud. "I've outsmarted you this time. He's gonna be dead by the end of the day anyhow."

Dog barked, as if in response.

"Shut yer trap, you damned wolfhound. I hope you get ate by a bear. More'n you deserve." As he talked he kept moving, then when he had enough space between himself and Dog, deliberately turned the horses.

"Hee-yah!" he shouted suddenly, kneeing his own horse and yanking at the reins of the other. In a cloud of dust, he galloped off, leaving the yowling wolf-dog to tend to his master.

McDill rode hard for a mile, then slowed to a more

even pace. It took him a few hours more to catch up finally with the trappers. But it gave him time to get his story straight.

"Well, boys, our friend Art is dead. Sorry to be the bearer of bad news and all."

"He wasn't no friend of your'n," Matthews said. He didn't like the sound of Percy McDill's voice, the barely concealed satisfaction when he told them of Art's passing. "He was a damn fine fellow, worth more'n ten of you and Caviness put together."

"Now no need to get bitter," McDill said in response. "We all did the best we could to help the man recover, but nobody could survive with those wounds—and you all know it."

The Hessian, Herman Hoffman, eyed McDill skeptically, watched him giving some secret hand signals to Caviness, his partner in crime. He suspected that something was not quite right about all this, but he could not afford to ride back to the campsite to see for himself what had happened. He had to take McDill's word that his friend was dead. It made him sad, and even angrier at McDill for his pompous stupidity.

They rode on till sunset, covering almost thirty miles. McDill was glad to put as much distance between himself and that damned Dog as humanly possible.

When the sun had gone down, Art's eyes opened. Dog was there, breathing in his face and occasionally licking it with his scratchy tongue.

A fever had gripped him, and he shivered as if it were wintertime and sweated as if he were lying under the desert sun. Because it was getting dark and the stars hadn't come out yet, he could not even see Dog, only a black shadow where the animal's head should be.

Where am I? he wondered. It took a while for him to recall what had happened to him. His fevered brain was

weak, and drifted away to strange places. He knew he was
thirsty, realized after a while that he was suffering from
a fever, and felt incredibly intense pain in nearly every
part of his body. After a while he lifted one hand and
touched his neck. He felt the bandage there, covered
with dried blood. He felt his face, a stubbly growth of
beard there, and winced when he ran his hands over the
still-open wounds from the giant bear's claws. He tried
to sit up, but could not. His head spun and he fell unconscious again. . . .

He dreamed about Jennie . . . the beautiful Creole
woman he had last seen in St. Louis. Their lives were in-
tertwined in ways he did not understand. He couldn't
have a regular woman in his life, not the life he had
chosen that kept him away from people and from civilization for months, even years at a time. It was no life for
a refined woman like Jennie. It would kill her. And he
loved her too much for that. Or did he? What was love
anyway? What did it mean to say, "I love you"? He had
never said that to any other person, even Jennie.

He saw her in his dream. She was dressed in a fancy
white dress that showed off her caramel-color skin.

She was calling to him, but he didn't know what she
was saying, couldn't hear her because there was a roaring in his head like a great wind. She beckoned with her
arms open, as if she wanted to take him in an embrace,
to be with him as a woman is with a man . . . but he
couldn't get any nearer to her, no matter how hard he
tried. The pounding pain in his head was so great that
he thought it would explode. Still, he strove with all his
might to reach her.

All the memories of his first wanderings and his own
captivity came rushing back at him when he saw Jennie's
face in his dream. Then the dream changed and he was
the young mountain man on his first journey in the
country of the upper Missouri, when the river became

his woman and he followed her to his destiny. He had been alone then. . . .

He had shot a turkey with his Hawken, and had built himself an oven to cook the bird when suddenly a voice startled him from his task. It was a man in soiled buckskin and homespun who called out to him.

"Hello the camp!" The man was tall, gaunt, bearded. "You campin' all by yourself, are you, young feller?"

Art thought for a moment about lying to the stranger, telling him that he wasn't alone, but he realized that the man had probably already scouted the area and would know that he was lying. And if Art lied, it would be a sign of weakness and fear, a sign that he was afraid to admit that he was alone.

In his fevered dream it was as real as if it were happening for the first time.

"I am alone," Art said.

The man stuck out his hand, calloused and gray. "Bodie is the name. How are you called?"

Bodie . . . he had driven a mule named Rhoda and traded her to Art for the horse the youth had stolen in his escape from Lucas Younger, who'd held him in slavery. He remembered how Younger had been about to shoot him when Art jerked at the chain that bound him and caused Younger to shoot himself—dead. Bodie then traded him the mule, a more surefooted animal for where Art was going. He also told Art about the Rendezvous, because Art was so green he had never even heard of such a thing. And most importantly, Bodie, the crusty old mountain man, had told Art to look up some friends of his.

Art heard Bodie's voice now, loud and clear in his mind:

"Listen, when you get up into the mountains, if you run into a couple o' ugly varmints—one is named Clyde, the other calls himself Pierre—why, you tell 'em that ol' Bodie says hello, will you?"

"Yes, sir. I'll do that," Art said. Then Bodie said some things that Art had never forgotten, even to this day.

"This be your first time in the mountains, boy?"

"Yes, sir."

"I thought so. Well, watch yourself up there. Winter comes early to the high country. Before too much longer you're goin' to be needin' to go to shelter. You any good with that there Hawken?"

"Tolerable," Art replied.

"Then I advise you to get you some meat shot, couple o' deer, an elk, maybe a bear. A bear would be nice 'cause you'd also have its skin to help you through the cold."

"Thanks for the advice."

A bear . . .

Now the image of the huge grizzly sow that had nearly killed him came back to Art in a feverish nightmare that took his breath away and left him sweating and panting for thirst. He was running . . . running . . . running . . . away from Jennie, away from the bear, away from McDill, away from Bodie, away from Clyde and Pierre, away from his family—away from everybody he had ever known in his life. His whole body ached from the running, yet he could feel the bear's hot breath on his neck, as if she was going to leap on him and devour him in that gaping pink maw of a mouth. Her razor-talons swiped at him, and he could feel their sharpness slicing into his skin. He was naked, alone, running—running for his life from the giant she-bear, and there was no way to escape, no way to fight, no way . . . no way . . . "You campin' all by yourself, arc you, young feller?" Alone . . . alone . . . alone . . .

Dog's breath in his face suddenly shocked him awake. He sensed it was nearly sunup. His body felt limp and damp from the night sweats. He wasn't even sure if he was alive or dead. Had he been dreaming all those things? He slowly moved his hands over his body under the blanket that Montgomery and Matthews had carefully placed over him. The morning air was cool and he gulped it in like water. His hands felt the bruises, bandages, and broken bones that he had become.

I'm in one hell of a mess, he thought, wincing with every slight move he made. But he felt that the fever had passed, and weak as he was, maybe there was a chance he could survive.

Dog stood there, slowly wagging his matted tail. It was the most beautiful sight Art had ever seen. He was still alive. He struggled for an hour until he could finally sit up. He looked around. No canteen, no food, no rifle, no horse.

"They really left us with nothin'," he said out loud to Dog. But he had his knife. He could feel its cool blade against his leg. That was something.

"Thanks for your help, Dog," he said. "Now, let's get something to eat. You know any fancy restaurant around here?"

12

For the first four days, unable to walk, Art crawled. He stayed by the river so he could be close to a source of water. It was already September, he calculated, and winter would come sooner than any man liked in this high country. Just as Bodie had told him so many years ago. He crawled, not knowing where he was going. He had to keep moving, somehow, to get back to the fort or to find some other human being—anyone.

He had heard some of the remarkable survival stories of other men who had been lost in the wilderness with no weapon, no food, no one else. He had been a man of the mountains himself for a dozen years, through every season, every condition of nature. He was determined that he too would survive.

He ate berries and nuts that he found close to the water's edge, and he crawled on, sleeping at night, moving during the daylight hours. Luckily, he still had his clothes and his knife. And Dog. So he felt he wasn't totally alone.

His fever lingered for several days, but slowly receded, lessening with each slow, agonizing mile and each troubled night of sleep. The nights were getting cold.

One day he rested on a flat, open table away from the

river, during the afternoon, with the sun warming his face. He dozed off for a few minutes, then awoke with a start. He noticed that Dog was silent, staring at something. Looking about five yards ahead, in the direction that he was moving, Art saw a rattlesnake coiled, sunning itself. He could have sworn the snake was looking at him too.

When he moved slightly to sit up, the snake's tail rose and rattled. It was on the alert and preparing to strike. Art moved his hand imperceptibly, feeling the dry grass, groping for something he could use as a weapon. He found a rock about the size of his own fist.

The rock felt hot from sitting in the sun. Art's hand closed around it. The snake rattled, raised and lowered its head. Art gripped the rock.

He tried to measure the distance and figure out how much time he would have when the snake moved to strike. Best to try when the snake was still coiled, which made a better target.

Holding his breath, he squeezed the rock and in a quick blur of motion flung it at the rattlesnake. He hit it, and the rock smashed the snake's head into the earth. Art forced himself halfway upright and half-crawled, half-walked over to the snake. It was still moving. He took his knife and quickly sliced the reptile's head off, then cut the body in half.

He was so starved that he started chewing on the snake, biting off a piece, chewing the innards and spitting out the skin. Then he bit off another piece and ate it. He didn't even think of the foul taste and the idea of eating a raw, bloody snake. He was so hungry he would have eaten anything that wouldn't poison him.

From that point he could walk, though slowly and with great pain. He cut a tall stick to use as a sort of crutch. He continued, day after day, to keep to the river, and he found edible roots that he could dig with the knife and stones. The water of the river brought new life into him, and even though he was incredibly sore from his injuries, he bathed in its cold current and washed away blood and ache and trail dirt. He lay out naked in the sun to dry and drink in the healing warmth and rays of the sun.

Dog stuck with him each painful step of the way. Day in and day out, the faithful beast was there. Dog was able to capture a stray rabbit or squirrel for himself, and sometimes ate the food that Art dug from the earth.

Art tried to keep track of the days, repeating the count to himself each morning and night: six days, ten days, fifteen days. . . . He headed toward the east and south as the great river wound its way through the badlands.

"Well, Dog," he said aloud one day, "where do you think we are? Any hope we'll find the fort or any human being soon?"

The animal looked up at the young mountain man, cocking its head and growling with impatience.

"All right, boy, if that's the way you feel about it. I was just asking a question. Don't bite my head off, now."

Art laughed. He couldn't remember the last time he had laughed. He lifted his head and felt the sun strike his face full on, and he breathed in the high plains air and swung his arms around. He realized that he wasn't in constant pain anymore. Oh, sure, there were pains and aches and bones still mending, and he depended a lot on his walking stick-crutch. But for a few minutes he felt better, felt that he might survive after all.

He thought about his men. Wondered where they were and what they were doing. McDill, no doubt, had taken over the leadership of the party—which he had felt was his all along. He vaguely remembered when McDill had returned to the camp to check on him. He felt then that he was going to die, but Dog had warned the man off, probably saved Art's life. McDill had taken Art's horse and rifle and canteen. He had left him there to die.

Art wasn't angry at McDill, but he knew that he would

probably have to kill him when they next met—if they ever met.

Three weeks into his arduous trek, the mountain man awoke one morning to the sound of something moving on the earth. He felt it first, then heard it: far away but getting closer. What the hell? Then he knew—it was a herd of buffalo moving across the land, probably approaching the river to ford.

The herd must be late in leaving the high plains for the lusher, taller grasses south of the Upper Missouri and the warmer hills and valleys of the lower country. Art looked around for Dog, didn't see him. The wolf-dog had heard the same thing he had and gone in search of the herd.

It took him two hours to walk about a mile through a densely treed area above the river and into an open hilly stretch. Clouds streamed across the sky, sometimes blotting out the sun and taking away the shadows from the land. He climbed a low hill, and when he got to the top he could see for several miles, and there, like a sea, was the wandering herd of buffalo.

He saw Dog, who stood like the wolf he was, salivating at the sight of enough meat for a thousand lifetimes.

If only he had his favorite Hawken, he could take down one of the huge beasts and have real food for the first time in weeks, and a buffalo-skin blanket for the increasingly cold nights! His body was still mending, and he could walk better and better each day, but he certainly couldn't run—yet. So there was no way he could hunt on foot.

The vast herd was moving south, rumbling over the brown-green grass of the low rolling hills. He couldn't even imagine how many there were. He followed Dog, who trotted closer to the moving mass of brown and black animals.

Dog's hunting instincts took over. Art watched with fascination as the wolf-dog got closer and closer to the western edge of the herd and watched, inspected the passing animals for potential targets. Dog would pause, run alongside the herd for about a hundred yards, circle back and look, then run again. The larger animals ignored the comparatively small beast who yipped and howled at them.

In the middle distance, about a half mile away, Art could see a pack of wolves out in the open, circling, trying to identify a likely victim, just as Dog was. Then Dog saw them too, some of his own kind.

He ran in their direction, barking and howling. The pack ignored the newcomer, sticking together tightly. Dog retreated, ran back toward Art, even wagged his tail, which was unusual for the mongrel.

"All right, boy," Art said. "We'll stay clear of them and they'll stay out of our way." He began hiking to the north, the direction from where the herd was coming. He kept the same wide distance between the wolf pack and himself, not wanting them to sniff him out as a potential meal himself.

Dog went about his business, plunging back into the fringes of the advancing herd of bison. It didn't take him long to cut out a youngster and turn him around and separate him from the rest of the herd. The calf was confused, scared, and it started to run away from Dog, to the west. Art moved after it. He knew Dog could take the calf down, but he didn't want to lose it to the wolf pack, who hadn't yet culled a calf or an injured adult for themselves.

The calf ran in crazy circles, and Dog pushed it farther away from the herd, over a low hill into a narrow ravine. Soon it could not see the herd at all, and bellowed like a wounded pig. Dog closed in. Art watched the whole thing happen. He drew his knife as he walked closer to the buffalo.

Even though it was a calf, the animal must have weighed more than four or five hundred pounds. It was unsteady on its legs in unfamiliar territory. It was scared of Dog and frightened to be apart from its family for the first time ever. It would be the last time too.

Dog attacked, leaping at the hapless calf's legs. It tripped and fell, breaking a spindly leg. It bleated in pain. Dog attacked again, this time going for the animal's throat. He tore into it viciously, immediately drawing blood. The buffalo calf tried to fight off the wolf-dog, but the harder it fought the worse it got—Dog held onto his prey, digging his teeth deeper into the poor calf's flesh.

Art hobbled closer, approaching with his knife drawn. He waited for his chance as the two animals struggled, then fell onto the calf and plunged the knife into its heart. He rolled off the big body as blood leaked out, soaking the earth.

Art heard the wolves approach from behind him. He swung around, holding his walking stick and knife. "Yah, yah, yah!" he challenged. Dog turned too and growled, his mouth dripping with blood and saliva.

The wolves—there were seven or eight of them— looked at these two creatures protecting their kill. Certainly they outnumbered the man and his dog, and might be able to fight them, but something about the threatening noises and movements of the two made them pause and back away. Then the pack leader turned and trotted off toward the buffalo herd, and the others followed.

"That's the way to do it, Dog," Art said.

Dog growled in agreement, then turned back to the kill. The young buffalo lay there like a small mountain, and Art set to work immediately dressing out the carcass as best he could by himself with a single knife. Dog patrolled the immediate area to make sure that none of the wolves came back to try again to claim the kill.

He wasn't finished by nightfall, so he and Dog slept right there at the site. The next morning he rigged a very primitive travois to carry away some meat and skin to a camp by the river. There he made a fire for the first time in weeks and cooked some of the meat for himself. Dog ate his supper raw, burped, and lay down for a nap.

Art ate his fill, then scraped the hide and washed it in the river and set it out, pegging it to the ground to dry. He felt better than he had since his encounter with the grizzly, finally healing and regaining some strength.

For the next few days he traveled with the travois, dragging it behind him, eating the meat each night for supper. He worked on the buffalo skin to soften it in order to make a blanket. The nights were fast getting colder, and he did not know how far he was from any human contact or civilization.

As the days passed, he resolved that he was going to catch up to his men—one way or another—to reclaim leadership of the expedition. He would have quite a story to tell Mr. Ashley—and Jennie—when they all returned to St. Louis.

The Blackfoot village had mourned their dead from the ill-fated attack led by Wak Tha Go against Art's exploratory party. Now, nearly two moons later, the people were restless for revenge. They had lost sons and brothers, and they had trusted the hotheaded war chief to bring them victory and count many coups against the white invaders. It had not happened.

Those who had returned alive had advocated another attack on the whites, with more men from the village. They were bitterly angry that Artoor had slain their leader, Wak Tha Go. They knew he had done it because he had left his hat pinned to the great warrior's chest in a gesture of defiance, like counting coup on the dead man. But he had not scalped the war chief, which surprised them.

They had also lost their great elder, Running Elk, who had died before the war party went out to fight the trappers led by Artoor.

The men sat around the council fire and smoked, talking about their village's misfortune and what could be done about it.

"We must bring war to the whites again," said Brown Owl, one of the younger men who had ridden with Wak Tha Go. He had lost a brother in the battle.

An elder named Buffalo Standing in the River, who was a respected nephew of Running Elk, said, "We cannot afford to lose any more of our young men. It is not our task alone, but for all red brothers to take up their war clubs against Artoor's men."

"But he has made peace with some of the others, like the Arikira," Brown Owl reminded the council.

"White man's peace." Buffalo Standing spat onto the earth in front of himself. "The word of such men is worthless. They know only war and destruction."

"It is true, Grandfather," another of the younger men said. "This is why our people will not make peace. But we must not sit here and moan like women. We must make another war party and seek out these white killes."

Others murmured agreement, and some spoke in favor of forming another war party. Brown Owl, though he was young, had earned the respect of the other men of his village. He joined the debate, speaking with confidence.

"I saw Artoor and the others with my own eyes. I shot arrows at them and I believe I wounded one of them. Even though we lost one battle, we must fight another. Then another after that, if necessary."

"Young men fight. Old men talk," Buffalo Standing said, nodding in agreement with what Brown Owl said, puffing on the long-stemmed pipe.

"Then let us prepare to fight," Brown Owl declared. He counted about ten warriors among the men around the council fire. "We will hold a war council tomorrow and make our plans."

"It is good," another of the elders said.

The men of the council whooped and cheered at

Brown Owl's words. They looked at this very young man with new eyes, with new respect. He would make a good war chief for their people.

But Brown Owl was frustrated after the council ended, and instead of going to his own lodge and the arms of his wife, he walked alone outside the village. He climbed the tall, one-hundred-foot bluff above the Yellowstone River from where he could look down on the village of his birth. It was past sundown and the moon, a shimmering crescent, had risen in the blue-black sky.

The land stretched out beneath him, the vast country that lay between the Missouri and Yellowstone Rivers, where his people had lived and hunted for generations. And they had fought wars there too, against many enemies, to defend what was to them sacred ground.

The young warrior thought back on the events of the past two months, beginning with a similar council discussion when Wak Tha Go urged them to go to war against Artoor. Then the death of Running Elk, who took with him some of the soul of his people and left an emptiness in the village with his passing. Then the war party itself, the attack on the island where the trappers fought back against Wak Tha Go's men, Brown Owl among them.

Wak Tha Go had been stunned, unhappy at the turn of events, and must have thought that the Great Spirit had abandoned him. In fact, Wak Tha Go himself did not survive that night. He had been killed and humiliated that very night. It was tragic that the war chief had not died in battle, but in his sleep. Stories would be told for many generations in the future of the defeat of Wak Tha Go.

Perhaps it was time for a new war chief to lead the people's best fighters against the whites. . . .

As he was thinking these thoughts, Brown Owl felt the presence of another, which was surprising because no one had walked with him to this place—nor had he seen anyone following him. He could see everything from this vantage point. He turned and saw, in the white-silver moonlight, an old man.

He had not heard the man approach, and wondered how he could have climbed the hill. He also wondered who this man was, for it was not a man of his village. Or was it?

The old man sat cross-legged on the ground, wearing a red shirt, trimmed in yellow. This was a ceremonial shirt, not the kind of clothing a man wore ordinarily. Also, the man's knife, bow and quiver of arrows, war club, and pipe all lay on the earth beside him.

"Who are you? How did you get here?" Brown Owl asked.

The old man said nothing.

"You are not of my village. Where did you come from?" Again no answer.

"Why do you say nothing? Why do you follow me?"

The old man remained silent, but more than silent, eerily still, as if dead. But he wasn't dead, or else how could he have gotten here?

"Speak to me, Grandfather," the younger man insisted.

The elder man's eyes were wide open and staring, black discs that were the opposite of the bright moon.

"And why are you wearing such good clothes and carrying your weapons and your pipe?" Brown Owl asked.

"I was dressed this way by the women," the old man said finally, breaking his silence. "The women of the village."

"What village?"

The strange old man turned and pointed over the side of the tall bluff toward Brown Owl's own village.

"How can this be?"

"What is past cannot be changed. What is future can be chosen, until there is no more future. Until death."

Brown Owl was confused and scared, and angry that this man should disturb his prayers with his nonsense. It was the way of old people, sometimes. Their minds wandered to many places and they did not make sense. He would have to help this man climb back down the side of the rise. But who was he?

"You speak of the future and of death."

"What else is there to speak of?"

"I have seen death."

"So have I, Brown Owl."

"You know my name."

"I know many names."

"Do you know the name of Wak Tha Go?"

"Yes, it is right you should ask about this man. I spoke to him before he led you into battle against the man named Artoor."

"He did not tell me of this conversation."

"He kept many things in his heart. He chose the way of war, the way of revenge against one man—a white man."

"Artoor killed him," Brown Owl said.

"I told him that Artoor would not be killed."

"How could you know this?"

"I know many things. I know things that are true. This I tell you: The one called Artoor will one day come to our village."

"How can this be? And why do you say 'our' village?"

The old man remained sitting, but his voice became stronger and more animated as he spoke. "I was born in this village and ended my life in this place. The women of the village took care of me. I married a girl of the village."

"But who are you then?"

"You know my name well, but I cannot speak it, for it is no longer my name," the man said mysteriously.

Brown Owl might have seen something of battle, but he was still young and naïve, and he could not figure out what the old man was trying to tell him.

"Speak to me, Grandfather, of what you said to Wak Tha Go."

"Yes, it is good that I should tell you. Know this— Artoor will not be killed. The people may capture him, but he will gain his freedom through his tongue, which will speak without ceasing from sun to sun."

"This sounds crazy. Why can we not kill Artoor?"

"Because he is a great man, and the Spirit who creates all men does not want Artoor to die. He has another name for Artoor."

"What is this name?"

"It is a name that white men and Indians alike will call him. It is the name Preacher."

"That is very strange," Brown Owl said.

"Not as strange as other things that will happen to the people. You are young and will live long to see many things change, many things pass from the earth. You will speak to Artoor with your own tongue and listen to him with your own ears."

"I intend to kill Artoor, to avenge what he has done to my people."

"This white man seeks the way of peace. But his people and our people will not know peace."

"What are these riddles that you speak, Grandfather? I do not understand."

"You will seek the white trapper, Artoor, and you will find him. Then you will know why I speak of these things."

Brown Owl turned to gaze down upon the sleeping village below. Many fires had burned out, and there was darkness in all but a very few tepees. It was time for the people to rest. Suddenly he felt tired, ready to go to his wife and sleep in his own bedroll.

"Grandfather, I—" He turned to speak to the old man again, but he was gone. There was no one sitting there, no war club or arrows or pipe. Where had he gone?

The young warrior ran down the side of the hill and ran toward his lodge. When he hurried past the tepee that had been Running Elk's, he realized who the old man was. A chill of fear and elation ran up his spine. He would tell no one of this vision that he had received.

* * *

It rained, hard and cold, for three days straight. Art sought shelter in a stand of trees near a sheltering bluff. He used the young buffalo skin as a makeshift tent to stay at least partially dry.

He had no more meat from the kill, but continued to subsist on roots and small game that Dog shared with him. It was a way to survive, but he didn't know how much longer he could exist in this way.

It was good to stay in one place for a few days. His arm and ribs had nearly healed. His beard was long and scraggly from lack of a razor, and his hair was long enough to have to pull back and tie with a thong made from the buffalo hide. He kept his knife sharpened and clean, free of rust or any blemish.

On the first day after the rain had stopped, about six weeks after his ugly confrontation with the grizzly, Art awoke to Dog's growling, snarling alarm. He got to his feet as quickly as he could, pulled down the buffalo skin lean-to, and erased traces of his campsite as best he could. Then he hid among the trees and waited.

Within a few minutes he saw a group of Indians approaching, armed and on horseback.

He counted ten, and he was sure they were Blackfeet. Although he couldn't be sure, he thought that some of them had been in the war party that had attacked his men on the island in the river.

Dog was nowhere in sight. He had run off to scout the oncoming party, and he was probably behind them by now, sniffing them out and trying to determine their intention. Art knew from looking at them what their intention was: to find and kill any white man, himself included. Especially him.

He held in his breathing in order to keep perfectly still, but there was little chance that the Indians would not spot his camp, if they were a serious search-and-fight party, as he suspected.

The leader was a young man, of average height but broad in the shoulders, bare-chested, the customary eagle feather in his scalp lock. He signaled for two of his men to scout the immediate area. He must have sensed the presence of someone by the way he looked around, his own nostrils flaring, his eyes sharp and penetrating.

The young war chief spoke in quiet tones to his men. Two more split off and rode to the rear, another two forward to the bank of the river. Now it was clear. They weren't going anywhere until they found what they were looking for—Art.

He had to decide what to do—hunker down in hiding or show himself and face the consequences. He hated the idea of them flushing him out like a timid rabbit, so he decided to come out and face them like a man.

He knew a smattering of several Indian languages, including Blackfoot, so he called out. "I am here," he said in their tongue. "I am here. I come out."

The Indians, especially the leader, stopped and looked.

From the thicket of trees and underbrush, Art walked forward, carrying the folded-up buffalo-calf skin. He kept his gaze locked on the leader of the party, who sat his horse proudly. He was sure this had been one of the attackers of the trappers' party.

"I am here," Art repeated. He stood in the clearing and threw the buffalo skin down on the ground.

"Yes, you are here," Brown Owl said. He called out to the others, the scouts who had split off from the main party. He stared at the mountain man, who looked haggard and worn with the scraggly beard and long, unkempt hair. Something had happened to this man, he realized.

Then he said, "You are Artoor."

Art nodded. "Yes, I am Art."

In his own language, the Indian said, "I am Brown

Owl of the people you call Blackfoot. You are our prisoner now."

Art understood some of what the man said, figured he had given his own name as Brown Owl and confirmed that he was a Blackfoot. Then he tried something, using sign language as well as speech. He said, "You and I have met before—in battle."

"Yes, I was with Wak Tha Go when we fought you. You killed Wak Tha Go."

So that was the name of the war chief whom he had killed. There would be no peace until these men had avenged their leader, and Art's chances of surviving that were nonexistent. He knew that. He wondered where Dog had gone, but figured that the animal was watching from a safe spot. No reason to show himself and get killed. Dog was one smart wolf-dog.

Speaking quickly, Brown Owl ordered one of his men to tie Art's hands behind his back.

"You will be our prisoner. We are not far from my village, and we will take you there to face the judgment of my people for what you have done."

Art was pretty sure he understood what the man was saying. He said, "I have done nothing. I want peace with your people."

"Yes, you talk of peace. You even make peace with some of the Indian tribes. But one day you will break the peace. It is the way of the white man who speaks like a god-spirit, then acts like a devil."

The mountain man knew he could not argue with the Indian, and he knew that the man was right in some respects. He thought of McDill and others like him who only wanted to give the Indians drink and addle their minds and kill them off. Art, on the other hand, truly believed that they could live together in the mountain country, that trappers could coexist with hunters and Indians of all tribes.

But too many promises and treaties had been broken

over the years for Indians such as Brown Owl to believe a white man.

After a while, they began the ride back to their village. Art was neck-tethered to one of the horses, and had to trot to keep up with the pace. After only a mile or so he was exhausted, ready to drop. His injuries began to ache again, and he grew incredibly thirsty. Once in a while the leader would look back at him to see if he was keeping up with the war party. At one point Art stumbled and nearly fell. The leader, Brown Owl, ordered them to slow down slightly. He could tell that Art had been injured somehow, and felt some pity for the white man.

They were only a few miles from the village, so they made it there by about noon.

A couple of scouts had ridden ahead to alert the people that a prisoner was coming. So, the entire village turned out to see Art, the famous "Artoor" they had heard so much about. They jeered at him and threw stones. Dogs in the village barked at him and bit him in the legs.

He could barely breathe, and he was dizzy from thirst and hunger. He was nearly crippled from the run, and wondered whether he had re-broken any bones. His ribs burned with pain. As he ran along the dusty path through the middle of the village, he gagged and nearly retched his guts out.

Finally, the party stopped in the center of the village, near the place where the council fire was held. Brown Owl dismounted and came around to Art, took the tether from the rider, and did not remove it from the white man's neck. Art's hands were still tied securely behind his back.

"Artoor, you will not be ill treated before you are judged by the council of the people. Come, you will go to my lodge and my wife will feed you. You will rest before tonight when the council fire is lit."

Art said nothing, but followed Brown Owl to his tepee.

There a woman, the war chief's wife, fed him a stew and gave him water. He had never tasted anything so good in his entire life, though he didn't even know what it was—and didn't want to know for fear it might be dog meat.

He tried to say thank you to Brown Owl and his wife, but they ignored him. She had prepared a resting place for him and, after he had drunk some more water, Art collapsed onto the skins and fell asleep immediately.

Brown Owl tied the neck-tether to a lodge pole. He said to his wife, "This is the man who killed Wak Tha Go. Now he will meet the judgment of the people and lose his own life."

"It is good, my husband," the woman said. "I am proud of you for having captured this man."

Brown Owl wanted to tell her about the dream-vision of Running Elk, how he had seen and spoken to the dead man the night before. But he held his tongue. She would not understand, or perhaps she would not believe him. It was something a man should keep in his own heart and not share with a woman.

Instead, he said, "Today I have become a war chief of my people. I have led the warriors and we have captured a prisoner. This day will be remembered for a long time to come."

"Yes, and I will always remember how my husband was a big man. I will take him to my bed tonight and show him that he is very important and loved by his people."

Brown Owl looked forward to this night, of all nights, with great anticipation.

13

Along the Southern Platte River

Jennie's party of women from the House of Flowers in St. Louis had found their way overland to Westport, then turned northwest and followed the Missouri River trail until it forked off along the Platte River. About a hundred miles west of the junction, where a trading town for trappers and explorers was located, lay a tiny, isolated settlement. The settlement consisted of a sutler and general store, a blacksmith, a three-room "hotel," and a small cluster of tent dwellings—about ten people in total, including Jennie's girls.

Ben, her faithful driver—and the only black man for five hundred miles in any direction, as far as she knew— rigged a place for himself in the back of his wagon. There he could attend to the horses and guard Jennie's valuable possessions: some cooking pots and a few dresses.

Clara, the young woman who had been caught up in the commotion surrounding the House of Flowers, stayed by Jennie's side as often as she could. Jennie and the few other girls did not try to talk her into becoming a prostitute to earn her keep, so she did some cooking and sewing and started a ledger book that recorded any money transactions—few as they were—that took place between Jennie and some "gentlemen customers."

The days were long and dry, hot during sunlight, and cool at night. The little village saw boatmen and trappers and a few Indians coming and going periodically. Most of the time, the men sat around in the front room of the hotel, which was a makeshift saloon with planks set over barrels and a few kegs of increasingly stale liquor that were rarely replenished. They played cards and gossiped like women—about the women in their midst.

Certainly, they didn't turn Jennie away when she came. They were glad to see women—any women—let alone women as pretty as she and as nice as her girls. They became occasional customers too, though they had little cash to pay. Jennie came up with a barter system, so that she and her girls could obtain food and supplies in return for their services. Within about a month, they had the system down, and it seemed to work well for them.

One day it rained, and the men gathered for a card game in the stale-smelling saloon.

"How did we get so lucky?" Bartholomew Wills, the owner and only resident of the Platte Hotel, said. He had come here from St. Louis, like Jennie, on the run from the law. He was a natural-born gambler, but unfortunately not very good at it. His debts had caught up with him, forcing him to flee as far west as he could. There was nothing beyond this little settlement, as far as he knew.

The others were men of similarly questionable backgrounds. They didn't probe into each other's pasts and didn't reveal anything about their own.

"I mean, to have Miss Jennie of the famous House of Flowers in St. Louie right here amongst us. Must have done something right at some time in our lives." He laughed. He was holding a winning hand.

The others were silent, concentrating on their cards. Compared to the rest, Wills was a chatterbox. He liked to boast of his business prowess and successes back in St.

Louis. No one believed him, and he didn't even believe himself. But it passed the time in this dreary, lonely place.

Thunder rumbled and crashed outside. The men smoked cigars and bet on their hands.

Just then Jennie came into the saloon-hotel lobby. She held a blanket over her head against the downpour, but it hadn't helped much. She didn't wear a hat, so her black hair was damp and hung down over her lovely face. The men stopped and gaped at her as she stood there and shook her head. Drops of water flew everywhere, even over the card table, but the men did not protest.

"Well, Miss Jennie," Bartholomew Wills said. "Welcome to our humble establishment. You light up the place like a lantern, like the sun, which we so sorely miss today."

"Thanks, Mr. Wills. One of my girls is sick and I need some medicine."

There was no doctor in these parts, unsurprisingly, so Wills kept some medicines and chemicals behind the bar. Mostly powders and potions that were months, if not years, old. He had won them in a card game with a traveling medicine salesman who had accidentally wandered far from civilized society. Word had it that the man had lost his scalp somewhere out on the plains after he had left the little village with no name.

"Hope it's nothing serious, ma'am," Wills volunteered as he rattled around among the bottles behind the bar.

Jennie said nothing. She thought she knew what was the matter with the girl: She was pregnant. It was probably the worst thing that could happen to the young woman. And it would be another mouth to feed for Jennie and the others. But her heart went out to the girl, who was desperately sick this morning.

"Thank you," she said finally when Wills handed her a bottle of powdered stomach medicine.

"You're quite welcome. Are you—er—that is, are the girls going to be around tonight?" he asked, somewhat sheepishly.

Jennie smiled, even though she didn't feel like it, and she said, in her best professional voice, "Yes, Mr. Wills. I would love it if you were to call on us this evening at any time. You're always welcome, as I hope you well know." She lifted a wet strand of hair from her eyes and put it behind her ear.

"Thanks, Miss Jennie," Wills said like a schoolkid.

The other men looked down in amusement and embarrassment. They would all probably come calling at some point that night.

Jennie took the medicine, put the blanket over her head again, and stepped into the rain. It was pouring hard, in sheets, and she stepped through mud puddles on her way back to the tent where the sick girl lay. She administered the medicine and helped the girl get comfortable, then went to her own tent. There, Carla was expertly sewing a torn undergarment for one of the other girls.

"Is Marie doing better?" Carla asked.

Jennie said, "Yes, but I'm afraid she's in for a long haul."

"What do you mean?"

"I mean she's probably expecting a baby."

"Oh, my!" Carla exclaimed innocently. "How can that be?"

"It probably happened in the usual way," Jennie replied.

"What way is that?"

"I hope one day you marry a nice young man and have lots of children, Carla. Then you'll find out."

"Oh . . ."

Jennie wished she were as naïve and trusting as Carla—then again, she certainly had been trusting with Mr. Epson, the damnable thief who had stolen not only her money, but her house and her livelihood, her chance at a normal life one day.

She felt almost like a slave again, trapped in a place from which there was little chance of escape. But at least she was her own mistress, she did not have someone telling her what to do every minute of the day. She vowed she would never go back to that life—not ever. She would die first.

"Do you think I'll ever get married, Miss Jennie?"

She was startled from her dark thoughts by Carla's voice. "Surely you will—one day," she lied to the girl.

Jennie went to the tent flap, opened it, and looked out on the rain. It reminded her of the old Bible story that she had heard as a girl, the story of Noah and the great flood that had covered the whole world. Maybe this rain would wash away her own cares and troubles. Maybe it would wash the whole world clean. Maybe, somehow, it would bring Art back to her—one day. . . .

In the Blackfoot Village

On his second night in the Indian village, Art was brought before the council fire. He had eaten and slept and regained some strength, and he knew he would need it for whatever ordeal lay ahead.

They had taken his knife and his buffalo robe when they had captured him. They'd left him only his clothes, which were ragged and dirty, and his moccasins, which were worn but still good. So he stood before them, the Blackfoot elders and warriors, with no weapon or means of defense except his own hands.

He had heard how they might make him run the gauntlet, which meant taking blows and taunts from every man, woman, and child of the village. And after that—he didn't know. But he assumed they would put him to death. How? Again, he had no idea, but he had heard stories of men being tortured or burned to death by various plains tribes. If he were a praying man, now was the time! But Art had never been particularly religious or churchgoing . . . though he did remember that preacher in St. Louis who had preached nonstop for hours and hours along the waterfront, and he had been spellbound by the man's gift for words and his faith.

The men began speaking among themselves around the council fire and passing the pipe from hand to hand. Each man took a few leisurely puffs of the smoke when his turn came. They seemingly ignored Art, who stood in their midst. He listened, but could only make out part of what they were saying.

"He must be put to death. Tomorrow."

"First we must hear his story. How did he kill Wak Tha Go?"

"What happened to him after the battle with our warriors? Why was he lost?"

"His own men turned against him and left him for dead."

"We do not know what happened. He must tell his story."

When the pipe had been completely around the circle, Brown Owl stood. He had gained stature among the people for his capture of this much-feared white trapper, Artoor. The men listened with respect to what he had to say.

"I agree with those who say we will hear his story. There are too many things unknown to us, too many questions."

The elder, Buffalo Standing in the River, agreed with the younger man. "Yes, let the white one talk. Even if he lies to us, we will learn more than we know already."

"I think he will not lie," Brown Owl said. "I think he is a man who speaks truth, even if we do not like what he says."

With sign and speech then, Brown Owl said to Art, the mountain man: "Artoor, you will tell us your story, what happened in the battle with Wak Tha Go and the others, then what happened to you that you were separated from your men."

Since it was his first chance to ask directly, he said to the warrior, "Were you there at the battle on the island in the river with Wak Tha Go?"

"Yes, I was one of the warriors."

"Were you the one who wounded my man Hoffman, the tall man with the yellow hair?"

Brown Owl smiled for the first time in a very long time. "Yes, my arrow struck his arm and drew much blood."

"Yes, it did. But Hoffman is a strong man. He was not badly injured."

"Then you will tell me, how did you kill Wak Tha Go?"

"It was not easy, but I sneaked into your camp. I stabbed him in his heart as he slept. I left my hat as a sign. I hoped your men would then go away. Which they did."

Brown Owl was unhappy to hear Artoor tell this part of his story. But he had to grant that it took much heart for him to have done this deed. He could have been killed by a sentry or by Wak Tha Go himself, if he had awakened.

"We retreated but vowed to fight again," Brown Owl said. "We will find your men and kill them one day."

"Well, I guess you might do just that," Art admitted. "Are you going to kill me?"

Brown Owl did not answer immediately. He spoke a few words to the other men in council. They grunted, nodded, and some raised their fists in a defiant gesture. None of it boded well for the trapper who was their prisoner.

"I guess that answers my question," Art said. He was resigned to his own death now, as he had not been after the mauling by the grizzly, after surviving in the wilderness for more than forty days. In fact, there had been many close calls in his life. Looking back, he was surprised that he had survived this long.

But this didn't mean he was going to give up without a fight. He had plenty of fight left in him. The only question was, how and who was he going to fight? He couldn't take on the whole village—or could he?

The man called Brown Owl was speaking to him: "Tell the men of my people how you came to be here. What happened to you? Why were you alone when we captured you?"

Art figured this would buy him some time, so he told the story of what had happened to him after the battle on the island. He told them of his encounter with the bear sow that nearly killed him, then about how his own men had left him behind—especially McDill, who probably would have killed him if it hadn't been for Dog's vigilance. He told them of his weeks of wandering and healing, of his killing the buffalo calf and eating its meat, crudely tanning the skin to make the robe that had sheltered him.

"My Great Spirit was looking out for me, I guess," he said in words and signs.

The men around the council fire could barely believe what he was saying. How could one man, a white man, do this—fight off a grizzly attack and survive for two moons without food or shelter? It was almost beyond comprehension. They nodded in admiration of this man.

"Truly, he is touched by the Great Spirit," one of the Indians said, echoing the thoughts of all the men around the council fire.

Brown Owl too felt a great respect for Art after hearing his story. But he knew that the trapper must die, could not be allowed to live since he was an enemy of the Blackfoot people. So Brown Owl put it before the council, for their judgment. "Now that we know the power of our enemy, who among you would want him to live to fight us in another battle and kill our warriors?"

"But must such a man be killed?" the elder Buffalo Standing asked, looking around at the others.

"Yes," Brown Owl said. "It saddens my heart in a way to say it, but this is the only answer; He must die."

Again, Art followed the discussion as best he could, but he knew immediately what was happening. It was his death sentence.

His mind went blank, free of fear or anticipation of what might happen next. The Indians kept talking, debating how and when he should be killed. They came to an agreement that he would be kept under double guard through the night, then killed the next day at noon. He could hear their voices, but what they said did not penetrate his consciousness.

Brown Owl was speaking: "This man has killed a great bear and survived for a long time with wounds that would have ended any other man's life. He has been alone in the dangerous country and killed a buffalo calf with just a knife. We must treat him carefully and with respect. He is a great warrior."

The others nodded and grunted in agreement with the plan to put two men on watch over the white man who had performed these great deeds of strength and survival.

He would not escape the judgment of the people, against whom he had fought so valiantly.

One by one the Blackfeet rose and filed away from the council fire, leaving Art there with Brown Owl and two men who were assigned to take the first watch. Art's hands were still bound with strips of buffalo hide, and they took him away to a tree near the council tepee and bound him to the trunk.

He stood there calmly, observing everything, watching Brown Owl who supervised the other men. Then the young Indian war chief spoke to him.

"You, Artoor, will die tomorrow. It will be a swift and honorable death for a warrior." He spoke in words and signs so that the trapper would understand.

Art just stared at Brown Owl. He did not defend himself or beg for mercy. That would not achieve anything but loss of respect from these men. The two guards stood on either side of the tree and watched him.

As Brown Owl walked away, Art thought back to his visit to St. Louis and Jennie. He thought of Mr. Ashley and their business arrangement, how he liked and respected the man for his seeming honesty. He remembered the great General Lafayette, who had visited the city to a warm greeting by the citizens and the town fathers.

Then he remembered the itinerate preacher who had been moving among the crowd down at the waterfront. The man had worn a long, black coat and a black stovepipe hat that had seen better days. He was skinny, probably hadn't eaten in days, with a narrow, hooked nose and pointy chin that almost touched each other, like a puppet that he had seen once.

The preacher's thin, bony finger had stabbed at the air, and his equally thin body had rocked and moved, as he spoke in a singsong voice, spouting Scripture and calling down God's wrath on the people of "sin and debauchery," on St. Louis itself, a "den of iniquity."

Art almost smiled as he remembered the scene and how the preacher had held him riveted, listening to his sermon, wondering if the man were crazy or just on fire with the word of the Lord. Crazy . . . the word of the Lord . . .

An idea formed in his head as the young mountain man stood there, a prisoner of the Blackfeet in their village, with no chance of help or escape.

Luckily, Brown Owl had made sure Art was comparatively well treated, and that he had drunk some water after eating a few bites of supper earlier, before the council meeting.

Art swallowed once and began to speak, to preach in the same tone of voice as the man he had heard on the wharf in St. Louis. "Hallelujah, hallelujah! Sweet Baby Jesus, come to me, Lord," he proclaimed like a bornagain, water-baptized, true believer in the Lord Almighty.

"Come to the aid of your servant who has wandered in the wilderness for forty days in search of your righteous blessing upon him. Deliver me, O Lord, from the hands of my enemies, from the clutches of the devil himself who has blasphemed your name. Release me from bondage as you did your people, freeing them from the Pharaoh. Release me from the lion's den as you did your prophet Daniel, against the king who would have him devoured by the lions. Open the doors of your heavenly city and let the sinner enter the gates of salvation!"

The two guards were startled by their prisoner's words, which were incomprehensible to them. But they were also mesmerized by them, by the outpouring of the rhythmic, chantlike prayers and proclamations.

"Lord, you sent hellfire and brimstone upon the evil cities of Sodom and Gomorrah who had raised up the devil to worship instead of the Almighty, and their evil deeds made a stink that could be smelled all over the world. You sent the plagues upon the Pharaoh, who would not let your people go, the water turned to blood, the frogs, the locusts and mosquitoes, the death of Egypt's cattle, the boils on man and beast, the hail that fell from the sky, the darkness that fell over the earth, and finally the death of the firstborn of Pharaoh. You have the power to make right what is wrong and to set free the unjustly imprisoned.

"You stayed Abraham's hand when he went to the rock to sacrifice his only son Isaac in obedience to you. You lifted up the suffering Job when he did not despair of your love. You made David a king when he was a simple shepherd and singer of praises to you, and gave him the power to slay the giant who made war on your people. Give this servant the strength to slay your enemies and to lift up your people in righteousness. Hallelujah, hallelujah! Even though I be spat upon and persecuted for your sake, you shall lift me up to glory if I am faithful to you O Lord. . . ."

* * *

In the morning, Art was still preaching. He had not
ceased all night long. He was amazed that the words and
stories from his youth came back to him, that he had the
strength to stand and to preach throughout the entire
night. Throughout the village the people were talking
about this amazing man.

Everyone knew the story of the grizzly bear and Art's
trek across miles and miles of the badlands even though
he was nearly dead. Over time it would become a legend
among the Blackfeet, but now it was still a freshly told
story, and the man who had accomplished these feats
was still among them, a prisoner tied to a tree near the
council lodge.

Like most of the village, Brown Owl got very little
sleep through the night. He made sure the guards were
replaced, and each time he came to the tree where the
prisoner was bound, he heard his ceaseless preaching.
He had never heard a white missionary preacher before,
though he had heard about them from others.

Over the years black-robed priests and black-coated
preachers had come among various tribes to try to convert them to their strange religion. They were called
Christians, and they taught that the Indians were bad for
not believing the same things that *they* did.

Brown Owl respected the stories of others and cher-
ished the stories of his own people. Why was one wrong
and the other right? That he did not understand. And it
made him angry that anyone would try to force their stories on someone who already had his own.

Before the sun rose, the young Blackfoot war chief
stood with some of the other people of the village and
listened to Artoor's strange and magical words.

"The Lord shall show portents in the sky and on the
earth, and blood and fire and columns of smoke will be
seen by all the people. The sun will be turned into dark-

ness and the moon into blood before the day comes, that great and terrible day. And all who call on the name of the Lord will be saved, for on Mount Zion will be those who have escaped the fires and plagues and the wrath of the one true God."

Whatever he was saying, it sounded frightening and powerful to all who heard him.

Art stood as straight and tall after several hours of preaching as he had when he had first been brought to the tree and bound there. His eyes were dark and glittery, as if he were under a spell. In fact, he was possessed by a powerful spirit.

He almost didn't realize what he was saying, but he kept talking, kept preaching, letting his voice roll out in the singsong cadence with the words that tumbled back into his mind from the times when he was a child and his parents dragged him to church services and traveling preachers' revivals.

"Proclaim this among all the nations. Prepare ye for war! Rouse the champions of the people, who will defend them in my name. Armies, prepare to advance. Hammer your plowshares into swords, your hooks into spears. Even the weaklings will be given strength in the Lord's name. Let the nations arouse themselves and assemble in the Valley of Jehoshaphat and be led by the champions of war!

"The sun and the moon will grow dark, and the stars will lose their brilliance. For the Lord God roars from Zion, He thunders from Jerusalem, and the heavens and the earth tremble at the sound of His mighty voice!"

For the rest of the morning, Art preached without stopping or faltering. The people of the village, men, women, and children, all came to the tree and stood and listened to him. All of them heard him, though they did not understand the strange white man's language.

The elders of the village huddled in an impromptu council nearby and whispered among themselves. They were amazed and concerned about this man, wondering whether he was a white devil who had come among them to destroy them.

As the sun rose in the sky, the mountain man preached on:

"When that day comes, the mountains will run with new wine and the hills will flow with milk, and all the streambeds of the country will run with water. A fountain will spring forth in the temple in the great city. Egypt will become a desolation and the land of the enemy a desert waste on account of the violence done to the Lord's people, the innocent children whose blood they shed in their country.

"But the land will be inhabited forever, and Jerusalem from generation to generation! 'I shall avenge their blood and let none go unpunished,' saith the Lord, and he shall dwell in Zion with the righteous ones."

Throughout the night the people of the village had heard him preaching without stopping. Very few had gotten any sleep that night. Throughout the morning women and children gathered around the tree where the man was bound and listened to his strange words. They talked among themselves, saying they thought he was crazy—that is, touched by the Great Spirit who created and protected all things.

Buffalo Standing in the River met with the other elders in the impromptu council. They watched and listened to Artoor, shaking their heads. They decided to call a full-fledged council meeting.

Buffalo Standing went to Brown Owl's tepee. There the younger man sat with his wife, who had been among the women listening to the prisoner preach throughout the morning. It was nearly noon, nearly time for the prisoner to be killed.

"Owl, my young friend, the men of our village must meet to discuss what we are going to do."

"The decision has been made. He is to be killed today. He is an enemy of our people."

"Yet he spoke of peace to many before Wak Tha Go came and told us we must fight him. And now we hear him speak and we think he is crazy. If this is true, he is under the protection of the Father and Creator of all."

Buffalo Standing led the young war chief to the council tepee where the others awaited. A pipe was lit and passed from man to man. Each one spoke his heart about this situation. All agreed that the prisoner should not be killed, that he should be released because he was clearly crazy.

When Brown Owl's turn came, he took the pipe and was silent for a moment. In the silence, from outside Art's words penetrated the council lodge:

"Listen, my people, to the words of the Lord. 'It was I who destroyed your enemies. It was I who brought you up from Egypt and for forty years led you through the desert to take possession of the Promised Land. I raised up your sons as prophets and warriors.

"'But because you have turned away from the Lord, I will crush you where you stand. Flight will be cut off for the swift, and the strong will have no chance to exert his strength, nor will the warrior be able to save his life. The archer will not stand his round, the swift of foot will not escape, nor will the horseman be able to rescue the fallen warriors. Even the bravest of men will throw down his weapons and run away on that day!'"

Finally, Brown Owl spoke. "The words of my brothers and fathers are correct. Although I have seen this man Artoor in battle and know that he is a skilled fighter, I see also that he is touched by the Great Spirit and we must honor the Spirit by letting him go."

All of the men nodded and grunted in agreement. Then, one by one, they rose and filed out of the tepee. Outside, the elders and warriors gathered by the white prisoner. Brown Owl ordered the guards to untie him.

Art stopped speaking for the first time in nearly eighteen hours. His mouth was parched and sore, and he staggered, had to steady himself by holding onto the tree. His vision was blurred, and he blinked to gain clear sight of all those who were gathered around him. At first he did not understand what was happening.

Brown Owl signed to him that he was free. Others stepped forward and gave Art a blanket, his own hunting knife, and a parfleche of food.

"You are free to leave us, for you have the protection of the Great Spirit. Do not come back to make war with our people, or else we will fight you, and this time we will kill you," the warrior told him.

Art took the gifts that were offered. Without a word, he walked away toward the east, away from the village. His head swam with words. His heart was full of strange emotions, but he was glad to be free. Now he would find his men, come hell or high water.

He wondered if Dog was out there somewhere waiting for him.

14

Junction of Platte and Missouri Rivers

Percy McDill had kept the trappers' party together, but through curses and threats rather than true leadership as Art had done. Along with Caviness, he bullied and cajoled the men, Matthews, Montgomery, and Hoffman, to stay with him when they threatened to split up and go their separate ways.

He practically had to kill Hoffman early on to keep him from going back to check on Art. The Hessian was certain that McDill had done something underhanded, and the others were too, though they didn't talk about it among themselves.

"You're taking orders from me now," McDill had told Hoffman with a sneer. "I say jump, and you jump. I say stay, and you stay. Got it?"

"Yes, sir." Hoffman had swallowed his pride and hatred and said the words that he was born and bred to say.

"That goes for all of you men. *Men*," McDill spat. "More like a bunch of women, if you ask me. I don't want no more trouble out of any of you—or else Caviness and me will deal with you."

That had been about eight weeks ago. Now, McDill led

the men back to the temporary tent-town where they had been in August, the settlement that was maintained for fur traders and trappers, where the mountain men stopped to resupply and get drunk and spend a few hours with some women.

The tents, some sod huts, and a few hastily erected log structures were the same. There may have been one or two more of each. And there were whites and a few Indians and mixed-breed children living there. There was a smoky, greasy pall over the whole encampment, a sense of impermanence and death.

McDill led the party into the settlement, coming from the opposite direction, the west, and met the stares and quizzical looks of the mountain men who happened to be there.

The big man didn't want to admit to anyone—including himself—that his leadership had been a complete failure. But he did what he did best: bluffed and blustered his way from one fiasco to another. His party had precious few pelts to trade, too few to bring back to St. Louis. This was because he was not an expert trapper, because he had not been able to stay in the mountains through the winter season when the furs were at their best. And because he wouldn't make alliances with any of the Indian tribes they had encountered on their journey after they left Art to die.

And his henchman Caviness was not very good either. The others were too green to know the ways of the wilderness well enough to salvage the mission. They knew that McDill was a lousy peacemaker—unlike Art—but they said nothing. They had decided to stick together rather than split up for the winter, and they went along with McDill's decision to return to St. Louis before the weather got too cold.

So, as they rode through this ramshackle excuse for a town, they were a pretty bedraggled, dispirited bunch. They had lost their original leader and had not recovered from that. Despite McDill's bluster, they all knew it.

He led them to a trading tent, where they offered their paltry supply of pelts—very few, and not very good—for sale to finance their trip back to St. Louis. He tried to demand the best price, but had to settle for much less. He kept all the money.

"I'm boss of this outfit and I'll take care of the money," he said, brooking no challenge to his decision. Behind the others' backs he looked at Caviness and winked. He'd take care of his friend, and the others could go to hell, as far as he was concerned.

"We're only gonna stay for a day or two here, rest up and buy some supplies for our ride back to St. Louie. Let's find a place to camp for tonight."

They walked their horses and gear over to a small clearing on the edge of the makeshift town. There was another two-man camp nearby with a campfire burning, the men sitting on a fallen tree trunk and tending the fire. There was a pot of coffee cooking in the fire.

McDill ordered his men to set up their camp and build their own fire, ignoring his neighbors.

After a while one of the men came over to the larger group and said, "You all are welcome to some coffee if you want."

"Maybe later," McDill said curtly.

"Sure we would," Montgomery piped up, poking Matthews in the ribs, and Matthews said he would too.

"Now look, you men—" McDill sputtered. "I told you we need to stick together here. We'll fix our own supper."

"Just tryin' to be neighborly, friend," the man said.

Then Hoffman said, "We met you before. You're a friend of our captain, Art."

"Yeah, I'm Jeb Law. We met before. And this here is Ed," he added, pointing to the other mountain man with whom he was sharing the camp.

McDill cut in. "Art used to be our captain. He's dead now. I'm the leader here."

"That so?" Jeb said, and left it at that. He returned to

his own campfire. He called over to them, "You're welcome to some coffee and grub—any time."

A little while later, Matthews and Montgomery drifted over to Jeb Law's campfire and sat down to drink a cup of coffee, the first they had drunk in many weeks. Then the Hessian, Hoffman, came over, and finally even McDill and Caviness gave in and came over, bringing their own drinking cups.

Jeb Law said, "Well, we heard you men ran into some trouble out there on the Upper Missouri."

"We're doin' fine," McDill said. "We did lose poor old Art. He got mauled by a big old grizz. It was painful to see him all beat up like that," he said with phony sadness, as if he had been a good friend of the young mountain man instead of a bitter and resentful enemy.

But Jeb Law wasn't fooled. He smiled. He had an ace up his sleeve. "That so? He was dead when you left him?"

"Yeah," Caviness lied. "We was on the run from some Indians, fought 'em off pretty good, but we had to keep moving fast."

Matthews shifted uneasily where he was sitting. He cleared his throat and started to say something, but McDill glared at him as if to tell him to keep his mouth shut.

The German couldn't help himself. He hated McDill and Caviness. He blurted out, "No he wasn't dead. He was hurt badly. We left him with his rifle and food. We don't know what happened to him."

"Really?" Jeb said. "Well, now, I wonder if he's the one the Injuns are all palaverin' about for the past month or so."

"What do you mean?" McDill spat.

"There's a man they're callin' Preacher. The Blackfeet captured him—seems he was wanderin' the country after he had been attacked by a bear. He had nothin' except his knife and a buffalo robe that he made hisself—I guess he kilt a buffalo to get it. Anyhow, the story is the Injuns caught him and brought him back to their village to kill him. But he started acting crazy-like, started preaching like from the Bible. Didn't stop talking for almost a whole day. Well, mister, seems like the Blackfeet couldn't bring themselves to kill him. They let him go and started calling him Preacher. Sounds an awful lot like my old friend Art."

McDill looked at Caviness. It was just about sundown and the shadows were long and dark. But McDill's face was white, like the moon. He and Caviness got up and left the campfire.

The others stayed and drank more coffee, and even ate some supper with Jeb and Ed. They pumped Jeb for all the information he had heard about Art. They were happy to learn that their old boss was alive and well. But the question in all their minds was: Where is he?

On the Missouri River, North of the Yellowstone

Art made his way back to the American Fur Company trading post on the river, commanded by Joe Walker. Along the way he had bartered for a horse from a friendly Indian, so he was able to save valuable time by riding the last fifty miles or so. Already it was past the middle of October and the days were getting shorter, the nights much colder.

He had been reunited with Dog after his captivity by the Blackfeet. The wolf-dog had remained outside the village, aware that his human companion was in trouble. He'd kept to the woods and brush throughout the day and night, and when Art had emerged a free man, he'd followed him for about a mile before showing himself. The young mountain man was glad to see his canine friend, but he wasn't surprised. Dog had proven himself many times over as reliable and faithful.

As he traveled, Art looked back on the events of the past few months. The primary mission was mostly a failure, though there had been some successful peacemak-

ing along the way. Still, Art wouldn't have much to
report to William Ashley besides his own adventures—
which he could barely believe himself.

Approaching the fortlike structure he saw that, like
before, the front gate was closed. The blockhouse that
overlooked the gate was still empty. He almost smiled at
the thought that he had been here before, that it was like
being in a play and repeating the same scene over and
over again. Then Dog barked, just as he had the time
before, which only confirmed the feeling that Art had.

"Who goes there?" came the voice from the blockhouse.

"I'm here to see Joe Walker. My name is Art."

"You again?" the voice said.

Minutes later Art was in Walker's lamp-lit, windowless
quarters, talking to the bald-headed, bearded commander of the trading garrison.

"You don't look too healthy," Walker said. He was
smoking a pipe, and the smoke filled the cramped space.
Papers and maps were strewn over the top of his desk.

"Well, I've had some tough days recently."

"So I hear—Preacher."

Art looked at Walker with surprise. "What did you say?"

"I called you Preacher. That's what the Indians are
saying. I just did some business with an Arikara scout
who told me all about it—all about your captivity by the
Blackfeet. I told you they were savages."

"They actually treated me pretty good, all things considered." Art scratched his beard. He wanted to shave
and to clean himself up. He couldn't believe that Walker
had already heard of his experience with the Blackfeet.
"What else are they saying about me?"

"Well," Walker said, "there is something about a fight
with a grizzly bear. Seems you won but came out the
worse for wear."

"Pretty near killed me," Art admitted. "She was a big mother bear with a bunch of cubs. I didn't mean to bother her."

"She couldn't have known that, I suppose. So your men left you behind, wounded?"

"They did what they had to do. I would have done the same if it was one of them."

"And where are you going now?"

"I'm looking for my party. You remember them from when we came here in August. They been through here?"

"Haven't seen them, but word is they're headed back to St. Louis. They don't have much by way of pelts."

"What?"

"Don't know why, but they were seen moving east just a few days ago. Probably they'll head down toward the Platte for resupply, maybe do a little trading, then head on down the Missouri to St. Louis. I've dispatched a message to Mr. Ashley to tell him to expect them. Didn't know about you, though. I'll write him a letter to tell him I have met with you." Walker puffed on his cigar. "And that you have a new name," he added.

Art said, "I will tell him myself what happened to me and to our expedition. Not sure what he will think about all this."

"Well, I hear Mr. Ashley is a reasonable man."

"I like him and respect him."

"I wish you good luck, sincerely. And I know you'll be back out here. You've never been a city man. You belong out in the mountains and the high plains, with men like me. That's who you are now, son."

"Well, I've got to keep moving. I'm going to try to catch up with my men. If I move fast I can do it."

"I have no doubt you will, Preacher. No doubt at all."

Jennie had made a decision. She was going to go back. Maybe not all the way to St. Louis, but she was going to take her girls out of this primitive place and back into something that resembled civilization. The settlement on the Kansas and Missouri Rivers, called Westport or

Kansas City, just beyond Independence, might be a place to settle. But it was hopeless out here, even though she had come to like the few bedraggled men who were trying to make a go of the little settlement.

It was getting close on to winter, so it was time to move. She told Ben and Carla Thomas and the other girls about her decision.

"I want you to pack up all your belongings and be ready to leave first thing in the morning," she said.

Then she told the men of the settlement. They couldn't believe their ears. They were sad because they had come to like her and her girls. It was beyond their wildest dreams that Jennie and the girls from the House of Flowers had come to their little village in the first place. What would they do without her when she was gone?

"You'll be fine," she assured them. "I'll miss you too."

But she wasted no time in gathering her girls, reloading the wagon, and ordering Ben to drive—east this time. First she would return to the trading settlement at the junction of the Missouri and Platte Rivers, and from there decide which direction to head next.

It took two days of hard overland travel to get there.

They rolled in near the end of the second day, the sun low in the sky. Jennie sat up front in the driver's seat with her old friend Ben, the freed black man. He had stuck with her through the worst of times and hundreds of difficult miles. He did not question her decision to turn back east—in fact, he was glad she was doing it. It would be safer for her and the girls.

"Look, Ben, this is a bustling community. There are even some women here. Most of them Indian girls as far as I can see. And a lot of trappers. Hmmm, I'll bet there's some money to be made here for a person of business."

"It's also pretty rough, Miss Jennie." Ben rarely ventured an opinion of his own.

The encampment was nothing pretty to look at—tents and crude sod and log buildings. The men hanging around stopped as the girls passed, and waved and whistled. No doubt, they were glad to see this train pull in to their humble way station.

"Look, there are some boats," Jennie said, pointing at some keelboats along the river's shore. "We could take a boat as far as Westport, maybe settle there for a while and see if we like it."

"Yes, Miss Jennie," the faithful black driver said simply. He knew by now that whatever Miss Jennie decided on was what they would do, no arguments from him.

They drove to one of the more substantial buildings, which was a fur dealer's headquarters, and Jennie went inside to get the lay of the land. She found out that they could camp anywhere they pleased, that there were no authorities in this place other than the gun and the fist, and that the trappers and traders and other men in the vicinity would be mighty glad to see them.

McDill got drunk during the second day in the sprawling tent-town. He spent a sizable chunk of the money that he had collected for the entire party's pelts. That left him with next to nothing to buy supplies, but he was too far gone by noon to care much.

He wandered the sprawling encampment looking for a woman. Any woman would do. He had almost forgotten about the time he'd been here before and the trouble he had caused by making a play for another man's squaw. But he hadn't forgotten how Art had sicced his wolf-dog on him, how Dog had bitten his knife hand and humiliated him.

"Shoulda shot that damn dog-monster when I had a chance," he muttered to himself drunkenly. He staggered through the makeshift "streets" of the town, glassy-eyed and angry. This time nobody was going to prevent him from getting what he wanted.

He headed toward the center of the settlement, where the Eastern fur traders had set up their frontier offices. A better class of people was living there, he had convinced himself. Maybe that meant a better class of woman.

Putting his hands in his pockets, he realized that he had very little money left. He'd given Caviness ten dollars off the top of their meager take, just to keep his friend off his back. The others were going to be mad when they found out he had spent all his money on liquor—and maybe a whore.

"Damn them to hell anyway," he breathed. "They got out of this thing with their lives, which is more than that young Indian-lover woulda done for 'em." Despite Art's skills and easy way with people, McDill wasn't about to give him credit for anything. "Like to get us scalped with his Injun-palaver. If I hadn't been there on the island, I don't know what woulda happened. Saved all of our damned lives . . ."

Percy McDill looked up and couldn't believe what he was seeing. There, directly in front of him, were the girls from the House of Flowers in St. Louis. At first he thought he was dreaming or maybe somehow imagining this sight. He had never gone into the famous house of prostitution—the likes of him couldn't afford the fancy prices for fancy women. But he had hung out nearby enough to recognize a few of the faces and figures of these girls.

What were they doing way out here in this Godforsaken place? A jumble of thoughts clogged up his brain and he couldn't think straight, couldn't figure out what was going on. All he knew was that he wanted a woman and here were some women. How lucky could a man get?

He smiled evilly and staggered forward.

* * *

Art wasn't sure why, but something propelled him forward. He rode without stopping to sleep, only to rest and water his horse. Turned out it was a good bargain, this horse: very sturdy and reliable and didn't seem to mind Dog tagging along for the ride. From Joe Walker, Art had obtained a rifle, shot and powder, a new canteen, a new saddlebag for food and supplies. He was all set now, and with each mile he felt stronger and more determined to find the men he had once commanded.

He hoped Hoffman, Montgomery, and Matthews were all right. He hoped McDill and Caviness were healthy too, so he could beat the hell out of them. He had no doubt that McDill had bullied the others and lied to them to make them do whatever he wanted. That was his way.

He remembered the first time he had encountered Percy McDill, in the tavern in St. Louis. The big man had been full of it then, a coward at heart, selfish, with nothing good to say about another human being. McDill had been so cocksure that the job of leading the expedition for Mr. Ashley would be his. And he'd been so angry when the assignment went to Art . . . and a thorn in Art's side ever since.

Late in the afternoon of the third day out of Walker's fort, Art rode into the tent city at the junction of the Missouri and the Platte. There was something familiar about the look and feel of the place, the men who populated it—for they were his kind of people, men of the mountains. As he rode through, he got more than a few hellos and howdies.

They looked at him differently, however. That dadblasted preacher story must have gotten to them too, he mused. He looked around for someone he knew well.

He found what he was looking for. There was Jeb Law, his old friend. Art rode over to Jeb's campsite. The old man looked up from his fire, broke out into a big grin. "Well, if it ain't my oldest and dearest friend and—" He looked down at the lean and hungry Dog. "And his pal Dog."

Art dismounted and shook Jeb's rough hand. Jeb looked him over, from head to foot.

"You be needin' a good meal, son. Let me fix you up some beans. Got coffee cookin' on the fire. Take a load off'n your feet."

"Thanks, Jeb. Good to see you too."

The two men sat. Jeb Law looked directly into the younger mountain man's eyes and said, "You came to the right place if'n you're lookin' for your explorin' party. They're right here."

"McDill and the others?" Art wasn't surprised except that it had taken him a lot less time than he had thought. He calculated that they'd be well on their way to St. Louis by now. McDill didn't like to linger in places like this, especially since he'd gotten in trouble over a woman last time through.

"They're all alive," Jeb said.

"I'll be damned. Well, that's a good thing. Guess they didn't need me after all."

"Ha! You should see the long hound-dog looks on those men. They sure missed you. They thought you was dead."

"McDill. He told them that, didn't he."

Jeb nodded. "Sure thing. The others didn't like it one bit when they found out he had lied to them. Other than that one that's joined to him at the hip—what's his name?"

"Caviness."

"Yep. He and Caviness are a pair of evil children if'n I ever laid eyes on any in my whole miserable life." Jeb smiled. "And you are a sight for sore eyes, boy. Here, have some of old Jeb's coffee. Best brew west of nowhere."

Dog sidled up next to Art, sat alertly right beside his leg. The coffee slid hotly into Art's belly, and he felt the effects of no food in three days.

"I told them all about you bein' called Preacher and all that. They were sure surprised."

"Now, where did you hear about that?"

"I hear things. Don't take long for stories to get passed around out here. You know that. And it was a pretty good yarn, about how you killed a bear and wandered around wounded and got yerself captured by Injuns. I said to myself, 'That sounds just like the Art I know.'" He grinned, showing the few yellow teeth he had left. "Sure 'nuff, it were you!"

"Where are my men?"

"Why, they're campin' right next door there." Jeb pointed. "They must be out galavantin' around. McDill got himself drunk early on today. He's either passed out or dead somewheres round about." He cackled like a woman. "That one's got death marked on him. It ain't gonna be long for him, I'll wager."

Art stayed and ate some of Jeb's beans cooked with a fistful of pork fat. He hadn't tasted anything so good since the last time he and Jennie had eaten together in St. Louis. His belly settled down and his mind became more focused on what he had to do: find his men and re-claim his leadership.

It wasn't going to be easy or pleasant, he knew. Not with McDill and Caviness fighting him every step of the way.

The sun had begun to fall below the distant hilltops. He had better get moving before it got fully dark. "Thanks, Jeb," he said. "I'll be back."

"I'll wager," Jeb said again.

He didn't know where to start, so Art just walked into the center of the tent town. He ran into some other ac-quaintances along the way and stopped briefly to say hello. All of them seemed to know about his adventures, and some of them even called him "Preacher."

Dog tagged along with Art, never leaving his side. He avoided other dogs, faded into the background if any barked or challenged him. Like his master, he didn't want any trouble or distraction at this time.

The mountain man came to one of the fur dealers' buildings, a squat log structure chinked with mud and sod. He went in. There were a couple of men there stacking pelts and going over their books. He asked about his men.

"Oh, yeah, they're here. Their captain, McDougal I think his name is, was around here earlier. Drunk as a skunk."

"Sold us a few pelts yesterday, not very good quality," the other man said.

Art thanked them and went out. He was close. Maybe he should just go back to the campsite and turn in and let them come to him.

15

In the darkness, illuminated only by a single candle, Jennie faced a terrifying apparition. Percy McDill had burst into her tent, and now moved toward her, his face twisted by lust and anger into a grotesque mask. The candle's reflection in his dark eyes gave Jennie the illusion of staring into the very fires of hell. She stepped backward, but found little room to maneuver in the confines of the tent.

Jennie screamed.

Outside, Art heard a woman's scream. It came from a nearby tent. It startled him—not because of the cry itself, but because he thought he recognized the voice of the woman who screamed. But it couldn't be . . . it couldn't be who he thought it was. Could it?

Running in the direction of the commotion, Art wondered what Jennie would be doing out here. It couldn't be her, could it? She was in St. Louis. And yet, something about the scream touched his very soul. He hurried toward the tent.

McDill lunged, clamping his dirty hand over her mouth. Jennie bit his hand and he ripped it away, howling like a wounded animal. She screamed again. Outside the tent she could hear people moving around, and she hoped someone would come to help her. She fought back, pummeling his chest and face with her hands, but he was so big and strong that it had no effect.

"You bitch!" he sneered, cradling his wounded hand. "I was gonna pay you, whore that you are, but now I'm not—I'm gonna take it for free."

"Stay away," she warned. "For your own good, mister. I don't want to hurt you."

"Ha! You don't want to hurt me?" he said with a lopsided, drunken grin. "Tell me, bitch, how you plannin' on hurtin' me?"

She couldn't stand the smell of him, and his ugly leer. Yet she realized that she had to be careful, that she couldn't rile him even more—or else he was liable to kill her. She had known men like him for her entire life.

She gathered what composure she could, and brushed a fall of hair back from her face. She forced herself to smile at him.

"Look, you're right, whoring is my business. But I was just getting ready for bed and I must look a mess. Why don't you go away now, give me a chance to get ready, then you can come back later," she said.

"No way, little lady, I'm here and here I am. You'll get to like me when you know me better. I promise."

Jennie doubted that she would ever be able to bear the sight of this man, let alone like him. He was grotesque, and it didn't matter that he was drunk. She had met this kind before, and he reminded her of her old master, among others.

"But you'll like me better if you give me a chance to get ready for you," Jennie said, making one last attempt to get through to him.

"I like you fine just the way you are," he said, starting toward her again.

Jennie felt the world closing in on her and smelled

blood in the air; she could only hope it wasn't her own. Again she screamed for help.

At that moment the tent flaps opened, and it was as if God himself had heard her plea. The one man in the world whom she truly loved stepped inside. It was Art, the man she had known as a boy, the man who was a part of her life even when they were not together. She had heard the stories of him over the last several weeks, how he had beaten off a bear attack, then wandered through the wilderness, surviving on berries, roots, and whatever he could kill with just a knife. She had also heard of his escape from the Indians, and of the new name the Indians had given him.

"Art!" she cried.

McDill turned to see the man he hated most in the world—the man he had thought was dead—moving at him swiftly and angrily. He ducked to avoid Art's first swing, and came up with a hard punch of his own, taking Art off guard, smashing into his chin. He laughed as the younger man staggered backward.

"Well, now, if it ain't my ole' pal Art," McDill said. "Only I hear tell the Indians call you Preacher now. Is that right? Are you goin' to preach to me, Preacher? Are you going to save my soul?" He laughed.

Art got to one knee, and shook his head, trying to clear away the cobwebs of the hammerlike blow. He stared up at McDill, and at the hideous leering grin on his face.

McDill held his hand out and curled his fingers, tauntingly inviting Art toward him.

"Well, come on, Preacher," he said. "You don't have a pistol under the table now, do you? Oh, wait, I forgot. It was a fork, wasn't it?" The leering grin left his face, to be replaced by an angry scowl. "Come on, you son of a bitch. I'm going to beat you to a pulp."

His head cleared, Art leaped up again and charged at

McDill. He buried his head in McDill's midsection, and both men went crashing to the ground.

Art scrambled to his feet and grabbed McDill by the collar, then dragged him outside. He wanted to take this confrontation away from Jennie. By now a crowd, drawn by the screams and the commotion, had gathered just outside. They surrounded the two men, who were locked in a deadly confrontation.

Among the people there were Matthews, Montgomery, and Hoffman, the big Hessian. They couldn't believe what they were seeing. Here was their leader, returned as if from the dead. They were overjoyed to see him, but not in these circumstances. He was locked in mortal combat with the larger, loathsome McDill.

The crowd cheered for Art and jeered McDill. Art, still exhausted from his long ride, and not yet fully recovered from all his injuries, stood still to catch his breath. That allowed McDill to get to his feet, and the big man charged like a bull. Art stepped out of the way, and McDill went hurtling into the crowd.

Laughing at his awkwardness, the men in the crowd caught McDill and pushed him back into the circle of combat. The two men faced each other again, and Art punched him as hard as he could. McDill doubled over. Art landed a strong right to McDill's jaw, straightening him out and sending him back on his heels. Art massaged the hand that had struck the blow.

Caviness was watching with the others in the crowd. He wanted to go to the aid of his friend, but he dared not, for fear of retribution from the others. McDill was on his own now. Caviness melted away into the growing darkness. Even as the fight was going on behind him, he saddled his horse. If Art won, he might come after Caviness. If McDill won, he would want to know why Caviness didn't help him. Under the circumstances, Caviness knew that this was no place for him to be.

"Art," Jennie said, coming out of her tent then.

Art turned toward Jennie, then held his hand out, as if telling her to stay away. "Jennie, stay back, keep out of the way!" he cautioned.

As Art looked away from McDill for just that quick second, McDill pulled his long-bladed hunting knife from its sheath and lunged at Art, the knife pointed at his guts. Now, enraged and humiliated by the beating he was taking from this younger and smaller man, McDill was more animal than human.

Jennie saw McDill and called out to Art: "Look out! He has a knife!"

Art turned just in time to see the blade flash in the flickering light of the nearby fires. He reared back to avoid the killing knife, then circled his enemy bare-handed. Someone from the crowd tossed him a stick. Art used it as a defensive weapon, swinging it at McDill to keep him at bay. With one swing, McDill's knife chopped the stick in half.

"What are you goin' to do now, Preacher?" McDill taunted, holding the knife out in front of him, moving the point back and forth slightly, like the head of a coiled snake. "You think that little stick is going to stop me? I'll whittle it down to a toothpick, then I'll carve you up."

Then Art realized he had no choice, he must fight this madman on his terms—no rules, any weapon at hand, and to the death. He drew his own knife, the same knife that had seen him through the past two months from the killing of Wak Tha Go, to the killing of the grizzly she-bear, and through his wandering and captivity. The same knife that had been returned to him by the Indians, when they granted him his freedom.

Art held the knife up, showing it to Percy McDill, saying without a word that he intended to kill the man who had threatened Jennie, who had left him for dead, who had lied and cheated his way through a worthless life. Well, that life was about to end.

Suddenly it seemed as if McDill had sobered up. The

taunting, leering grin left his face and he became deadly serious and focused. With a steady hand he held his own knife up, challenging his opponent, his face now a mask of calm determination.

"I should've killed you when I had the chance. You'd better start preachin' your own funeral, Preacher," McDill said. "It's time for you to die."

Now, for the first time, Art grinned. It was neither taunting nor leering. Instead, it was confident, and it completely unnerved McDill. "I don't think so, McDill," Art said easily. "I think you are the one who is going to die."

"I'm going to kill you, and that damned mutt of yours," McDill said with false bravado, trying now to bolster his own courage.

Out of the corner of his eye, Art could see Dog, standing near Hoffman on the edge of the watching crowd. If it hadn't been for the wolf-dog, McDill probably would have slit his throat and left him for dead some two months earlier.

The young mountain man put aside all thoughts other than one: McDill must die for his crimes. Trying to hurt Jennie was the last evil thing this son of a bitch would ever do.

The two men circled each other like gladiators in a Roman arena. The crowd became silent. Even Jennie, who watched in horror, could neither speak nor cry out. Dog stood at alert. He could've attacked McDill, but somehow seemed to sense that this was something Art needed to do by himself.

McDill moved first. He swung his blade at Art, missing his face by only a few inches. Art felt the wind of the swift knife blade and jerked his head back. In almost the same movement, he swung his own knife low and hard, aiming for McDill's belly. He missed.

The big man then punched Art on the side of his head.

Art was stunned, and for a second couldn't see anything. He backed away quickly to avoid the oncoming McDill, then stepped to one side. As McDill shot past him, Art stabbed with his knife blade and felt it slip into McDill's midsection.

He pushed the knife in as far as it could go, then held it there. The two men stood together, absolutely motionless, for a long moment. Art felt McDill's warm blood spilling over his knife and onto his hand.

Howling like a stuck pig, McDill pulled himself off the knife. He stepped back several feet, then came back toward Art. But before he could even lift his own knife, he gasped, dropped his knife, and put his hand to his wound. Blood filled his cupped palms, then began oozing from his mouth as well. His eyes turned up in their sockets, showing the bloodshot whites.

From her position by the front of her tent, Jennie looked at McDill's eyes. They had caught the reflection of the campfires and, once more, she had the illusion of staring into the pit of hell. She shuddered, and wrapped her arms around herself as she realized that, within minutes, McDill would be there.

"Damn . . . you . . ." McDill managed to gurgle through the blood and spit that filled his mouth. "Damn . . ."

Art took one step toward the dying man, then stopped. McDill's big body shuddered, then collapsed in a heap on the ground. Beneath him the blood pooled darkly from his leaking wound.

Jennie ran up, threw her arms around Art, and kissed him. He stood there unmoving, unable to take his eyes off the crumpled heap that had once been a man.

His own men now came forward: Montgomery, Matthews, and Hoffman. Dog followed warily, his nostrils filled with the blood scent from the dead man.

"Well, Boss, good to see you again," Matthews said. The others clapped him on the back. There were tears in their eyes.

Jennie said, "Yes, so good. You're alive. You saved my life. If you hadn't been here—I don't know what might have happened."

Still, Art said nothing. His body and mind were spent. He didn't feel good about killing McDill, even though the man was a bastard and nothing but trouble for everyone around him. He had never enjoyed killing for the sake of killing, but only killed as a last resort. In this case, it had been a necessary last resort—no question.

Finally, he spoke: "I'm glad that you're all alive and well. Where did Caviness go?"

"I think we will never see him again," Hoffman said with his heavy German accent. "I saw him sneak away like a dog."

"Careful when you say that," Art said, nodding toward Dog, who cocked his head at the big Hessian.

They all laughed. Dog even wagged his tail, sensing that they were talking about him.

"Let's clean up this mess and bury it," Art said.

"I tell you, Art, that's more than he would have done for you," Montgomery observed.

"Call me Preacher," Art said.

"Preacher? Yeah, I heard you'd picked up a new moniker. That's what you want to be called, huh?"

"Yeah," Preacher said. "That's what I want to be called."

Later that night Jennie washed off the blood and trail dust that clung to the man who would now, and forever more, be called Preacher. She coaxed him to eat some supper, then to sleep off the aches and pains of his long ordeal. She lay beside him until he fell asleep.

The next morning Preacher set out early, before Jennie awoke. Dog followed him to the edge of the settlement. Preacher rode toward the ford. He would cross the Missouri and ride back to St. Louis to report to William Ashley as he had promised to do. It seemed a long time ago since that last trip to St. Louis. A lot had happened, and he felt like a different man now. It was good that he had a new name to go with this new man. Maybe he had grown up. He was still young, but he had been through more in the last few months than most men would go through in a lifetime.

"Dog," he said, "I want you stay here with Miss Jennie. She needs you. I don't. I'm on my own now."

The wolf-dog stopped. Preacher stopped too, turned his horse, and faced his faithful companion. "You understand what I'm saying, don't you?"

The animal cocked his head and wagged his tail again. At this moment he looked more like a dog than a wolf, though you couldn't separate the two canine natures. Dog seemed to speak; he barked twice, looked at Preacher, then slowly walked back toward the settlement.

Now the lone rider, a man of the mountains who had left the only home he had ever known more than a dozen years ago, reined his mount around and headed toward the river.

The man called Preacher would start a new chapter in his life—and he would be alone, as the men of the mountains always were.